Also by Piers Paul Read

THE
PATRIOT

PIERS PAUL READ

THE PATRIOT

Random House
New York

Grateful acknowledgment is made to the following for permission to
reprint previously published material:

DOUBLEDAY, A DIVISION OF THE BANTAM DOUBLEDAY DELL PUBLISHING
GROUP, INC.: Fourteen lines from "My Beloved Will Arrive at Last" from
From Desire to Desire by Yevgeny Yevtushenko. Copyright © 1976 by
Doubleday, a division of the Bantam Doubleday Dell Publishing Group,
Inc. Reprinted by permission of Doubleday, a division of the Bantam
Doubleday Dell Publishing Group, Inc.

PENGUIN BOOKS LTD.: Excerpt from *Faust Part One* by Johann Wolfgang
von Goethe, translated by Philip Wayne (Penguin Classics, 1949).
Copyright © 1949 by the Estate of Philip Wayne. Reprinted by
permission of Penguin Books Ltd.

REED CONSUMER BOOKS: Excerpt from *The Russian Tradition* by Tibor
Szamuely, published by Martin Secker and Warburg. Reprinted by
permission of Reed Consumer Books.

A. P. WATT ON BEHALF OF THE ESTATE OF CONSTANCE GARNETT: Excerpts
from *On the Eve* by Ivan Turgenev, translated by Constance Garnett.
Reprinted by permission of A. P. Watt on behalf of the Estate of
Constance Garnett.

Library of Congress Cataloging-in-Publication Data
Read, Piers Paul
The patriot / Piers Paul Read.
p.   cm.
ISBN 0-679-44544-7
I. Title.
PR6068.E25P38   1996   823′.914—dc20   95-11598

Manufactured in the United States of America on acid-free paper

24689753

First U.S. Edition

It has been hard for outsiders to realize that Russian national feeling is a spiritual emotion largely detached from the mundane things of life, that for centuries past Russia has meant for her people much more than just a country to be loved and defended: "Russia" was more a state of mind, a secular ideal, a sacred idea, an object of almost religious belief—unfathomable by the mind, unmeasurable by the yardstick of rationality.

TIBOR SZAMUELY, *The Russian Tradition*

I

1991
August 30

I

The neighbor on one side was an old woman living alone. She was deaf and remembered nothing. The house on the other was divided into apartments. The owners were questioned when they returned that evening. One, a middle-aged spinster, remembered music, loud choral music, in the early hours of the morning ten days or so before. She had telephoned the police to complain. Sometime later the music had stopped and she had fallen asleep.

A cassette remained in the tape deck. None of the team investigating the deaths could decipher the Cyrillic script on the label, so Kessler, the senior detective, played the tape for a moment or two: Slavonic church music, undoubtedly the music that had kept the woman awake. He turned up the volume, taking care not to superimpose his fingerprints on any that might be there already.

The sergeant, Dorn, put his hands to his ears. "Why so loud?"

Kessler said nothing. Instead, he hit the walls of the large living room with his fist. The music must have been played at full volume to have woken the woman next door; the windows had been closed, the walls were thick, and the houses on this stretch of Dubrowstrasse were at least fifty meters apart—large Teutonic villas built at the turn of the century in the heyday of the German empire.

"They go for over a million marks, houses like this," said Dorn, looking around at the large rooms with bare walls. "And when the government moves here from Bonn, they'll double again. I bet the children of the woman next door can't wait for her to pass on. She's squatting on a fortune."

Why so loud? Kessler stopped the tape and switched off the system. To muffle the sound of the shot that killed the man? No. His body lay in the hall at the bottom of the stairs; he must have been killed as they entered. To smother the screams of the woman? Surgical tape had covered her mouth. Stooping over the body tied to the chair and studying her face through a magnifying glass, Kessler could see traces of white adhesive above and below the edges of the tape; on the sticky side, dangling loose on her chin, several small black hairs from her upper lip lay on top of one another, suggesting that it had been removed on several occasions. To let her talk? Or scream?

Kessler stepped back because of the stench. A robust Berliner who had seen many a corpse in his time, he was shaken all the same by the sight of this woman. She wore a light cotton dress, but in her writhing the dress had torn, rucked, and twisted to uncover most of her body, and the folds were now brittle where the sweat had dried. Sweat had matted the strands of dark hair that had fallen over her face and now seemed glued to her skin. There were black stripes where ropes bound her wrists and ankles, and discoloration where her back and buttocks pressed against the chair. There were patches on the upholstered seat, too, that gave off a pungent odor distinct from that of rotting flesh, but there seemed to be no blood on her body, only red weals where they had burned her skin, almost certainly with cigarettes, so that it now looked as if she had suffered from smallpox or bubonic plague.

There were shreds of tobacco on the floor. Kessler crouched and picked one up with a pair of tweezers. It was dark and finely cut, probably from a Turkish or a Bulgarian cigarette. He laid the shred in a small transparent plastic bag and put the bag into his pocket.

The woman's head lolled back, the open eyes gazing at the ceiling. From the lines and the complexion, Kessler estimated that she was at least forty, but attractive in a swarthy Levantine way. The face was untouched, but the sight of it disturbed Kessler more than the marks on her skin—particularly the way in which her features were set in the expression of an agony that could all too easily be taken for rapture.

"Did they fuck her?" asked Dorn.

Kessler turned away. "Tied like that? And with her clothes on?"

"Shall I look in her mouth?"

"Leave that to them." Kessler nodded toward the team of forensic technicians.

"How did she die?"

Kessler pointed to a small circular bruise on the back of her neck. "An injection, I'd say. Probably cyanide."

"To save a bullet?"

"Possibly."

"Not just cruel, but stingy too."

Kessler was called to the telephone in the hall. The police post at Schlactensee had received a complaint from an apartment on Dubrowstrasse at 3:32 A.M. on Tuesday, August 20, 1991. A patrol car had called at the house in question. A man had come to the door, apologized, and promised to turn off the music. He had been tall, in his late thirties or early forties, and had spoken German, but the officer had thought he might be a foreigner—perhaps a Yugoslav or a Russian.

This information helped Kessler establish the approximate time of death for the two corpses; certainly it smelled about right. It also added weight to his hunch that neither the victims nor the murderers were German. The dead man in the hall had the kind of pudgy face and potato nose that Kessler associated with Slavs, and the woman's eyes, cheekbones, black hair, and sallow skin suggested a touch of Tatar blood. The tape label was in Russian, and most of the books in the house were printed in Cyrillic script.

Clearly they had passed themselves off as Germans. The bills for gas and electricity that he found in a drawer were addressed to Hermann Ludwig, and in the same bureau was writing paper, some headed HERMANN UND KLARA LUDWIG with the address on Dubrowstrasse, some headed LUDWIG KUNSTGALERIE, again with the address on Dubrowstrasse. Despite the absence of pictures, it seemed likely that the large rooms on the ground floor had been used as a gallery. There was little furniture, and spotlights pointed at rectangles of discoloration on the bare walls.

Only the kitchen and one of the bedrooms upstairs looked lived-in: the double bed was unmade and dirty dishes remained on the drainboard of the sink. In the kitchen, Kessler wrinkled his nose at the new odor of rotting rubbish.

"Whew!" said Dorn at his elbow.

"Russische Gemütlichkeit," said Kessler.

"You think they're Russians?"

"Yes."

"Mafia?"

"Perhaps."

"Come back, DDR, all is forgiven."

Kessler smiled. Like many West Berliners, he looked back with some nostalgia to the days when the Wall had made it easy to control crime in their half of the city. As a boy living in Wilmersdorf, he had watched U.S. planes fly supplies into Tempelhof to break the Russian blockade, and less than two weeks ago, when watching the attempted coup in Moscow on the television news, he had felt a twinge of that old angst. But by and large, life had been good in the divided city—certainly less complicated for a policeman than it was today with whole quarters of the city inhabited by Turks, Croats, Serbs, Hungarians, Czechs, Poles, Russians, and even Vietnamese and Ethiopians, each with their own network of criminals and racketeers.

"What do you think?" he asked Dorn as they returned from the kitchen into the hall.

"Could be theft with trimmings."

"Theft of what?"

"Paintings?"

Kessler looked around. "And the trimmings?"

"The woman."

"Why?"

"Why not? A little bit of what you fancy. Particularly if you've got to kill her anyway."

Kessler looked uncertain. "A professional thief wants to be in and out as quickly as he can."

"Usually, yes."

"He doesn't want to hang around listening to music or torturing women."

"Unless the thief happens to be a pervert."

"I don't think he did it for fun."

"Why not?"

"Because every now and then he took the tape from her mouth."

"To kiss her?" Dorn laughed.

Kessler remained grave. "To let her speak. To give her a chance to tell them what they wanted to know."

"And did she?"

Kessler hesitated. He thought of the look on her face. "Yes, in the end I think she probably did."

Dorn shook his head. "They can be really nasty, these Russian mafiosi."

"They're certainly learning."

"Well, so long as they only kill one another," said Dorn, "I don't really care."

II

1992
September–December

2

Nikolai Gerasimov looked down from the office of General Savchenko in the Lubyanka at the bare pedestal in the middle of Dzerzhinski Square. Where the statue of Felix Dzerzhinski had once stood, there remained only a stump. Nothing had yet replaced the founding father of the Cheka, the first Soviet secret police.

It was an unusually warm, even sultry, September day. The Lenin Hills were hidden behind the haze over Moscow. There was a move to call them the Sparrow Hills once again. Gerasimov had no view on the matter; he was neutral, even indifferent. Indeed, if anything had surprised him over the past months, it was the discovery of how little he cared when Marx and Lenin had followed Dzerzhinski into the trash can of history. He had been an enthusiastic member first of Komsomol and then the Party, but when President Yeltsin suspended the Party with a stroke of a pen, his only thoughts had been: Will I lose my job? Will they abolish the KGB?

Both were unnecessary anxieties. Without the Party, the secret police became the only effective means of governing the country, and Gerasimov had all the necessary qualities for preferment by the new regime. He was young, fit, good-looking, and spoke flawless English and German. His father was a retired army general, his wife the daughter of a physicist. Above all, he had that indifference to ideology, now called "professionalism," which qualified him as an officer in the new

11

Security Service of the Russian Federation and had led to a request for his transfer from Service A for special duties under General Savchenko in the Twelfth Department.

Others had been sacked to placate Yeltsin and the democratic forces. Officers responsible for the nastier measures taken against dissidents had gone. So had those known by Western intelligence agencies as the authors of some of the old KGB's more unsavory operations, as well as a group suspected of aiding the KGB commander, Kryuchkov, in planning the coup.

Gerasimov's own superior, General Savchenko, who now came back into his office, was secure. Posing for ten years as the London correspondent of a Moscow magazine, he had picked up some British mannerisms and habits of thought, as well as a certain tolerance for eccentricity and an aversion to dogma. Now a senior officer on the staff of the Twelfth Department of the First Chief Directorate, one of the few sections that still had offices in the Lubyanka, he was known to be close to Vadim Bakatin, chief of the KGB since the coup.

Savchenko was not uncritical of the actions of the new regime. He had confided to Gerasimov that it had been a mistake to let such dangerous men loose on the world with only a small pension in inflationary times, and now he had been given the task of "damage control" (he had used the American phrase to describe his role to Gerasimov), restructuring or closing networks that the sacked officers had controlled and doing what he could to recover the large sums in foreign currency that they had been allocated by the KGB to finance their operations abroad.

"Enjoying the view?" he asked as Gerasimov turned away from the window.

"I was wondering who would replace Dzerzhinski on the pedestal."

The colonel rolled his eyes and sighed, as if to say, Don't start on that! He was a squat, heavy man in a crumpled, shiny suit who, before the coup, had been trying to cut down his smoking to a pack a day. Now he was back to three.

"Save your energy," he said to Gerasimov. "Dzerzhinski is dead. We have trouble enough with the living."

Savchenko threw onto his desk the fat green file he had brought into the office. Both men sat down, Savchenko behind the battery of telephones on his desk, the most prestigious of them, the one with the hammer-and-sickle emblem which had connected him directly to the Central Committee, being now a museum piece. Gerasimov faced him in a comfortable leather chair. The wood of the desk and the other furniture matched the yellow-beech veneer of the walls. The door to the office was upholstered with purple plastic, as was common in Russia, to preserve privacy by muffling the sound—a pretense in the past, thought Gerasimov, since there had been microphones hidden behind the wooden veneer. And now? The microphones were probably still there, but he doubted whether anyone could be bothered to listen.

"Orlov," said Savchenko, patting the file on his desk. "Andrei Orlov. Captain. Did you know him?"

"No."

Savchenko gave a quick, penetrating look at Gerasimov, not mistrustful so much as thorough. "Are you sure? He was at the Foreign Intelligence School."

Gerasimov blushed at having answered so quickly. He thought back to his days at the Yurlovo. There had been a Gennady Orlov in his year, but he could remember no Andrei. He shook his head. "I don't remember him."

"No, well, he's a few years older." Savchenko opened the file. "And you never met him here, in the canteen or socially, with some of your friends?"

"Not that I can recall."

"There are a number of Orlovs. It is a common name."

"Yes, of course. I know a Gennady Orlov. . . ."

"But not an Andrei?"

"No."

Savchenko seemed satisfied. He looked down at the contents of the file and scratched the skin beneath the tousled hair on his head. "This Orlov was one of our best men." He paused, his breathing wheezy. "For most of his career he was with the First Chief Directorate. He did a spell in Africa for the Ninth Department, then in Washington for the First, and then worked in Moscow on the Washington desk. Two years ago he was transferred to work in the Second Chief Directorate under General Khrulev. Khrulev, as you may know, committed suicide after the coup."

"I heard," said Gerasimov.

"He too was one of our best men. A good comrade. Zealous, too

---

13

zealous. A true believer at a time when . . ." Pause. Wheeze. "At a time when it is prudent to retain a little skepticism, about everything and anything." He looked up at Gerasimov. "Loyalty to one's country, of course, and to the government of the day, but not to one's own convictions. Not to a cause."

"I understand."

"Professionalism . . . professionalism." Savchenko repeated the word as if he was trying to inculcate that quality in himself as much as in Gerasimov.

He lit another cigarette.

"You know, with Kryuchkov in prison and Khrulev dead, and most of Khrulev's people fired or in disgrace, it is difficult to pick up the trail of what they were doing just from the files." He paused, wheezed, and flicked through the papers.

"Were they involved in ongoing operations?" asked Gerasimov.

Savchenko gave a sigh. "Not according to the files. About two years ago, Khrulev put Orlov in charge of a particular operation in Germany. At one time Khrulev had served with the Eleventh Department, so he had good contacts in Berlin."

"The operation?"

"Kryuchkov had told Khrulev to stop the illegal export of icons. It was big business, as you know, but no one had thought much of it; in fact, many of our own people packed the odd icon in their suitcase when they went abroad, to get hold of some extra currency. It was a perk that went with the job. But Kryuchkov disapproved of it: squandering the national heritage, cheating the state of foreign earnings, that kind of thing. Orlov was considered something of an expert." He pushed the file over to the younger man.

Gerasimov looked first at the mug shot of a handsome clean-shaven man with strong features and plenty of wavy brown hair.

"As you can see," Savchenko said, "Orlov's background is unusual. He is the son of Anatoly Orlov."

"Anatoly Sergeyevich? The painter?"

"Precisely. Brezhnev's favorite artist."

Gerasimov nodded. He remembered trudging around art galleries as a child, looking up at the enormous canvases painted by Anatoly Orlov portraying triumphant workers with square jaws and grim faces, clutching red banners against a radiant sky.

"They had not only an apartment in Moscow," Savchenko went on, "but also a dacha in Zhukovska, a gift from the Central Committee. Anatoly Sergeyevich held the Order of Lenin and any number of state prizes. His paintings are in every gallery in the country." He laughed, coughed, and laughed again. "They were still there, at any rate, when I last went into a gallery, but they may not be there now."

Gerasimov looked down at the file. "Andrei Orlov was not a painter?"

"No. But he knew and cared about art. Khrulev felt he could trust him, for that and for other reasons which do not appear in the file."

"What other reasons?"

Savchenko waved his hand. "He had good connections . . . but that is beside the point. He was an excellent chekist. At the time of the coup, Orlov was out in the field. He was closing in on a man in Berlin named Maslyukov."

"An icon smuggler?"

"A smuggler and a receiver. But more than that, an organizer and a fixer. Almost a mastermind. In one of the memos, Khrulev estimates that more than half the icons smuggled out of the Soviet Union ended up with Maslyukov in Berlin."

"Did Orlov find him?"

"Yes. He found him, but it was messy. Three of them went in— Orlov and two others. Either they were expected or Maslyukov guessed who they were. Maslyukov was killed. His wife—" Savchenko continued his train of thought for a moment in silence. "They used extreme methods and persuaded her to talk. They recovered the icons. Orlov sent back ninety-seven, many of them major works, with a junior officer. His name's in the file."

"Partovski?"

"Yes. Partovski took a Volkswagen van on the ferry from Travemünde to Tallinn and then drove from Tallinn straight to the Tretyakov Gallery, where the icons remain today. Orlov flew back a week later and was sacked."

"Why? If the operation was a success?"

"Because of Khrulev. Not only had Orlov worked for Khrulev, it was thought he shared Khrulev's point of view. He was offered a job on the security staff of the Tretyakov, along with Partovski. Partovski accepted but Orlov refused."

"So what did Orlov do?"

"He disappeared."

"What do you mean?"

Savchenko frowned. "What I say. He left the service. No one bothered to find out what he was up to. But now that we want him, he can't be found."

"Why do we want him?"

Savchenko sighed. "In reviewing the past operations of General Khrulev, I have come across certain . . . irregularities. Some of his files are missing, not just ones like these"—Savchenko nodded at the file in front of Gerasimov—"but also computer files, erased from the hard disk and with the backups removed from Khrulev's safe. Khrulev, you see, was permitted to work on his own. The icon operation in particular had to be secret, even within the Lubyanka, because so many of our own people had done business with the Maslyukovs. For this reason, Khrulev may have used agents in Germany who were known only to him. It is the files relating to these agents that have disappeared."

"Could Khrulev have erased them before he killed himself?"

"It's possible."

"Or do you think Orlov might have taken them?"

Savchenko shrugged. "That too is possible."

"Why would he want them?"

Savchenko lit another cigarette. "I don't know. That's what we would like to ask him. And there is something else. There is reason to believe that Orlov may have got hold of the Maslyukovs' money, but he only returned the icons. He may therefore be guilty of appropriating state funds."

"So he may simply have gone back to the West to live on the Maslyukovs' money?"

"If you study the file, you will see why that is unlikely. Orlov was not chosen by Khrulev simply for his talents. They were like-minded—zealots—and shared the same ideals. I cannot believe Orlov has changed simply because of the failure of the coup."

"So why did he want the money?"

"I don't know, but consider this: Khrulev sends Orlov to Berlin to recover the icons. Just as Orlov is about to pounce on the Maslyukovs, the coup occurs. Khrulev commits suicide. Does Orlov abort the operation? No. He goes ahead, feeling, perhaps, that he now bears the responsibility for Khrulev's mission—not just the mission to recover the icons but the mission in a much wider sense. Indeed, the failure of the coup, followed by the suspension of the Party, must have made it clear to Orlov that if the Party was to survive it would have to go underground, and that if it was now cut off from the resources of the Soviet government, it would have to raise funds as best it could."

"But if he got hold of the Maslyukovs' money, why has he now gone back to the West?"

"That is what I want you to find out."

"Do we know where he is?"

Savchenko shrugged. "The only thing we know for sure is that he took a night train to Kiev on October twelfth of last year. From there it is possible that he flew to Vienna on one of his Western passports, possibly posing as a German microbiologist who had been in Kiev for a convention."

Gerasimov could not restrain a feeling of excited anticipation at the thought of a trip to the West. "Do we know the names on his Western passports?"

"We know the passports he used for the icon operation, but he may have new ones. He had friends in Directorate S. It's quite possible that someone arranged for replacements."

Gerasimov leafed through the file. "Who was the third man?"

"A noncommissioned officer, a Chechen called Kastiev. He returned, but not with Partovski, and was then sacked."

"And now?"

"He too cannot be found."

"Was he fired for his links with Khrulev?"

"No. He was—" Savchenko hesitated "—his methods, his specialty as it were, belonged to an earlier era."

"Kryuchkov's?"

"More like Beria's. It is regrettable, in my view, that such people should ever have been employed by our state security. We may all have to do unsavory things from time to time, but the Chechen is the kind of man . . . well, in my view, he should be either in a prison or an asylum, not the KGB."

"Do you think he's with Orlov?"

Savchenko shrugged. "Kastiev is cunning, even fanatical, but he speaks no languages. He would not have gone West without Orlov, so where we find Orlov we will find Kastiev too."

"What about their wives?"

"Kastiev was not married, and Orlov hasn't lived with his wife for several years."

"All the same, she might know where he is."

"Yes, but leave her alone for the moment. Her father still has powerful friends."

"So should I pick up Orlov's trail in Vienna?" asked Gerasimov, trying not to show his eagerness.

Savchenko shook his head. "No. At least, not yet. There must be someone in Moscow who knows where Orlov can be found. Read the file. Talk to the people here who knew him. Talk to the officers still in the Lubyanka who served under Khrulev. There is also Partovski at the Tretyakov and, if you get nowhere with other sources, Orlov's father and Orlov's wife. But be tactful. People's respect for our State Security Service is not what it was."

At six that evening, Gerasimov drove out of the Lubyanka in a beige Samara, his briefcase with the file on Andrei Orlov on the seat beside him, and at once became caught in traffic. Before the coup he might have sped up one of the emergency lanes, confident that if stopped by the militia he could get away with it as an officer in the KGB, but now, in these democratic times, not even the generals in their Zils used this privilege. It was prudent to be discreet.

Nor did Gerasimov resent the time spent in his 1989 Samara, a small car with only two doors but one of the only Soviet models with a modern Western design. He had bought it with all his savings and a loan from his father the general, and he had added accessories—a Blaupunkt radio and a radar scanning device—brought back from trips to the West.

He crossed the ring road and continued north on Prospekt Mira toward Sputnik Park. The engine hiccuped, and the car faltered but then picked up again. Gerasimov cursed the dirty gasoline that clogged the carburetor. He would have to phone Georgi. When the traffic stopped he shifted into neutral and revved the engine to prevent it from dying. He looked at the faces of the other drivers, then at the people on the pavement making for the Rizhskaya metro station. As always, their expressions were gloomy and inscrutable. Two generations of terror had taught them to hide their feelings, and the present political changes were too recent to persuade them to drop their masks now.

Gerasimov looked at his own face in the mirror of the Samara. Did he look different? He was fitter and healthier than most Muscovites; the staff restaurant at the Lubyanka might not be quite as lavish as it was in the days of the KGB, but it still provided a better bill of fare than the average office or factory canteen. He also had regular medical checkups, access to a gym, and, before the coup, an annual vacation with his family at the KGB's holiday complex on the Black Sea. He still had marks on his face from acne in adolescence, but so did Harrison Ford; Gerasimov liked to think that when he stuck out his jaw he bore a close resemblance to the American star.

Gerasimov also showed a certain confidence in his bearing; an ordinary Muscovite could sense he was one of the few who was accustomed to kick the many around. But even the most confident can face frustration, and as the Samara chugged forward his forehead creased in a frown. He was hungry but was not sure there would be anything for supper. The conference with Savchenko had gone on longer than expected, so the special store in the Lubyanka had been closed when he came out, and the canteen had run out of supplies. He had called his wife to warn her, but her reply—a deep sigh—did not encourage him to hope that she had then gone out to join a line at a state shop or to squander her housekeeping allowance at the free market. More likely, she would suggest going to some astronomically expensive cooperative restaurant, if one could be found that would take rubles rather than dollars.

Gerasimov had run out of dollars. Surely some would have to be allocated for his investigation of Orlov? Without a trip to the West, this was a tacky assignment. Gerasimov was trained to use his wits against an enemy, but now he was being asked to investigate a colleague; for all Savchenko's talk of professionalism, there was a political whiff about the job, a quiet purge by the democrats of those officers who might suffer from too much nostalgia.

Not that he had much sympathy for the likes of Orlov. Gerasimov had first gone to the West in his twenties and been stunned by the prosperity, but he was prepared by years of ideological training in school and university, the Komsomol, and the Party to believe that the capitalist countries were richer because they had got off to an earlier start. It was only when he was sent to Singapore early in 1986 to pick up the products of some industrial espionage that he realized that in one generation the Asian nations had overtaken the Communist nations of the Soviet Union and Eastern Europe. Why, if socialism was superior, did Russians have to steal secrets from Chinks?

No doubt Gorbachev had reached the same conclusion; Gerasimov had returned to the new policy proclaimed at the Twenty-seventh Party Congress: glasnost and perestroika. But two months later came the catastrophe at Chernobyl, and after that things had gone from bad to worse. A leopard can't change its spots. Too many had a vested interest in the status quo. Gerasimov had seen the way in which his own superiors had paid lip service to glasnost and perestroika while working behind the scenes to frustrate them. It was not just that they wanted to hang on to their privileges; it was also the impossibility of envisaging any other way. Free speech? Free elections? These were the slogans of the imperialists and capitalists they had been trained to fight. A free market? The only entrepreneurs in the Soviet Union were the gangsters the KGB were supposed to prosecute—currency speculators, icon smugglers, and black marketeers. It was like being told to surrender to the enemy without a fight.

But when it had come to the crunch during the attempted coup a year ago, no one could face the thought of a return to the old days either. Seeing "Vremya," the nine o'clock news on television, was like watching a newsreel of Stalin's days that someone had dug up from the archives. The old rhetoric and bombast had raised the blood pressure of Gerasimov's father, the old general, but the officers of the KGB's Alpha group had refused to storm the "White House." The coup had collapsed, and Yeltsin had triumphed, and Gerasimov's only worry had been for his job.

Any Muscovite who knew the building on the Ulitsa Academika Koroleva where Gerasimov now parked the Samara would have understood why. The apartment that went with his job was easy to reach from the center of town, had a fine view over Sputnik Park, and had been built to a far higher standard than that usually found in Soviet dwellings. Some of the apartments were assigned to Western journalists, and one of Gerasimov's duties was to keep his eyes and ears open in the lobby and the elevator—a small price to pay for two bedrooms, a living room, and a kitchen and bathroom with Finnish fittings.

The furniture was Russian, the same glass-fronted bookcase and three-piece suite that could be found in a million other apartments. The large color television had been made in Riga, but there was a Panasonic video recorder brought back from a trip to Frankfurt and a Sansui stereo system from the trip to Singapore. Of the books in the bookcase, some, like Jack London's *The Iron Heel*, were English-language editions published in Moscow dating from Gerasimov's days as a student in the Institute of International Relations. Others were Russian classics by Chekhov and Gorky, and there were a few Western bestsellers whose tattered covers betrayed how often they had been lent to the Gerasimovs' friends.

Since the advent of the VCR, neither Gerasimov nor his wife Ylena had read much. Thanks to Georgi, they were able to get pirated editions of most Western movies, some of which Ylena watched two or three times. Her job in the library of the All-Union Institute of Geology was not challenging; she had persuaded her doctor to certify that she was susceptible to migraines and so often returned in the early afternoon to watch yet again a grainy copy of *Pretty Woman* or *Gone With the Wind*.

She also followed all the soap operas, both Brazilian and home-grown, and when Gerasimov entered his flat that evening he was greeted not by the smell of cooking but the sound of the TV. He hung up his coat in the closet in the hall, removed his shoes, put his briefcase in his bedroom, and went into the kitchen to confirm that there was nothing either in the fridge or on the stove. This established, he went to the living room to try to disengage his wife's attention from the television and discuss what they should do about dinner.

Ylena was curled up on the sofa, a box of cookies at her side. She looked at Gerasimov for less than a second, to let him know that she knew he was there; then her attention returned to the screen.

Gerasimov's spirits sank when he saw that most of the cookies had been eaten; Ylena was a woman who acted on whim and only thought about food if she was hungry. Like Gerasimov, she was in her early thirties and was still attractive, with brown hair, blue eyes, and a porcelain complexion, but already the soft femininity found in Russian girls had been replaced by a fixed look of dissatisfaction. In the former Soviet

Union, dreams had faded fast, and if Ylena as the wife of an officer in the KGB had been pampered in comparison to other Soviet wives, with the nice apartment, the car, and holidays in the Crimea, her life still fell far short of the glossy luxury she saw on videos from the West and now, since the coup, had fallen shorter still.

Nor had Ylena's privileged status saved her from the wear and tear of a married life where the pill was unobtainable, even for the wife of an officer in the KGB, and condoms so precious that they were washed after use and hung on a line to dry. She had had a baby, Sasha, soon after they had married, then four abortions in seven years, then nothing—neither sex nor abortions—until Georgi came up with some pornographic videos, after which came a short-lived revival of their sex lives, followed by two more abortions.

Gerasimov suspected that she slept from time to time with some geologist at the institute, probably behind the cupboards containing specimens of rock, or even with her boss, Professor Bloch; someone had recently supplied her with tights and tampons, and he had noticed a box of Roger et Gallet soap in the bathroom. She had told him that her girlfriend Lubov had been given some by a French scientist who visited the botanical institute where Lubov worked. Gerasimov had let it go; after all, he had affairs from time to time with typists and translators at the Lubyanka.

They stayed together, or had until then, partly because of Sasha, partly because it served their interests. Ylena liked the apartment and the perks that went with her husband's job. Gerasimov knew the apparent stability would help his career, as did his connection with his father-in-law, who was in good standing with the Party. Now, of course, the Party had been suspended and even those like Gerasimov who had kept their jobs in the Security Service of the Russian Federation could no longer count on the perks that had kept Ylena happy. The cursory glance and the sour look she had on her face when she finally turned off the television were the punishment meted out to the now not-so-mighty hunter who had failed to bring home a rabbit for the pot.

"Where's Sasha?"

"He's with my mother. She had a chicken."

"Couldn't you have bought a chicken?"

"You said you could get some sausage."

"I missed it. I was busy."

She pouted and shrugged. "It was too late to go out, and anyway, do you know what they cost now, on the market? Who can afford a chicken except the profiteers?"

"Your mother—"

"She was given it by her friend Natalia. She's been at their dacha."

"That was kind of her."

"She's done things for them."

Gerasimov glanced at the cabinet, where he knew there was a bottle of vodka still a third full. He longed for a drink but knew that if he started drinking on an empty stomach, with Ylena in this mood, it might end in a squalid quarrel.

To placate both his wife and his growling stomach, he gave up all thought of thrift and suggested eating out.

This did not produce the enthusiasm in Ylena that he had expected. She sighed. "Where?"

"The place on Petrovski Boulevard."

"They only take currency."

"Since when?"

She shrugged. "Lubov told me. They went there last week."

"What about the new cooperative near the Kazan station? I was told that they take rubles."

"They won't let you in unless they know you."

"I'll show them my service card."

She laughed—with derision, not merriment. "Then they'll cut your throat."

"I'll call Georgi. He'll get us in."

"Don't call Georgi."

"Why not?"

She wrinkled her nose.

"I've got to call him anyway about the car."

She looked away. Gerasimov went to the telephone in the hall. It had only been a year since Georgi had acquired a telephone and his number had been added to the list pinned on the wall. Gerasimov dialed the first digits, then stopped and disconnected the line. Inexplicably, he suddenly felt that he should collect his thoughts and consider the tone to adopt in talking to Georgi.

He frowned, irritated with himself for hesitating in this way. After all,

Georgi Nazayan was his creation, a young fixer who in the old days would have been condemned as a work-shy parasite but who in the Brezhnev years became an indispensable bridge between the theory and practice of life in a socialist state.

Gerasimov had first met him outside the apartment house in the grim suburb where he had lived before his promotion: a sly, ingratiating young Armenian who had offered to clean his car. Gerasimov had given him the job for twenty kopeks and then casually asked if he knew where he could get any windshield-wiper blades; he had forgotten to remove them the night before and they were gone in the morning.

Georgi delivered new blades that evening and offered replacements for the old Lada's balding tires. Gerasimov had known they would certainly be stolen, but he agreed, and in the years that followed he came to rely upon Georgi not just to maintain his car but to provide the mundane things that were not to be found even in the KGB's special stores: washers, drain plugs, fuse wire. In return he would supply Georgi with surplus Western goods that were easy for him to acquire: packs of razor blades and Marlboros, bottles of cognac, jars of Nescafé, and tins of ham.

By the time Gerasimov and Ylena had moved to the apartment on the Ulitsa Academika Koroleva, Georgi, now in his twenties, had expanded into more complex transactions for a wider clientele, including some of the foreign journalists who lived in the same building. Foreign currency, airline tickets, and residence permits were available to all those who could pay. But Gerasimov remained his most favored customer; Georgi had found him the Samara and would himself fetch and deliver it just to change the oil. In return, Gerasimov protected Georgi from the militia who were always on his tail. He let it be known that Georgi's dealings were of some value to the KGB, and such was the residual fear of this organization that impending charges of illegal currency dealing and black marketeering were dropped.

In the year since the coup, all this had changed. With its boss behind bars, the KGB was demonstrably no longer above and beyond the law. Now it was not Gerasimov's influence but Georgi's bribes and intimidation of potential witnesses that kept the militia off his back. He could well afford the bribes; his business was booming. He had a team working under him, some looking less like fixers than like thugs. He still saw to the Samara, sending someone to fetch it whenever Gerasimov called, but he himself had a two-year-old Mercedes and a three-room apartment near the Kremlin.

It was the realization that it was becoming absurd to phone this flourishing entrepreneur about clogged carburetors that made Gerasimov hesitate before making his call. He turned toward the living room, as if to consult Ylena, but then remembered that she was opposed to the call. He looked back at Georgi's number on the list above the telephone. Why was he so nervous? Nothing Georgi had said suggested that he was no longer willing to fix the Samara; in fact, he had been exceptionally friendly and unctuous when they last met. Almost certainly—and quite rightly—Georgi still felt indebted for services rendered in the past. Nevertheless, it might be more in keeping with his new status to mention the clogged carburetor in passing and to ask about the restaurant first.

When Gerasimov dialed the number his call was answered by Georgi's wife. He could hear music and voices in the background, and then Georgi came to the telephone.

"Georgi."

"Nikolai. Just one moment." He shouted to someone to turn the music down.

"We thought of going out tonight to that cooperative near the Kazan station. Do you know if it's any good?"

"Don't touch it."

"Ah. Where would you suggest?"

"Are you at home?"

"Yes."

"I'll pick you up in half an hour."

"If you really—"

"Don't worry. I'll be there."

The Mercedes was driven by one of the bulky bodyguards. Georgi sat in the back; he was without his wife.

"Ylena sends her apologies," said Gerasimov as he climbed in beside Georgi.

"She's not hungry?" The young man grinned, showing some teeth capped in gold.

Gerasimov shrugged. "She says she's tired."

"Never mind."

The car moved off, the driver barging into the traffic as if the Mercedes were an official Zil. "It's good to see you, Nikolai," said Georgi, in a slightly patronizing tone. "You've been on my mind. There are many matters we could talk about. This is now the land of opportunity, you know, for those who know how to seize it."

"I daresay." Gerasimov glanced uneasily at the young man beside him. He had grown plumper in the months since the coup and wore a dark blue suit. He was balding at the temples, which made him seem as old as Gerasimov, when in fact he was not yet thirty. His breath smelled of garlic and tobacco.

"Did you get the videos I sent over?"

"Yes."

"Pretty Woman?"

"Yes."

"A classic. I show it to the girls so they can learn. Class! Style!"

Gerasimov was not sure what girls Georgi was speaking about—certainly not the friends of his daughter, since the little girl was only two.

"The place I'm taking you to is new. I want to know what you think. I have a fifty percent interest in it."

Again Gerasimov smarted at the patronizing tone but felt relieved to think that Georgi would pay the bill.

"There's good money in these cooperatives, but they can be a nightmare because you have to ensure your own supplies, which means payoffs right down the line." Georgi stretched out an arm and pointed his finger out of the window. "I mean *right* down the line—to Georgia, Armenia, Azerbaijan."

He continued to explain the economics of owning a restaurant as they drove down the Nikitski Boulevard and finally came to a stop in a side street near the Arbat. There he went to a door on the ground floor of a nondescript building that could have housed an office or a flat and knocked twice. A small hatch cut into the door opened and a pair of eyes looked through. When Georgi said his name the hatch closed, the door opened, and they were let in.

The inside of the building had been done up in style. Gerasimov had been to half a dozen of the better cooperatives, and this was on a par with the best. A girl took their coats and the headwaiter, wearing a black tie, led Georgi to a corner table with a civility that was quite unknown in the former Soviet Union. The carpet, chairs, tablecloths, and cutlery were all certainly from abroad.

The restaurant was about half full. The light was dim and there was an air of discretion about the diners, who either kept their eyes down or looked at those at the same table. Gerasimov thought he recognized a senior officer from the Lubyanka but he was with a younger woman, so Gerasimov looked away. Almost half the diners had the swarthy look of the Caucasus, and some were greeted by Georgi as he crossed the room.

Almost as soon as they sat down, a carafe of vodka was placed on the table, soon followed by small plates of chopped herring, celery, tomato, and a medium-sized jar of caviar. Georgi poured out the vodka. "To our wives," he said, and they clinked glasses.

It was the first of a number of toasts. The first carafe of vodka was soon emptied and, without their having to ask, a second appeared. The food took longer; they were given salad but then had to wait half an hour for some borsch. Finding Georgi's conversation irksome, Gerasimov only too readily allowed him to fill his glass. He talked about the past and the future, about business and pleasure, about taking pleasure in business and making a business out of pleasure. What he said was of little interest—increasingly drunken drivel—but it was the tone rather than the content that annoyed Gerasimov, vacillating between unctuousness and condescension, both appealing to him for approbation and yet somehow sneering at him for being there, sponging off his former minion.

Both men became drunk. Georgi sent for a bottle of French wine—Gerasimov dared not think what it cost—and then insisted that his guest help him drink it. Three quarters of an hour after the borsch, the waiter served them with dry pork chops and some noodles. By now Gerasimov had lost his appetite, but he could hardly forgo such a luxury. He forced the food down, listening as he did so to Georgi's increasingly slurred exposition of what he called "a Russian interpretation of the new world order."

"You see, Nikolai, my dear friend, we have to understand that there is only one path to take and that is the same path taken by the Americans, because Russia is like America—a big, big country—and that is the path we should have taken and would have taken if that swine Lenin and all those Jews hadn't hijacked the country and led us down the road to our present ruin. Decades lost. How many decades? 1917, 1927"—he started to count them off on his fingers but became muddled—"years. Years and years, wasted, going down the wrong road, but now we're on the right road, but way back, way back. We're like America a hundred years ago, and we have to go through the same historical processes they did, with gold rushes and Al Capone. . . ."

Gerasimov scarcely listened to what Georgi was saying. This lecture by the little twerp on world history was as pretentious as it was patronizing. What did he know? He had never even graduated from high school, and here he was droning on like a professor. Yet despite his inattention and the effect of the vodka and wine, Gerasimov remembered his clogged carburetor and all the time was wondering how he could slip it into the conversation.

"And *The Godfather*. Did you see the videos of *The Godfather*? Yes? Marlon Brando, Al Pacino. You know, some of the boys think I look a little like Al Pacino?"

"Why not? They say I look like Harrison Ford."

Georgi laughed. "Well, I'd say Kevin Costner. Elliot Ness in *The Untouchables*? You must have seen that. I sent it over to Ylena. It was bit fuzzy, but still . . . you should learn from movies like that. The militia, they're corrupt, like the Chicago police. You KGB men, you're the G-men, the Untouchables."

Gerasimov frowned. Had he seen *The Untouchables*? He could not remember. "I don't think I saw it."

"I'll send another copy. And some Dutch porn—fantastic stuff. Women with women! You can't imagine."

Gerasimov forced a grin, to establish that he was one of the boys, but at the same time shook his head. "No, thanks. We're not into that at present."

The waiter put some pink ice cream in front of Gerasimov. Georgi waved his away, lit a cigarette, and took a long look at Gerasimov through narrowed eyes as he exhaled the smoke toward him across the table. "Not into *that*," he asked, "or not into *her*?"

While Gerasimov had discussed his defunct sex life with a number of his friends, he had never considered that he was on such terms with Georgi, but having eaten caviar and drunk a good pint of vodka at Georgi's expense, and faced now with a goblet full of pink ice cream, it seemed churlish not to confide in him, man to man. "Well, you know how it is."

"Sure," said Georgi, "but a man's a man."

"I get by," said Gerasimov, the roguish grin back on his face.

"And a woman's a woman."

"Sure."

"We're friends, aren't we?"

"Of course."

"So let me give you a bit of advice."

Gerasimov kept the grin on his face and nodded.

"A woman's a little like a car."

At last! thought Gerasimov. The carburetor!

"She needs fuel."

"Don't we all."

"The higher the octane, the better she runs."

"Unless the carburetor—"

Georgi raised his hand, frowning at this interruption. "Wait. Let me finish. She runs better on high octane: pretty clothes, nice restaurants, holidays in the Crimea."

"Sure."

"Not just Ylena. They're all the same."

Gerasimov nodded, waiting patiently to return to the carburetor.

"But they also need servicing, Nikolai. Regular servicing, thorough servicing."

"I know."

"And Ylena hasn't been getting that from you."

"Well, from time to time—"

"Nikolai." Georgi looked at him almost with reproof. "I know the score. She told me."

"She told you?"

"Tell me if I'm wrong."

"You're not wrong, but . . . but when did she tell you?"

Georgi sighed. "Nikolai, we're friends, aren't we?"

"Of course, but—"

"Nikolai, I can't bear to see a good woman go to waste. I've been seeing Ylena."

"You've been seeing . . . you've been *fucking* Ylena?" Gerasimov gripped the sides of the table, his knuckles white with the force of his grip.

Georgi sighed and stood up. "Let's get out into the fresh air." He sauntered away from the table and signed a chit of some kind at the headwaiter's desk.

Gerasimov followed him dumbly. He was dizzy from the drink. They stood side by side, silently, waiting for their coats. Gerasimov could not decide what he should say or do. He could pound him into a pulp. Once out in the street, he *would* pound him into a pulp; his KGB training would more than make up for the extra years. But then who would see to his Samara?

Out in the street, the fresh air increased the dizziness and sense of dislocation. Had Georgi really said that he had been sleeping with Ylena? He gripped the lapel of Georgi's fancy Italian overcoat. "Are you telling me, just like that, that you've been screwing my wife?"

"Your wife? She's not your wife. She's Ylena, a fantastic woman, Nikolai: getting plump, the way our women do, but really fantastic." He shook his head in wonderment. "I mean, how you could let something like that lie fallow?"

Gerasimov drew back his arm to strike Georgi, but before he could bring his fist forward he felt it gripped from behind. He was held by Georgi's driver.

Georgi shook his head in affected sorrow, as if Gerasimov had let him down. "Come on, Nikolai. Don't get so upset. If it wasn't me, it would have been someone else."

Gerasimov dropped his arm and, released by the driver, staggered a few paces away. He looked up to the top story of the building on the other side of the street, then higher up to the sky. There were no stars, just dreary cloud, colored by the dim orange light of the streetlamps.

Georgi took him by the arm. "Come on."

Gerasimov allowed himself to be led back to the Mercedes and slumped into the backseat with Georgi beside him. For a while they sat in silence; then, in a flat tone of voice, Gerasimov said, "Send someone to see to the Samara, will you? There's something wrong with the carburetor."

Georgi looked ahead. "I'll do that and more." He leaned forward and said to the driver, "Go to the Cosmos." Then he turned to Gerasimov. "I daresay you could do with servicing, too."

"What?"

"Let's go see some of my friends."

Gerasimov closed his eyes, his head resting on the back of his seat. He longed to go to bed, but not with Ylena. How could she? With Georgi! With the greasy Armenian errand boy! Why? For the soap? The tights? Was it just Russian women, or did all women barter with their cunts?

The Mercedes drove up a ramp of the Cosmos Hotel. Gerasimov opened his eyes and looked up at the tall Western-style building: still no stars. He climbed out after Georgi. Four or five girls, beautifully dressed and made up, clustered around them. "Get us in, Georgi, please." Georgi glanced toward the doorman, then turned to two of the girls. "You're with me."

As he passed the doorman, Georgi slipped him a roll of dollars. In the immense atrium of the hotel, Gerasimov waited with the driver while Georgi went to the desk. The girls hovered a short way off, their faces straining to give an air of sophistication.

Georgi returned with a key, and they all went up in the elevator. Georgi gave the key to the driver, who gently took Gerasimov's arm and led him along the corridor while Georgi kept the two girls by the elevator. Gerasimov looked back and saw them talking. The driver opened the door and led Gerasimov into a suite. "Look, TV, minibar, bathroom." He showed him around with a certain pride.

Then the girls came in, Georgi behind them. "Have a good time," Georgi said to Gerasimov.

Gerasimov looked at him with no expression. "Tell the bitch—"

"Forget it. I've got other things to do."

"The Samara—"

"Sure. I won't forget the Samara."

When Georgi left the room with his driver, the girls came back into the room. One pouted and the other giggled. The pouter sidled up to him. "So, sexy, how do you like it?" She loosened his tie and undid a button of his shirt. The giggler was smaller and blond. "Both together, or one at a time?" A hand went under his shirt and stroked his skin; another undid the buckle of his belt. "He's generous, your friend Georgi," said the pouter. "You've got both of us all night."

"So take your time, big boy," said the blonde, "take your time."

He lay back on the bed like a patient in a hospital, and like nurses the girls removed his clothes. Then they took off some of their own, careful not to crease the blouses and skirts, climbed onto the bed in their exotic Western underclothes, and started kissing and nibbling his skin. Like eager young actresses, they did what they had seen on Georgi's videos, but inexpertly confused the roles of tooth and tongue. Typical Russian whores, thought Gerasimov as he flinched at the pain. They even get a blow job wrong.

3

The young American art historian Francesca McDermott had slept little while crossing the Atlantic from Boston to Frankfurt, so she dozed off on the connecting flight to Berlin. She awoke only as the plane approached Tegel, now one of the two airports serving the city. She looked out the window. It was September, and the trees of Spandau Forest were already losing their leaves. The pale sun reflected off the water of the Tegeler See. When the plane turned to make its approach, Francesca could make out the Radio Tower and the Olympic Stadium.

Ten years before, when Francesca had last been to Berlin, Tegel had been in the French sector of the city. Now that Germany and Berlin were reunited, there was little sign of occupation by the Western powers beyond the fact that Lufthansa was not yet permitted to fly from Frankfurt to Berlin; the line carrying Francesca was Air France. Everything else about the airport was German—West German: the cleanliness, efficiency, and brisk courtesy of the airport personnel. Since Frankfurt to Berlin was now classified as an internal flight, there was no passport check, but no one curious about Francesca's nationality would have had to see her passport to know she was a citizen of the United States. She was tall, healthy, and handsome, pert Irish features on a body that had been fed steak, not potatoes, went jogging every morning, and played squash on weekends. She walked toward the baggage carousel with the assurance of a well-educated, well-dressed, and well-paid professional woman from the land of the free: a competitive glint in the eye, an elegance that is composed rather than seductive, and a similar sexual allure, healthy rather than lush, proclaiming that a woman is a woman, not just the plaything of a man.

Ten years before, Francesca McDermott had looked different—not quite a hippie, because she was already a graduate student, but rarely out of jeans, and with her hair, now so well cut at great cost, gathered into a ponytail by an elastic band. For this reason, when she came to the gate the woman she recognized as Sophie Diederich did not recognize her, which was just as well. Surely Francesca's face betrayed the shock she felt at the sight of Sophie, not simply because Sophie—who was in any case five years older than Francesca—now looked a good ten years older, but because in all other ways she was so entirely unchanged, her hair in greasy wisps, her clothes the same dungarees worn in dissident circles back in the 1980s.

All sorts of reasons for Sophie's wretched appearance passed through Francesca's mind: stress, diet, persecution, not least the month she had spent in prison in the old DDR. Even so, she thought, a woman can make the best of herself or at least appear to try, and a look of sisterly determination crossed her face as she pushed the baggage cart toward her friend.

Sophie Diederich, who had not had the advantage of recognizing Francesca in advance, could not hide an expression of confusion as she realized that the tall, elegant woman in a beige suit and red silk scarf held at her throat by an antique brooch was the same Francesca she had known ten years before. Though her face broke into a smile of unreserved delight, she checked the impulse to hug her as if it might be somehow inappropriate. Francesca, both more composed and more controlled, pushed the cart aside and with a cry of "Sophie, I can't believe it!" embraced and kissed the small woman.

They went to the parking lot, where Francesca was again taken aback by the sight of Sophie's car, an East German Wartburg with a two-stroke engine that puttered like an overworked sewing machine as they set off down the motorway toward the Stadtring. Surely the wife of the new Prussian Minister of Culture should be driving a BMW or, at worst, a Volkswagen?

"We'll go down the Ku'damm," said Sophie cheerfully, "so you can see how it's all changed."

She drove haphazardly, as if realizing that the shiny Western cars would give her old Wartburg a wide berth. She chattered in German as she drove, and Francesca, her German now rusty, sometimes found it hard to follow. "Dearest Francesca, it is so wonderful that you are here; there is so much to tell you. And you, you are a professor? No, a lecturer, but Dr. . . . *Dr.* McDermott, and from that thesis that you were working on here on the Bauhaus, yes?"

"That's right."

"It was just like fate when they said we must get an expert from America, perhaps even Francesca McDermott, because then the Americans will be more likely to lend their paintings, and Stefan agreed, and, in the end, so did even the Russian, and it never occurred to me that this was you, *our* Francesca. But then Stefi said it was you, and he had invited you over because now he—you know he's a minister?—he can decide these things. He has only to flick his fingers and there is the money because all the parties want the New Grouping—that's Stefi's party—to support them in a coalition, and they know he can influence them one way or another."

"Is he the leader?"

"You know, the group has no leader. We had too much of leaders before, with Ulbricht and Honecker. Anyway, it's not a party as such, only a group, because we had too much—much too much—of the word *party*."

"I can believe it."

"But Stefi really is a first among equals. The candlelight vigils—you must have read about them or seen them on television?—he was among the first to organize them when it was still dangerous, very dangerous. No one imagined—no one even dreamed—that the whole thing would collapse so quickly."

"It was incredible."

"Incredible, yes. And if it wasn't for Gorbachev and Shevardnadze there would have been no change from communism to democracy. The Wall would still be standing. And thank God for Yeltsin too, but he is unfair to Gorbachev, I think. At any rate, for us Germans, Gorby is a hero, a big hero, but there also had to be little heroes, and Stefi was a little hero. He organized the vigils, and he was on the citizens' committee that took control of the Stasi headquarters here in Berlin."

"With all those files?"

"The files! God help us. Six million of them! They started to burn them, you know, because they thought the Stasi would be back, but then they realized they were burning the records of the spies themselves—the IMs, the 'unofficial collaborators.' But Francesca, if you knew. . . . Our friends, our dearest and closest friends in the Evangelical Church, the Peace Now movement, and the Ecological Group—Stasi spies, all along! Spies and provocateurs!"

"I read about it, Sophie. It must have been terrible, as bad as anything that went before."

"In a way it was worse. . . . Look, here we are in the Ku'damm. You remember? You had a room near Savignyplatz, didn't you?"

"Yes. On Schlüterstrasse."

"It's so nice around there, so lively. Of course then we could only imagine it."

"You haven't moved to the West?"

"No. God forbid. That's what they expect. A house in Charlottenburg, a Mercedes. But Stefi won't hear of it. We are where we always were. You'll see; nothing has changed."

Francesca looked out at the shops and cafés on the Kurfürstendamm—not so very different now from what she remembered from ten years before. "And have you seen your Stasi file?" she asked Sophie, to return to the subject they had touched on before.

"No."

"Are you going to?"

Sophie sighed. "Perhaps. I don't know. Stefi's against it."

"Why?"

"He says the wounds will never heal if we keep reopening them and that he would rather not know if some of our friends were Stasi spies. He prefers to give them all the benefit of the doubt."

"I can understand that."

"You see, when the Wall came down, we were all deliriously happy; we could not believe it. But now, three years later, we see the problems."

They had now passed the Kaiser Wilhelm Memorial Church at the foot of the Kurfürstendamm, its ruins preserved as a memorial to

World War II, and turned toward the Tiergarten. "There are so many *practical* problems," Sophie went on. "The sewers, the electricity. Did you know that the grid supplying East Berlin is controlled from Kiev? There are industrial and economic problems. Politically we are now one country, but economically the two halves of Germany are half a century apart. But there is also the *moral* problem, the lack in the provinces of the old DDR of any positive values, any values at all. . . . Look, here's the Goddess of Victory on top of her column, and there's the Brandenburg Gate."

Francesca looked out at these landmarks through the windows of the Wartburg. "No more checkpoints?"

"No more checkpoints, just traffic jams. There still aren't that many places where you can cross from one half of the city to the other." She jerked the car forward. "I'll try the Invalidenstrasse. We can see Unter den Linden some other time."

"There's no hurry."

"Does that mean you'll stay?"

"I would certainly like to," said Francesca, "if it can be arranged."

"Oh," said Sophie with a laugh, "they don't understand about contracts or salaries. You can ask for anything you like."

Francesca blushed. She had not been thinking so much of remuneration—her salary on sabbatical would pay the mortgage on her apartment in Boston—but rather of status and authority. But that would come later. Now, while she was alone with Sophie, she wanted to catch up on her friend's personal life.

"Sophie," she said quietly, "what happened to Paul?"

"Ah, Paul. . . ."

"I mean, not just *to* him, but *between* you and him, because when I was here—"

"We were married. I know."

"And you seemed so happy."

For the first time since Francesca's arrival, Sophie Diederich appeared almost subdued. "Paul," she began; then she hesitated and said, "Poor Paul." And added, "You know, after the Communists were thrown out, he was made mayor of his village."

"Where's that?"

"North of Berlin. Bechtling, not far from Dierberg."

"Does he live there?"

37

"He is the pastor."

"Wasn't it kind of quiet after his position here in Berlin?"

"Of course, but you see he was ill, very ill. He was in a sanatorium. He simply couldn't cope."

"With what?"

"His work, his position, the expectations people had of him." She became agitated as she spoke. "Now we are finding out what terrible things they did to men like Paul."

"Who?"

"The Stasi. They had a word—*Zersetzung*—"

"Subversion?"

"Obliteration. They planned to undermine, crush, or destroy anyone who opposed them in any way, and Paul, because he was first the chaplain to the Protestant students, then a dissident—"

"But Stefi was a dissident too."

"Of course, but Stefi was stronger because he could be humorous about everything, whereas Paul was so earnest. You know, it was enough to worry about the Stasi, but he was also always anxious about God and the Devil."

"So what happened? Did he have a nervous breakdown?"

"Yes. He really almost went mad, and it was terrible for him, but also for me and the children. Thank God Stefi was there. He was really wonderful to Paul and to me, when Paul could no longer cope with anything: with his work, but also with me and with his family. You see, when he left the sanatorium, he would not come home. He went back to his parents in Bechtling. He would not see me or talk to me. It was then that Stefi took care of us."

"I guess Stefi loved you a little as well?"

Sophie brightened. "Do you think so? Do you remember that?"

Francesca looked out the window. "He was always one for the girls."

"Yes," said Sophie sweetly. "He was one for the girls, and yet he chose me."

As Sophie said this, they crossed the railway bridge on the Invalidenstrasse and reached the band of raked earth that had been the free-fire zone on the eastern side of the Wall. Now in East Berlin, Francesca was astonished by how little had changed, not just since the reunification of the city but in the ten years that had passed since she had last been there. The buildings were uniform, drab, and poorly maintained, mile upon mile of apartment houses with only an occasional shop or café.

When they reached Friedrichshain, Sophie turned into Wedekind-strasse and stopped the car outside the prewar apartment building that Francesca remembered vividly from ten years before. Here again, nothing appeared to have changed. The vestibule was dark and shabby, and all at once she felt conspicuous in her Burberry raincoat and beige suit. Embarrassed by the size of the smart suitcase that Sophie now heaved out of the back of the Wartburg, she tried to take it from her. "No, no," Sophie insisted. "We're used to hard labor." And as she lugged it up the two flights of dank stairs, she added, "There were no deliveries under socialism. We had to carry our furniture—refrigerator, everything—up these dreadful steps."

Sophie opened her door and went in. Francesca stood on the threshold, remembering the conspiratorial visits she had paid to this same apartment, either to attend readings of the dissidents' unpublished works or simply to spend an evening with Sophie and Paul. Then it had been furnished with old pieces of furniture given Paul by his father, including a piano at which Paul accompanied Sophie singing Schubert lieder, his earnest features gradually relaxing as the music calmed his mind, his eyes looking gently up at his wife, whose thin little voice enchanted them all.

Now Paul was gone and the appearance of the apartment had completely changed. Gone were the carpets and rugs, the oil paintings and photographs of Paul's parents and grandparents—everything, in fact, that had given the apartment a flavor of Germany before the war. Now the floors were sanded and the furniture was Scandinavian in style: a squat white sofa and two beanbags, one black, the other red. In place of the piano was a large television, and there were contemporary prints and paintings on the wall—of a mediocrity, Francesca decided with her professional eye, that could only be found in Eastern Europe.

"My, it's changed, Sophie," she said.

Sophie took this as a compliment. "The hi-fi comes from before unification, also the records. They were cheap in the DDR."

"So were books, I guess," said Francesca, looking at the shelves, which on two of the walls went from floor to ceiling.

"There was not much else to do but read," said Sophie.

"Well, they do furnish a room."

"Cheaper than wallpaper, even if one could get it."

"And the paintings?"

"That one's by Brigitte Schönemann, a friend. That's by a Czech friend, Jaroslav Zermak. . . . In fact, they're all by friends."

Francesca crossed the room to study the paintings: the Schönemann a drab pastiche of 1960s abstractionism, the one by the Czech a daub like a squashed cockroach, except that the real thing would have been more impressive.

"Of course, you're an art critic now," said Sophie.

"Not an art critic, no, an art historian. I know very little about anything outside my field."

"Russian art?"

"Experimental Russian Art: 1863 to 1922." She rattled this off; it had been the title of her thesis.

"Wonderful," said Sophie.

Francesca turned and smiled. "Well, it's a happy coincidence if that's what Stefi wants to know about."

Sophie almost jumped up and down with excitement. "Listen, we mustn't talk about it now. Wait until Stefi gets back this evening. Now we'll have some coffee and cake." She patted her stomach over the dungarees as she made for the kitchen. "I'm so fat I don't normally touch them, but in your honor, Francesca—"

"And what about me?"

Sophie looked back. "You're thin as a rake; anyway, you can afford a little fat because you're so tall. Now come into the kitchen, while I boil the water, and tell me about your life."

What each woman wanted to know about the other was the state of their affections, but as Francesca had already discovered, the story of Sophie's divorce from Paul was clearly a painful one for her to remember. While she had many friends in the United States who were or had been divorced, Francesca could not get over a sense of sadness and perplexity that Sophie was now married to the quick-witted, devious Stefi rather than the gentle, heroic Paul. She was therefore quite willing to wait until she and Sophie had reestablished the intimacy that had existed ten years before, and to be first to unload the secret details of her life—that in any case were hardly secret, since Francesca had nothing to hide. Her parents were fine, still in Ann Arbor—her father was now retired and they traveled a lot; her brother worked for NASA in Cape Canaveral; her sister was an associate editor on a magazine in New York City. Francesca herself lectured on Russian art at Boston University; her book on the Russian Constructivists had come out two years before and had been well received. She had a nice apartment in Boston with a view of the Charles River that she had shared for a while with a friend who taught at MIT but now lived in alone.

"You aren't married?" asked Sophie.

Francesca laughed, a touch of bravado mixed with the hilarity. "Not yet. But I have a friend."

"Tell me about him."

"Well, he's nice and intelligent and amusing and handsome."

"And rich?"

"Rich enough. He's a publisher in New York, which is a bore, but we see each other most weekends. Either he flies up or I fly down."

"How old?"

Francesca pondered. "I guess he's getting on for forty."

Sophie frowned. "And not married?"

"He's been married. He has a son who lives with his ex-wife."

"But he's divorced?"

"Yes, for five or six years."

"So why not marry again?"

"He's kind of cautious . . . and so am I."

"But if you want babies, Francesca . . ."

Again the brave laugh. "Yes, I know, the biological clock is ticking away."

"So?"

"So I don't know. I mean, we've talked about it—having babies, marrying. . . ."

"And?"

"Well, maybe we're getting there, but he has his job and I have mine. You know."

Sophie sighed. "He should catch you while he can."

"Or I should catch him. In America these days we don't just wait for the men to make up their minds."

"Then propose to him. What is his name?"

"Duncan."

"Propose to Duncan."

"We haven't got quite *that* far—I mean, the woman going down on bended knee. But—you know, both parties make a mature decision at the right time."

"But what is the right time?"

Francesca laughed. "When Duncan's analyst says so, I guess."

Sophie wrinkled her nose and frowned. "Analysts. I hate them."

"You have them here?"

"Very few. But Paul went to a psychiatrist and he became worse, far worse."

Sophie served coffee and brought out two huge slices of cheesecake. The women sat down at the kitchen table like happy teenagers: Francesca because her shining skin and healthy hair did indeed make her seem several years younger than she was; Sophie because her disheveled hair, naive manner, and trilling, almost yodeling voice—together with the dungarees—gave the impression of a determined childishness that only the lines on her face and the gray strands in her hair belied.

Stefan Diederich was due home at seven, and Francesca, resting on the sofa in his study, which served as the Diederichs' guest room, awaited his return with a certain nervousness. In her unworldly way, Sophie had not realized quite how many clothes were contained in her huge suitcase and so had not thought to offer Francesca somewhere to put them. Some had to be left in the suitcase, others were draped over the chair at the desk, and her cosmetics were laid out on top of a filing cabinet. As always, Francesca regretted her inability to travel light.

At five, Sophie's two children arrived, and Francesca could hear their voices amplified by the bare boards of the living room. The voice of the elder, Martin, had already broken; the high-pitched tones of the daughter, Monica, might have been those of any American fourteen-year-old girl complaining to her mother about something that had gone wrong at school.

Francesca knew it would be fatal to fall asleep; she would never get over her jet lag if she did. She got off the sofabed and walked around the room. It was large, with high ceilings, the walls lined with more books. She had forgotten how erudite and earnest all those dissidents had been—how protected, despite West Berlin television, from the mass culture of the West. Compared to her own small den in Boston, with its bright curtains and English watercolors on the wall, Stefan's study was severely functional, saying little about his character or taste. There were no bowls or vases, no photographs or framed diplomas—simply books and papers and a manual typewriter on the desk. The very anonymity of the presiding spirit brought a temptation to look through the papers, but her forthright nature came from a good conscience, and the temptation was resisted.

Francesca met the children when she emerged from the study to take a shower, shortly after six. They were eating in the kitchen but stood up and greeted her with an old-fashioned formality. Monica even gave a form of curtsey as she shook her hand. Sophie showed her guest to the bathroom, apologizing for its inadequacy as she looked uneasily at Francesca's fluffy terry-cloth bathrobe. But the shower was fine; it worked, and the water was hot. She had known many worse, particularly in London, but she started to rehearse the phrases with which she would suggest moving to a hotel without hurting Sophie's feelings.

Francesca faced a dilemma after her shower about what to wear for supper, for her simplest evening costume would seem offensively elegant. She therefore chose her designer jeans as the nearest thing to Sophie's dungarees, only to find when she emerged that Sophie had changed into a dress which belonged in a museum of bad taste. It was too late to change back, and Sophie seemed patently relieved that at least her guest had not put on a ball gown. She offered her a glass of wine from a half-empty bottle that Francesca remembered as being unopened that afternoon.

The wine relaxed them both, and they were chatting easily on the sofa when they heard the sound of a key in the latch. Immediately Sophie's face tightened; she stood and went toward the door. Stefan entered, his brow creased with a look of mild irritation. He handed his briefcase to Sophie and kissed her cursorily on the cheek.

Even if she had not been expecting him, Francesca would have recognized Stefan at once: small, alert, hair spare at the front, close-shaven on the neck, graying now, the face still lean, the same thin lips and clipped mustache, but with deeper wrinkles around the eyes. At first he did not notice her. Then Sophie said quietly, "Francesca is here," whereupon Stefan's eyes started to flutter like the departures board at a train station, stopping finally in an expression of genial delight.

"Francesca!" he said while walking forward, as if, like Sophie, he was one of her long-lost friends. Since he was now married to Sophie, Francesca responded in kind, suppressing her misgivings as she kissed him on the cheek.

"My dear Francesca," Stefan went on. "This is wonderful . . . and so *right*, so *apposite*, that you should be here *now* when you were here *then*." He went to an armchair and sat down, pointing to the sofa like an executive who was used to having his way. "You know, there are thousands of people from the West—from the Federal Republic, from Scandinavia, from the Netherlands, from America—who are now claiming to have been with us in those dark days—Sophie has probably told you—journalists, politicians: when in fact it was quite the contrary; it was the policy of the Federal government to woo Honecker and the others and to ignore us, even work against us, because we were rocking the boat." He took the glass of wine Sophie held out for him. "But you came, you befriended us, you took risks, even, I think, with your own government. You really *are* an old friend, and if we can persuade you to join in this project that we have in mind, it will really be a kind of happy ending—no, not so final: a happy ending to volume one."

"I'm all ears," said Francesca, who had sat down on the sofa as she had been told. "Sophie has given me some tantalizing hints, but she wanted to wait for you."

"This is the idea: an exhibition, a *major* exhibition, a definitive retrospective here in Berlin, of forbidden Russian art, the Russian art of the diaspora, the art that kept the Russian spirit alive during the dark days of Stalin and his dogma of Socialist Realism."

Francesca grew alert. "Do you mean all the painters who left Russia and came West?"

"I do."

"Chagall, Kandinsky, Gabo, Pevsner—"

"Yes, but also those who stayed behind, like Tatlin and El Lissitzky. I don't think people have any idea what they were doing at the time of the Russian Revolution—how dynamic their work would have been had it not been obliterated by Stalin's Neanderthal conception of art."

"Would it be a . . . significant exhibition?" Career considerations reined in the excitement that had been Francesca's first reaction to Stefan's idea.

"Listen," said Stefan. "Thirty-five years ago, in 1958 or 1959, there was a major exhibition in the Haus der Kunst in Munich of *entartete Kunst*—decadent art: all the paintings the Nazis had removed from Germany's public galleries because they were considered decadent or were painted by Jews. That is what we want to do here. We want to show the young people of East Germany and Eastern Europe—and that includes Russia, Belorussia, and Ukraine—just how crude and stupid and philistine the Communists were with their imbecilic Socialist Realism."

As Stefan was speaking, Francesca's emotions were drawn in two conflicting directions. On the one hand, she was swept up by the undoubted truth in what he said and by the urgency and enthusiasm with which he said it; on the other, she could not quite shake off the doubts about his sincerity that remained from the impression she had formed of him ten years before. Perhaps it was because Stefan had once been an actor that he now sounded like an actor speaking his lines. He used the right words, the right cadences, the right expressions, and yet he left Francesca with the impression that the role he was playing had been created by another and the ideas he expressed were not his own.

Despite this, however, Francesca found herself increasingly excited by the idea of an exhibition of the kind Stefan described: of Russian art that had flourished in the first years of the Revolution but had then been banned and execrated by the Soviet regime. Her friends in America—Duncan was one of them—believed the Russians had simply chosen the wrong political and economic system in 1917, just as one might choose a lemon for a car; as a result, they now felt that all you had to do was change to democracy and free enterprise for everything to go well.

Francesca knew it was much more complicated than that. The Russian soul faced two ways, toward the East and toward the West, and it had to be coaxed to accept its own liberation by more than trade agreements and hard currency loans. If the Russians could be shown that they were not outsiders, knocking at the door of contemporary Western culture, but could claim as their own some of the artists who had created that culture, it would be far easier for them to be assimilated by the new world order.

There were also, of course, the secondary but still powerful considerations of what organizing such a major international exhibition would do for Francesca's career. She needed to know what her role would be but was afraid to appear too pushy. It was better to appear sought-after than seeking.

"When would it be?" she asked, calculating that with a sabbatical of only a year it might mean giving up her post at Boston University.

"In July," said Stefan.

"This coming July? That's impossible."

Stefan leaned forward. "Of course it's impossible. Normally, an exhibition of this size would take two, three, even four years to plan and stage. But we don't have the time, Francesca! History will not wait for us! It must be now or never, and I believe that with the right political backing we can achieve the impossible and put on the exhibition in nine months' time."

Francesca shook her head. "We would need a lot of help."

"My ministry would be at your disposal. The city of Berlin, the Federal government in Bonn, all would help."

"And I would organize the whole exhibition?"

"You and Günter Westarp."

"Who is Günter Westarp?"

"Günter is harmless," said Sophie, without making it clear whether she meant this as a compliment or an insult.

"Günter is director of the New German Foundation, which will sponsor the exhibition," said Stefan.

"Is it a gallery?"

"No. It is simply a cultural foundation, set up here in Berlin. We have yet to decide where to stage the exhibition. It depends, to some extent, on how many galleries are prepared to lend their works."

"Of course, but how about funding?"

"No problem. Our state government has already put up the money to develop the idea. That was within my power, as it were, and there are a number of private sponsors lining up to join in. It is a project that will attract much publicity and bring great prestige."

"Is Günter Westarp an art historian?"

Stefan smiled. "Of a kind. To be quite honest, Francesca, his appointment was a reward for his work as a dissident in the DDR."

"Did I meet him here in the old days?"

"No, he was in Leipzig and was made to suffer by the Stasi."

"He is sweet," said Sophie. "A good man, but not very bright."

"That is why we need you," said Stefan.

"But aren't there German experts?" asked Francesca.

"Of course. We were given a whole list of them. But I made the case that having you as organizer would reassure the galleries and collectors in America, where in fact many of the works of art are to be found."

Francesca nodded. Certainly, no one in the States would have heard of Günter Westarp or the New German Foundation.

"So what do you think? Will you do it?"

"I'd certainly like to," said Francesca.

"What can we do to make up your mind?"

"It's a question of a contract, I guess."

Sophie glanced uneasily at Stefan.

"We must discuss that with my officials," said Stefan, "but I can assure you that we see you as a valuable commodity in—what do you call it?—a sellers' market."

Francesca laughed and said "Great" but felt afraid that she might have given her friends the impression that she was mercenary. She put her arms around Sophie's shoulders. "It's worth much more than money to be back with you in Berlin."

"Come, let's have supper," said Sophie.

They walked toward the kitchen; then Stefan stopped. "Ah, yes. I had forgotten." He turned back to Francesca. "There is, I am afraid, one further condition."

"What's that?"

"We have already taken on a Russian. It was thought . . . well, you can imagine, for all the reasons we have given, it was thought tactful to have an art expert from Moscow to assist you."

Francesca frowned. "But are there any experts in Moscow on their experimental art?"

"Apparently, yes. Dr. Serotkin. Andrei Serotkin. Do you know of him?"

"No."

"I have met him. He seems knowledgeable enough."

"Well, I guess if you can work with him," said Francesca, "so can I."

4

Shortly after ordering Nikolai Gerasimov to find Andrei Orlov, General Savchenko left Moscow on a tour of inspection of Russian intelligence-service residences abroad. Every now and then Gerasimov would receive cryptic messages sent via Savchenko's office—from Washington: "Spoke to Kirsch about our friend; he knew him well; Kirsch is prepared to speak to you when he is next in Moscow"; from Toronto: "Any progress?"

Gerasimov had made no progress and began to dread Savchenko's return. It was difficult enough to get anything done in Moscow, where no one returned calls or kept appointments. Also he had been distracted, to say the least, by complications in his personal life, moving out of the apartment that he shared with his wife to lead a nomadic existence on the sofas of family and friends.

Gerasimov rehearsed in his mind the arguments he would advance for his lack of success. First, Orlov had had few friends. Second, those few had been unwilling to talk to him. As Savchenko himself had said, the Security Service no longer struck terror into those it questioned, least of all officers who outranked Gerasimov. Savchenko would surely accept that the chaotic conditions in the Caucasus made it impossible to trace Kastiev, the Chechen, but he might find it more difficult to understand why Gerasimov had not yet got around to interviewing Partovski, Orlov's adjutant, at the Tretyakov Gallery in Moscow.

Soon after receiving Savchenko's message from Toronto, Gerasimov was called by an officer in Savchenko's office to say that Kirsch had arrived from Washington and would await him in an hour's time. Gerasimov went down to the canteen, bought a cheese roll and a cup of coffee, and took them back to his office, where he unearthed the fat file on Andrei Orlov. He quickly refreshed his knowledge of Orlov's background: his father, a celebrated painter; education at Moscow's exclusive School No. 6; top marks in English, German, math, and gymnastics. Were the marks genuine, or had the teachers given a helping hand to the son of an illustrious father?

It seemed clear from the file that Orlov himself had known from an early age how to get along under the system. He had been a team leader in the Pioneers at the age of ten and secretary of the Communist Youth Movement, the Komsomol, in his last year at the Institute of International Relations at Moscow University. Tatiana, his future wife, had been a member of the committee, and when Orlov had been made a Party member at the age of twenty-five, Ivan Keminski, Tatiana's father, had been one of his sponsors. Full marks for opportunism. If you must date a fellow student, choose the daughter of a top official in the Secretariat of the Central Committee.

Orlov had graduated from the institute with the highest marks of his year. From the KGB's Foreign Intelligence School at Yurlovo, he had gone to Department Twelve of the First Chief Directorate. His first work in the field had been under the cover of an interpreter at international conferences both in the Soviet Union and abroad. In 1976, he recruited an Indian physicist at a scientific congress in Kiev. In 1978, he accompanied a group of Russian scientists to the United States, again posing as their interpreter, writing meticulous reports on their contacts with their American colleagues and guarding them against approaches from the CIA.

In 1980, Orlov was transferred to Department Nine, and after two years on the Africa desk went with his wife, Tatiana, to the KGB residence in the Soviet embassy at Dar es Salaam. Again, a creditable performance: an up-and-coming civil servant in the president's office recruited as an agent of influence in his first twelve months. Reports from the residence chief and from the Africa desk in Moscow both praised Orlov to the skies. It was decided that he was wasted on the Africans. He was recalled to Moscow, and, after a year on the U.S.

desk, Andrei Orlov was sent to Washington under the cover of a cultural attaché in the Soviet embassy.

The telephone rang: Kirsch was waiting for him in Savchenko's office. Gerasimov swallowed the cold dregs of his coffee, closed the file, and went up the stairs with the dread feeling in his stomach of a student about to be examined in a subject he has not prepared. He should know more about Kirsch beyond the fact that he had served for a number of years in the Washington residence and was presumably a Jew.

Kirsch was sitting in a chair by the coffee table in the corner of Savchenko's office, smoking a cigarette. He was small and dark, with sparse black hair: age, Gerasimov estimated, late fifties or early sixties; trim, even dapper, in well-cut Western clothes. As Gerasimov entered, a girl brought in a glass of tea and a plate of cookies on a small metal tray and put it down beside Kirsch. Nothing was offered to Gerasimov. Nor did Kirsch get up.

"You want to know about Orlov?" he asked as Gerasimov sat down on the empty sofa.

"If you could give me some background."

"I understand he has disappeared?"

"We have not been able to trace him since he went to Kiev a year ago."

Kirsch nodded and sipped his tea.

"There has been no sign of him in the United States?"

Kirsch sniffed derisively. "If Orlov is up to something, he is unlikely to be leaving his calling card at Russian embassies around the world."

"We do not know that he is up to something."

Kirsch looked at his watch. "I am unable to help you in your principal task, that of finding Andrei Orlov, but if you think it would help I can tell you something about his tour of duty in Washington."

"He went there, I believe, in 1988?"

"Yes. '88 or early '89. He came with his wife, Tatiana, and their young son. They were both an immediate success. They were young and good-looking. They became a popular couple on the political and diplomatic circuit. We paid for elegant clothes and subscriptions to country clubs. Both played tennis. Orlov was good at squash. We instructed Tatiana Orlova to befriend the women. She joined a reading group organized by a Congressman's wife. She became interested in art, took up sculpture, and went to classes once a week. We encouraged them both to present a soft image. They could even be apologetic, if they thought it appropriate, about our involvement in Afghanistan or our record on human rights."

"That must have gone against the grain."

"For Orlov? Yes. But what you should understand is that he is a man who is unusually adept at concealing his true feelings." Kirsch took another sip of his tea. "He could enter into American life with great gusto, while at the same time . . ."

Gerasimov waited.

Kirsch put down his glass. "He gave the Americans the impression that he loved them, though I have yet to find anyone who held them in greater contempt."

Gerasimov took out a notebook and wrote *Master of duplicity.*

"Of course, we were all, as it were, adversarial in our approach. We were still fighting the Cold War. But there were very few of us who had such a visceral dislike of Americans and the American way of life."

"Do we know why?" asked Gerasimov. He was genuinely puzzled.

"Why what?"

"Why he hated the Americans so much?"

Kirsch shrugged. "He was hardly trained to love them. We were all Leninists, after all. The Americans were capitalists, imperialists, exploiters." Kirsch took out a pack of Marlboros. "But Orlov also saw a cultural dimension. You must understand that culturally he was a cut above most of our officers—a result, no doubt, of being the son of a painter." He removed a cigarette from the pack but did not offer one to Gerasimov. "He had a particular loathing for abstract paintings— icons of emptiness, he would call them—and the great art galleries where these icons were venerated."

"Yet his wife studied sculpture."

Kirsch lit his cigarette. "Yes. That was to become a problem."

Gerasimov waited for Kirsch to expand on this, but he went off on a tangent.

"Orlov was good at his job. It was after President Reagan's Star Wars. The American defense technology was outstripping ours. Moscow told us to get hold of the microchips and computer components that might help us keep up. The pressure was intense. We were reminded that atomic secrets from Los Alamos had reached the Kremlin within a week. Through offshore trusts and secret bank accounts,

Orlov set up bogus companies in the U.S. to get hold of what we wanted and smuggled them out of the country in the baggage of Sandinista sympathizers flying to Nicaragua."

"If he did so well," said Gerasimov, "why was he recalled?"

Kirsch sighed. "There were two problems. First, his wife. You realize she is Keminski's daughter? That was a great embarrassment to us in Washington, because she began to get serious about her art and then about religion. Psychologically . . . well, I think she was upset when Orlov on a couple of occasions found himself in a position where he could obtain important information by entering into intimate relationships with certain American women. You understand what I mean; he was acting under orders. It goes with the job. And Tatiana Orlova must have known this, but when she lost faith in our system she no longer saw the necessity, and so they became estranged. We knew what was going on from Orlov. But I think he loved his wife and took it personally."

"Was he recalled because of that?"

"Orlov has one failing: he can be arrogant. That not only irritated some of the other officers at the residence who were envious of his success but also made him enemies in Moscow. On his own initiative he started writing position papers and sending them back to Keminski, who passed them on to the Central Committee. They were highly critical of Soviet policy since the war. In his view, this had exaggerated the *military* threat posed to the Soviet Union when it was the *cultural* imperialism of the U.S. that posed the greatest danger to the long-term viability of the Soviet system."

"Was he wrong?"

"Probably not, but our military-industrial complex had its patrons on the Central Committee, and this was not what they wanted to hear."

"But with Keminski behind him—"

"Keminski's position was made awkward by the conversion of his daughter. Her religiosity was not just a cover; she had ceased to submit reports." Kirsch stubbed out his cigarette. "But that was not the reason for Orlov's recall. As I understand it, these position papers came to the notice of Khrulev just as he was recruiting a team for his icon operation. It was Khrulev who had Orlov recalled."

Gerasimov doodled in his notebook. What more could he ask

Kirsch? "Could you hazard a guess," he said, "as to what Orlov might be up to now?"

Kirsch shook his head. "No. In my view, it was a great mistake to have dismissed him. I know that attitudes are changing, but a man like Orlov should be kept busy, if only to prevent him from getting up to anything else."

"Can you think of anyone who might know where he is?"

"Yes. His father-in-law, Ivan Keminski."

"He has been placed off-limits."

"And would not tell you what you want to know. What about Orlova?"

"They are separated."

"Even so. They have a son."

"If Keminski will not talk, why should she?"

"Keminski remains a Communist, but if Orlova is a believer, she should sympathize with the reforms. And try the old father. Andrei was fond of his parents. For all his Bolshevik zeal, he was always a family man."

A bored-looking secretary at the Tretyakov Gallery showed Nikolai Gerasimov to the office of former KGB lieutenant Alexander Partovski. He was young—much younger than Gerasimov had expected—with a shy manner and an intelligent expression. Gerasimov found this disconcerting. It was bad enough to be investigating a fellow officer, but worse to be asking someone to tattle on his last operational commander. He could see that Partovski was ill at ease—not afraid, as so many were when being questioned by state security, but rather embarrassed, as if the whole exercise was somehow squalid.

"I have been asked to make inquiries about Captain Andrei Orlov."

"Yes."

"You knew him well, I think?"

"I was with him in Berlin."

"Precisely."

"We recovered more than ninety illegally exported icons."

"So I understand."

Partovski nodded toward the door of his office. "Some of them are now on exhibit."

"The operation was successful, then?"

"Yes, thanks to Comrade Orlov."

"He was competent?"

"More than that."

"But it was messy."

"How?"

"People were killed."

"That was expected. It was kill or be killed."

"What about the woman?"

Partovski blushed. "She had information. . . ."

"About bank accounts?"

"Yes."

"She told you?"

"In the end."

"You persuaded her?"

"Yes."

"You tortured her?"

"I—" He stopped. "Our orders were to use whatever means were necessary."

Gerasimov made no reply to this but looked down at his notes. "And then you returned with the icons?"

"By Travemünde. Yes."

"With *all* the icons?"

There was a slight hesitation. "All the icons, yes."

"And the bank accounts?"

"They were left to Orlov."

"Did she tell you how much they contained?"

"I was not present at her interrogation."

"Who was there?"

"Comrade Orlov and Comrade Kastiev."

"The Chechen?"

"Yes."

"Did Orlov tell you how much money the bank accounts contained?"

"No."

"There is no record that any of these funds were repatriated."

Again there was a slight hesitation. "Perhaps Comrade Orlov failed to gain access to the accounts."

"He flew to Zurich?"

"So I believe."

"And then returned to Moscow?"

"Yes."

"Did you see him in Moscow?"

"Yes."

"Did he tell you whether or not he had gained access to the accounts?"

"No. We did not talk about it."

"What did you talk about?"

"Our future. The country. The Party. Things had happened while we were away."

"He too was offered a job here at the Tretyakov, I believe?"

"They were grateful to us for recovering the icons."

"But Orlov turned it down?"

"Yes."

"Why?"

Partovski shrugged. "It didn't appeal to him."

"It suggests he had something else in mind."

"Perhaps."

"Did he tell you what that was?"

"Not specifically."

"In general?"

Partovski struggled to find the right words. "He is . . . a patriot."

Gerasimov sniffed. "What does that mean?"

"He was more concerned for Russia than he was for himself."

"One can afford to be patriotic with access to bank accounts in Zurich."

Partovski looked angry. "It is inconceivable to me that Comrade Orlov would have spent state funds on himself."

"Then how does he live?"

"I don't know. He may have savings."

"Despite inflation?"

"His father, as you know—"

"Yes, I know. The famous painter."

"He must have money."

"Perhaps."

"And then . . ." Partovski hesitated.

"What?"

"As I understand it, Orlov had friends in the Party. They might have supplied him with funds."

"Did you know he had gone back to the West?"

"I assumed he would."

"Why?"

"There was some unfinished business."

"To do with the icons?"

"No."

"The bank accounts?"

"Possibly. I don't know. He didn't confide in me. He merely asked me . . ."

"What?"

"To go with him."

Gerasimov became alert. "He asked you to go with him to settle some unfinished business but did not tell you what that business was?"

Partovski looked unhappy. "It was understood that I could only be told if I was committed to the general idea."

"Of what?"

"Of saving Russia."

Gerasimov was genuinely confused. "Orlov went back to the West to save Russia?"

"He had some project."

"What was it?"

"I don't know. He didn't tell me. But the icons . . . the operation . . . torturing the woman . . . it affected him."

"You said it had nothing to do with the icons."

"Nothing as such. But the way the icons were smuggled out of Russia and sold to the West by slime like Maslyukov and even corrupt chekists"—here Partovski darted a look at Gerasimov—"and the way the police in the West knew all about it and did nothing to stop it . . . The icons were Russian, part of our heritage, our culture. To see them traded as commodities, just to decorate the houses of the bourgeois in Frankfurt and New York!" Partovski was agitated. "You must understand that Comrade Orlov was not only efficient and courageous but also had great conviction. He believed in what he was doing."

"And you?"

"I obeyed orders."

"And when you returned?"

"As you know, I was dismissed from the service and was advised to take this post at the gallery."

"And you would like to keep it?"

"Of course."

"Which you would not if it was felt that you were concealing information to the detriment of the state."

"I have told you all I know," said Partovski glumly.

"Why should we believe that?"

Now a slight look of contempt came into Partovski's eyes. "You are still in the service, Comrade Gerasimov. I am not. Nor is Orlov. But we have all had the same training. If you were Orlov, if you had something in mind, would you let out any information to someone who was not part of the operation?"

Gerasimov did not answer.

"If I had agreed to join him, Orlov would have told me. But I did not."

Gerasimov saw the sense of what Partovski was saying and changed the subject. "General Khrulev, I think, had his own agents in Germany?"

"So I understand."

"Did any of them help you recover the icons?"

Again a slight hesitation. "There were two cars and a van. I am not sure how Orlov got hold of them."

"No Germans were with you?"

"No."

"Only"—Gerasimov looked down at his notes—"you and the Chechen?"

"Yes."

"What happened to him?"

"I don't know."

"And the van?"

Partovski shrugged. "The van? I don't know. It was picked up by someone from the Center and returned to the pool."

Gerasimov stood up. As he did so, he noticed a look of relief come onto Partovski's face. Undoubtedly he had revealed only as much as he felt he had to about Orlov, things he judged Gerasimov might discover from other sources. Almost certainly he knew more, or at any rate could hazard a guess.

"You must look at the icons," said Partovski, leading Gerasimov down the corridor toward the gallery. "This is the cream of the Tretyakov collection, and the gallery, as you know, has been recently restored."

"By Finns, I believe."

"Superb, don't you think? And our security is state of the art—" As he spoke, there was a loud electronic bleep.

They came into the gallery. There, on the walls, were a series of magnificent icons: of Christ, of the Virgin, of St. Nicholas, of St. Parascevi, among them the celebrated icon of Our Lady of Kazan and Andrei Rublyev's *Holy Trinity*. A number of visitors were shuffling from painting to painting, watched by lethargic attendants. The only sounds were the hum of the humidifiers and an occasional loud electronic bleep.

"What's wrong with the security system?" asked Gerasimov, more interested in Western technology than he was in the icons.

"As you can see," said Partovski proudly, "there is an electronic beam in front of the exhibits which when broken triggers an alarm." There was another bleep. He pointed toward an icon of the Virgin of Kazan. "But look."

Gerasimov turned. An old peasant woman wearing felt boots and a tight head scarf had knelt down and now bowed forward to kiss the icon, blocking the beam. There was a loud bleep. The attendant yawned.

"Why don't you stop them?" asked Gerasimov.

Partovski shrugged. "The equipment is state of the art," he said, "but our people, I am afraid, are not."

5

At the request of the Prussian Minister of Culture, Stefan Diederich, an apartment was found for Francesca McDermott in the Hansa quarter of West Berlin. It was on the fourth floor of a modern apartment house near the Academy of Art with views over the Englischer Garten. Francesca was told that her Russian colleague, Dr. Serotkin, would be given an apartment in the same building when he returned to Berlin.

Because telephone communications were still poor in the eastern half of the city, the office provided for the exhibition's organizers was in West Berlin, in the same building on the Schöneberger Ufer used by the New German Foundation. It looked out over the canal onto the New National Gallery and, beyond the new National Library, to what remained of the Berlin Wall on the old Potsdamerplatz.

The proximity of this office to Francesca's apartment enabled her to establish an agreeable routine. At seven every morning she would jog in the Englischer Garten under the watchful eye of the Goddess of Victory, eat her usual breakfast of yogurt, muesli, and Lapsang souchong tea, and then drive to the office in a leased Volkswagen Golf.

From the start, her mood was good; indeed, she had to rein in a sense of exhilaration. Whether it was the celebrated Berlin air or the challenge of a job that was tailor-made both for her ambitions and her qualifications, Francesca felt charged with an unusual energy and sense of liberation.

In part, she recognized, this came from getting out of the rut of her life in Boston—a pleasant enough life, certainly, with a nice apartment, tenure at the university, and Duncan in New York, but one that had changed little since her appointment five years before. Here, in contrast, was both a challenge and a change but an undemanding change, with everyone appearing to fall over themselves to smooth her path and make things easy. Finding a place to live in a crowded city might have been difficult, but she had had to spend only two nights with the Diederichs on the Wedekindstrasse before moving into the apartment.

Matters were just as well arranged at the office. Theoretically Günter Westarp, the director of the New German Foundation, was the co-organizer of the exhibition, but it was clear from the start that the two assistants borrowed from the New National Gallery—a young man and an older woman—as well as the two secretaries, all regarded Francesca as the one in charge.

Westarp had some knowledge of the Bauhaus in its Weimar phase, and it had been his attempt to speak up for modernism that had antagonized the authorities in the DDR. However, he had no academic standing and no natural authority, and Francesca feared that if the director of the Museum of Modern Art in New York or the National Gallery in Washington should ever set eyes on him the project would be doomed. He was short, almost squat, with a docile yet dogged look on his sagging, fleshy face. His hair was thin and dirty, and its graying, greasy strands reached halfway to his shoulders. He always wore jeans—not crisp denim designer jeans like Francesca's but tawdry East-bloc imitations, creased and molded around his crotch and precariously close to being bell-bottomed. His thick knitted cardigan seemed as greasy as his hair; his only luxuriance was the large, drooping, Günter Grass mustache upon which, after eating, fragments of food hung like baubles on a Christmas tree.

The other members of the permanent staff scarcely disguised their contempt for their Ossie cousin. Knowing full well that Günter only spoke German, they spoke English in their discussions with Francesca; at times she found herself translating what they had said back into German for his benefit. But Günter appeared quite content with his subordinate role. He sat at his desk in the offices of the New German Foundation on the floor below, signing the letters and memos that were set before him after only a cursory glance. If any question was put to him directly, at a meeting of the secretariat or the exhibition committee, he always looked to Francesca to provide an answer; soon the incoming letters and faxes were passed directly to her.

Francesca's only worry was Serotkin. She understood the necessity of having a Russian work on the project. She could even see some advantage in having a man with good contacts in Moscow as part of the team; they would want many paintings from the public collections in Moscow and St. Petersburg and there was archival material that she would dearly love to bring to Berlin. However, she could not discover why this particular Russian had been chosen, nor could she find anyone in her field who had heard of him or his work.

Günter Westarp knew nothing about him; he said it was Stefan's choice. But Stefan, when Francesca questioned him, said Serotkin had been proposed by the Ministry of Culture in Moscow. Stefan could hardly say what the Russian was like, having only met him on two or three occasions; he was dark, middle-aged, taciturn, and bearded. He spoke German well, possibly English also. He had seemed knowledgeable about art and enthusiastic about the exhibition.

As she waited for Serotkin's return, Francesca formed an image of him in her mind. He would be pedantic, donnish: his beard clipped like Lenin's, his manner cautious, occasionally evasive, as Soviet academics so often were, bullied in their studies by the dogmas of Marx. He would probably be lazy and indecisive, happy to leave the researchers to do the work and let her or Günter have the responsibility. Indeed, the more she thought about this bumbling professor, the less anxious she became that he would cramp her style. After a couple of weeks she had almost ceased to think about him, distracted as she was by the momentous task of getting the exhibition off the ground.

The first details for Francesca and her team were to decide on the scope and the name of the exhibition, choose the artists to be represented, and discover the whereabouts of their works. Then they would have to approach the lenders, a delicate matter that was crucial to the success of the whole enterprise. Francesca knew that many people in the United States would be reluctant to allow major paintings by, say, Kandinsky or Chagall to cross the Atlantic. It was therefore essential to approach them in the right way—to appeal to the idealistic impulses of major lenders like the Museum of Modern Art and the Guggenheim in

New York, whose participation was essential if works from lesser collections were to follow.

Francesca told Stefan time and again how important it was that he seek endorsement for the exhibition at the highest level—if possible, from the Federal government. An approach should be made to the cultural attachés of the different embassies in Bonn; letters to the major lenders would have to be signed by Stefan himself, as the provincial minister, before Francesca made her requests for the loan of specific works of art.

All this was agreed. The New Grouping, in coalition with the Christian Democrats in the Prussian provincial government, could count on the support of the Federal government in Bonn. The Federal government would also provide the usual indemnity in lieu of insurance for the works of art if the arrangements for security were satisfactory.

There was a long discussion by the exhibition committee about the title of the show. Francesca's thesis had been called simply "Russian Experimental Art," but it was argued by the female researcher, Frau Doktor Koch, that the art in question was, in retrospect, hardly experimental because the word "experimental" suggested a trial that might fail. Stefan thought the title should be something like "The Indomitable Spirit: Russian Art in Exile" or "The Russian Role in Contemporary Culture." Other ideas were thrown up by different members of the committee. Why not simply "Russian Art: 1917–1993"? Francesca said this was too bald and academic. Surely the title must contain the message that the exhibition was meant to convey; she therefore preferred Stefan's original suggestion, "The Indomitable Spirit: Russian Art in Exile"; and it was on this that the committee eventually agreed.

The next question to be considered was the exhibition's scope. Was it to be huge and comprehensive? Or should it confine itself to a few fine examples of the work of the artists involved? Francesca argued forcefully for the latter; in her view, the impact would be greater if the visitor was not overwhelmed by a large number of works. There was also the danger that artists with a relatively small output would be lost in the plethora of works by more prolific ones or might not be seen at all by visitors who gave up from cultural satiety or sheer exhaustion.

In this Francesca was backed by the director of the New National Gallery, who also sat on the committee. Günter appeared to agree until he caught the eye of Stefan Diederich, whereupon he brought his contribution to the discussion to an indecisive end as quickly as he could. Stefan's intervention was more decisive in tone but equally confused in content. He suggested that it was not a question they could decide there and then but should be put on the agenda for the next meeting. Francesca objected that this would hold up the whole enterprise: the letters had to go out to the lenders and a decision had to be made about whether they would need more than one site. But the most Stefan would do to meet her objections was to bring forward the date of the committee's next meeting.

Francesca returned from the offices of the Prussian Ministry of Culture where the morning meeting had been held to her office on the Schöneberger Ufer in a mood of simmering irritation. It was a wet day. She had missed her morning jog in the Englischer Garten. She had drunk regular coffee at the meeting because no decaf was offered, and though no one had come up with any argument against it, her "quality over quantity" proposal had been put on hold. It was her first setback and it triggered the release of a number of other pent-up annoyances, most of them imprecise and irrational, like her hatred of the bland antiseptic decor of the office, of Frau Doktor Koch's rubber plant, of the eager zeal of the young researcher, Julius Breitenbach, who as she passed his office was looking through the 1989–90 catalogs of Sotheby's auction house in London.

Seeing that Francesca had returned from the meeting, Julius rose and followed her into her office. "Do you know, by any chance," he asked, "who bought Kandinsky's *Fugue* in—"

"No, I don't," Francesca snapped at him, throwing her folder down on her desk.

Julius blushed and backed away. "I'm sorry."

"No. Wait." Francesca frowned. "Wasn't that in the Guggenheim?"

"Yes. They sold it at auction in 1990, but I don't know who bought it."

"You'd better call Sotheby's. It's an important work. We ought to have it."

Julius retreated again, closing her door. Francesca had just kicked off her damp shoes under her desk when there was a knock on her door.

"Yes?" she said, unable to suppress a note of exasperation. Frau Doktor Koch, the older researcher, looked in. "Dr. Serotkin is here," she said.

"*Here?*"

The Russian stood behind her; Frau Doktor Koch stepped aside to let him pass. Francesca stood to greet him but, feeling the ridged carpet beneath her stocking feet, realized she was not wearing her shoes.

"Shit," she muttered and, before taking more than a glance at Serotkin, she crouched down behind her desk to recover them. "I'm sorry," she mumbled as she stood up again. "I lost my shoes."

The man who stood before her was so unlike the man she had imagined that at first she thought he must be someone else. Later, when she described Serotkin to Sophie, she used the word "dashing" because he reminded her of the Bulgarian patriot Insarov, in Turgenev's *On the Eve*. When she mentioned Serotkin to Duncan over the telephone to New York, she avoided using the word "dashing" only because he might take this to mean attractive, which it did not. To start with, Serotkin had a beard—a black beard matching the thick black hair on his head—and Francesca hated beards. Then his eyes were a murky color, his face was too long, his cheekbones were too high, his nose was too straight. He was also formal and solemn as he shook hands with her, and she liked men to be friendly and smile.

Francesca realized, of course, that this first encounter could be something of an ordeal for a Russian art historian who, whatever his professional abilities, might be a little intimidated by a more sophisticated colleague from the West. She therefore asked him to sit down and did her best to put him at ease. She buzzed the secretary to bring some coffee and, rather than sit like a boss at her desk, crossed to the sofa next to the chair chosen by Serotkin.

"Have you come from Moscow?" she asked.

"No," he replied shortly.

Francesca waited for him to say something further, but he did not. "I guess we all assumed you were in Moscow or St. Petersburg."

"No."

"But you are *from* Moscow, aren't you?"

"Yes."

Francesca did not want to give the impression that she was interviewing Serotkin, but she was eager to know the extent of his knowledge and the value of his qualifications. "Do you teach there," she asked, "or are you at a gallery or a museum?"

"I was at the Ministry."

"I see."

"Our system was different from yours. We had experts in different fields working in the Ministry."

"Of course. And you were the expert in this field: experimental Russian art?"

"Of course." His voice was deep, his English flawless. There was no trace of a Russian intonation.

"But you have traveled abroad?" Serotkin was wearing gray flannel trousers and a dark gray herringbone sport jacket, a blue shirt, and a dotted tie, elegant Western clothes that he carried with a certain ease.

"Yes, I know your country a little. London also. And Germany, of course." There was a touch of mockery in his eyes, as if he was thinking things he was not prepared to say.

"I understand that you speak German."

"Yes."

The secretary brought in the coffee. Francesca balked at more caffeine but felt she must drink with Serotkin, as though smoking a pipe of peace. "While you've been away," she said, "we've gotten off to a fairly smooth start. The only difference, I think, is over the scope of the exhibition."

"Yes. And the title, I believe."

"We settled on that: 'The Indomitable Spirit: Russian Art in Exile.' "

"It is imprecise."

She frowned. "How do you mean?"

"Well, this art we are considering was not all created in exile. Some was in Russia."

"But most of the artists went abroad."

"Some remained: Malevich, El Lissitzky."

"Sure, but they were censored and suppressed."

His eyes flashed. "Certainly."

"So even if the painters remained in the Soviet Union, the spirit was forced into exile."

"Nevertheless it is imprecise."

Francesca frowned. She disliked being crossed, particularly on something that had been decided, and she was also irritated that Serotkin was not responding to her friendliness as he should. "And the scope?" she asked, somewhat sharply.

"It must be . . . comprehensive."

"I took the view—" she began.

"I know. Diederich told me. But I feel that only a comprehensive collection will do justice to the theme."

"You mean *all* the Kandinskys? *All* the Chagalls?"

"As many as possible."

"I just don't know if we'll get people to lend, and the shipping costs will be enormous."

"Diederich has money for that."

"And the insurance. Some of these paintings are now worth a great deal."

Serotkin paused. "I realize that."

"We're talking about millions of dollars."

"Of course."

Francesca stood, went to her desk, and picked up her phone. "Julius, what did that painting by Kandinsky sell for at Sotheby's?" She listened. "Uh-huh." She put down the phone and turned back to Serotkin. "In 1990, Kandinsky's *Fugue* went for over twenty million dollars."

"Yes," said Serotkin. "And I believe Chagall's *America,* also from the Guggenheim, was sold for more than fourteen million at the same sale."

Francesca frowned as she sat down again; Serotkin was clearly better informed than she had supposed. "So we're talking of *hundreds* of millions of dollars."

Serotkin appeared unimpressed. "I understand that in exhibitions of this kind insurance is not a direct expense because the government provides an indemnity."

"Sure. And it's highly unlikely that the paintings will be burned or stolen. But all the same—"

"I think it's for Diederich to worry about things like that," said Serotkin.

"I agree. But we have to know the scope to draw up our lists."

"Of course. I have to some extent, with the aid of colleagues, drawn up a list of works in my country."

"That's fantastic, because really we don't know what you have in your collections."

"No. They were not . . . advertised." He smiled, and since this was the first smile to have appeared on his face, it raised Francesca's spirits, which, starting low because of the damp day, had raised briefly at the first appearance of the "dashing" Serotkin and then begun to sink under the impact of his obtuseness on the questions of the title and scope of the exhibition.

She took the smile as an invitation to venture a more personal approach. "It must have been difficult," she said in a compassionate tone, "to study experimental and abstract art in the Soviet Union."

"It was."

"I guess you weren't encouraged."

"No."

"You couldn't teach?"

"No."

"Or publish."

"No."

"Which is why no one has ever heard of you." It came out baldly; she did not quite mean it that way.

But Serotkin smiled. "No. Such a field of study was not very much . . . esteemed under communism. However, if you have doubts about my abilities—"

"Not at all."

"—I could give you the names of colleagues and officials."

"Don't be ridiculous. Would Stefi have invited you if he didn't know you?"

"I trust not."

"All I meant was how shameful it was that for ideological reasons your studies were suppressed."

He smiled again. "Yes. They were suppressed. But now this exhibition gives me an opportunity to realize my life's ambition."

"Mine too."

In an office it is often awkward to draw lines between professional cooperation and personal involvement. When it came to lunch, for example, which most of them ate in the staff restaurant of the New German Foundation, the two researchers, Frau Doktor Koch and Julius

Breitenbach, who already kept their distance from Francesca by calling her Dr. McDermott, clearly did not consider it appropriate to join her at a table. Her only colleague of the same rank was Günter Westarp, who in the first few weeks had often accompanied Francesca to the restaurant, boring her to death with anecdotes about his days as a dissident in Leipzig or with obscure items of information to establish his encyclopedic knowledge of the Bauhaus—encyclopedic but also indiscriminate; he had gathered facts like a train buff who knows the numbers and types of the locomotives passing through a station but has no interest whatever in their destination.

To escape from Westarp, Francesca either brought a sandwich to the office, which she ate at her desk, or waited a good half hour after Günter had left for lunch before going down to the restaurant herself. The Germans all ate early in any case—a heavy meal at midday or shortly after; if Francesca waited until quarter to one, she could be reasonably sure of eating some soup or a salad alone with a book or a scholarly review.

The day of Serotkin's return she followed this tactic only to find that the Russian had done the same thing, and finding themselves side by side at the counter, and at the desk where they paid for their food, they could hardly avoid sitting at the same table.

Held under Serotkin's arm as he carried his tray was a copy of *The Economist;* like Francesca, he had clearly hoped to be able to eat in peace, but he put on as brave a face as she did and after the initial awkwardness looked at her with almost a twinkle in his eye. "You don't like German food?"

Francesca glanced down at the salad. "We aren't used to eating hot food in the middle of the day."

"We like to eat hot food both at midday and in the evening." He dug into the dish of the day: smoked pork, red cabbage, and dumplings.

"But you don't get fat," she said, glancing at Serotkin's slim figure.

"We don't always get to eat as much as we would like," he said.

"Are there shortages?" she asked, the compassionate note again in her voice.

"Sure."

"Do you have a family, Andrei?"

He hesitated. "Yes."

"You don't mind my asking?"

"I have a wife and a son," he said, "but I am separated from my wife."

"I guess there's as much divorce in Russia as there is in the United States."

"We are separated, not divorced."

She stood corrected. "Are they in Moscow?"

"Yes."

"You should have them visit you here in Berlin. I'd like to meet them."

Serotkin did not respond to this but took another mouthful of food. "Are you married?" he asked eventually.

"I'm not married but I have a friend. He's divorced."

He nodded. "You should be married."

"Why?"

He shrugged. "You are a beautiful woman, but you are no longer young."

Francesca was taken aback by this abrupt double-edged compliment, delivered in an offhand manner. "Marry in haste, repent at leisure," she said with a slightly forced laugh.

"Is that a proverb?"

"Sort of."

"But not true."

"I think it's true enough, if you think of the growing number of divorces."

"They are not caused by the haste with which people marry but by their false expectations of what marriage should be."

"Such as?"

He shrugged. "Rapture, fulfillment, Hollywood romance."

"Is that what you and your wife wanted?"

He frowned. "No. Our differences were . . . ideological."

"She was a Communist?"

"No." He hesitated, as if about to say one thing but, thinking better of it, said another. "Under our system there were particular difficulties. It was impossible for a young couple to have their own flat. And women were expected to work. They were expected to work by the government, but they were also expected to look after the home and care for the children."

"By the men," said Francesca.

"By tradition," said Serotkin.

"Didn't the tradition change?"

"Traditions will not change if they stem from ineradicable aspects of human nature."

Francesca's face became a little flushed. She put down her fork. "But surely no one in Russia believed that it was inherent in human nature that women should work in a factory but also do all the chores in the home?"

"They believed that women should work in the factory because it followed from the principle of equality between the sexes."

"Of course, but in the home—"

"Marx and Lenin never pronounced on who should wash the dishes or iron the clothes."

"So it was left to the women?"

Serotkin shrugged. "Of course. That was the tradition."

"The women shouldn't have put up with it," said Francesca.

"But it was the women who wanted it that way."

"*Wanted* it?"

"No Russian woman could love a man who washed dishes or ironed clothes."

Francesca scowled. "Then they've sure got a long way to go."

Serotkin finished his plate. "Does your . . . friend do his own cooking and cleaning?"

"Sure. Well, he has a maid, and we usually eat out because we're both busy."

"Do you have a maid?"

"Yes."

"A woman?"

"Yes, a Jamaican."

"Because you're busy?"

"Yes. But that actually doesn't have anything to do with it."

"Of course not."

Francesca looked up from her yogurt; she could not tell because of the beard whether or not Serotkin's smile was ironic. "The fact is," she said, "that if Duncan and I were to get married, we would share the chores."

"And the labor to earn your living?"

"Yes."

71

"But . . ." He hesitated as if considering how far he should go. "If there is no division of labor within a marriage, if all the earning and all the chores are shared, then what binds the man to the woman or the woman to the man?"

"Well, love."

"And if love goes?"

"Then . . . nothing, I guess."

"Which puts a heavy burden on love."

"I don't see how else things could be arranged."

"In the past, you see, among our Russian peasants, a man could not survive without a woman or a woman without a man. They remained together because separated they would not survive."

"And that was *good*?"

His eyes flashed. "Yes. I think it was good, because it meant that necessity held families together instead of mere . . . whim."

Francesca found herself growing almost angry. "So you'd like to see women back in the kitchen?"

Serotkin took a pack of cigarettes out of his pocket and offered one to Francesca. She shook her head, surprised that anyone could imagine that she might smoke. "Have you read the work of Valentin Rasputin?" he asked.

"Rasputin? The monk?"

He frowned, just as a tutor might frown when a student gave a particularly crass answer to one of his questions. "No. Valentin Rasputin. He is a contemporary writer, a Siberian. Some of his works have been translated."

"I'm sorry. I don't know them."

Without asking Francesca whether she minded or not, Serotkin lit his cigarette. "Rasputin depicts an ideal woman who comes from the Russian tradition. She is not assertive and ambitious—a scientist or a writer or an engineer—but someone warm, stable, affectionate, and strong: a mediator, if you like, between the sky and the soil."

A cloud of heavy blue smoke with an unusual, sweet aroma drifted toward Francesca. She fanned her face with her hand. If Serotkin saw this gesture as a complaint, he did nothing to show it.

"It seems to me," he went on, "that Western women no longer see themselves as the companions of men but rather as their competitors, their rivals."

"They just want their due," said Francesca irritably.

"Their due?"

"Well, their rights."

Serotkin smiled. "To what?"

"To equal treatment."

He nodded. "In the factory . . ."

"And the office."

"Yes."

"And the home."

He drew smoke into his lungs. "By equal you mean the same?"

"Sure. Equal means the same."

"A nut and a bolt may be equal but they are not the same."

"And is that how you see men and women? As nuts and bolts?"

"More or less."

"And what if a bolt doesn't want to be a bolt but would rather be a nut?"

"We are what we are."

"That's fatalistic."

"Yes."

"And un-American."

"I daresay." He took another drag on his cigarette.

As if by tacit agreement, Francesca McDermott and Andrei Serotkin kept their distance in the days that followed this first encounter. They met in the office, of course, and Serotkin did indeed prove invaluable in tracing paintings in collections in the former Soviet Union. Francesca's knowledge of Russian was rudimentary, and none of the others knew any at all. It was therefore Serotkin who made all the calls that required a Russian speaker and, on a Cyrillic typewriter obtained by Julius Breitenbach, typed the letters to the lenders.

However, his presence in the office was a mild irritation. It was not so much the recollection of his obnoxious opinions as her own inability to figure him out. Serotkin did not fit into any of Francesca's predetermined categories. She was not someone who allowed her first impressions of a person to become her definitive judgment and, while confident in her ability to judge character, she was not so arrogant as to imagine that her experience of human nature in Wisconsin, Michigan, New England, and New York qualified her to assess those from an entirely different culture. She was also always ready to encounter the enigmatic, but to her enigma meant silence and reserve, whereas Serotkin had been open, almost insolent, in the way he had assaulted her with his offensive ideas on the position of women. How could anyone, even a Russian, hold such antediluvian views? But then how could anyone in this day and age smoke unfiltered cigarettes?

Francesca had been thrown, she realized, by her assumption that a Russian academic would be like the European academics she had encountered from time to time. She had been encouraged in this assumption by the quality and good taste of his clothes. She should have been alerted, she now realized, by her very first impression—that quality she had referred to as "dashing," which she could now neither analyze nor define. Was it only because she had expected a stooping old professor that she had been taken aback by the appearance of a man so fit and slim? He had moved with confidence around her office, as if used to having his own way with the objects and people around him. And there had been the look in his eyes—those murky eyes whose color she could not remember—that at times encouraged a kind of camaraderie but then betrayed a sneer, even a trace of cruelty and contempt. Sky and soil! Nuts and bolts! Had he been teasing her over lunch or had he meant what he said?

She soon discovered to her consternation that, when it came to the exhibition, Serotkin's opposition to her ideas was in earnest. The postponed decision on the scale of the exhibition was on the agenda of the next meeting of the organizing committee, which Serotkin attended. Francesca argued as before for a show of limited size on a single site showing only major works by the artists chosen. "Having looked at the different galleries," she said, "I would favor the New National Gallery in West Berlin. It is the only one with the kind of facilities we require."

"I disagree," said Serotkin abruptly. "It should be a comprehensive retrospective exhibition of the entire body of Russian experimental art."

The meeting was held in the overheated conference room at the Prussian Ministry of Culture. Stefan Diederich was in the chair. He looked down the table to Günter Westarp. "What do you think?"

"I think, Herr Minister, that while I appreciate the force behind Dr. McDermott's argument, which she advanced so eloquently at our last meeting, there is also something to be said, in terms of our political objectives, of thinking on a grander scale."

"Grand does not always mean large," said Francesca.

"That is unquestionably true," said Westarp, glancing nervously around the table at everyone but Andrei Serotkin. "And from the purely artistic point of view, which is naturally the point of view that one would expect Dr. McDermott to take, she is undoubtedly right, but it would hardly help those living in East Berlin and eastern Germany to feel that this was part of their tradition if the exhibition was confined to a gallery in the western half of the city."

"I concur with this last stated opinion," said Dr. Kemmelkampf, the civil servant in the Ministry of Culture with responsibility for the exhibition. "There is something to be said for the more comprehensive option simply because it would permit the use of sites in the two halves of the city. The symmetry of two architectural gems from different epochs, Mies van der Rohe's New National Gallery in West Berlin and Schinkel's Old Museum in the east, would itself symbolize the reintegration of the old and the new."

"What is in the Old Museum at present?" Serotkin asked Diederich.

"Social realists like Strempel and Cremer."

"Paintings of heroic labor by Willi Sitte," said Günter Westarp, "and Waldemar Grzimek's statue of a worker on a collective farm."

"So wouldn't it help make the point to remove their paintings to make way for works by Kandinsky and Chagall?"

"Most emphatically," said Diederich.

"But think of the expense and the organization," said Francesca. "As it is, we have set ourselves the almost impossible task of mounting a major exhibition in under a year. If we aim to bring to Berlin every work of art by all the artists on our list—"

"As far as finance is concerned," Stefi interrupted, "the bigger the better. The foundations to which we are looking for funding are far more likely to be enticed by something grandiose than by something . . . refined."

"And if the political will is there," said Kemmelkampf, "the organizational means can always be found."

Stefan Diederich turned to Francesca. "Are you persuaded?"

She shrugged. "I guess so, if that's how you all feel."

The meeting proceeded to consider less controversial matters and drew to its end toward four in afternoon.

"Is there any other business?" asked Diederich.

Serotkin raised his hand.

"Dr. Serotkin?"

"I was unfortunately absent at the last meeting when this committee reached its decision on the title of the exhibition, which was, I believe, 'The Indomitable Spirit: Russian Art in Exile.' "

"Do you object to the title?" asked Stefan Diederich.

"In my view, it is imprecise and should be reconsidered."

Francesca could not withhold a sigh of exasperation. "We went into it at great length, Dr. Serotkin. We have already had stationery printed—"

"The title is misleading," said Serotkin, "since much of the work we are considering was done in Russia. It would make it more difficult— perhaps impossible—to secure loans from Russian museums if we persist with a title of this kind."

Frowning, Stefan Diederich turned to Günter Westarp. "Can you remember what other titles we had in mind?"

Günter Westarp nervously tugged at his mustache. " 'Triumph of the Spirit: The Modern in Russian Art.' "

"That was rejected," said Kemmelkampf, "because it was thought to have a resonance with Riefenstahl's film made under the Fascists, *Triumph of the Will*."

"I have a proposal," said Serotkin.

"Please," said Diederich.

" 'Excursus: The Cosmopolitan in Russian Art.' "

There was silence. Diederich looked up the table. "Would anyone like to express a view on this proposal?"

"I think it's terrible," said Francesca.

"Would you care to elaborate?"

"Well, why 'excursus'?"

"It is a short word," said Serotkin, "that seems to encapsulate most aptly what we want to convey."

Francesca was close to losing her temper. She turned to the chairman, Stefan Diederich. "With no disrespect, it seems to me that perhaps Dr. Serotkin does not understand the precise meaning of obscure words in the English language. 'Excursus' comes from the Latin and means 'digression.' It is untranslatable into some modern languages. For those who know what it means, it will suggest that the art exhibited is somehow an aberration, and if placed alongside the word 'cosmopolitan' it will give the impression that we do not regard it as a genuine manifestation of Russian culture."

Serotkin smiled at her with the condescension of an adversary in a game who knows he will win. "It is precisely because 'excursus' *is* universal and untranslatable that it will provoke interest in the exhibition." He stretched out his hands. "Imagine, in large lettering, on a poster: EXCURSUS. It will catch the eye. It also has an affinity with the word 'exodus' and as such will be a subtle reference to the exile of so many of the artists who, as latter-day children of Israel, escaped from the oppression of the Russian pharaohs into a land flowing with milk and honey."

Francesca frowned; she could not make out whether or not Serotkin was serious. "I think you mean," she said, *"like* latter-day children of Israel, not *as* latter-day children of Israel."

Serotkin said nothing.

"Unless you meant to refer to the fact that some of the artists were Jews."

"Presumably not," said Diederich hastily.

"As to the word 'cosmopolitan,' " Serotkin went on, opening a *Webster's Pocket Dictionary* on the table in front of him, "it is defined here as 'belonging to the whole world; not national, local,' but it would also be a reference to the suppression of such art because 'cosmopolitan' was the term of abuse used for such art by Stalin and the advocates of Socialist Realism."

"Just as the word 'degenerate' was used by the Nazis," said Günter Westarp.

"And that word was used, I seem to remember," said Dr. Kemmelkampf, "by the exhibition in Munich in 1957."

"Which in a sense," said Diederich, "is the model for our exhibition."

There was a short silence. Then Dr. Kemmelkampf cleared his throat. "I have to say—of course, this is purely a personal opinion—that the title proposed by Dr. Serotkin does seem more *arresting* than the title we had provisionally chosen."

"It would certainly look good on a poster," said Günter Westarp.

"And I think the embedded reference to the show in Munich," said Stefan Diederich, "is an important consideration."

They waited in silence. Francesca looked around the table for allies. The director of the New National Gallery shrugged in a gesture of surrender, and Frau Doktor Koch and Julius Breitenbach, present in an advisory capacity only, avoided meeting her eyes.

"Dr. McDermott?" asked Stefan Diederich.

She too shrugged in capitulation. "OK. If that's what you want, Excursus it is."

6

Andrei Orlov's wife lived in an old-fashioned building on the Malaya Bronnaya, an area favored by writers and artists. The elevator was antique: an ornate cage of the czarist era quite unlike the functional tin boxes that carried most Muscovites up to their apartments.

Nikolai Gerasimov pressed the button for the fourth floor with a skeptical look on his face. Despite recent events, he still had faith in progress and therefore doubts about anything old. With a clank, the elevator started moving. Gerasimov looked at his watch. It was past four. The little boy would be back from school. There was no record of a resident babushka. Tatiana Orlova should be at home.

He rang the bell. A woman came to the door. He first saw the back of her head because, as she opened it, she had turned to shout behind her, "Come, Igor, it's Drusha!"

Then she turned and saw it was not Drusha, whom she was expecting, but a tall, muscular, slightly pockmarked man who, from the look in her eyes that momentarily followed the expression of surprise, knew that she knew who he was, where he came from, and why he was there.

"I am Nikolai Stefanovich Gerasimov," he said politely, instinctively deferential to the daughter of a man as powerful as Keminski had once been. "If it is not inconvenient, I would like to make some inquiries."

Because she knew, Tatiana Orlova did not ask what the inquiries were about but stepped aside to let him in. "A friend of my son's is coming soon," she said in a matter-of-fact manner, her eyes avoiding Gerasimov's by looking at the ground.

"This won't take long." He started to remove his shoes, but with a wave Tatiana Orlova told him to keep them on. "There's clay all over the floor," she said, as she closed the door and led the way down the corridor. As he passed the kitchen, Gerasimov glimpsed a little boy drawing at the table.

They came into a large room—immense for a private apartment—that clearly served as her living room and studio and probably her bedroom too; there was a single bed behind a screen in the corner. In the center of the room, about five feet from the window, a tripod stood on a square of linoleum, and on top of the tripod, on a square board, was a lump the size of a human head swathed in cloth like a turban. From the marks on the linoleum, Gerasimov assumed it was a lump of clay covered to retain the moisture. Against the wall, on a shelf, were some finished works, abstract shapes with no resemblance to any natural forms.

Tatiana Orlova invited Gerasimov to sit down on the sofa that divided the area used as a studio from the rest of the room. She herself sat on a wooden chair, crossed her legs, and leaned forward—the posture of someone ready to listen. She was wearing blue workman's overalls, smudged with clay. She was tall and could have been beautiful if she had not been so thin. With more flesh on her bones, her nose would not have seemed so angular, her cheekbones so protruding, her bosom so flat. The leanness of her face made her eyes seem large—certainly in contrast to Ylena's piggy slits. In the sunlight from the window, Gerasimov saw gray strands in her black hair.

"Well?" She looked up, impatient to get the interrogation under way.

"I am from the State Security Service of the Russian Federation."

"Yes." She waved her hand as if to say, Dispense with the formalities.

"You will doubtless be familiar with—"

"Yes."

"Your husband, Andrei Anatolyevich Orlov, as you know, worked for the former Committee for State Security."

"Yes."

"We are now trying to make contact with some former employees, in order to, as it were, tie up loose ends."

To his irritation, Gerasimov found that he was speaking with a certain nervousness without understanding why. Was it because of her connections, or because she seemed so indifferent to his presence in her home?

"I have had no contact with my husband," she said. "As far as I know, he is not in Moscow."

"He is in the West."

She acknowledged neither that she knew nor that the information caused her any surprise.

"Did you know this?"

"What?"

"That he was in the West?"

She hesitated. "I did not know it, but I assumed it."

"Why?"

"He has not been to see Igor."

"Normally he would come to see his son?"

"Yes."

"How often?"

She shrugged. "When he's in Moscow, once or twice a week."

"When he last came, did he say when he would come again?"

"He said he would be gone for a time."

"Did he say for how long?"

"No."

"Or why?"

"No."

"He gave you no clue at all as to why he was going to the West?"

"Perhaps to look for work?" She said this coolly, looking Gerasimov straight in the eye. "After all, he lost his job."

"He was offered a post at the Tretyakov."

"That was given to one of his men."

"He could have had a job there as well if he had wanted it."

"Not one suited to his talents."

"Your husband was, I think, a convinced Communist."

"Not only my husband."

"No."

"And"—she hesitated—"it was more complicated than that."

"You must forgive me if I appear to be intruding on a private matter, Tatiana Ivanovna, but I understand that your separation from your husband was caused by ideological differences?"

She smiled again, a sour, sad smile. "Are you married?"

"Yes."

"Sometimes ideology is an excuse for other things."

"But there was no other woman and no other man."

"Oh, but there was."

Gerasimov looked perplexed. "That was not our understanding."

"The other man was Jesus Christ." She said this evenly.

"I see. And the other woman?"

"Mother Russia."

She spoke with no trace of irony, and it struck Gerasimov that perhaps her impassive, incurious manner was the mask of someone who was mad—that the insanity of believers, like the insanity of dissidents, was not, after all, a contrivance of the Fifth Chief Directorate. In the present circumstances, however, he was more likely to achieve his objective if he treated Tatiana Orlova as if she was sane.

"You became a believer?" he said.

"Yes."

"And he did not?"

"He believed," she said, "but not in God."

"In Russia?"

"Not just in Russia. In the Union."

"He was therefore against the plans of Mikhail Sergeyevich Gorbachev for a new treaty between the republics?"

"Yes."

"And so he was in favor of the coup?"

"He was not in the Soviet Union during the coup."

"And if he had been?"

She looked at him coldly. "Your guess is as good as mine."

"He remained a Communist?"

"As far as I know, he has not torn up his Party card."

"But he believed."

"In what?"

"In Marxism and Leninism."

She hesitated. "It is some time since I discussed such things with him."

"And then?"

"Then? He believed in Marxism and Leninism, yes, but only, I think, as a means to an end."

"What do you mean?"

"He would say—" She stopped. "Is this relevant?"

"It might be."

"He would say that a nation must share a belief, whether or not it was true."

"Then why not become a Christian like you?"

"Because religion is the opium of the people." She smiled. "He thought Christianity was too gentle."

"While communism was strong?"

"Yes."

"Our people no longer seem to share his point of view."

Again, she smiled. "They have turned to worship the golden calf."

Gerasimov looked puzzled. "What golden calf?"

"When Moses was on the mountain receiving the Ten Commandments, the people of Israel turned away from God and started to worship a golden calf."

Gerasimov nodded. "Do you think," he said, "that in view of recent political developments, your husband might have felt authorized to retain state funds?"

"Again you ask me to speculate."

"It is my duty."

She sighed. "Would he feel authorized? By whom?"

"General Khrulev, for example."

"I was told that Khrulev is dead."

"Then certain figures in the parliament: Rutskoi, for example, or Khasbulatov?"

"I don't know."

"Or even, perhaps, by himself?"

"You mean would he steal state funds like everyone else?" She laughed. "No, comrade. Whatever else he may be, Andrei is not a thief."

The doorbell rang, and Tatiana Orlova got to her feet. "That must be Drusha. Will you excuse me a moment?"

Her courtesy annoyed Gerasimov. After she had left the room, he stood up to look around. The room lacked any of the luxuries he would esteem—a color television, a video recorder, a compact disc player—but had an old oak wardrobe, a table covered with a silk cloth, and a huge old samovar, all from before the Revolution, antiques like her beliefs. Privileged bitch, he thought, pretending she never fucks or farts.

He looked behind the screen at her narrow single bed. Georgi's words came back to him—"Women need servicing, regular servicing, thorough servicing"—but it looked as if there was no one to service this dried-out, stuck-up, would-be nun.

He could hear children's voices from the corridor. A single woman with one child in an apartment this size! Perhaps he should offer to move in with her. He would fuck some color back into her cheeks.

A brave idea. When Tatiana Orlova returned, Gerasimov saw that her first glance, a wistful one, went not to the Russian Harrison Ford but to the turbaned lump of clay. Then, impassively, she looked over to where Gerasimov was standing by the bookcase next to her bed and asked, "Are there further questions?"

He was on official business; he must be correct. "Can you think of anyone else—a friend, perhaps—who might know where he has gone?"

She did not sit down. "You probably know about his friends better than I do."

"He had no girlfriend?"

"What does it say in his file?"

"Nothing."

"Is that so difficult to understand?"

Even before he answered, Gerasimov could see that she regretted putting the question, because it enabled him to say, "Not now that I have met you, Tatiana Ivanovna."

The compliment was unwelcome. "The children—" she began.

"Yes, I am going." He walked toward the door. "I would be grateful if you would tell me if you hear from him."

She said nothing.

As he walked past the kitchen, he glanced in and saw that the boy now sat at the table with a girl of twelve or thirteen. Tatiana Orlova made no move to introduce them, and Gerasimov moved on down the corridor. "A fine boy," he said. "His father must be proud of him."

Again she did not answer. Gerasimov sensed that she was impatient to get him out of the house. "Remember, a telephone call or a post-card," he said as she opened the door.

"You will know," she said, leaving it uncertain as to whether he would know from her or by intercepting her mail and her calls; then, without bothering to say good-bye, she closed the door.

Gerasimov was angry. At first he did not know why—whether it was at the condescension of Orlov's wife or because of the frustrating lack of results of that day's investigations: probably both. It was quite apparent that Partovski and Orlova were holding something back. Both were too well acquainted with the methods of the former KGB to try to conceal what Gerasimov might discover from other sources, both appeared to give straight answers to his questions, but neither had cared to confide or to speculate. Both had seen him as an adversary; both in their own way were aiding and abetting the absent Orlov by their minimal cooperation.

Partovski he could understand. No one likes to turn in a fellow officer, particularly a former commander whom one has admired. Gerasimov would have sympathized with Orlova, too, if she had still been Orlov's wife; no woman can be expected to betray the man she loves. But they were separated and ideologically opposed. Tatiana Orlova should welcome the defeat of the coup, the death of Khrulev, and the dismissal of hard-line officers like Orlov from the new Security Service of the Russian Federation. She should have seen Gerasimov as her protector, a knight in shining armor. Instead, she had treated him as a vulgar interloper who had no business poking his nose into her life.

"Privileged bitch." He said it out loud this time, as if the coarse words spoken into the cold air of dusk could somehow wipe the impassive expression from her face. He was angry not just with her but also with himself—for having fancied her and for having paid her a compliment, knowing quite well it would be thrown back in his face. The overalls had angered him; like her religion, her art was the kind of pretension only the elite could afford.

Gerasimov returned to the Lubyanka and spent what remained of the day planning the evening ahead. He had been sleeping for the last fortnight on his sister's sofa but sensed that he had already outstayed his welcome. He remained determined not to return to Ylena. He wanted her to suffer. In the end he would move back to the Ulitsa

Academika Koroleva, but first he would have to get over the rage he still felt at the thought of Ylena with Georgi and of that night at the Cosmos Hotel. He was running short of old friends to descend on. The patience of most of them had worn thin. The last resort would appear to be Klaudia, an old girlfriend whom he saw from time to time. She would certainly give him a bed for the night unless someone else happened to be in it, but she lived out in Prazhskaya and he could not turn up empty-handed. It would mean sacrificing the bottle of vodka locked in the bottom drawer of his desk—a high price to pay for a night either on Klaudia's sofa or in her bed.

He could stay in a hotel, but that would be tricky. It would not be easy to find a room. It would be recorded by the militia and so would find its way into his file as an example of "domestic instability" that might affect his career. In the end, Klaudia seemed the most satisfactory solution. When he called her, her drowsy voice answered the telephone. She said he could come but warned him that she had nothing to eat.

Gerasimov scrounged some ham and a tin of herring from the Lubyanka canteen and, since there was no gasoline in the Samara, set off for the suburbs on the metro, changing at Prazhskaya to a bus. He reached Klaudia's apartment by nine. It was clear that she had made no effort to tidy up or improve her own appearance. As always, it was hard for him to recognize the bright-eyed blonde he had screwed when she was eighteen in the fat slut of thirty-five with unbrushed hair and worn slippers.

Gerasimov was not offended; Klaudia's great advantage was that though she gave nothing she expected nothing in return. He went through the routine pretense of being pleased to see her. She looked indifferent until he gave her the bottle of vodka, at which point she perked up. He brought out the ham and the tin of herring. She had some bread, and they ate and drank. Klaudia started on a long, plaintive story about how she had been done in by her supervisor in the typing pool at Radio Moscow, where she worked. Gerasimov tried to listen, but he longed to sleep. His mind wandered. He filled their glasses. He was getting drunk. When Klaudia started shaking her finger at him, he tried to focus once again on what she was saying. It was the old story that they should have married; it was because of him that her husband had walked out on her; he was so jealous; just because she was seeing . . . and so on. He had heard it all before. Like the bottle of vodka, it was the price he had to pay for a night's lodging.

By the time they finished the bottle, the vodka had produced illusions of desire. They staggered from the kitchen into Klaudia's bedroom and fell onto her bed. Gerasimov went to work, too drunk to feel much pleasure, simply doing what had to be done, but as he groped her flabby body, he began to imagine that she was Ylena. His grunts became angry, his thrusts became blows. Then he thought of the lanky stuck-up sculptress and became angrier still, yanking back strands of Klaudia's hair. Being mistaken as a sign of passion, this only heightened her excitement until, after a few more brutal thrusts, Gerasimov slumped onto her in a stupor, spent and steeped in self-disgust.

7

That evening, while Nikolai Gerasimov found solace with Klaudia Spizenko, Tatiana Orlova changed out of her overalls into a dress, left her son Igor with Drusha, the thirteen-year-old daughter of her neighbor, and walked up to Tverskoi Boulevard, where she caught a bus.

She got off the bus after it had crossed the Kalininski Bridge over the Moscow River, where the huge Hotel Ukraine faces the "White House," parliament of the Russian Federation. Barbed-wire entanglements, tanks, and barricades still remained as relics of Yeltsin's defiant resistance against the coup the year before.

Next to the Hotel Ukraine is a second skyscraper of the Stalinist era with a grandiose entrance and pale gray walls. As she walked toward it in the dusk, Tatiana shuddered. Since she had learned that so many millions had died in the gulags at the time this building was built, she had always imagined that the bricks had been made with their ground-up bones.

Tatiana was admitted by the concierge who kept watch on the door. "Are they there, Katerina Petrovna?" she asked.

"So far as I know." The grim-faced woman did not smile but her tone was familiar, even friendly.

Tatiana took the elevator to the ninth floor and, as she came out onto the landing, took a key from her bag and let herself into an apartment.

"Hello!" she shouted as she closed the door.

"Tania?" came the voice of an older woman.

"Mother?"

"We're in the kitchen."

Tatiana's mother had no need to say this, for though it was a large flat with big rooms, some facing across the river to the parliament, Tatiana's childhood had been spent in that kitchen and it was there her mother felt at ease.

Her parents were eating: her mother standing at the stove, her father sitting at the table. The mother embraced her; the father, gruffly but with evident pleasure, patted the seat beside him on the bench that ran along the wall.

Tatiana sat down where he had suggested, her thin body slipping easily between the bench and the table. Her mother, a small, broad woman with a round face and gray hair combed back into a bun, put a bowl of soup and a spoon in front of her daughter. Tatiana glanced at it, smiled up at her mother, thanked her, and picked up the spoon, but instead of dipping it into the soup she turned to her father and asked, "Where is Andrei?"

Ivan Keminski frowned. He was a man of around sixty with dark features, a grave look, and the same high cheekbones and pointed nose as his daughter's. "You know," he said. "He went west."

"They were asking about him."

"Who?"

"Someone from the Lubyanka."

"What did you say?"

"That I didn't know where he was or what he was doing."

"Which is true."

"Yes, but if they are suspicious . . ."

"What?"

"I am afraid."

"For Andrei?"

She blushed. "Not just for Andrei. Also for you."

Her father laughed, but as he did so Tatiana glanced at her mother and saw that she too was anxious.

"I know that you and he have something planned," she said.

"A joint venture, that is all."

"What kind of joint venture?"

"Nothing. Just a bank."

"A bank? The last two Marxists in Russia are starting a *bank*?"

"Not starting a bank, no. Just opening a branch of a Western bank."

"But Father—"

"They have suspended the Party. There is no more Central Committee. No more Secretariat. I am out of a job. Andrei too."

"But a bank!"

He frowned again. "What would you want me to do, sell apples from the dacha in the market?"

"No." She shook her head. She knew—she saw, she could not avoid it—how terribly recent events had upset her father, who had given his life to the Communist cause. Since her conversion to Christianity, she had often argued with him and, being young and quick-witted, had sometimes got the better of him. But in those days he had always had his position to sustain him as a leading ideologue at the center of influence of one of the two great powers of the world. Now, since the coup and the suspension of the Party, it had become impossible to argue against him without appearing to gloat over the downfall of the Soviet state.

"Why not a bank?" asked Tatiana's mother, still standing at the stove. "We have plenty of room in the apartment. All you need is a telephone, a typewriter, and a fax—that's a bank!" She said this with childlike enthusiasm, but it was unconvincing because of the worried look on her face.

"But what do you know about banking, Father?" Tatiana asked.

"You don't need to know much. There are banks in the West that want to invest in Russia. They need people with contacts. I have contacts. That is my capital, my contacts."

"And what do they bring?"

"Money. Currency."

"And what has Andrei to do with it?"

"Well, he is in Europe to arrange things, to set it up."

Tatiana looked uncertain. It sounded plausible, and would have been so had the idea been put forward by two other men. "Is there no more to it than that?" she asked.

"What more should there be?"

"Andrei served under General Khrulev, and General Khrulev was involved in politics up to his neck."

90

"Maybe. Perhaps that's why they want to question Andrei. But the coup failed. Khrulev is dead. Now we have to change our ideas to survive."

Tatiana put down her spoon, her soup untouched. "I know you love Andrei," she said to her father, "and that you were sorry when we separated."

Keminski shrugged. "What's done is done."

"I know that perhaps you think it was my fault, that my becoming a Christian made it impossible for Andrei—"

"No man wants to be married to a nun."

Tatiana blushed. "I wasn't a nun, Father. I was always—well, a wife."

"Don't talk about these things," her mother muttered.

Tatiana looked up. "I am afraid, Mother. I am afraid not just for him but of what he might do. And I blame myself, because a man with a family will think twice before he does anything dangerous."

"But there is nothing dangerous about a bank," said Ivan Keminski.

She turned on her father. "Whatever you may say, Father, you will not persuade me that Andrei has now become a bourgeois businessman. I know him better than anyone. He is a believer, a true believer, a Soviet patriot, a Bolshevik dreamer, and I fear he will stop at nothing to make those dreams come true."

"Not a dreamer," said Ivan Keminski, "an idealist, as any chekist worthy of the name should be."

The telephone rang. Ivan Keminski left the room to answer it. Tatiana was relieved. When her father became bombastic, she knew the time had come to change the subject.

"Ah, Nogin, at last." Her father's voice boomed from the hallway. "I've been trying to get through to you for several days. Did you get the message? . . . My nephew, yes, in Jena. I'd be most grateful. . . . Bored, I think. Without currency they can hardly afford to breathe. . . . Yes, that would be kind. . . . Here? Don't ask. Terrible. To think we fought for this. . . . Courage, my old friend. Courage of a different kind."

When Keminski returned to the kitchen, Tatiana rose to go. "Is Piotr in Germany?"

"No, in Satarov. Why?"

"Then who is your nephew in Germany?"

For a moment, the old man looked confused. "What nephew in Germany?"

"I thought you just said, on the telephone, that you had a nephew in Jena?"

"Ah, yes. It's Piotr. Of course it's Piotr. I only have one nephew, after all. He's going there, briefly, on some business or other, and I told him to look up my old friend Nogin. He's still stationed there. You won't remember Nogin. We were in the army together. Back in 1945, our tanks ran neck and neck in the race from Stalingrad to Berlin. Brave soldier. Good comrade. He got there first. And now, I daresay, he'll be one of the last to leave."

8

Colonel Yevgeni Mikhailovich Nogin, Ivan Keminski's old comrade-in-arms, commanded the Soviet base at Waldheim, fifty miles north of Berlin. His most pressing duty during the short dark days that winter was finding something for his men to do. There was no reason now to train for a war with NATO. They knew they were to return to Russia when, if ever, quarters were built where they could live. What reason was there to get up in the morning, let alone turn up on parade? The most Nogin could hope to get out of his men was an hour or two each morning spent servicing the tanks before they were loaded onto trains at the Tucheim sidings on the first stage of their journey back to the scrap heap in Russia.

By midafternoon, most of Colonel Nogin's men were tipsy; by sunset, they were dead drunk. If they had no vodka, wine, or cognac, they stole pure alcohol from the dispensary or even antifreeze from the workshops. Since Nogin himself was not immune to this national weakness, he was usually flushed when the time came to eat dinner with his fellow officers in the mess. Not only was his face red in patches but one or two buttons on his tunic were often left undone. Most of his subordinates were in the same condition.

Only Captain Sinyanski was always sober. At one time Colonel Nogin had been afraid of Sinyanski, who was known to report back to the Third Directorate of the KGB. At the time of the coup, Sinyanski had become agitated—plotting, Nogin suspected, to arrest and incarcerate those officers whom he considered ideologically unsound. But after the collapse of the coup and the subsequent restructuring of the KGB as the Security Service of the Russian Federation, Sinyanski had become dejected. He was now a toothless tiger, and Nogin no longer feared him. He even came to like him. Sinyanski was more intelligent and hence better company than most of the other officers, and the colonel shared many of his feelings, particularly his anger at the way Gorbachev and Shevardnadze had surrendered Germany without a fight.

Although it was now stranded in the middle of hostile territory by the receding tide of Soviet power, the garrison at Waldheim was little affected by the collapse of the Communist government in the DDR. There were no more May Day parades in the nearby town of Tucheim, where girls with blond pigtails from the Freie Deutsche Jugend had once presented their "fraternal liberators from fascism" with bunches of flowers. But neither were his men stoned by the local inhabitants when they went to Tucheim on leave, as Nogin had once feared.

It was not until December that Nogin heard from Piotr Perfilyev, Keminski's nephew in Jena. He immediately invited him to stay at the base for the weekend. They were glad to see a fresh face and were hardly short of space. In due course, Perfilyev turned up at Tucheim on the train. Nogin sent a junior officer, Lieutenant Vorotnikov, to meet him.

Perfilyev was brought straight to Nogin's house. He wore civilian clothes and told Nogin that he was working in Jena as an engineer. Perfilyev was a tall, dark, bearded man well into his thirties, perhaps even forty, who bore no resemblance either to his uncle, Ivan Keminski, or his mother, Keminski's sister, whom Nogin had met in Moscow after the war.

Perfilyev produced as a gift for the garrison six bottles of Stolichnaya vodka. The five that found their way to the officers' mess ensured a warm welcome for the visitor, who was placed next to Nogin at dinner. Perfilyev's health was the first of many toasts that were proposed in the course of the evening.

As they became drunk, the officers lost their inhibitions and an argument started up between Captain Sinyanski and Lieutenant Vorotnikov about the slander in a new guide to the former concentration camp of Sachsenhausen, situated between Waldheim and Berlin.

"If it's true, it's true," said Vorotnikov. "Hitler used Sachsenhausen. Stalin did too. Think of the kulaks in Ukraine. The one was as bad as the other."

"Untrue!" shouted Sinyanski. "Certainly Stalin did what had to be done because he faced desperate odds. People died, I grant you that. Perhaps innocent people were killed. But the end justified the means. Without collectivization there would have been no industrialization, and without industrialization there would have been no tanks to fight the Fascists at Stalingrad and Kursk. Where would those swine in the West be now if our fathers and grandfathers hadn't laid down their lives in the Great Patriotic War? The concentration camps would still be in business and there wouldn't be a Jew left alive."

"That's as may be, Alexander Sergeyevich," another junior officer broke in, "but you can't build the future on the courage and heroism of past generations. It won't help our economy. It won't buy food."

"Lenin and Stalin imposed communism," shouted another, "and communism doesn't work!"

"Who says it doesn't work?" countered Sinyanski. "No country on earth has achieved so much in so short a time. In 1918 we were a bankrupt nation of muzhiks. In 1945 we were a major world power."

"And now we're a bankrupt nation of muzhiks once again," said Lieutenant Vorotnikov.

"Only because so-called reformers have bartered the achievements of three generations for a loan from the World Bank."

"They had no choice!"

A number of voices now clamored to be heard, but since none could rise above the others, and since most were now too drunk to sustain a cogent argument of any kind, they all eventually petered out, whereupon Nogin, from curiosity as well as politeness, turned to Perfilyev, who until that point had remained silent. "Have you a view of the current situation, Piotr Petrovich? You know better than we do what's in store for us when we get home."

"I sympathize with our friend here," said the visitor, nodding toward Sinyanski, "but I am afraid that we have to acknowledge that we have been outmaneuvered by the enemy."

"Outmaneuvered?" asked Nogin, hoping that the conversation was moving on to military matters he could better understand.

"Outwitted is perhaps a better word," said Perfilyev.

"How do you mean?"

"It was a mistake to spend all our resources on defense and on prestigious projects like the space program and foreign aid. We should have invested in the quality of life at home."

"I agree," said Nogin. "To think of all those rubles going to Cuba, Nicaragua, and Ethiopia when our own people were going short."

"What Marx and Lenin promised, after all," Perfilyev went on, "was not wealth but justice, a society in which each gave according to his ability and each received according to his needs."

"But after seventy-five years of socialism," said Vorotnikov, "there are still millions who do not receive according to their needs."

"Yes," went up a cry. "What about our housing?"

"We are impoverished," said Perfilyev, "precisely because we concentrated our resources on preparing for a war that would never be fought. If they had been used instead on public welfare, we could have shown the world the superiority of our socialist way of life."

"But the Americans and Germans would still be richer," said Major Ivashenko, Nogin's second-in-command, "and they would enjoy liberties that were not permitted under our Soviet system."

"Liberties?" asked Perfilyev, who, though he had drunk little, was now flushed. "I have lived in America, comrade, and I can tell you that their so-called liberty is only the cant of their corrupt intelligentsia. In reality, it is the most intolerant and unequal society the world has ever seen. You can become rich, true, but once you are rich you are imprisoned in your suburban villas behind chain fences while drug-crazed hoodlums prowl the streets, hunting, pillaging, and murdering their own kind. That is what liberty means in America, comrades—to exploit if you can and rob if you cannot."

"I get the impression," said Nogin, "that you did not warm to the Americans."

"Warm to them? No. I loathed them. They are a nation of malcontents, descendants of all the miscreants and traitors who abandoned their native lands in the Old World—sectarians like the Puritans and Quakers, greedy English colonists, slave owners who preached liberty as an excuse to turn against their king, runts of the litter from every slum in every minor nation from Latvia to Sicily, from Ireland to Greece. What is the driving spirit of every colonial culture? Greed! To hell with the people; every man for himself. From the conquistadors in Mexico to the cattle barons in the Wild West—exploit the soil, enslave the people! And if they will not work as slaves? Herd them onto reservations and let them die!"

As he was speaking, Perfilyev's eyes had widened and their expression had grown intense. His deep voice, rising in pitch as he proceeded, held the attention of his intoxicated audience. Sinyanski looked at him with evident satisfaction. Nogin, too, could not suppress a sense of exhilaration to hear the old enemy attacked in this way. Even the young lieutenant, Vorotnikov, appeared impressed by Perfilyev's fervor, if not by the substance of what he said.

Only the adjutant, Major Ivashenko, retained his skepticism. "You may be right," he said, "but if our people now reject socialism, what can we do but follow their example?"

"It will be fatal to try," said Perfilyev. "Socialism suits the temperament of our people; they were always averse to capitalism of any kind. They resisted Stolypin's reforms after 1905; they will resist Yeltsin's now. Unless, of course, the so-called reforms are forced upon us by the Americans and the World Bank. Then, comrades, you have only to look south over the border to see what the future holds. Look at Turkey, a once-great empire reduced to the condition of a third-rate power, its people transported to Germany to provide cheap labor for Krupp and Thyssen in the Ruhr."

"There are Russian workers," said Ivashenko, "who would be only too happy to work for Krupp and Thyssen."

"Of course," said Perfilyev, an angry look now in his eyes, "because they are enticed by the thought of riches and imagine that the higher their standard of living the happier they will be. But some things matter more than money, comrade major: justice, dignity, honor. We may have been poor under Brezhnev. There may even have been cases of corruption. But what comparable country was better off? Thailand, where a quarter of a million children work in brothels? India, where children are mutilated to make them more effective beggars on the street? Mexico, its people admitted over the Rio Grande to work as serfs in cities with the sacred names of Los Angeles and San Francisco, now the Sodom and Gomorrah of the modern world?"

It was late. The bottles were empty. The officers were sobering up, their moods sinking from joviality into melancholy. The future seemed grim. Even those like Ivashenko who did not agree with Perfilyev found it hard to contradict him, above all because here was a rare Russian who appeared to have seen something of the world.

"So what's to be done?" asked Nogin, accepting a cigarette offered by Perfilyev.

"Another coup," said Sinyanski. "And next time no scruples!"

"Things must get worse before they get better," said Perfilyev. "But when the moment comes—" He clenched his fist, as if catching and then crushing a mosquito hovering in the air.

"And in the meantime?" asked Nogin.

"We should learn from the Germans," said Perfilyev. "After World War One, they were only permitted an army of one hundred thousand men. They therefore made officers serve as NCOs, and NCOs serve as privates. That way they kept the nucleus of an army ten times the size."

"But can the Americans dictate the size of the Russian army?" asked Nogin. "Has it come to that?"

"It is not so much the army that has to be prepared," said Perfilyev. "It is the Party."

"Ah."

"Why do you think Yeltsin suspended it right after the coup, with the stroke of a pen? Because the Americans, who helped him defeat the coup, knew that without the Party the Soviet Union was ungovernable and would fall apart."

"But now that the Party has no state to support it, how can it survive?" asked Sinyanski, also accepting a cigarette offered him by Perfilyev.

"It will go underground once again," said Perfilyev, "as it did before the Revolution." He struck a match and lit first Nogin's cigarette, then Sinyanski's, then his own.

Nogin inhaled and then sighed as he blew out the smoke. "I don't pretend, comrade, that I was ever a good student of Marx or Lenin, and I joined the Party because it seemed the thing to do. But there's no doubt in my mind that it was the Party, as you say, that held the Union together and was the guarantee of the greatness of Russia. Without the Party—well, it's as you say, and quite evident for anyone to see.

We're going down to God knows what depths of poverty, chaos, and degradation."

"It's worse than you think," said Perfilyev darkly.

"Worse?"

"Take the job our team is doing here in Jena. Our Ministry of Medium Machine Building had some top-secret projects with our German comrades—first-rate military research. We've been told to dismantle the equipment so it can be sent back to Moscow, but I happen to know that some of Yeltsin's people in the Defense Ministry mean to sell it to the Americans."

"Impossible!"

"You can't imagine what it's like back in Moscow, comrade colonel. Anyone will do anything for dollars."

"Can't you denounce them?"

"To whom? Everyone is getting a cut."

"Then stop them!"

"How?"

"I . . . you could . . . couldn't you destroy it? That would surely be better than letting it fall into the hands of the Americans."

Perfilyev pondered. "Where? In Germany now we are watched."

"Bring it here."

"Here?"

"To the base. Why not?"

"It is bulky. . . ."

"We have plenty of space." He turned to Sinyanski. "Don't we have space enough, comrade?"

"Of course. The hangars, where the tanks used to be."

"And to destroy it?" asked Perfilyev.

"Burn it. We have some gasoline. Or we can use it for target practice for the tanks. The one thing we're not short of is shells."

III

1993
January–May

9

In the first months of 1993, Francesca McDermott worked harder than she ever had before. The challenge she faced was not so much how to make the Excursus exhibition a triumph as how to save it from becoming a fiasco.

From the start, she had been warned by friends and colleagues in the United States that she had bitten off more than she could chew. A major exhibition could not be arranged in less than a year. In the beginning, she had reassured herself that the backup provided by the Germans for a show on the limited scale she envisaged could be mounted for the following July, but by the time the decision had been made to make it a mammoth two-site exhibition, it was too late for her to pull out.

Even then, Francesca did not believe they would be lent all the works they had requested. However, Excursus had been endorsed at the highest political level and aroused enthusiasm wherever it was mentioned. Pledges of backing were pressed upon the organizing committee by banks, conglomerates, and foundations. In December, the Museum of Modern Art in New York had agreed to lend all the works of art that had been requested. By January, it had become clear that where MOMA led, every major national gallery was eager to follow. Directors and private collectors wrote from all over the world, offering works that Francesca had not known existed.

Many of the practical arrangements were handled by Dr. Kemmelkampf and his civil servants in the Prussian Ministry of Culture; however, it became quite clear to Francesca that they had little experience in mounting exhibitions of this kind. The timetable presented particular problems. Günter confided to Francesca that a fierce dispute had broken out between the ministry and the two gallery directors, who had already had to cancel the exhibitions they had planned for July and the first half of August. Those that were scheduled earlier also had to be curtailed to make way for Excursus, provoking considerable ill feeling in members of the museums' staffs who had been working on these projects for several years.

The differences had come to a head, according to Günter, over the issue of where the Excursus works of art should be stored upon arrival in Berlin. Normally they would be sent straight to the gallery with the best facilities, in this case the New National Gallery, but because of its commitment to a major retrospective, it did not have the space to handle even a part of the Excursus works of art.

"But surely there is space in one of the galleries or museums in East Berlin," said Francesca, discussing the question with Günter one morning in his office.

"Of course there is space," said Günter, "but the facilities are too primitive to satisfy the lenders—or, for that matter, the people in Bonn."

"What does the ministry propose?"

"The ideal solution would be a secure warehouse where the paintings could be held until the moment came to hang them."

"Does such a warehouse exist?"

"Of course. There is one in Tegel."

"Then why don't we use it?"

Günter shrugged. "You may well ask. It all has to do with budgets and precedents. Exclusive use of the warehouse would be expensive. Kemmelkampf has told Stefi that if the galleries are given the facility for this occasion, they will regard it as their right in the future."

"But surely they realize that Excursus is exceptional?"

"Of course, but you must know about such bureaucratic wrangles. We are now in a position where everyone knows that an outside warehouse is the only solution, but no one feels able to suggest it."

"Why don't you suggest it?"

"I have. I have even offered to pay for it through an additional grant from the New German Foundation. But Kemmelkampf is still worried by this question of precedent."

"To hell with Kemmelkampf," said Francesca. "I'll tell him that the lenders will pull out unless the paintings go to that warehouse."

"Perhaps you should look at it first."

"Do I need to?"

"I would feel more confident. We are not as experienced as you are about this kind of thing."

They drove out to Tegel the next day in Francesca's Golf. It was only a short way up the Stadtring, but it took them some time to find the warehouse belonging to Omni Zartfracht GmbH—Omni Fragile Freight Company. The manager of the company's Berlin office was there to show them around.

Francesca was enormously relieved. The warehouse was ideal. It was newly built behind a chain and barbed-wire fence, with state-of-the-art temperature and humidity controls and the security of Fort Knox. It was large enough to store all the works of art if they could stipulate exclusive use until the exhibition was over. Günter, too, seemed impressed.

At the next meeting of the organizing committee, Francesca proposed storing the works as they arrived at the OZF warehouse. The anticipated argument by Kemmelkampf about precedent seemed of less interest to the gallery directors than Francesca had been led to suppose. She argued forcefully that the American lenders would insist upon the very highest standards. Günter pointed out that it would certainly be expensive, but if the committee felt there was no other solution, the money could be found. Dr. Kemmelkampf hoped the company would make an allowance for the prestigious publicity they would gain if a contract was agreed upon. Stefi said the Federal government would have to be satisfied about the competence of the company and the measures taken to protect the works of art. Francesca agreed. "But I imagine that all concerned would feel as I did that we are extraordinarily fortunate to have something like this available on such short notice."

Only Dr. Serotkin made an objection; he said the Soviet galleries would find it irregular to entrust works of art from public collections to a private company.

"Perhaps only because there are no private companies in Russia," said Francesca tartly.

"I defer to your superior experience," said Serotkin, with one of his ironic smiles.

"Are there any other objections?" asked Stefan Diederich. There were none. "Then I suggest it be recorded in the minutes that at the suggestion of Dr. McDermott the committee authorizes Herr Westarp and Dr. Kemmelkampf to enter into negotiations with the Omni Zartfracht Company for the exclusive use of their warehouse in Tegel."

With no dissenting voice, the motion was carried.

After this satisfactory solution to the problem of storage, Francesca's chief task became the preparation of the catalog, a major document that would not only survive for years after the end of the exhibition but would also carry Francesca's name and her achievement all over the world. The catalog obsessed her. Every now and then she would have to have lunch with some visiting cultural dignitary—a museum director from Paris, a cultural attaché from Tokyo—and though she behaved properly on such occasions, her mind never left her office, where, with Frau Doktor Koch, she was assembling illustrations and information for the catalog from the different galleries and collectors.

It was a tormenting task. By and large, the major galleries were able to provide Francesca with what she wanted, but even the galleries often had no suitable photographs of the paintings they planned to send and only a hazy idea of their provenance. Some private collectors had no idea who had owned their paintings before them. Francesca made calls and sent faxes to such far-off places as Nagasaki and Bogotá. Her own and Frau Doktor Koch's research into the history of the paintings was frequently frustrated by the professional envy of scholars and experts. Some had to be flattered into cooperation and asked to contribute to the catalog but then would fail to send their copy.

A large number of works were in galleries in the former Soviet Union, and for these Francesca was at the mercy of Andrei Serotkin. When Stefi Diederich had first told her that he was to be a member of the organizing committee, she had accepted him with some reluctance; later, she had come to see the advantage of enlisting someone with contacts in Russia, and finally she had had to acknowledge to Stefi that Serotkin was indispensable, having got agreements from the Tretyakov in Moscow and the Russian Museum in St. Petersburg for the loan of all the works she had requested, including Tatlin's *The Sailor,* Goncharova's *The Cyclist,* and Popova's *Italian Still-Life.*

By February, however, Francesca began to wonder whether or not she could rely on Serotkin's assurances. She had only his word for the galleries' consent, usually based on no more than a telephone call, occasionally backed up by an indecipherable fax. When she asked him for letters from the galleries concerned, confirming their consent, Serotkin would laugh without saying what his laugh denoted. She would send him memos asking, say, if color slides were available from the Tretyakov of Malevich's *Dynamic Suspension* and, getting no answer, would go to his office and ask if there was any news about the slides.

"Ah, that."

"We've got beautiful slides of the early Maleviches from the Stedelijk, and of his *Yellow Quadrilateral on White.* It would be a pity if we couldn't illustrate any of those in the Russian collections."

"It's not so simple. In Moscow, good color reproduction is not always possible."

"If it can't be done, Andrei, it can't be done, but we have to *know.*"

To compound Francesca's frustration, Serotkin would absent himself every now and then, sometimes for as long as a week. He never said where he was going or when he would return. Francesca suggested to the committee that they take on another Russian-speaking researcher, but this was vetoed by Günter Westarp on the dubious grounds of cost. She therefore had to wait for answers to her queries until Serotkin chose to reappear.

When she complained about Serotkin's absences to Stefi, he said he suspected that Serotkin had a mistress whom he visited from time to time. Sophie said he probably got drunk "like Yeltsin; all Russians do." Their explanations only added to Francesca's irritation. It was intolerable that Serotkin should leave his post without a good excuse. On occasions, upon his return, she would ask him where he had been but he would always make an evasive reply, such as, "Ah, well, you know, we Russians are not used to hard work," or he would say in German, *"Geschäft ist Geschäft,"* business is business, without explaining what his business was.

Julius Breitenbach, who overheard one such exchange, confided to Francesca that most Russians in Germany went in for a little import-export on the side, and it was perhaps to some enterprise such as this that Serotkin referred. "They have so little money," said Julius. "Quite possibly he is investing his stipend in fax machines or video recorders and shipping them back to Moscow."

Francesca found this explanation degrading, but she could not be sure it was not true. Part of the irritation caused by Serotkin's unexplained absences was that it added to his mystery. She had never had any reason to revise her first impressions that he was dashing, even handsome, and earnest, yet with a twinkle in his eye. She noticed that the secretaries, Dora and Gertie, and even Frau Doktor Koch, became downcast whenever he was absent and perked up whenever he returned.

After almost six months in the same office, Francesca still could not make Serotkin out. Was he intelligent? He spoke English and German with remarkable fluency, but his knowledge of Russian experimental art was merely adequate for someone who was supposed to be an expert in the field. Was he amusing? It was hard to tell. After that first discussion in the canteen about the position of women, their only exchanges had been about Excursus. He was always courteous and correct, but at times his politeness seemed almost ironic. At meetings of the organizing committee, he always spoke with a certain wit, and he often smiled when Francesca spoke, but she had the impression that he was amused by who she was rather than by what she said.

Of course it was Francesca herself who had drawn the line of demarcation between their professional and private lives, and she had been relieved that Serotkin respected her decision, limiting their contacts to the office and their exchanges to matters concerning the exhibition. But as the months passed, it began to irk her that he made no attempt to question the rules she had laid down. She became curious, not just about his absences but about what he did on weekends and during his spare time. It even occurred to her that since they were both alone in Berlin, it might make sense to go to a play or a movie together, but it was difficult to think of an unobtrusive way to change the pattern she had established.

Francesca hinted to Sophie that she and Stefi could ask them over one evening, but Sophie said Stefi hated Russians and preferred to see as little of Serotkin as he could. It was therefore up to Francesca to get across to Serotkin that as far as she was concerned the time had come to change the rules, but whenever she made up her mind to say something to him, she backed down at the last moment, finding that she was unwilling to risk the embarrassment of his turning her down. She was humiliated by the memory of how she had thought Rasputin the writer was Rasputin the monk; in fact, to make up for that gaffe on some future occasion, she had found a book by Valentin Rasputin and had read a number of his stories. However, conversation with Serotkin in the Excursus office never turned to literature from art, and Francesca was on the point of abandoning the idea of getting better acquainted when fate intervened in an unexpected way.

Although Francesca McDermott and Andrei Serotkin had apartments in the same building, they rarely met in the lobby; Francesca did not even know on which floor Serotkin lived. Each morning she went jogging in the Englischer Garten and she knew that Serotkin jogged there too; she had seen him from the window of her living room. He seemed to get up about half an hour before she did and so had usually finished his round before she set out.

In December it was too dark for a single woman to venture safely into the park, and Francesca had given up her jogging in favor of working out at a gym when she could. At the beginning of February, however, when the mornings grew lighter, Francesca had resumed her jogging and on one or two occasions saw Serotkin, either in the lobby or in the Englischer Garten. Both would exchange a curt "Good morning," Serotkin sweating, Francesca bleary-eyed. She preferred to avoid these early-morning encounters; she hardly looked her best.

One morning in March, Francesca was doing her round of the Englischer Garten in her charcoal-gray track suit when she was joined by three men wearing running shoes, jeans, and grubby sweatshirts. From their appearance, she judged them to be Turks. This in itself did not alarm her; she had been told that, after Istanbul and Ankara, Berlin had a larger Turkish population than any other city in the world. The three men had as much right as she did to exercise in the Englischer Garten, and it was only paranoia induced by comparison with New York's Central Park that aroused her alarm at the sight of their dark skin.

After a few minutes, however, the three men crowded her, one on each side, one behind, and as they ran tried to engage her in conversation. *"Guten morgen, Fraülein. Schönes Wetter, was?"* As she ran along the path, puffing somewhat—she was still out of condition after the winter break—she asked them to leave her alone: *"Bitte, lass mich in Ruhe."* She also looked around to see if there was anyone to whom she could look for help. There was not. Finally she stopped, gasping for breath, and told them with as much authority as she could muster to fuck off.

The tallest and oldest of the three, a man of around thirty, now looked around, and he too saw that no one else was in sight. He moved even closer to Francesca. *"Aber, warum so unfreundlich?"* he asked with a leer.

Francesca was now alarmed and tried to dodge past him, but the Turk grabbed her by the sleeve of her track suit. The two others leaped forward, gripped her by her arms, and, while the first covered her mouth, dragged her off the path and behind some shrubs. She was thrown backward to the ground. The first man took his hand off her mouth, but before she could shout he covered it with his own mouth, climbing onto her while unzipping his jeans.

Francesca struggled, and for a moment managed to kick him off, but the two other men still held her arms and the first man, picking himself up, his jeans around his knees, hissed in Turkish to the other two, one of whom then grabbed both her wrists while the other held a leg. She was able to shout and did so, but she was unable to get up off the ground. While the second Turk held on to her left leg, the first tugged at her track-suit bottom and pants and eventually removed them. Then he climbed on her, the wobbling pink point of his penis protruding from the black fuzz at his groin. Stifled by the smell, Francesca still struggled beneath his heavy body. She felt his hand move like a wedge between her legs and begin to prize them open . . . and then a hand pulled him off her by the hair and she saw, towering above her, Serotkin.

Hobbled by his jeans, the first Turk could do little to keep Serotkin from throwing him aside, but while the third still held her, the second let go of her leg, took a knife out of his pocket, flicked open the blade, and went for the Russian. Serotkin, only now turning back from the first Turk, dodged the lunge of the second and caught him with a kick in the stomach that sent him gasping to the ground.

Now the third let go of Francesca and—while she scrambled to get her right leg back into her pants and track-suit bottom—threw himself at Serotkin, but once again Serotkin easily stepped aside and struck the Turk on the back of the neck with a blow of such force that it left him lying motionless on the gravel path.

The first Turk, who had by now fastened his jeans and buckled his belt, saw what had happened to his companions and turned to run away, but before he could escape, Serotkin kicked him in the groin and then landed a blow on his chest that made him stagger, choke, and finally fall beside his companion on the ground.

Despite her shock and humiliation, Francesca had the composure to feel astonished that this Russian art historian should dispatch her three assailants with such ease. Indeed, from the expression on his face, it even seemed that he took a certain pleasure in the escapade, and though he now came to help her to her feet, asking if she was all right, there was nonetheless the same hint of irony, as if even this atrocity had its amusing side.

"Shall I go for the police?" he asked.

"No, don't leave me." Involuntarily she clutched his arm.

"Very well."

She started to walk toward the path and after only a few steps realized that her feet were bare. "I've lost my running shoes," she said.

They turned back. One of the Turks looked up but, seeing Serotkin, closed his eyes and lay still. Serotkin found Francesca's shoes and, while she kept her balance by putting her hand on his back, crouched to help her ease them back on her feet.

"Like the first time," he said as he stood up.

"What?"

"Don't you remember? No shoes."

She laughed and then she wept, sobbing without constraint as they walked back to their building, his arm around her shoulder, one of hers around his waist. But even as she cried, Francesca thought her tears were odd, because mingled with the shock of what she had just endured was a certain joy that he remembered she had been barefoot when they first met.

Serotkin accompanied Francesca to her apartment, where she called the police. When two uniformed officers arrived, they each made a statement, Serotkin's overly modest about his heroic role. He then went up to his own place to take a shower and change. When he returned half an hour later, Francesca too had bathed and changed. She insisted on going to work and accepted Serotkin's offer to drive her to the Excursus office in his Opel. At times she trembled; she had no appetite for breakfast because of the shock, and when she got to her desk she found it difficult to concentrate on her work.

In the middle of the morning, two plainclothes detectives from the Berlin police came to make some further inquiries and to ask Francesca and Serotkin to sign the statements they had made that morning. "You're a lucky woman," the detective sergeant said to her, "to have had this particular man come along."

Francesca agreed. The detective looked up at Serotkin. "You must be trained in unarmed combat."

Serotkin shrugged. "In the army, you know. We all did our national service."

The detective looked down at the statement. "Sure, but even so . . ."

The policemen left, Serotkin went back to his office, and Francesca telephoned Sophie to tell her what had happened. Sophie immediately insisted on driving over from the Wedekindstrasse and taking Francesca out to lunch. They went to the restaurant on the top of the KaDeWe department store. Sophie's sympathy was overwhelming and sincere, and Francesca listened to her chatter about how dangerous Berlin had become, especially for women, and how the police were often quite lackadaisical when investigating cases of rape because they were men and could not imagine what it felt like to be a woman and in fact often seemed to regard all single women as fair game. But even as she listened to this burbling stream of ideas that she could not help recognizing as her own, Francesca found that she was thinking of Andrei Serotkin and wishing that he, not Sophie, were sitting opposite, eating his pork and red cabbage and exhaling the smoke of his dark unfiltered cigarettes.

Sophie departed after eliciting a promise from Francesca that if she would not come and stay with her in the apartment on the Wedekindstrasse, she would at least let Stefi pick her up and bring her home to supper. As the afternoon wore on, however, Francesca felt less and less like an evening with the Diederichs. At half past four, she called Sophie and begged off, saying she was tired and wanted to go home to sleep. Then she left her office and went down the corridor to Serotkin's. It was empty. Tears came to her eyes. She crossed the corridor and looked in on Frau Doktor Koch. "Has Dr. Serotkin left?"

"Perhaps, I don't know. I haven't seen him."

Francesca turned and, as she did so, saw Serotkin enter his office. She went to the door. "Andrei?"

He looked up.

"I was wondering if by any chance you were free this evening."

He smiled. "Have you work for me to do?"

She blushed. "Not work, no. I thought perhaps you might like to have dinner."

"Ah." He hesitated, looking troubled. Then he appeared to come to a decision and said, "Yes. I would like that very much."

Francesca told herself that this was only a friendly gesture toward a man who had saved her from a fate worse than death. She told herself that it only made sense to take the opportunity presented by the day's events to pursue her nagging curiosity about Serotkin. She told herself that since she could not face work, solitude, or Stefi Diederich, it was only logical to seek the company of a colleague who knew what had happened and so would make allowances for her fragile state. She told herself everything except that she was already more than half in love with Andrei Serotkin.

Back in her apartment, Francesca persisted in this self-delusion as she got ready to go out. Serotkin, who had brought her to the office, also drove her home. They agreed that they would meet in the lobby at eight. Francesca therefore had a couple of hours to soak in the tub and then, swathed in her towel, to lie on her bed. She considered calling Duncan in New York but decided against it because he would still be in his office and it would be awkward for him to express sympathy in front of others. She could call him later, when she got back from dinner—and as her inward focus moved from the gentle American in New York to the violent Russian in Berlin, she felt an involuntary spasm of crude desire.

She jumped off the bed as if she had been touched by something more tangible than a message from her brain, returned to the bathroom, unwrapped the towel, and for a moment looked at her naked body in the full-length mirror on the wall. Serotkin had seen part of that naked body, but this knowledge, rather than inspiring shame or embarrassment, now induced a sense of vulnerability that only increased her feeling of bodily longing.

She went back to her bedroom, straightened the cover, put away her discarded clothes, sat down at the dressing table, and, with meticulous care and precision, put on mascara and eyeshadow. She chose an outfit that was both sober and alluring: her best underclothes, bottle-green tights, a black skirt, and a green cashmere sweater that matched the tights. Around her neck she put a string of black pearls given to her by a former boyfriend, a banker in New York. She brushed her thick blond hair, nodding it back from time to time, and picked off a stray that had dropped onto the sweater. Finally, she put on a pair of simple black leather shoes and sprayed some Amarige on the inside of her wrists and around her neck.

Serotkin was waiting in the lobby. He too had changed his clothes: gray trousers, a navy blue blazer, a light blue shirt, and striped tie. He smiled when he saw Francesca, a smile that seemed somehow melancholy, and led her out to his car.

"Where shall we go?" she asked.

"I thought you would benefit from a change of scenery," he said.

Francesca was quite happy to let Serotkin make the decisions. They drove in silence around Ernst-Reuter-Platz, past the Charlottenburg Palace, onto the Stadtring and then the Avus, leaving at the exit leading onto the Potsdamer Chaussee. Serotkin then doubled back into the Grunewald, turned up a track, and stopped the car outside a restaurant in the middle of the woods.

"Have you been here before?" he asked.

She shook her head. "No."

"It's nicer in summer, of course, when you can sit out on the terrace."

They went up the steps into the restaurant and the headwaiter led them to a table by a window from which they could see the sun setting over the water of the Wannsee.

"This is lovely," said Francesca.

"It may help you to feel that you are out of the city, at least for a while."

"Thank you." She wanted to bask in his solicitude but could not decide whether he was being considerate because he cared for her or merely because he felt obliged by circumstances to do the right thing.

"You must try to forget about this morning," he said.

"There would be more to try to forget if it wasn't for you."

"It was nothing." He picked up the menu, and they chose what they wanted to eat and drink.

"You have a proverb, I think," said Serotkin. " 'Every cloud has a silver lining.' "

"Yes."

"I think the silver lining to this morning's cloud might be to oblige you to work less hard. It is not good for you."

"The work has to be done."

"You can delegate some of it to others."

"I'm not good at that."

"It is part of the art of leadership."

"I guess I'm not much of a leader."

"Oh, but you are."

"Unattractive in a woman?"

"In an attractive woman, everything becomes attractive. That is the danger."

"The danger?"

He hesitated, then turned with seeming relief to the waiter, who had come to their table with a glass of schnapps and a bottle of wine. The food followed, and all the while Francesca was considering how she could return to the danger that Andrei had mentioned without appearing to fish for a compliment.

"Do you think," she asked, "that there are big differences in nationalities? I mean, in the way we feel and the way we think?"

"Yes. There are big differences."

"Do you think they matter?"

"In what way?"

"Well, in art or love or international negotiations?"

"In international negotiations, clearly, each country employs experts who are specialists in the way the other party feels and thinks. This suggests that they think it matters."

"In art, then."

"There are specialists too."

"But the eye is universal. You can appreciate a painting by an American and I can appreciate a painting by a Russian."

"Perhaps."

"You don't think so?"

"Your thesis, I think, was to *explain* Russian experimental art. Therefore you too are a specialist and must have been drawn to the subject by some curiosity, and curiosity implies something unknown."

"I don't think it was the national differences that interested me. After all, a painter like Malevich, whose father worked in a sugar factory in Kiev, is about as deep-rooted in his ethnic culture as you can get, but his artistic influences were blatantly international."

"May I take notes, Frau Doktor?"

Francesca blushed. "I'm sorry. You know all that already."

"If it was not because the painters were Russians, what led you to choose that theme?"

"Well . . ." She hesitated, then shot a secret smile across the table. "You will be horrified to hear that I was led into it from a course I took in Women's Studies. I had meant to write a thesis on women painters— which was hardly original; in fact, in American faculties it's well-trodden ground. But in doing the preliminary research, I came across Natalia Goncharova, Liubov Popova, Olga Rozanova, and Alexandra Exter. They gave me the idea."

"They were talented."

"Thank you!" The gentle tone of Francesca's ironic rejoinder was a measure of how far her attitude toward Andrei Serotkin had changed.

"But they were not innovators. They merely imitated what was in fashion."

"So did the men."

"Precisely." There was a flash in his eyes. "They followed the fashions set in Paris. They had lost touch with their own people."

Francesca was puzzled. "They *thought* they were in touch with the people. After the Revolution, they took agitprop trains around Russia, carrying books and films and paintings to the peasants and workers."

"They were taking their idea of art to the people, not letting the people's idea of art come to them."

"And didn't the people benefit?"

Serotkin was about to answer but then seemed to think better of what he had intended to say. "We are talking shop," he said.

"I'm sorry."

"I would like to know more about Francesca McDermott the woman and less about Dr. McDermott the art historian."

"What would you like to know?"

"Where you were born. What family you have."

She gave him a brief curriculum vitae, describing her childhood and the different members of her family, now scattered around the United States.

"None of you still lives in Wisconsin?"

"I think Susan might go back there. I guess it depends on who she marries."

"And you? Does it depend on who you marry?"

She looked away. "I like the East Coast."

"So you should marry someone from New York."

"Perhaps. Or Boston."

"A publisher, perhaps?"

She looked at him across the table. "Hey, have you been doing some background research?"

Serotkin laughed. "Diederich mentioned that there was someone. But I don't want to pry into your private life. Tell me about your career."

"There's not much to tell. I went to high school in Madison, then to Ann Arbor, and then to Harvard."

"That can't have been easy."

"It's easier if your father is a college professor."

"Influence?"

"No. Home tuition for the SATs—the entrance exams."

"What did you major in?"

"German. But I also took courses in Russian and Art History."

"And Women's Studies."

"Yes. Then, after Harvard, I spent a year in Berlin."

"That was where you met Diederich?"

"I met Stefi through Sophie, who was then married to Paul Meissner. I was living in West Berlin, doing research on the Bauhaus. A magazine in New York asked me to write a piece on an East Berlin painter—I can't even remember his name—who was part of a group of dissidents around Paul and Sophie."

"Diederich was part of the group?"

"He was on the fringe. I remember him, but not well. Paul was the leader. He was a wonderful person. Brave, gentle, charismatic, and incredibly kind to me."

"Were you in love with him?"

Francesca laughed. "God, no. Paul was an evangelical pastor and married to Sophie. They had two kids. He was chaplain to the students at the university, so the Stasi gave him a really rough time. He was harassed in every imaginable way, and his own church gave him only lukewarm support. They were crazy to let me visit them so often; in those days it was really compromising to be seen with a foreigner, particularly an American. But I got hooked on the atmosphere in that apartment. They were so brave and cheerful and kind of . . . pure. I've never known anything like it, before or since."

Serotkin was silent.

"Then my year came to an end and I went back to the United States. Later, I heard that Paul had a severe nervous breakdown. The marriage broke up, and Sophie married Stefi." She shrugged. "And here we are."

Serotkin's expression had become somber. "It was a cardinal error of the regime to fail to appreciate the cultural value of religious belief."

Francesca was puzzled. "Are you religious, Andrei?" she asked.

"No, I am an atheist. And you?"

"My grandparents were Irish Catholics, but my parents didn't practice and I wasn't even baptized."

"So you are an atheist?"

"More of an agnostic, I guess. I don't know how you can know."

"I am an atheist," Serotkin said again, "because if a God was even a possibility—" He stopped.

"Then what?"

"Then men and women would not be free. They would be his playthings, his children, his slaves."

By now they were eating their dessert—Francesca a crème brûlée that she had allowed herself as consolation for her earlier ordeal. She was feeling a little woozy; she had noticed that after an initial glass of schnapps Serotkin had let her drink most of the wine. She tried to pull herself together enough to steer the conversation away from the gloomy subjects of religion and politics to something more appropriate for a date with a handsome man.

"Now tell me about you," she said to Serotkin.

"You already know most of what there is to know."

"I know you're an art historian who works for the Ministry of Culture in Moscow, that you have a son, and that you're separated from your wife."

"That's about it."

"What about your parents?"

"My father was a soldier. He fought in World War Two."

"And you were in the army?"

"Yes. It's obligatory."

"Which is where you learned unarmed combat?"

"I was in a parachute regiment."

"And you've kept yourself in shape."

He shrugged. "Once you learn these things, you never forget them."

"Like riding a bicycle?"

"Yes."

"And—" She wanted to ask if he had a girlfriend but did not quite dare. "And are you happy?" she asked.

He darted a look at her, almost of anger. "There is not much to be happy about in Russia just now."

"Is it really true that people are starving?"

"Not starving, no, but they have trouble finding food."

"Your parents?"

"Even my parents."

"And your wife?"

"She is younger. It is worst for the old."

Francesca shook her head. "It's unbelievable. A superpower that can't even feed its own people. I'm surprised they don't string up all the Communists on the nearest lampposts."

"It is not—" he started, then bit back his words. "There are not enough lampposts."

"I guess there aren't, but all the same it must make you angry."

"It does."

"And you want to do something about it."

"Yes."

"And here you are, stuck in Berlin with a hysterical American. Poor Andrei."

"You are not hysterical. I am impressed by how calm you have been."

"I might have been less calm if it had actually happened."

"Yes."

"So if I'm calm, it's thanks to you."

"Anyone would have done it."

"So you keep saying, but I'm not so sure."

"You have such assaults in America, I believe."

"Sure. Nowhere's safe."

"It will not serve the feminists' cause if once again women need men for their protection."

"There's always Mace."

"Mace?"

"You know, canisters of gas that you keep in your purse. They're sometimes more effective than men."

"But you don't need it."

"Why not?"

"Because you have your friend."

"Duncan? Sure. But he's in New York and I'm in Boston, and anyway . . ."

"What?"

"He's not the type to go in for macho heroics."

"Which may be the reason why you love him. A new man for the new woman."

"Do I love him?"

Serotkin looked embarrassed. "I'm sorry. I assumed—"

"Sure. Well, I guess I *did* love him, at least I thought so, but real love would survive a long separation, wouldn't it?"

"I'm not an expert on love."

"You must know *something* about it."

"Yes. Real love would survive a long separation."

"It wouldn't depend on time or place?"

"No."

"Or nationality?"

"No."

"So, since I no longer feel it, I guess I never really loved Duncan."

"It is over?"

"Yes."

As she said this, Francesca did not feel that she was betraying Duncan or misleading Serotkin. On the contrary, only as she spoke did she realize that what she was saying was true. It *was* over. Neither she nor Duncan had admitted it, either to themselves or to each other; there had been calls twice a week—dreary, affectionate, long-drawn-out conversations over the transatlantic lines—with each exchanging bits of news that were of little interest to the other and expressing encouragement and affection that was no more than routine. Perhaps there was a trace of deception in the way she now suggested to Andrei that she had been free of any kind of commitment over the past few months, but it seemed no different from the kind of deception that resulted from applying mascara to her eyelashes or Amarige to her body. She did not want to give the impression that men drove bumper to bumper into her heart and into her bed.

"And you?" she asked Serotkin. It seemed she had the right to ask him now.

"I am not in love," he said.

"I'm sorry."

"Why?"

"Wouldn't you like to be in love?"

"I have been very busy."

"We've all been busy."

"Not just with the exhibition. There are other things."

"Your mysterious absences. Stefi thought you must have a mistress." Serotkin shook his head. "No."

"So where do you go?"

"I visit colleagues."

"In Germany?"

"Yes, and in Switzerland. After all, when Excursus is over, you will go back to America, but my future is not assured."

"Won't you have your job at the Ministry?"

"It was a Party job, and the Party is now suspended."

"I'm sorry." She thought for a moment. "I'm sure, if you wanted to, particularly if Excursus is a success, that you could get some sort of teaching post in America."

"Perhaps."

"Unless you prefer import-export."

Serotkin looked puzzled.

Francesca laughed. "Julius thought you were running some kind of business on the side, shipping fax machines and video recorders back to Russia."

He frowned. "Some of us are reduced to that."

"He wasn't serious," she said quietly.

Serotkin looked sorrowfully into her eyes, as if rebuking her for saying something that was not true.

She blushed. "*I* didn't think it was true."

"Thank you." He did not seem grateful.

"But I had my suspicions about the mistress."

"That is more plausible," he said acidly. "Americans regard love as a form of recreation."

Francesca recoiled at the bitter tone with which he said this. "That's a little unfair."

"Is it?"

"How much experience do you have of Americans in love?"

"I am judging from the cinema."

"They're more about sex than love."

"Sex, then, as recreation. The hero and heroine go to bed together before the end of the first reel."

Francesca looked down, afraid that what he said might be true. "Happiness is so often elusive. Americans want to snatch it while they can in case they wake up the next morning and find it gone."

"Happiness lies in more than a satisfactory one-night stand."

"Sure. It lies in love."

"Yes, in love, but not just in sexual love."

"What other love is there?" It was a stupid question, and she regretted asking it before the words were out of her mouth.

"There is love of one's parents and one's children."

"Of course."

"And one's country."

"Yes."

"I have never known anyone to die for a woman," said Serotkin, "but I have known several who have been happy to die for their country."

"And kill for their country," said Francesca.

"Of course," said Serotkin. "If you are prepared to die, you must be prepared to kill. To kill, and worse."

They said nothing as they drove back through the Grunewald. It was not a hostile silence; on the contrary, Francesca felt the intimacy that had been fortuitously forced upon them that morning had been confirmed by the evening spent together. However, it was intimacy of a kind that she had never previously encountered and that therefore left her somewhat baffled. In the United States, after a date, the traffic signals usually shone green or red or perhaps amber. With Andrei, it was as if there were some technical malfunction. All the lights were flashing on and off at the same time. Using a cruder but well-worn metaphor, Francesca felt as if she had hooked a fish, as she had intended, but had then been dragged off balance into the water as the fish tried to escape downstream. Andrei was drawn to her; she could tell from the way he behaved in her presence. But for some reason she could not fathom, he was doing his utmost to resist the attraction, considerate at one moment, almost angry at another. Why would a man who wanted a woman deliver a diatribe against sex on the first date? They were both adult and uncommitted, both alone in a foreign city. They had known each other for six months. Why should what seemed proper to her seem depraved to him?

Francesca thought that when it came to the point, Andrei's actions would belie his words. She so longed for him to embrace her that she almost wished for a rerun of the morning's assault to give her the excuse once again to sob on his shoulder. In the car he smoked his strong unfiltered cigarettes, and as he exhaled she took a certain pleasure in drawing into her lungs the same smoke that had been in the deepest recesses of his body. This intimacy was better than none. She would rather he laid his hand on her leg, the leg he had seen naked that morning. But he did not even reach over and take her hand. Why? Was he being high-minded? Did he desire her but feel it would be wrong to take advantage of her vulnerable condition? She felt now that she had loved him for much longer than she had supposed, just as she now realized that her affair with Duncan had ended some time ago. But while she could present this second revelation as a retrospective truth, and would tell Duncan in due course, she could hardly confess to the first until Serotkin had owned up to his own feelings for her. Then she could draw in the line and lift him out with a net.

Even as they stopped the car in the garage beneath their building, she thought it might happen that night, that their yearning would be too strong to allow either of them to go to their separate apartments. She thought of the conventional tactic of asking him up for a drink or a cup of coffee, but after what he had said about Hollywood morals it seemed impossible.

In the lobby they entered the elevator together. Serotkin pushed first the button for the fourth floor, then the button for the ninth. Francesca stood close to him and, when the door opened, turned her face toward his.

Serotkin clasped her hand. "Good night."

"Good night." She turned to go, then remembered that she should at least be polite. "Thank you, Andrei."

He smiled. "I thank *you*."

"You should have let me pay my share."

"Please. I am a Russian." The automatic door started to close, and his foot went forward to stop it. "By the way, do you play squash?"

"Yes."

"Shall we play a game together?"

"I'd like that."

"It will be safer than jogging."

He removed his foot, and the door closed. Francesca went into her bedroom. She was embarrassed to remember how she had straightened the spread. She sat down on the bed and called Duncan. She did not tell him about the assault but said as kindly as she could that their relationship was over. Duncan listened and said little in reply, but his few words were enough to convey that he not only agreed but was relieved that she had come to this decision.

10

Despite the efforts of detectives Kessler and Dorn over more than eighteen months, the investigation into the murders in the Dubrowstrasse had made little progress. By the spring of 1993, Kessler—who used to boast that he knew everything that went on in West Berlin "before it happened"—felt at a loss for the first time in his life. All he had established was that the victims were Russians, a married couple, Grigori and Vera Maslyukov, nominally art dealers, in practice receivers of stolen goods—go-betweens for those who smuggled icons out of Russia and the more reputable dealers and collectors in the West.

Kessler's contacts in the Russian underworld in Berlin had told him that Maslyukov was a KGB agent, but in his experience every Russian émigré regarded every other Russian émigré as a KGB agent. Their suspicions meant nothing. The idea that Maslyukov had been an active agent, or even a sleeper, seemed farfetched.

More probably, Kessler's first supposition was correct: the Maslyukovs were casualties in a war between different factions of Berlin's Russian mafia. The icons were long gone, undoubtedly stolen by whoever had killed Maslyukov and tortured his wife. This hardly pointed to the CIA or the West German Office for the Protection of the Constitution or Bundesamt für Verfassungsschutz, the BfV.

Kessler's best hope lay in a tip from one of the Russians living in Berlin. But so much had changed since the breach of the Wall. Illegal immigrants were flooding into the city and new gangs had taken over from the old ones. There had been gun battles in the streets of Kreuzberg; Russians had been shot dead in a restaurant on the Kurfürstendamm. The detective had asked for names, but his usual informants knew nothing about the new networks of Georgians and Azerbaijanis and were clearly too prudent to ask.

Dusting down the furniture in the Dubrowstrasse had produced no fingerprints. The murderers had worn gloves. The shreds of tobacco on the floor by the feet of the tortured woman were almost the only clue. Analysis showed that they were from BTs, Bulgarian cigarettes made for the Soviet market. Before the fall of the Communists, they had been sold in East Berlin; now they were hard to find. Dorn had spoken to scores of tobacconists, finding a few who still stocked them; he had even identified a number of regular buyers, but none had the profile of a killer or a thief. If the murderer lived in Berlin, they had yet to find him, and as month had followed month with no progress, Kessler fell back on a second hypothesis: the cigarettes had not been purchased in Berlin at all but had been brought by the murderers from the Soviet Union itself.

It then became a matter of checking arrivals and departures at East Berlin's Schönefeld airport and the border crossings at Frankfurt an der Oder, both by road and rail—a tedious task that had used manpower and time. Kessler's superior, Commissar Rohrbeck, became irritated. He could hardly deny his subordinate resources—a murder was a murder—but like Dorn he could not summon up much outrage about the death of a couple of Russian crooks.

Nor could Kessler. Indeed, the more he learned about the Maslyukovs, the less he liked them. Their files showed how little they paid the smugglers and how much they charged their Western clients. The markup on the icons was several thousand percent. It was also clear that their declared income, upon which they paid taxes, was a small fraction of their profits. Their account at the Berliner Bank had only 32,000 deutsche marks; the rest of their assets were probably in Liechtenstein or Switzerland. There were references on the hard disk of their Nixdorf computer to the existence of such accounts, but no files or documents that identified them were found.

However, it was not the tax evasion that led Kessler to dislike the Maslyukovs but the image he formed from the evidence of those who had had dealings with them—not their friends, because they did not seem to have had any friends, but other dealers, in particular a middle-aged German woman, Katerina von Duse, who had a gallery off the Kurfürstendamm. "I tell you," she said to Kessler in an almost hysterical voice, "these Maslyukovs were the very lowest sort, quite pitiless. I am not at all surprised that they were killed."

"Why do you say that?" Kessler had asked.

"A young couple—Russians, clearly; they spoke very little German—came into the gallery and offered me an icon: a beautiful St. Nicholas, early sixteenth century. It was wrapped in a cloth and carried in a briefcase. They had some kind of bill of sale from the Patriarchate in Moscow, almost certainly a forgery, but all the same I made them an offer. I cannot remember exactly what it was—say, ten thousand marks. Not a bad offer, but I could see what was going through their minds. They were astonished that it was worth so much, but just because I had offered them more than they had imagined, they now thought perhaps it was worth even more, so they said they would think about it and went away. I heard nothing for a week, but then the girl came in alone and asked if the offer was still open. I said it was but she looked frightened. She said the boy had gone to Maslyukov, who had offered them only one thousand. She said she would come back with the icon that afternoon, but she never returned, and ten days later, Maslyukov offered me the same icon—for thirty thousand."

"Did you buy it?"

"No. It was overpriced."

"The young couple never returned?"

"No."

"Perhaps Maslyukov put up his price."

"No. He frightened them. That was his style. So many had no proper visas or bills of sale, and if threats did not work . . ."

"What then?"

"I don't know. There were stories."

"Of what?"

"Accidents. Maslyukov had some very unsavory friends."

"A charming profession!"

She frowned. "Are there no corrupt policemen?"

Kessler laughed. "So I am told. But tell me, did you ever come across Maslyukov's wife?"

Katerina von Duse wrinkled her nose. "Once or twice. A dreadful woman."

"Why?"

"Worse than her husband. Grasping. Also vulgar."

"Would she have known details of the business?"

"Certainly. She was cleverer than he was. An Armenian, I think, or a Jew."

"Could they have been killed by a rival dealer?"

"He had no rival," the woman had said. "Not in Berlin, at any rate. They had all disappeared."

Even before he heard this opinion from Katerina von Duse, Kessler had come to dislike Vera Maslyukov. The image of her fat, putrid corpse had lodged in his mind. The set of her features in death, twisted in that horrible caricature of sexual ecstasy, still disturbed him after all those months. She had been tied up, tortured, and then killed. He should feel sympathy, pity, outrage; instead, he only remembered the hair from her mustache: some on the tape, some still on her upper lip. The pungent aroma that still lingered in his nostrils made Kessler imagine that she had somehow wallowed in her agony just as she had wallowed in pleasurable sensations, that she was primitive, indulgent, a grotesque blob of flesh around her own nerve endings. He loathed the victim but still had to find the man who had killed her. That was his job.

Kessler's obsession with Vera Maslyukov had distracted him from a close scrutiny of her husband's corpse. It was only when he seemed to have reached a dead end with the tape that had gagged her, and the shreds of tobacco on the floor, that he returned to the report from the forensic experts on Grigori Maslyukov.

His body had been found at the bottom of the stairs, five or six meters from the front door. His hand held the butt of a revolver on the inside pocket of his jacket. No bullet had been fired. Presumably they had shot him as he was reaching for his gun. His revolver was a Smith and Wesson; the bullet extracted from his body was from a Beretta. Both were common weapons. The specialists had been unable to make much of the markings from the bullet that had gone through Maslyukov's heart. Only one comment in their report attracted Kessler's attention: "The subject was killed by a single bullet entering the heart, a remarkably accurate shot from a short-barreled weapon of this kind, if fired across the hallway from the front door."

Remarkably accurate. Anything remarkable was unusual, and anything unusual was a clue. If the revolver itself was not significant, the use of it was, because it is far harder than people suppose from watching television to bring down a man with a single shot unless it is from point-blank range. From the position of Maslyukov's body and the path of the bullet, it seemed he had been shot from the direction of the door. Had the killer entered with his weapon drawn, or had he beaten Maslyukov to the draw? Either way he had no time to take careful aim, yet he had fired a single shot that had gone straight to the heart.

So what? Kessler had the plan of the hallway spread out before him with the position of Maslyukov's body marked in ink and the probable path of the bullet in a black dotted line. Had Maslyukov recognized his assailant? Who had let him in? Had they had a key, or had Vera opened the door? All in all, it suggested a more accomplished operation than one would expect from Russian mafiosi.

Dorn came into Kessler's office. "We've got nowhere," he said. "It's a waste of time."

"Have you looked into people *leaving* for the Soviet Union the day after the crime?"

"Yes. From Schönefeld, nothing—or nothing convincing. There were direct flights from Frankfurt to Moscow and Kiev. But if they were taking the icons with them, they could hardly have packed them into suitcases."

"No."

"They were more likely to have left them in Munich or Frankfurt, or even here in Berlin."

"Or Switzerland. Or Liechtenstein."

Dorn shook his head. "We're wasting our time, chief. What's the point of checking all these entries and exits? It won't be Russians from Russia who bumped them off, and if it was, they would hardly fly in and out like a trade delegation."

"No."

"Can we drop it then?"

"Yes."

Dorn turned to go but Kessler held him back. "What about this?"

He tapped his pencil on the dotted line showing the trajectory of the bullet.

"What about it?"

"One shot. Straight to the heart."

"Luck?"

"Or skill."

"They don't have skill, these gangsters. That's why they use Uzis or sawed-off shotguns."

"Precisely."

Dorn looked puzzled. "So what do we conclude from that?"

"That he was a good shot, a very good shot."

"Experienced?"

"Trained."

"Ex-army?"

"Not with a Beretta."

"Then what, intelligence?"

"More likely."

"Ours or theirs?"

"Could be either."

"Any noise from the BfV?"

"No. But then, we never inquired."

"It's a long shot."

"Yes." Kessler looked down at the plan. "Precisely. A long shot. Let's see where it takes us."

There were official channels for liaison between the West Berlin Police and West Germany's Office for the Protection of the Constitution, the BfV, but Kessler chose not to use them. They were slow; besides, it would mean briefing his superiors on the progress of his investigation, which in itself would be awkward since there was none. He had also found that the local BfV people were reluctant to put things on the record. Requests went to Cologne, authorization was arbitrary, and he always ended up with a fraction of what he wanted to know.

Kessler also knew that the BfV still had their hands full dealing with the disbanded East German secret police, the Stasi. His request would go into an in-basket and might not be considered for weeks. He therefore said nothing to his superiors but telephoned a contact named

Grohmann and arranged to meet him that evening in a bar in Wilmers-dorf.

Grohmann was hardly a friend. Kessler felt no particular fondness for him or anyone else in the BfV. Their paymasters were the Christian Democrats in Bonn, whereas West Berlin was a socialist city, and the occupational anticommunism made the BfV suspicious of the West Berlin police, whose leftist sympathies dated from the days of the Weimar Republic. Kessler was hardly soft on communism, and he appreciated that West Berlin had been sustained by the grants it received from the Federal Republic; he nonetheless felt no particular affection for the government in Bonn.

But just as Berlin needed Bonn, so Bonn needed Berlin, not just as a showcase for capitalism and democracy but also as a center for its operations to the east. They might treat the city police as auxiliaries but they needed them all the same, and if Kessler now wanted some help from Grohmann, he was only calling in favors he had done for him outside channels in the past.

Grohmann was ordinary in appearance: medium height, glasses, brown trousers, a green shirt. He might have been a math teacher on his day off, or perhaps the company secretary of a small firm. He looked at his watch when Kessler came in, even though Kessler was on time, and after a curt nod of greeting asked him what he wanted to drink.

Kessler ordered a beer. Grohmann paid—not from generosity, Kessler suspected, but to be able to leave without waiting for the barman to return.

"Maslyukov," said Kessler.

Grohmann sipped his beer. "Grigori Maslyukov?"

"Yes."

"The art dealer. I remember reading about it."

"In the papers or in a memo?"

"In the papers."

"He was murdered. So was his wife."

"So I read."

"They tortured her first."

"I didn't read that." Grohmann peered into his glass as if looking for a fly in his beer.

"We didn't release it."

131

"Why was she tortured?"

"We don't know. In fact, we know very little. We need help."

"As it happens," said Grohmann, "when I read about Maslyukov, I checked to see if we had him in our files."

"And did you?"

"Yes."

"And?"

Grohmann put down his glass. "Nothing much. He came west in 1982, was given asylum, imported icons, made a fortune."

"An entrepreneur?"

"Yes."

"Not an agent?"

Grohmann shrugged. "If he was, he wasn't active. They may have been saving him for something."

"Any reason to think that?"

"No. I think he was probably what he seemed to be."

"So there was no reason for anyone here to kill him?"

"Here?"

"Any of you people, or the Americans."

"Certainly not us."

"The Americans?"

"I doubt it."

Kessler glanced at Grohmann, trying to assess whether or not he meant what he said. "Whoever killed him was a good shot."

"What weapon?"

"A Beretta."

"Ah."

"What?"

"Much favored by the KGB."

"Could it have been them?"

"Possibly."

"Why?"

"Because of the icons. They may have come to reclaim them and met with . . . resistance."

"If they were stolen, why not go through Interpol?"

"Official channels? No. Too corrupt in Russia, too slow in Brussels. Anyway, it would be difficult to prove they were stolen."

"So they send a team to recover the icons, are recognized or ambushed, and shoot Maslyukov before he shoots them?"

"That's possible."

"Why torture the wife?"

Grohmann shrugged again. "To find where other icons were hidden, perhaps. Or the numbers of bank accounts."

"Have you any idea who might have led such a team?"

Grohmann scratched his chin. "In the past, the KGB did some of the smuggling of icons. It was a perk that went with foreign travel. So if they mounted an operation to get them back, it would have to be insulated or else Maslyukov's former customers would tip him off."

"Which means?"

"That it wouldn't have been done through the usual KGB personnel. It would have been a special operation, mounted directly from Moscow."

"So the chances of identifying the killer would be small?"

"I can make inquiries, but even if we identify the killer, it's unlikely that he could be extradited."

"Unless Yeltsin wanted to establish his law-abiding credentials."

"In which case it might make sense to play the game strictly according to the rules and ask Interpol for help from the Russian police."

"Would they give it?"

Once more Grohmann shrugged. "They'll send someone, certainly, because Interpol pays. Whether he helps or hinders is another matter." He drank down the rest of his beer. "But you're going to a lot of trouble. Does it matter so much who killed the Maslyukovs, after all this time?"

"It matters," said Kessler. "Not because of the Maslyukovs, but to get the message across that Berlin is not going to become like Chicago at the time of Al Capone."

11

On the day General Savchenko was due back in Moscow, Nikolai Gerasimov drove out to Zhukovska to visit the celebrated painter Anatoly Sergeyevich Orlov. He used a Volga from the Lubyanka car pool; his Samara was once again in the hands of Georgi Nazayan. Ease of access to Georgi's mechanic was one of the reasons why Nikolai had returned to live with his wife in the flat on the Ulitsa Academika Koroleva. He had neither forgiven nor forgotten, but he had grown tired of sleeping on sofas, wearing dirty shirts, and traveling by bus.

It took some time for Gerasimov to find the dacha. The straight roads cutting through the pine forest all looked alike. Each house was set back behind a fence on its own hectare of land. Some had no numbers. They were all large by Soviet standards, most built in the 1950s with three or four bedrooms and given by the Party to those considered to have made an outstanding contribution to their country in science or the arts. Rostropovich had lived there; so had the physicist Sakharov until he had been turned into a dissident by his second wife, Elena Bonner. Gerasimov's lip curled at the thought of Sakharov. Times had changed, but not his instinctual distaste for those who had betrayed the Soviet cause.

He finally found Orlov's villa and parked the Volga outside the gate. A drive led from the gate to a garage and the back door of the house. There was a lawn in front of the house, a small clearing in the forest.

The grass was uncut and was half covered by damp, dead leaves. The doors to the garage had moss growing between the planks of wood; they did not appear to have been opened for years. Gerasimov looked up and saw a large north-facing window that he took to be that of the artist's studio. Some slates were missing from the gable. Ferns grew out of the gutter. More moss had grown where there was moisture on the walls.

Gerasimov knocked on the door. There was silence. He had telephoned, he was expected, but so strong was his impression that the house was empty that had it not been for the window of the studio he might have decided he had come to the wrong place. He knocked again and, after waiting and listening a few more minutes, heard a shuffling of slippered feet.

The door opened. A tall woman, between sixty and seventy years old, invited him in. Like Tatiana Orlova, she did not ask who he was or why he was there.

Gerasimov stepped into a pantry. Muddy boots stood on the floor; empty vases stood in a low sink.

"Natasha Petrovna?"

"Yes. Come this way."

She led him through from the pantry into a dark hallway and from there into a living room that was scarcely lighter; it looked out onto the garden but the garden itself was enclosed by pine trees, their shade welcome in summer, no doubt, but on a cloudy day in April shrouding the house in gloom.

"If you will wait," she said, "I will tell my husband that you are here."

Gerasimov remained standing. From the look of the furniture, it seemed that little had changed since the house was built. The chairs were made of varnished wood, with upholstered backs and seats. The same veneer had been used for the dining table and for the glass-fronted bookcases that ran along the wall. A grand piano was at one end of the room; displayed on a sideboard like birthday cards stood leather folders containing certificates from different Soviet institutions—the Academy of Sciences, the Central Committee—commending Anatoly Orlov for his services to the arts. On one, Gerasimov saw the signature of Stalin; on another, Khrushchev; on a third, Brezhnev. There was an Order of the Red Banner, an Order of Lenin—all the honors that could be bestowed on a favored artist—and when he looked up at the pictures hanging on the walls, he could see that several had been painted by Orlov, some of them portraits, early works, before he had evolved the distinctive style so familiar to every Soviet child—faces of workers set in the heroic proletarian mold with square jaw, grim look, clenched fist, unyielding eye.

Over the mantel was a portrait of Lenin, again one of the kind that had hung in galleries in every major city of the former Soviet Union. It was on a smaller scale, of course, which made it unsuitable for a public collection. There was even a twinkle in the Soviet leader's eye.

"That is an early work."

Gerasimov turned. Behind him stood an old man wearing a dressing gown. Beneath it he wore loose trousers, a shirt, and a badly knotted tie. On his head was a tasseled fez.

"It is entitled *Lenin Amused* and was thought unsuitable for public exhibition. Prophets are not supposed to have a sense of humor."

For all his professional training, Gerasimov could not suppress a look of astonishment at the old man's costume.

"Ah. I see that you're amused too. Well, it's cold in my studio, damned cold, so I have to wear a hat, and a fur hat is too heavy and a peaked cap cuts out the light."

"I am sorry to disturb you, Anatoly Sergeyevich," said Gerasimov, assuming the kind of deferential posture he thought appropriate in the presence of a man who, however eccentric his appearance, remained one of the most celebrated painters in the former Soviet Union.

"Don't worry," said Anatoly Orlov, still referring to Gerasimov's astonished expression. "People are always puzzled when they meet me. They expect me to look like one of the heroic figures in my paintings. They are not puzzled by my wife; she looks the part. She was the model for some of those heroines holding the red flag. You met her, didn't you? Of course you did; she let you in. Monumental. A strong woman. A good woman, a good wife, a good mother, a good citizen. And now she's angry."

"Angry?"

"With events. The counterrevolution."

"I see."

"She thinks you've been sent to spy on us."

"Only to ask—"

136

"We've nothing to hide. We're Bolsheviks. We've always been Bolsheviks, and if that drunkard Yeltsin wants to drag me off to prison or throw me out in the street, I'll be proud to go." He clenched his fist and raised it to the level of his shoulder. "They can suspend the Party with the stroke of a pen, but they can't suspend the Bolshevik spirit in the Orlovs, the spirit that made this country great, that sent a shiver down the spine of every damned capitalist and imperialist west of Brest and east of Vladivostok!"

"Comrade Orlov—" Gerasimov began.

"Comrade? Are you being ironic? Am I your comrade? Or are you a lackey of the pusillanimous Gorbachev and the drunkard Yeltsin? Reformers! Democrats! Ha! Traitors, more like, out to sell Russia to the Jews in America and make us serfs of the World Bank."

He spoke in a declamatory style, as if addressing a crowd, striding to and fro, his dressing gown swirling around his ankles. "So what do you want to know? What am I painting? Not Yeltsin's ugly mug, that's for sure. Not the sly Asiatic eyes of that Siberian opportunist, no! I'm painting . . . come, I'll show you." And quite suddenly he turned, took the far larger Gerasimov by the arm, and led him back across the hallway and up the stairs.

"What do you know about art?" he asked Gerasimov.

"I have—"

"Not much. I know." Orlov said this kindly. "We had such a huge task—to educate the masses—that what we taught had to be rudimentary. Yes." He paused on the landing to catch his breath, looked into Gerasimov's eyes, and repeated the word: "Rudimentary. And of course art had to serve the cause." They continued up the stairs. "There was no room for fancy theorizing, none of your 'art for art's sake' "—he spoke those words with derision—"which gave rise to all those flowery pictures by the Impressionists that now sell for millions in the West, all mirrors of their decadence. The mad van Gogh: to elevate the distortions of a lunatic and call that art! And Renoir: pornography! 'I paint with my penis.' He admitted it; he never pretended otherwise."

They had come to a door at the end of a corridor on the second floor. Anatoly Sergeyevich Orlov paused; he still held Gerasimov by the arm. "And in Russia? A few pathetic imitations, always running after the latest Western fad. Just like now. But that wasn't our authentic tradition. Have

137

you read Chernyshevski? 'The true function of art is to explain life.' And the Wanderers put that thought into action. Repin, Surikov—they knew what they were doing. The Moscow school. But then Vrubel came from Petersburg and the rot set in. Bloody foreigners, charlatans who jumped on the bandwagon, just like now. Experimental art. Abstract art. Cubism. The Suprematists, Constructivists—rubbish, all rubbish. And they thought *they* were the revolutionaries! Ha! They were the frauds. Cunning Yids who bamboozled the critics—and even, for a time, the Party. But they were never Bolsheviks. Never. They didn't care a damn about the people. They despised the workers and poured scorn on anyone who scratched their heads in front of their paintings and asked what their scribblings were all about. Tatlin? Bits of wood. El Lissitzky? Squares and circles. Chagall? Yiddish kitsch. Kandinsky? Disintegration! Disintegration of form, disintegration of meaning, doodles, ravings. The icons of nihilism. The delirium of a drunk!"

He opened the door and led Gerasimov into his studio, a huge room with the high window that Gerasimov had seen from outside, a patch of brown on the white ceiling beneath the missing slates. It faced north, making the room even darker than the living room below. "Damn cold, eh?" said Orlov. "We can't get anyone to deliver coal for the stove. And no lightbulbs. I paint in the dark. Dim light, dim eyes, but color in the painting, yes?"

And there *was* color, a bright red in the flag held aloft by an armed worker as he stormed the gates of the Winter Palace. "*Lest We Forget.* That's what I've called it. Lest we forget!" Suddenly the old man fell silent, brooding over his painting.

To Gerasimov it was familiar; he had seen dozens like it in different art galleries as a child. The storming of the Winter Palace had been one of the subjects he preferred—better, certainly, than the realistic depictions of workers surpassing their quotas in steel mills or on collective farms. "It's very fine," he said lamely.

"But no one will buy it," said Anatoly Orlov, quieter now, his brow creased in a frown. "Look." He turned and pointed to a stack of canvases in the corner of the studio. "They've started to return them. Some just arrive; others have a covering note: *We've no room in our storerooms, Anatoly Sergeyevich, and yours are no longer the kind of pictures the public enjoys.* That from Perm. And from Lvov no paintings,

138

only a letter: *If you would like your works returned, kindly forward the cost of transporting them; otherwise they will be destroyed."*

"I am sorry," said Gerasimov with real sincerity.

"The question is this," said the old man. "Is art to lead or is it to follow? Is it to teach? Can it help but teach? And if it teaches, what does it teach? The earliest paintings—the buffalo in the caves at Lascaux—were they there for decoration? No. The statues of the Greeks? The expression of an ideal. The Bayeux tapestry? A celebration of victory in war. And our Russian art, comrade chekist, our venerated icons? Were they there simply to decorate the churches, or were they the embodiment of the people's faith? When the icon of the Virgin of Smolensk was paraded in front of the troops before the battle of Borodino, was it just to show the soldiers a pretty picture, or was it an invocation to a higher power, the power of the Mother of God which it portrayed? We are a nation, comrade chekist, to whom the icon was also the idea. And now"—he turned to look at the stack of his rejected paintings—"now there is no more art in Russia because the Russians have lost faith in the idea."

There was a moment of silence. If Anatoly Orlov had any further thoughts, he did not choose to share them with Nikolai Gerasimov.

Eventually, Gerasimov cleared his throat and said, "Anatoly Sergeyevich, it is my duty to ask you whether you know where we can get hold of your son, Andrei Anatolyevich."

The old man snapped out of his reverie. "Andrei? No. I don't know where he's gone."

"He has left the country."

"I'm not surprised."

"As you know, he is no longer—"

"They got rid of their best man."

"There were—"

"Afraid of him, I daresay. I'm not surprised."

"There were changes in the personnel."

"It always happens when there's a shake-up. The dregs float to the top."

It occurred to Gerasimov to point out that the October Revolution had been just such a shake-up, but he did not want to set Anatoly Orlov off on another tirade. "His abilities were respected—" he began.

"Nonsense. He was dismissed because he still believed."

"It was thought that officers who could not adapt to the new conditions—"

"Who wouldn't be lackeys of the West."

Gerasimov was becoming irritated. For all the old man's distinction, he could not permit him to waste his time. "There are loose ends," he said. "We have to find him."

"Then find him."

"We had hoped you would help."

Now Anatoly Orlov seemed to feel that time was passing to no avail. He led Gerasimov out of the studio and down the passage toward the stairs. "He has gone to the West. He had business there. A joint venture, I believe. Import-export. How should I know? You fired him. He had to live. To use his talents. He can speak five languages. Did you know that? He can pass for a German or an American or a Frenchman. You trained him well."

"Has he contacted you?"

"No."

"Have you an address or a number?"

"No."

"Has he called you?"

"No. He was a chekist, remember? We never expect to hear from him when he's away on an operation."

"You said he was on business."

The old man looked confused, as if he might have said something to compromise his son. "We haven't heard from him," he said. "I don't know what he's doing. He would never tell me anyway. I'm a painter, not a politician."

They had reached the landing halfway down the stairs. "So he did talk to politicians?"

"I didn't say that."

"If he had talked to politicians, who might they be?"

"Who said he talked to politicians? Damn it, there were no politicians in the Soviet Union before Mikhail Sergeyevich had those damned elections in '89. Elections! A beauty contest among weasels!"

Gerasimov did not want to engage in a debate about glasnost and perestroika. "I would greatly appreciate it, Anatoly Sergeyevich, if you would let us know if by any chance your son should get in touch with you."

"Hmph." The painter reached the hall where his wife, Natasha Irenovna, was waiting for them. She looked fleetingly at her husband, an anxious look in her eye, then turned to Gerasimov with no expression.

"I was just saying to Anatoly Sergeyevich," said Gerasimov, "that we are most anxious to talk to your son Andrei."

She nodded.

"If he should call you—"

"Of course." She led him toward the pantry and the back door.

Gerasimov turned to take his leave of the painter. "Thank you for receiving me, Anatoly Sergeyevich."

The old man laughed. "It was no favor. I have time on my hands."

"The lightbulbs," Natasha Irenovna whispered to Gerasimov as she opened the back door. "The large ones, for the studio lamps. They are so hard to find."

"I will see what I can do," said Gerasimov.

She nodded, not to thank him but merely to acknowledge that she had heard what he had said.

"These are difficult times," said Gerasimov.

"Indeed." For a moment she watched as Gerasimov walked back down the damp drive toward the gate. Then she closed the door.

Back at the Lubyanka, Gerasimov was told that General Savchenko had returned and wished to see him at once in his office. He was ushered straight in. The general sat at his desk, leafing through the thin report that Gerasimov had prepared for his return.

"I realize," he said sharply, before Gerasimov could open his mouth, "that you may have had other duties, and that this investigation which I entrusted to you posed particular problems. I realize too that I may have given the impression that there was no particular urgency in the matter. Nevertheless it astonishes me that—" He stopped, flicked through a few more pages, then went on. "No, nothing astonishes me. But it surprises me, comrade lieutenant, that in—what is it now, eight months?—you have accomplished so little."

Gerasimov cleared his throat. "As you say, comrade general, there have been particular problems associated with this case. First of all, because of the secrecy of the icon operation, very few officers had any contact with Orlov in the period preceding his disappearance."

He waited to see if this excuse impressed Savchenko.

"And?" asked the general.

"Well, you yourself imposed limitations. For example, I am quite sure that Orlov's father-in-law, Ivan Keminski—"

"You saw the daughter?" Savchenko interrupted.

"Yes."

"Unforthcoming?"

"She said she knew nothing."

"And Orlov's father?"

"I saw him this morning. The same."

"Keminski," said Savchenko, rummaging through another pile of papers on his desk, "has apparently just registered as the agent of a private Swiss bank."

"That could well be something to do with Orlov."

"I know."

"Can I go and see Keminski?"

Savchenko hesitated. "Better not. He still has friends who—it's all very delicate. If we tread on the wrong toes, we could be ordered to leave Orlov alone."

"So how should I proceed?"

Savchenko considered for a moment, tapping his nicotine-stained teeth with the end of a pencil. "Although I had hoped you would have done better than this," he said eventually, tapping Gerasimov's report with the pencil, "I have to concede that the inquiries I made on my travels also proved fruitless. You talked to Kirsch?"

"Yes. He provided some useful background."

"But nothing more. I know. No one in our Western residences has seen or heard of Orlov. It's quite possible, of course, that some may have done so but were unwilling to admit it. A large number of those still in the service are unsympathetic to the reform program. They do not think it will succeed, and fully expect that in a year's time we may see Rutskoi or Khasbulatov in the Kremlin instead of Yeltsin."

"I don't see what more we can do unless Orlov himself breaks cover."

"We've got nowhere with people," said Savchenko, lighting a cigarette, "but there may be something we can learn from *things*."

"Things?"

"First of all, there are the passports. Orlov must have some false identity, and the papers to support this identity must come from Moscow." The cigarette dangled from Savchenko's lips as he once again rummaged through the papers on his desk. He found what he was looking for, glanced at it, and then pushed it over the desk to Gerasimov. "There is a protégé of Khrulev's—"

Gerasimov looked down at the memo. "Peshkov."

"Peshkov, yes. He was placed in Section Six by Khrulev and handled the documentation for the icon operation. I suggest you visit him at home. Lean on him. Threaten him if you like."

"On whose authority?"

"Mine. And you can mention the chief, Bakatin. He's as keen as anyone to find Orlov."

"Very well." Gerasimov half rose to go but Savchenko had not finished with him.

"And then there's the van," he said, exhaling the smoke of his cigarette.

"The van?"

"It struck me when I was in Germany that the Volkswagen van used by the young officer, I forget his name—"

"Partovski."

"Yes, Partovski. That van he used to bring the icons back to Russia is the only material link to Orlov's operation in Berlin. Orlov may have bought it, or some associate may have bought it for him. Perhaps Orlov still has links with that associate. Certainly it is worth looking at the van to see if it provides some kind of lead that you have failed to get from people."

The white Volkswagen van had disappeared. It was reported in the log of the center's transport office that it had been collected from the Tretyakov two weeks after Partovski's return. A driver named Akinfiev had brought it to the Lubyanka, but then it had been moved to the central depot on the outskirts of Moscow by a driver whose scrawled signature appeared to read *M. Gorbachev*.

Nikolai Gerasimov drove out to the depot in the Volga that afternoon. He looked through the log book with the duty officer to make sure there was no record that the van had arrived. The duty officer readily admitted that it had almost certainly been sold by one of the drivers. "We have no M. Gorbachev on our list, comrade captain, not even Mikhail Sergeyevich—even though he's out of a job."

"We have to find it," said Gerasimov, not smiling at the officer's joke. "It's not merely a question of the theft. It's an operational matter."

"Try the militia," said the transport officer. "They know the people who handle stolen goods."

A counsel of despair. No one in the militia would want to help the former KGB, particularly not Gerasimov, who had so frequently stymied their moves against Georgi. But the very thought of Georgi gave Gerasimov an idea, so instead of returning to the Lubyanka, he drove back into Moscow on the Prospekt Mira and stopped off at his flat on the Ulitsa Academika Koroleva.

Ylena was watching a video. She looked miserably at her husband. He did not greet her but went straight to the bedroom to take off his clothes, then to the bathroom to take a shower. As he passed through the hall on his way to the bathroom, Ylena shouted, "The Samara's ready." He made no reply. He took his shower and then, with a towel around his waist, went to the door of the sitting room and asked, "Is it here?"

"No. He said to call when you wanted it."

"Tell him I want it now."

"You tell him."

He looked at her with an expression of menace in his eyes.

She sniffed. "I don't want to talk to him."

"Call your fucking lover and tell him to bring the car."

He heard her sniffling as he went back to the bedroom and then a click as she picked up the telephone.

"And tell Georgi I want to talk to him!" he shouted. The sniffs became sobs. "Tell him it's business, nothing personal. Tell him, 'What's a fat slut between friends?' "

The sob became a yowl but slipped back to a sniff as she delivered his message over the telephone. Then she went back to the television while Gerasimov, in fresh clothes, lay on the bed, reading while he waited.

Georgi came with his heavies. It was the first time the two men had met since the night out that had ended at the Cosmos Hotel, so possibly Georgi feared that Gerasimov had planned some revenge. But Gerasimov, greeting him at the entrance to the building, was all charm. "Georgi, it's been a long time. And I never thanked you for the great time I had with your girls—better, I should think, than you've ever had with that fat slut of mine."

Georgi darted an uneasy look at him, trying to guess whether or not rage lay behind this male bravado, but Gerasimov was too well trained to betray his real feelings. He put an arm around Georgi's shoulder and gave him a genial smile. "Do you want to come up?" he asked.

"I have things to do," said Georgi. "The Samara's clean. She's humming like a bird."

"I'm grateful. But now I have another favor to ask you."

"Fire away."

"A Volkswagen van."

"You want a van?"

"A specific van. A white Volkswagen van that disappeared sometime in September 1991 on its way from the Lubyanka to the transport-department depot."

"Stolen?"

"Sold. A private deal by one of our drivers."

Georgi narrowed his eyes. "You want the man?"

"No, not the man, the van. But not to keep, just to examine. It's a lead in an investigation. I can't say more."

Georgi looked uncertain. "It's a long time ago."

"I know, but there can't have been many vans like that from the Lubyanka."

"I can ask around."

"That's all I ask. From our end, these days, everything's a pale shade of gray. But you, from your end—well, quite honestly, Georgi, when a police state falls to pieces, matters depend on people like you."

Again Georgi narrowed his eyes. Was this a compliment or an insult?

Gerasimov retained his genial facade. "It would be a big favor," he said. "I mean, not just to me but to the people above me. They'd owe you one."

Georgi nodded. "And you don't want it back?"

"No. Just a look."

"At the Lubyanka?" He looked uneasy.

"No. Here will do."

Georgi walked back toward his Mercedes. "I'll do what I can."

Gerasimov drove back to the Lubyanka and handed in the keys of the Volga.

"Did you find the van?" asked the dispatch officer.

"No. Let's look at the log again." Gerasimov followed the duty officer to his desk. "M. Gorbachev. Who's the joker?"

The officer shrugged. "I don't know."

"Who was on duty that shift?"

"I was."

"Aren't you meant to check that the drivers sign their names?"

"In theory, of course."

"And you can't remember who took the van?"

Now the man began to look uneasy. "Offhand, no. So many vehicles come and go."

"But not brand-new German vans."

"If I could remember the bastard, I swear—"

"Swear all you like. It still looks bad."

The man began to look afraid. "What can I do?"

"Do you want my advice?"

"Yes."

"Report it stolen. That's what they said at the depot. Call the militia. Let them find it."

The young officer put his hand on the telephone. "Right away, comrade. Now that I have been informed that it never reached the depot, I'll report it stolen."

It was now dark, and time to pay a visit to Peshkov, the man in the second division of Directorate S of the First Chief Directorate, the KGB's counterfeiters, the best in the world, purveyors of everything from United States passports to British birth certificates, German *Ausweise*, French share certificates—anything and everything required for operations abroad.

Gerasimov decided not to call on Peshkov in his office. The visit might come to the attention of Orlov's friends in the Second Chief Directorate. It would be equally compromising if Gerasimov were to go to his home in a conspicuously official car like the Volga. He therefore took a bus back to the Ulitsa Academika Koroleva to pick up the Samara.

The car purred down the Mira Prospekt toward the center of Moscow. Georgi's mechanic had serviced the car well—as well as Georgi had serviced his wife. This thought, that would once have made Nikolai grind his teeth, now produced only a sardonic smile.

Gerasimov knew the building where Peshkov lived; it had been built to house Directorate S personnel. With the air of a friend paying a visit, he showed his service card to the concierge and took the elevator to the fourth floor.

Peshkov's wife came to the door. With the same nonchalance, Gerasimov said, "Trouble at the office," and walked through the door.

"Grigori!" she shouted.

Peshkov was eating his supper off a low table in the living room while watching television. Two children appeared. The elder, a girl, stood staring at Gerasimov; the younger, a boy of eight or so, dangled from exercise bars on one of the walls of the hall.

Peshkov came out of the living room, frowning and wiping his mouth. With a nod of his head, he sent his wife into the kitchen and the children followed. He gestured to Gerasimov, who had taken off his shoes, to follow him into the living room, where he turned down the sound on the TV.

"I'm sorry to interrupt you at home," said Gerasimov.

"Never mind," said Peshkov. He was only forty—Gerasimov knew this from his file—but being bald looked older. Perhaps he was ill.

"I've been ordered to make certain internal inquiries."

"By?"

"General Savchenko, but it has been authorized by Bakatin."

Peshkov nodded. "Go ahead."

"Khrulev."

"What about him?"

"He ran his own outfit within the Second Chief Directorate?"

"Yes."

"The last operation was insulated."

Peshkov was looking at the television. Was he bored by what Gerasimov was saying or trying to hide the fact that he was scared?

"It was insulated," Gerasimov went on, "because it was an operation to recover icons, and some of our own people had been selling them in the West."

"We are never told about operations," said Peshkov.

"But you knew that this one was for Khrulev's eyes only?"

"Yes."

"Orlov was your liaison."

Peshkov said nothing.

"Not even your department head knew."

"No."

"You answered to Khrulev."

"Yes."

"And now Khrulev's dead."

"So I hear."

"So who ordered you to provide new passports for Orlov?"

Peshkov did not move. With his eyes still on the television, he picked up a slice of bread from his plate.

"Orlov left the service," said Gerasimov. "He's now in the West. We have reason to believe that you provided the passports. We want to know the names."

Peshkov took a bite of the slice of bread and chewed it slowly. "Orlov left the service?" he asked.

"Yes. You must have known that."

"To provide documents for an ex-officer would be a serious offense," Peshkov said.

"Yes," said Gerasimov.

"Why would one do it?"

"You tell me."

"I would if I knew."

It was clear that Peshkov was not going to admit to what he had done. "Listen," said Gerasimov, leaning forward, resting his elbows on his knees. "No one is interested in prosecuting anyone who, through misplaced loyalty or even for a dollar or two, gives a little help to a friend. No one's interested in knowing who's a progressive and who's a hard-liner in your department because, quite frankly, as long as you do your job, no one cares. What interests us is a list of names, nationalities, passport numbers: on my desk or sent through the post. No questions asked. No one told."

"And if not?"

"The Cold War is over, comrade. There are ten times too many people doing our jobs. Some are going to have to go, and to be honest there aren't that many opportunities for someone in your line of work."

Gerasimov left his card on the table, put on his shoes, and let himself out, leaving Peshkov in front of the television while his wife and children cowered in the kitchen. He was hungry, but he was also tired—too tired to eat out or go back to any bed but his own. He drove back to the Ulitsa Academika Koroleva.

There was a smell of cooking in the apartment. In the kitchen the table was set for two. A fat round candle stood between the salt cellar and the pepper pot. Hearing him enter, Ylena shuffled out of the bedroom. Both her lips and her eyes were red—the lips from lipstick, the eyes from tears.

"Expecting company?" Gerasimov asked sarcastically.

She sniffed, shuffled into the kitchen, and lit the candle.

Gerasimov shook his head, incredulous that after ten years of marriage he could still be surprised at the depths of his wife's vulgarity and sentimentality. A reconciliation dinner! He washed his face and hands in the bathroom before going to shut himself in the bedroom, but he was waylaid by the smell of borsch and his appetite got the better of his resolve. He sat down at the table. Ylena ladled the soup into his plate, then sat, her plate empty, sniffing soulfully and looking pathetically into his eyes.

When the telephone rang, Ylena went to answer it. "Yes, yes, yes." She came back into the kitchen. "He thinks he's found your van. He'll bring it around tomorrow night."

Gerasimov left for work at the Lubyanka at seven the next morning. Before going to his office, he had a word with Melnik, the transport officer. When he got to his desk, he found a letter. His name was handwritten. There was no stamp. Inside was a sheet of paper with a list of names, numbers, and nationalities: the passports forged for Orlov by Peshkov—one American, one German, one Swiss, one French, and one Soviet.

Gerasimov went to see Savchenko. "The list of passports, comrade general."

"Well done." Savchenko took the list and studied it. "Why a Soviet passport, I wonder?"

"I asked myself the same question."

"Did Peshkov have any ideas?"

"Peshkov admitted to nothing. This list is off the record."

Savchenko nodded. "So we have no way of knowing whether our friend Orlov is traveling around Europe as the American Edward Burton, the German Hans Lauch, the Swiss Franz Grauber, or the Frenchman Marcel Jeanneret?"

"No. Presumably in Germany he will be a German, and to get at the bank accounts in Zurich he will be Grauber, the Swiss."

"And the Russian, Serotkin?"

"To return to Moscow incognito."

Savchenko nodded. "Do we know if photographs had already been affixed to the passports?"

"No."

"Almost certainly not. Orlov will have changed his appearance."

"So even with the names and the passport numbers, he won't be easy to find."

"Unless . . ." Savchenko leaned forward and took a piece of paper from the top of the pile on his desk. By its shiny surface and smudged Latin lettering, Gerasimov judged that it was a letter from the West that had been faxed and refaxed a number of times. "There has been a request through Interpol for our assistance in the case of the murders of the Maslyukovs in Berlin."

Gerasimov frowned. "How will we respond?"

"How indeed." Savchenko sat back in his chair. "The usual thing is to send some dumb ox from the militia who speaks no German and would act more as a hindrance than a help. But in this case—"

"We tell them about Orlov?"

"Who was acting on our orders? No. That would be most damaging to our relations with the Federal Republic. But if we sent *you* to Berlin, and if you could gain access to their database, you should be able to find Orlov before they do."

"And when I do?"

"Find out what he's up to."

"And if he won't tell me?"

"Bring him home."

"And if he won't come home?"

"Insist. Point out the danger he runs of being prosecuted for the

Maslyukovs' murder and the harm it would do to Russia's credibility as a civilized nation."

"And if he *still* won't come home?"

"*Then eliminate him*. If Orlov were to fall into the hands of the Germans, there might be a public trial. Think of the harm that would do to the reputation of the Russian Federation. If there is the slightest risk, you must do your duty and eliminate him. However admirable his services may have been in the past, he cannot be allowed to compromise the future." And, as if to illustrate the point, Savchenko drove the butt of his cigarette into the base of the glass ashtray with a savagery unexpected in such a portly, amiable man.

Once the decision was made and the order given, the different departments of the new Security Service of the Russian Federation went to work with all the efficiency of the old Soviet KGB. There was a minor dispute as to whether the deutsche marks required should be charged to the department of the militia that dealt with Interpol or the foreign-currency account of Directorate S, but it was quickly resolved and Gerasimov was told that he would leave for Berlin on his own passport in two days.

All he needed now was any evidence he could glean from the Volkswagen van. He telephoned Partovski at the Tretyakov Gallery, to say that his presence would be required that evening, and at 6 P.M. went to fetch him in the Samara. Partovski looked uneasy as he climbed into the car, and Gerasimov's high spirits made him more nervous still. "It may be difficult for me to say for sure that—" he began.

"There must have been some documents," said Gerasimov, "to get you onto the ferry."

"Yes, of course. The log book, the insurance, that kind of thing."

"What happened to them?"

"They were left in the van."

They reached the Ulitsa Academika Koroleva. Gerasimov parked the Samara by his building; Partovski accompanied him up to the apartment. Again there was a smell of cooking. Ylena was keeping up the blitz on his baser instincts, doubtless with Georgi providing the sausage and the wine. She looked disconcerted when Partovski came in behind her husband and, like Partovski, regarded Gerasimov's high spirits with suspicion.

Gerasimov introduced his companion. "He's here to identify the van."

The two men took off their coats and shoes and went into the living room.

"Some vodka?" asked Gerasimov.

"No, I—"

"Come on." Gerasimov went to the glass-fronted cupboard and took out a half-filled bottle and two glasses. "After all," he said, "we've found the Volkswagen. That's something to celebrate."

Ylena came in. "Will you eat with us?" she asked Partovski.

"No, thank you. My wife—"

"Of course he'll eat with us," said Gerasimov. "Who knows when Georgi will turn up?" He turned to Partovski. "Call your wife and tell her you'll be late."

"Very well. If you insist." Partovski acquiesced but made no move to the telephone.

Gerasimov raised his glass. "To Comrade Orlov, wherever he may be."

"To Orlov," said Partovski, also raising his glass and then adding, with a touch of defiance, "to Andrei Orlov, a brave man."

They emptied their glasses, and Gerasimov refilled them. "And to our wives."

"To our wives."

"As faithful as the day is long."

Ylena sniffed. "Dinner's ready," she said.

"Then let's eat."

In the kitchen a third place had been set by Ylena and the candle taken away.

"I have a wife who can not only cook," said Gerasimov, "but who to acquire the food will do what has to be done."

"You're a lucky man," said Partovski.

"Lucky indeed."

Ylena served up the borsch and they ate, silent except for an occasional slurp.

"We have a son," Gerasimov said eventually, "but I rarely see him."

"He's with my mother," said Ylena to Partovski.

"The Russian babushka," said Gerasimov. "What would we do without her?"

"Do you have a child?" Ylena asked Partovski.

"Yes. A daughter."

"How nice."

For a moment Gerasimov was almost touched by the wistful, child-like look on his wife's face. But it was too late for pity.

The doorbell rang. Ylena went to answer it, then returned to the kitchen. "It's Georgi. He'll wait downstairs."

Gerasimov looked at his watch. "Excellent." He turned to Partovski. "Would you like some more?"

"No, thank you. I've had enough."

"Would you like some coffee?"

"No, thank you."

"Another time."

The two men put on their coats and shoes. Ylena hovered in the kitchen as Partovski followed Gerasimov out of the flat to the elevator.

"All we need to know," said Gerasimov, "is whether or not this is the van you brought from Germany to Tallinn."

"I understand."

"The question of how it disappeared need not concern you."

Partovski nodded.

There was a Dutch journalist with a Russian photographer in the elevator. Gerasimov and Partovski stood in silence side by side as it descended to the ground floor.

Georgi was waiting in the lobby. Two of his men were outside the door. He narrowed his eyes at Partovski. "Who's this?"

"He brought the van to Russia. He can tell us if it's the right one."

"Is it his?"

"Is it yours?" asked Gerasimov, smiling.

"No," said Partovski. "It isn't mine."

They went out to the parking lot, where a white VW van with Soviet license plates was parked next to Georgi's Mercedes.

"It wasn't easy to find," said Georgi, his eyes flitting to and fro between Gerasimov and Partovski, as if trying to discover why Gerasimov should be in such an ebullient mood.

They reached the van. A third thug sat at the wheel of the Mercedes. Georgi slid back the door of the VW. "Was it a diesel?" he asked Partovski.

"Yes."

Gerasimov looked in the glove compartment. It was empty. "No documents," he said.

Georgi laughed. "Not likely."

Gerasimov pulled the lever that opened the hood and went around to the front of the van. The plates with the engine and chassis numbers had been chiseled off. "No numbers," he said to Partovski.

"I never noted them anyway," said Partovski, "but it's the van, all right."

"How can you tell?"

"Come and look."

Gerasimov walked around to the back of the van. Beyond the parking lot he could see four men in a Lada peering in their direction.

"Those scratches on the inside. I remember them, because the van was more or less new."

"Anything else?"

"There are still two empty Fanta cans under the seat and some sandwich wrapping. Those were mine."

"They file off the numbers," said Gerasimov, "but don't take the trouble to clean it out."

"And the name of the garage," said Partovski. "I remember that. On the back window. Look: Autohaus Bedaur, Leipzig. There can't be two white VW diesel vans in Moscow from the same garage in Leipzig."

"So you'd swear to it?"

"Yes. This is the van."

Georgi, who had been following their examination of the Volkswagen, now turned away to find himself facing two plainclothes detectives from the militia.

"We have reason to believe," said the first, "that you are in possession of stolen state property."

Georgi darted a look over their shoulders; his three men were already handcuffed to uniformed policemen. He turned to Gerasimov. "Tell them."

Gerasimov shrugged. "You're asking too much, I'm afraid." He turned to the detective and shook his head. "Inflation. The prices people ask, and for stolen goods!"

With a roar, Georgi lunged at Gerasimov, but before he could reach him he was seized by the two detectives, handcuffed, and led away. The older detective said nothing but merely nodded to Gerasimov before turning to follow his men.

Gerasimov took Partovski by the arm. "Thank you, comrade. You have been a great help. The militia have been after that scoundrel for years. It's been hard to get evidence against him, but this, I should say—state property, after all—should put him away for quite a while."

12

Francesca McDermott, who had been a junior squash champion in Wisconsin and a member of the women's team at Harvard, anticipated that her skill might make up for a man's natural advantages when playing Andrei Serotkin. So it proved in the first couple of games. He was good but she was better—or so she thought.

In the third game her presuppositions were shaken by a defeat. Francesca was puzzled. She could not quite make out what had gone wrong. Perhaps unconsciously she had been unwilling to humiliate the man she loved by winning three games in a row. She tried harder in the fourth game and won. She tried equally hard in the fifth game and was beaten. Only then did she realize that Serotkin far outclassed her. He had been playing with her like a cat with a mouse, letting her win only when he chose to do so.

"My God, Andrei," she said, panting. "This just isn't fair. You must have played on the Soviet team."

"No."

"So where did you learn to play like that?"

"There were courts at the Ministry. And in Washington, of course."

"You were in Washington? You never told me that."

His expression did not change. "Briefly, at the embassy. I stood in for the cultural attaché."

"No wonder your English is so good."

Francesca thought no more about it. As Stefi had once pointed out, Russians had learned the hard way the importance of keeping themselves to themselves. She knew she was only going to get to know Serotkin little by little, and she did not want to jeopardize these friendly meetings by appearing too inquisitive.

Francesca also recognized that a measure of mystery was a necessary ingredient in love, and she was in love; there was no question about that. When Andrei Serotkin entered the room, her heart lifted; when he left it, her heart sank for the few moments it took to conjure him up once again in her imagination. That they were not lovers did not dishearten her since the exhibition brought them together every day, and she felt confident that his feelings, although undeclared, were nevertheless engaged.

The squash games were the proof. Andrei had suggested them, and he seemed to enjoy the opportunity they provided to compete with Francesca and win. She had known competitive men before, and she had known some who had appreciated her ability to give them a good run for their money. All sports bind players together with mixed strands of rivalry and friendship. With Andrei, however, the game seemed to be more than a game, and the objective was not merely to win. It was as if he felt challenged by her in ways that possibly he did not fully understand, and that he must establish not only that he could beat her but that he could tease and manipulate her—physically on the squash court, intellectually in the office. She always rose to the bait. Her mind was out of kilter with her emotions and, though ready to surrender her body should he choose to take it, she was not prepared to defer to his judgment when they disagreed on art.

Serotkin had defeated her in the early days on the scope and title of the exhibition. Now they joined battle on the question of texts. At an earlier meeting, Frau Doktor Koch had proposed that blown-up photographs be displayed alongside the paintings, either portraits of the artists or pictures of places pertinent to the exhibition, such as the church at Abramtsevo or Tatlin's model for a monument to the Third International.

Francesca had argued against this on the grounds that the place for photographs of this kind was in the catalog, not on the walls. Rival images among the exhibits would dissipate the impact of the art. The committee had agreed. Defeated on this issue, Frau Doktor Koch regrouped and mounted a new offensive on the question of displaying excerpts from the manifestos of the different artistic schools—the Futurists, the Constructivists, the Suprematists—as well as quotations from the writings of Kandinsky. Here again, Francesca argued, large placards would distract from the paintings; they would make visitors feel that they were there to learn rather than to enjoy. The gallery directors and Dr. Kemmelkampf agreed; Stefan Diederich had no view; Günter Westarp was undecided. It seemed that the texts would go the same way as the photographs when Andrei Serotkin raised his hand.

"Dr. Serotkin?" asked Stefan Diederich.

"I should like to ask Dr. McDermott whether she is confident that, without texts of the kind proposed by Frau Doktor Koch, those who look at the works of art will understand what their creators had set out to achieve."

"I believe they explain themselves," Francesca answered.

"I was thinking, for example," said Serotkin, "of Larionov's Rayonnist Manifesto of 1914." He read from a book open on the the table in front of him:

"We declare the genius of our days to be: trousers, jackets, shoes, tramways, buses, aeroplanes, railways, magnificent ships. . . . We deny that individuality has any value in a work of art. . . . Hail nationalism! We go hand in hand with house painters.

"Or there is Kandinsky's *Concerning the Spiritual in Art,* the bible of the modern movement. Don't you feel that we should at least display some quotations from that?"

"I'm not sure," said Francesca.

"Perhaps we could use the opening sentence: 'Every work of art is the child of its time: often it is the mother of our emotions.' "

"Isn't that a truism," asked Julius Breitenbach, "and so comes across as somewhat banal?"

Andrei Serotkin turned to Francesca. "Perhaps Dr. McDermott could tell us whether or not it is banal."

Francesca cleared her throat. "I think Kandinsky's writing is interesting, but more as an adjunct to his art than in itself. To display excerpts like that would only tend to confuse people—"

"Because they are too stupid to understand them?" asked Serotkin.

"Not necessarily."

"Or because the writings themselves are nonsense?"

"Because, as I said, the writings are not really theories as such but more the expression of the kind of ideas that inspired Kandinsky: not so much his philosophy of art or aesthetics but more like the prose poems he was writing at the time."

"Ah, yes," said Serotkin. "The prose poems." He read from the book:

> "A circle is always something or other
> Sometimes even a great deal.
> Sometimes—seldom—too much.
> Just as a rhinoceros is something too much.
> Occasionally it—the circle—sits in com-pact violet.
> The circle the white circle.
> And grows indisputably smaller. Even smaller.

"Perhaps this," suggested Serotkin, "should be exhibited on a board?"

Francesca frowned. Was Andrei sincere in what he said, or was he mocking Kandinsky? "We have put some of his poems in the catalog," she said. "I would have thought that was enough."

"Speaking for us Ossies," said Günter Westarp, "I think we have had quite enough of slogans pinned up on walls. Let's just have the paintings with some labels and have done with it."

Serotkin raised his hands in a gesture of capitulation. "Very well. My suggestions are withdrawn."

On the following Wednesday, Francesca and Andrei played squash after work and afterward went to a nearby café for a drink.

"You know, Andrei," said Francesca, "I sometimes think you have a mischievous side to your character."

"Mischievous? How?"

"At Monday's meeting. Were you serious about putting those texts on the wall?"

"Were they serious when they wrote them?"

"Probably. But that doesn't mean they should be taken seriously. In my experience, artistic talent and intellectual rigor rarely go together."

"Yet artists have ideas, and if their works of art are really the mother of our emotions they have influence too."

"I should have thought the influence was largely subliminal and imprecise."

"That has not been the view of those who have used art to promote their interests."

"Like?"

"The dominant classes throughout history, in particular the clergy and the bourgeoisie."

"That theory denigrates the genius of the artists," said Francesca.

"Not their genius, no. Their integrity, perhaps, but even then . . . an artist has to live."

"And what interest is promoted today through modern paintings?" asked Francesca. "What are they meant to do to our emotions?"

Serotkin darted a quick look of anger, even contempt, toward Francesca, but when he spoke he chose his words with care. "The argument would go, I think, that with the collapse of communism and the worldwide triumph of pluralism, capitalism, and democracy, we see not just the end of history but also the end of art."

"From where I sit, there's never been more interest in art."

"Of course. Art is revered as never before. It has replaced religion. In Western Europe, and above all in the United States, the great art galleries are the temples where people come to revere the icons of their age. But what are these icons? The squiggles of Jackson Pollock, the daubs of de Kooning, the monochrome canvases of Rothko. When you look at contemporary American paintings, you marvel not at the skills of the artist or at the beauty of what he has depicted—because in essence he has depicted nothing—but at the fact that these empty canvases are sold for millions of dollars. It is this that gives them their status as icons of the new religion. They could have been painted by anyone, even by machines. They bear no trace of the human hand, let alone the human mind or the human eye. When you revere a work of abstract art, you are worshipping capitalism in its purest form: added value for added value's sake."

"Is this what *you* believe?" asked Francesca.

"These were the ideas that were put forward by some of the people in the Ministry in Moscow."

"And what did they say about contemporary realists whose paintings also go for millions of dollars: Francis Bacon, say, or Lucian Freud?"

"My colleagues would argue that if these are the mothers of the emotions of the Western world, no wonder it is so diseased, degenerate, and depraved."

"Artists cannot look at the world through rose-tinted spectacles."

"Of course not. But when Grünewald portrays the cruelty of the crucifixion or Goya the horrors of war, the works are protests against what they portray and there is the implicit promise of redemption. The paintings of Bacon and Freud hold no such promise. They are the icons of despair."

"It almost sounds as if you agree with your colleagues."

Serotkin smiled. "If I did, would I be here?"

Francesca, who went on to have supper with the Diederichs, told them what Serotkin had said about modern art. "And at the end of it all, I still can't make out what Andrei himself actually believes."

"He may not believe in anything," said Stefi.

"But it's his specialty, isn't it?"

"You have to understand the way things worked under the Soviet system. Most of them only wanted to find a well-paid sinecure and then keep their heads down. Serotkin would never have been allowed to specialize in experimental art if he had actually believed in it; that would have made him a dissident on cultural matters. He most certainly would not have been given a post in the Ministry of Culture. He probably drifted into the job because it gave him the chance of occasional foreign travel."

"Yes. He said he'd lived in Washington for a time."

"Did he? I didn't know."

"Apparently he stood in for the cultural attaché."

Stefi shrugged. "There you are. A second-rank cultural bureaucrat."

"I think he's worried that there may not be a job for him when he goes back," said Francesca.

"I daresay."

"Couldn't you find him something here? He really is very knowledgeable, and he speaks both German and English so well."

"Wouldn't you rather he got a job in America?" asked Sophie with a smirk.

Francesca blushed. "I was only thinking that if there was some way we could help him—"

161

"I get the impression," said Stefi, "that Dr. Serotkin is quite capable of looking after himself."

"And sometimes others," said Sophie. "Even damsels in distress."

Again Francesca blushed. "He certainly did me a good turn. I'd like to do one for him in return."

Sophie giggled. "The easiest way would be to marry him. Then he could get an American passport."

"He hasn't proposed," said Francesca.

"I'm sure he will," said Sophie. "You work together. You play squash together. You live in the same building."

"But we don't live together," said Francesca emphatically. "I've never even seen his apartment."

"But he's been to yours."

"Only once, after the attack, to call the police."

Stefi frowned. "I would advise you," he said, "not to get romantically involved with Serotkin."

"You would say that," said Sophie, "but it's only because you hate Russians. But he wasn't responsible for the DDR, and Francesca isn't an Ossie, so there's no reason why she should feel the same."

"Russians are deceptive," said Stefi. "They look like Europeans, but under the skin they are Asians, as cruel as Mongols and as contemptuous of women as the Turks."

"I have always found Andrei very considerate," said Francesca.

Stefan shrugged. "You are grown up, Francesca. You can make your own judgments. But I advise you to be cautious."

"And where would we be if *we* had been cautious?" asked Sophie. "You take a risk when you fall in love."

Later that evening, Stefi told Francesca in confidence that Bonn had let it be known that the President of Germany, Richard von Weizsäcker, might be willing to come to Berlin to open the Excursus exhibition on July sixth. It was a tentative offer because the President realized that the exhibition's organizers might not want a political leader or, if they did, might prefer an East German or even a prominent Russian dissident. Stefan asked her to think about it and perhaps discuss it in the strictest confidence with Andrei Serotkin and Günter Westarp.

When Francesca saw Günter in the office the next morning, he lobbied against the idea. It would be insulting for Gustav Kiepert, the

Minister President of Prussia, who had been asked to open the exhibition six months before. "It's typical of the Wessies. When they think something is going to be successful, they want to take it over and make out that the idea was theirs all along."

Francesca could see why Günter would think this, and she pretended to agree, but she was somehow irritated that he could not shake off his Ossie inferiority complex and rise to the occasion. From her point of view, it could do no harm to her reputation if her name was associated with an exhibition opened by the president of a major nation, rather than by the minister president of a minor province. Who in the United States had heard of Kiepert? She was sure Andrei would feel the same, or could be persuaded to feel the same, and she waited impatiently for him to arrive at the office.

He did not come. She grew fretful and, late in the morning, went to the secretaries' office and casually asked if anyone knew what had happened to Professor Serotkin.

"Oh, yes," said Gertie. "He called in sick."

"You might have told me," said Francesca.

"I'm sorry. There was no meeting, so I thought—"

"Did he say what was wrong?"

"Influenza."

"Have you his home number?"

Gertie flicked through the cards on a Rolodex and jotted down the number.

"And his address."

"He's in the same building as you, Frau Doktor."

"I know. But what's the number of his apartment?"

Gertie could not help giving Dora a quick smirk before writing down the address. "There," she said, handing the piece of paper to Francesca. "And I've put down the postal code too!"

Francesca went back to her office. She picked up the telephone to call Andrei but then thought better of it. He might be sleeping. He might also decline an offer of a sick call, but he could hardly turn her away if she looked in on him when she got home.

It felt odd to Francesca to go up in the elevator beyond the fourth floor. On the ninth-floor landing everything was replicated—the color of the walls, the pattern of the carpet—yet was in some intangible sense different. Like hers, Serotkin's apartment was in the northwest corner of the building. She straightened her clothes, brushed back her hair, pursed her lips to bring up their color, and rang the bell at his door.

There was silence. Her briefcase weighed heavily on her arm. She waited, doing her best to keep the casual "I just thought I'd stop by" look on her face. She rang again. Again there was silence. Perhaps he was asleep, drugged with a sleeping pill. Or perhaps he was not there, his illness a pretext for another of his mysterious trips out of town. She rang for a third and last time. As she did so, she imagined she heard a shuffle behind the door, and the peephole seemed to darken.

There was another shuffle, then the sound of muffled voices. Curious but also embarrassed, she was about to leave when suddenly the door opened. She said "Hi, I was just—" but then stopped. The man who faced her was not Serotkin. He had black hair and dark skin, like an Arab or perhaps a Turk. His face had no expression. He neither smiled nor frowned nor seemed surprised that she was there.

"I'm sorry," she said. "I thought this was Dr. Serotkin's apartment."

The man stepped back, no words but only the movement indicating that she was to come in. She walked into a hallway, of the same dimensions as her own, and then, following a silent gesture from the man, into the living room. Again it was the same as her own, with a kitchen at one end and a fireplace at the other. The same furniture was upholstered in a different color and was arranged in a different way, but what immediately struck Francesca was the magnificent icon of Christ above the fireplace, its severe eyes watching her, almost rebuking her, as she stepped forward to take a closer look.

She knew little about icons, beyond the influence they were said to have had on artists like Goncharova, Tatlin, and Kandinsky. However, this one was patently old, probably sixteenth or seventeenth century, and was almost certainly Russian, not Balkan or Greek. To judge from the somber expression, it was probably of Christ as the universal judge. How on earth, she wondered, did Andrei Serotkin get hold of a work like this that normally you would only find in a church or a museum?

"*The Savior* from Pskov."

She turned. Serotkin stood behind her; the other man was nowhere to be seen. He was wearing pajamas and a bathrobe. His face was pale. From its expression, she could not tell whether or not he was pleased by her visit.

164

"What do you think?" He nodded at the icon.

"It's wonderful."

"I find it a source of solace. It instills a mood of great calm, but it is also inspiring."

"A mother to emotions?"

"Precisely."

"Is it yours?"

"It is on loan. A little corner of Russia while I am here in Berlin."

"You're very lucky."

"Yes." As he said this, Serotkin started to cough.

This reminded Francesca of the pretext for her visit. "I'm sorry to burst in on you like this. I was told you were ill and I wondered if I could do anything to help."

Serotkin smiled and pointed toward a chair. "That is kind." Francesca sat down. "As you can see, a friend from Moscow happens to be passing through Berlin. He is able to get me a few things." Serotkin did not sit down but went to a cupboard. "Would you like a drink?"

"No. Really. I just thought . . . I mean, have you seen a doctor?"

"No. I am not so ill. I shall be better tomorrow."

"You should have called me."

"I had my friend."

"Am I not your friend?"

He took out a bottle of vodka and two small glasses. "I hope so." He sat down and placed the glasses on the same low coffee table that Francesca had in her living room. "You must have a drink to keep me company."

"All right."

"Russians believe that vodka is the best cure for all diseases." He laughed, then coughed, then laughed again. He handed her a glass filled with vodka and took one himself. "Your health . . . and mine!"

They touched glasses.

"Is your friend staying with you?" asked Francesca.

"No." He turned toward the door. "You should be introduced to him, except that he has gone out for some aspirin. He is an interesting fellow, a native Chechen, but unfortunately he speaks little English or German."

"What does he do?"

"He is a scientist, a biologist."

"And what is he doing here?" Francesca could not help feeling a certain antipathy toward the Chechen.

"A conference of some kind."

"Well, if he's busy, I can always come up and make you some supper."

"Thank you, but I can manage."

She frowned. "It would be a favor to me, Andrei. I would like a chance to try and repay you for what you did for me."

"I did not regard that as part of a transaction."

Francesca blushed. "No, of course not. I didn't mean that."

He appeared to relent. "Come tomorrow, then. By tomorrow my friend will have gone."

Francesca awoke with a start at three in the morning with the idea in her head that Andrei Serotkin was gay. Had she dreamed it? The more she thought about it, the more it seemed to make sense of his behavior—his narcissistic fitness, his strange absences, above all his failure to respond to her advances. The Chechen must be his boyfriend! She had sensed his antagonism when she entered the flat—he must have realized she was a rival—and for the same reason she had taken an instant dislike to him. At the time she had put this down to his being an Arab—not, of course, that there was anything wrong with being an Arab or, for that matter, gay—but in love and war . . .

These thoughts prevented Francesca from going back to sleep. How could she have been so stupid as not to have realized it? Clearly, Russian gays were not as open as American gays; because homosexuality had been frowned on in the old Soviet Union, Russian gays had to be particularly discreet. Was it this that had broken up his marriage? It would explain why he had never bothered to get divorced. It would also explain his choice of profession; gays were common in the art world.

At around six, Francesca fell asleep. At seven her alarm went off. She rose feeling awful, mixed her yogurt and muesli, and boiled the kettle to make her Lapsang souchong tea. She felt depressed. She assumed at first it was because she had slept badly but then remembered the idea that had woken her during the night.

In the cold light of dawn, she was less sure. Andrei had withstood her advances, true, but she was quite certain he found her attractive. A woman can always tell, either by the way a man looks at her, or by the way he avoids looking at her, or by the way he only looks at her when he thinks she is not looking at him. Francesca also had to admit that neither Andrei nor the Chechen had any gay characteristics, nor did the clothes each had been wearing show the kind of fastidiousness that Francesca had observed in her gay friends. The Chechen had worn scruffy jeans and a nylon shirt; Andrei, though his clothes were elegant enough, let them get rumpled and never bothered to brush off the ash that fell from his strong cigarettes.

Of course not all gays were neat and dapper, and perhaps the Chechen was a passing fancy, a bit of "rough trade." The issue remained open in her mind as she drove to work and festered in the back of her mind throughout the day.

The proofs of the catalog were in. Francesca wondered if she could get Serotkin to check the Russian entries while he was still ill. She made a number of calls to Milan and Paris about the dispatch of some of the paintings. At twelve she had lunch with Stefan Diederich and the cultural attaché from the U.S. embassy in Bonn to discuss the possibility of taking Excursus to New York. She told Stefi that Serotkin was ill and asked if he knew anything about his Chechen friend. For a moment Stefi seemed confused; a morsel of poached salmon remained poised on the end of his fork between his plate and his mouth. Then he said, "A Chechen? No. What is a Chechen?" which permitted the U.S. attaché, who had served in Moscow, to deliver an impromptu lecture on the different nationalities found in the Caucasus and around the Caspian Sea.

After lunch Francesca drove out to the Omni Zartfracht warehouse in Tegel with Günter Westarp, Julius Breitenbach, and Frau Doktor Koch to supervise the unpacking of the first paintings. Such was the security that they were refused entry, and they had to wait for an official to arrive from the Ministry to get them in. Even after they had been admitted and stood admiring El Lissitzky's celebrated *Proun* from the Yale Art Gallery in New Haven, they were watched by the special security guards—young men in beige uniforms, black belts, and leather gloves.

Leaving Julius Breitenbach in charge of the unpacking, Francesca returned to the Excursus office with Günter Westarp and Frau Doktor Koch. A number of calls and faxes had already arrived from the East Coast, and at 6 P.M. the traffic started with the West Coast and the southern hemisphere. It was seven before Francesca got back to her apartment and eight before she went up to Serotkin's, carrying two plastic bags containing the ingredients of a light supper.

Serotkin opened the door. He was still in his bathrobe but looked much better. At her insistence he retreated to his bedroom while Francesca went into the kitchen. She put the bags down on the counter that divided it from the living room. From the wall above the fireplace, the eyes of Christ the Savior looked severely at what she was doing, as if discerning the ulterior motives for her mission of mercy.

Francesca unpacked the bags, taking out a carton of milk, a can of pheasant broth, a package of chicken breasts, and some string beans. She frowned as she realized that the director of the Los Angeles Museum of Modern Art might try to call her at home and wondered whether or not she should call and leave Serotkin's number. But it could wait. Of more interest to her at the moment were the contents of Andrei's kitchen cupboards—a few cans, a few jars, packages of tea, coffee, and rice.

When supper was ready, Francesca went to the door of Serotkin's bedroom. It was ajar. She knocked gently. He asked her in. He lay on the bed—the same kind of bed as in her place below—propped up against some pillows. A book, in Russian, lay open on the bedclothes.

"Shall I bring you a tray?" she asked.

He shook his head. "No. I'll come to the table."

Francesca went back to the kitchen and Serotkin followed in his bathrobe and slippers. He sat down where she had laid a place on the dining table in the living room, and she served him the pheasant broth. "What would you like to drink?" she asked. "Some vodka?"

"Why not? Yesterday's dose did me some good."

"You don't think milk would do better?"

"Milk? Yes. The national drink of the Americans, after Coca-Cola."

She filled a glass from the carton and placed it on the table. "We went out to the warehouse this afternoon," she said, "and unpacked the first painting."

"Wonderful."

"Their security's really tight. At first they wouldn't let us in."

"Better too strict than too lax."

"I guess so." She started her soup. "And the proofs of the catalog are in."

"At last."

"We've got to turn them around in three weeks."

"Have you brought them? I can do them in bed."

"It might tire you."

"I feel much better. I shall return to work Monday."

Francesca wanted to ask Andrei about his friend the Chechen, but she held back. It might seem nosy. Instead, she asked, "What have you been reading?"

"Dostoyevsky."

"The Brothers Karamazov?"

"Crime and Punishment."

"I haven't read it."

"The hero, Raskolnikov, is a murderer."

"You mean the antihero."

"No. He is the hero. That is what makes it an interesting novel. At the beginning of the book, Raskolnikov murders an old woman for her money yet retains the reader's sympathy throughout."

Francesca frowned. "How can you sympathize with a murderer?"

"He acts from the highest motives. He feels he is destined to do great things for humanity, like Napoleon. But he lacks the means—the seed money, we would call it today. The only way he can think to raise it is by killing a dreadful old crone, a pawnbroker. He dares himself to do it, not just for the money but to prove to himself that he is a man of destiny by overcoming the inhibitions of conventional morality."

"But that's not right, is it? That all great men are above morality?"

"I would say so, yes."

"We would have impeached President Nixon."

"Perhaps Nixon was not a great man."

She laughed. "There's no perhaps about it."

"But Abraham Lincoln?"

"He was great."

"Only because history went his way. Imagine how you would judge him now if the South had won the Civil War."

"Isn't that kind of cynical?"

"To the victor goes the spoils, including the luxury of deciding what is right and what is wrong."

"You mean there's no objective morality?"

Serotkin hesitated. "Dostoyevsky believed that there could only be an objective morality if there was a God to define it."

"And you?"

"I don't believe in God."

"I wish you'd finish your soup," said Francesca.

Serotkin smiled. "Women are fortunate. Instinct serves as conscience, and all reasoning is made superfluous by intuition."

Francesca frowned. "Is this Dostoyevsky speaking or Andrei Serotkin?"

"Perhaps just Mother Russia."

"Dostoyevsky at least had the excuse that he lived in the nineteenth century."

"Whereas I should know better because I live in a more enlightened age?"

"Yes."

"The age of Auschwitz and Hiroshima."

"You can hardly blame them on feminism."

"They are part of the same phenomenon."

"What is that?"

"The rejection of Christian order that followed the rejection of Christian faith."

"Serotkin or Dostoyevsky?"

"Dostoyevsky."

"Does Serotkin agree with Dostoyevsky?"

"Up to a point."

"What point, if he doesn't believe in God?" She was speaking from the kitchen, where she was taking the chicken breasts out of the oven.

"Man does not live by bread alone."

"So let him eat chicken." Francesca put a full plate in front of him.

Serotkin did as she said, but she sensed that thoughts continued to ricochet around in his brain. He seemed agitated, even feverish, and showed little interest as she prattled on about what had happened in the office during the day. When she told him they had unpacked El Lissitzky's *Proun* from Yale, he frowned. "In the end, I think, we will have most of the modern Russian paintings in American collections?"

"Yes."

He thought for moment, then said, "There is an interesting character in *Crime and Punishment* called Svidrigailov. At the end he has to choose between shooting himself and going to America. To Dostoyevsky, I think, they amounted to the same thing."

"And what does he do?"

"He shoots himself."

Serotkin ate only half his chicken and turned down Francesca's offer of fruit or yogurt. He said he would like some coffee, and she said she would bring it to him in his bedroom once she had cleared away the dishes.

Francesca put the dishes in the dishwasher and filled the kettle to make coffee. While waiting for it to boil, she went to the bathroom. It was the same as her own. There were spots of dried soapsuds on the mirrored door to the cabinet above the basin. She wondered whether anyone came in to clean for Serotkin or whether he cleaned his flat for himself. She wiped off the dried soapsuds with a damp tissue, then opened the cabinet in which downstairs she kept shampoo, foundation cream, cleansing lotion, and contraceptive pills. Serotkin had only a bottle of Odol mouthwash, shaving cream in a pressurized can, aspirins, and a square bottle labeled *Polyman Color. Tönungs Shampoo. Natur Schwartz.* It was black hair dye. So the philosophizing Andrei was not so high-minded after all!

It was a sign of how much Francesca was in love with Andrei Serotkin that she found this touch of vanity endearing. Little by little the veil was being lifted from the inscrutable Russian to reveal him to be a man as vulnerable and fallible as any other who caught flu and worried about looking old.

She went back to the kitchen, made the coffee, and took the pot with two cups on a tray into the bedroom. He lay on his bed, propped up against pillows, reading. She put the tray on the dresser, filled the cups, handed one to Serotkin, drew up a chair, and sat down next to the bed.

Now that she knew, his hair did seem a little too good to be true. The beard too. Of course he was silly. He would be just as attractive, perhaps even more attractive, if a few of his hairs were gray. It would add gravitas. She could just imagine him in an amphitheater of enthralled students at BU.

"What are you reading?" she asked.

"Poems by Mayakovsky."

"Would you read one out loud?"

Serotkin started to recite from memory, the book unopened in his hand, his voice suddenly both dramatic and melodic as the words in his native Russian tumbled out in his deep bass voice.

> "Does the eye of the eagle fade?
> Shall we stare back to the old?
> Proletarian fingers
> Grip tighter
> the throat of the world:
> Chests out! Shoulders straight!
> Stick to the sky red flags adrift!
> Who's marching there with the right?
> Left!
> Left!
> Left!"

"I guess you prefer that to Kandinsky's poem?" said Francesca.

"It was written around the same time."

"But Mayakovsky killed himself," said Francesca.

"Yes. Like Svidrigailov. Whereas Kandinsky went to America, like Solzhenitsyn."

"If I had been Mayakovsky, I think I would be happy to know that sixty years later people were still reciting my poems."

"Even though his poems no longer give birth to emotions?"

"There are emotions other than Bolshevik zeal."

"Of course.

> "How fearful, in and out of season
> to pine away from passion's thirst,
> to burn—and then by force of reason
> to stem the bloodstream's wild outburst . . ."

As Andrei recited Pushkin's verse the daylight faded, but neither of them moved to switch on the electric light. Serotkin gazed at Francesca as if Eugene Onegin's words to Tatiana were addressed to her, while Francesca kept her eyes fixed on the open neck of Serotkin's pajamas. The triangular patch of skin, pale-colored in the gloom, seemed to make him vulnerable, like the patch of skin on Achilles' heel. Just as he had glimpsed her nakedness in the Englischer Garten, so she now felt that she was glimpsing his, and she felt an urge to lean forward and lay her hand on his chest with a protective caress.

He began to recite, again from memory, a poem by Yevgeny Yevtushenko.

> "My beloved will arrive at last,
> and fold me in her arms.
> She will notice the least change in me,
> and understand all my apprehensions.
> Out of the black rain, the infernal gloom,
> having forgotten to shut the taxi door,
> she'll dash up the rickety steps,
> all flushed with joy and longing.
> Drenched, she'll burst in without knocking,
> and clasp my head in her hand;
> and from a chair her blue fur coat
> will slip blissfully to the floor."

Both were now silent. Francesca could not tell in the dusk whether Andrei's eyes were open or closed. She got silently to her feet, stepped closer to the bed, and looked down. His eyes were open. He took her hand. She sat down beside him on the bed and with the hand that was free obeyed the urge to touch the skin beneath his neck. With her finger and thumb she could feel the strong lines of his collarbone and, beneath it, the pulse of his blood. She held her hand there for a moment; then she felt his arm come around her shoulder and drawn her down.

"Andrei," she whispered. She meant to say You are ill, you are weak, but it was she who felt weak while his arm felt strong. They kissed. Her hand moved farther over the warm skin beneath his pajamas. Is it true, she wondered, that with women intuition and conscience are one and the same thing? Then he held her more tightly and she wondered no more.

IV

1993
May–June

13

When Nikolai Gerasimov arrived in Berlin, his principal objective was to spin out the assignment for the maximum length of time. His expenses were paid under an arrangement with Interpol by the city government of West Berlin; the per diem allowance in deutsche marks, if he stayed long enough, should buy him a fax machine, a compact disc player, or even a secondhand Mercedes.

Pursuit of this strategy was made easier by Gerasimov's instructions from General Savchenko to play the plodding officer from the militia and on no account let it be known that he was an officer in the Security Service of the Russian Federation or that the Maslyukovs had been killed by a team from the KGB. His mission was to find Orlov, not help the Germans find him, and, when he did, either to bring him back to Moscow or, if necessary, stub him out like Savchenko's cigarette.

Gerasimov was met at Schönefeld airport by two men who introduced themselves as Inspector Kessler of the Berlin police and Herr Grohmann from the International Police Liaison Department of the Federal German Ministry of the Interior. They drove him to a two-star hotel in a small street off the Hohenzollerndamm and waited in the lobby while he took his suitcase to his room. They then drove him to the headquarters of the Criminal Police on Gothaerstrasse in Schöneberg. There, in his office, Inspector Kessler described the murder, showed Gerasimov photographs of the scene of the crime, and produced a thick file of papers: transcripts of interviews, analysis of forensic evidence, lists of exits and entries from Schönefeld and Tegel. Good, Gerasimov thought to himself. It will take me a while to wade through all of this.

His own initial contribution was small. Following the plan worked out by Savchenko and outlined to him by the general, who had himself accompanied him to the airport, Gerasimov told Kessler that it was the view of the Russian militia that the Maslyukovs had almost certainly been killed by a rival group of smugglers and racketeers. "We have been on their trail for some time. Their chief is a man we call Ivan the Terrible. Ruthless—"

"And cruel," said Kessler, pointing to the photograph of Vera Maslyukov.

"What are those marks on her body?" asked Gerasimov.

"Cigarette burns. She was tortured."

"Typical, I am afraid, of Ivan the Terrible."

"Do you have any idea who he is?" asked Grohmann. As he asked, a younger man came into the office and was introduced as Sergeant Dorn.

"We are fairly sure he is an Armenian called Georgi Nazayan. But you must realize, gentlemen, that the Soviet Union—that is, the former Soviet Union—is no longer as well policed at it once was. We used to know everything that happened almost before it happened, but now, among other Western imports, we have a crime wave."

"Clearly," said the younger detective, "there was little crime in the country when half the people were in the police."

"I have one or two leads I should like to discuss with you," said Gerasimov, ignoring Dorn's jibe. "And doubtless you have things you would like to discuss with me."

"We have to confess," said Kessler, "that we have made almost no progress. We are fairly sure that the Maslyukovs' icons were stolen, and we have reason to believe that one of the assailants smoked Bulgarian cigarettes."

"That would be enough for Hercule Poirot," said Gerasimov, who had recently seen the video of *Death on the Nile,* "but real life is rarely as straightforward as it appears in the books of Agatha Christie."

"Perhaps you would like to look through the file," said Grohmann, "to see if anything there links up with your own investigation."

"Of course."

"Could you do that overnight?"

"Ah . . . I am afraid I am slow at reading German. Perhaps you could give me twenty-four hours?"

"As you like."

"It's been some time since the murders," said Dorn. "Another day more won't make much difference."

"And perhaps we could see your file?" asked Kessler.

"Can you read Russian?" asked Gerasimov.

"We have people who do," said Grohmann.

"Then I shall send for it from Moscow."

"You brought no copy with you?"

"I am afraid our copier was kaput. But it can be easily arranged."

"Good."

"It may take a day or two."

"Of course."

"Perhaps even a week."

"We understand."

"But in the meantime there is this." Gerasimov patted the file he had been given. "And, if you will allow me a certain freedom of action, there are one or two leads I might follow up on my own."

Kessler looked at Grohmann. "Of course," said Grohmann. "The old Cold War suspicions are a thing of the past. You have your visa, go where you like. And if you need help of any kind, just let us know."

Gerasimov found German women the most attractive in the world. There was something about their long limbs and serious faces that drove him to a high pitch of erotic excitement. Their coldness, their matter-of-fact manner, their sensible approach to life, and their disdain for the silliness of the English or the flirtatiousness of the French made it all the more exhilarating when things got under way, their bodies rising and falling like pistons on some precision-made machine from Krupp. What a contrast to the lazy, dumpy, squat, inept sluts in Russia!

Back in his room at the hotel, Gerasimov dumped Kessler's file on top of the television, took a shower, changed his clothes, went down to the hotel restaurant, and, while he was eating, planned his strategy for the night.

The choice was between doing a tour of the bars and nightclubs, in the hope of finding a *Mädchen* who would appreciate his rugged good looks, or squandering a chunk of the deutsche marks that had been handed over to him by Kessler on a tall no-nonsense German whore. It was some time since he had been west, and he was not sure what he would have to pay. But since it was his aim to save his allowance, Gerasimov decided to try the bars and nightclubs first.

He walked up the Kurfürstendamm, then down to the area around the Zoo Station. It was too seedy. Everyone seemed either an Arab or a Turk. Where would the German girls go who were out for a good time? He walked west on the Kantstrasse, then turned left into Savignyplatz. This was more like it; there were innumerable little restaurants and *Stuben* with young people spilling out onto the street.

He came to a bar, Der Riesige Liliputaner: the Giant Midget. Berlin humor. Gerasimov went down the steps into a cellar. It was dark—he had to stoop to avoid hitting his head on the low ceiling—and almost empty. A couple sat in the corner, two men at the bar. Gerasimov turned and went out. Farther down the same street, he went into a crowded café, sat down at a table, and ordered a beer. He looked at the menu: alfalfa salads, nut cutlets, cottage cheese on sourdough rye. It was for vegans and other vegetarians; no wonder the waitress had looked surprised when he ordered a beer.

Gerasimov studied the people. They all seemed young, and although they gabbled away in German, none of the girls had the blond, blue-eyed, long-legged look he was after. Perhaps they no longer existed, the Prussian look smothered by dark-haired dark-eyed dwarfs from Saxony and Bavaria.

Gerasimov finished his beer, paid the waitress, and went back to the street. Perhaps he should try the bars at the grander hotels—the Hilton or the Kempinski—but there any woman would probably be a whore and would cost him a fortune. He still hoped he could get what he wanted for the price of a few drinks, but as he stalked the pavements, crossing the Kurfürstendamm and the Lietzenburgerstrasse and turning right into Pariserstrasse, his confidence began to wane. The brightly lit shopwindows displayed elegant clothes at prices that terrified him. He could not help converting the price tags into rubles, which showed that a whole year's salary would hardly buy him a pair of shoes.

The cars, too, seemed larger and shinier than he remembered: Mercedes Benzes, Audis, and BMWs were crammed up against the curbs of every street or clustered at every intersection, their drivers slim, suave women or well-groomed men. What have I got to offer them? he asked himself glumly. All the women are much richer than I am. They would have to be perverse to want to sleep with a penniless muzhik.

It was one of Gerasimov's strengths that these moments of self-doubt did not last long. He not only had a confident personality, he had been trained to work on the assumption that every problem has a solution. His mind began to turn toward possible ways of making money beyond reselling an imported stereo system or video recorder. Clearly, Orlov was onto some scam. He had probably pocketed the Maslyukovs' money and was setting up some racket of his own. He might like a partner; certainly, until he found him, Gerasimov should keep an open mind.

He was beginning to feel tired. He had been on the move since he left Moscow that morning, where the time was two hours ahead. He took out his map of Berlin and fumbled with its folded pages by the light of a shopwindow to find where he was and plan a route back to his hotel. It was not far. He put the map back into his pocket and walked north along Uhlandstrasse. Within a block of his hotel, his eye caught the sign of a bar called Whisky-a-Go-Go. A Scotch would help him sleep. He went into the bar—plush, carpeted, and filled for once with adults, not the young.

Gerasimov sat down on a stool at the bar and ordered a J&B. Next to him sat a couple, a man of around fifty with close-cropped hair, the woman with long henna-dyed hair, perhaps in her mid-thirties; it was hard to tell in the subdued light. They were talking in German but the man spoke it badly. Gerasimov thought he must be a Swede or a Finn. They made some arrangement to meet the next day, at which point the man slapped DM 100 onto the bar, shook hands with the woman, and left.

She turned back and called the barman to give her another drink. He seemed to know her; he gave her a long look that Gerasimov could not quite interpret. Commiseration? For a moment Gerasimov simply sat studying the bottles ranged against the wall. He fancied the woman but could not decide how to proceed. She seemed respectable. She was elegantly dressed. She was probably a businesswoman, in Berlin for a meeting with customers from abroad. Gerasimov had to be cautious. Better not admit to being a Russian. He would say he was Canadian. His English was good enough, and in his experience no one had a pre-conception of what a Canadian was like.

Gerasimov turned to the woman and said, in deliberately faulty German, "Are you from Berlin?"

She gave him a long look of appraisal before she answered. "Yes."

"I just flew in today."

She took out a cigarette, allowed Gerasimov to light it, took a drag, and, as she blew out the smoke, asked, "From where?"

"Regina, Saskatchewan."

She frowned. "Is that in America?"

"Canada."

"You are Canadian?"

"That's right."

"I am afraid I speak little English." She said this in English.

"My German isn't too bad."

She gave him another appraising look from under her eyelashes. "Are you a businessman?"

"Yes. Pharmaceuticals."

She nodded and took another drag on her cigarette.

"And you?"

"Fashion."

"You're a model?"

She shook her head. "No, I choose designs for foreign buyers."

"Was that one of your clients?"

She blew out the smoke. "More or less."

"Can I buy you a drink?"

She looked down at her glass, which was still half filled with wine. "In a moment perhaps."

This was not going to be easy. "I haven't been in Berlin for a number of years. It seems to have changed."

"Yes. The Wall came down, you know." She almost smiled.

"I read about that."

"But even before, it was full of foreigners: Turks, blacks, and now Gypsies from Romania." She wrinkled her nose.

"That can't be easy to take for someone born in Berlin."

"To be cosmopolitan is one thing; to become a refugee camp is another."

"Sure."

She finished her glass of wine. Gerasimov bought her another and started to tell her about the company he worked for in Regina. At an appropriate lull in the conversation he introduced himself. "You don't even know my name. Nick Turner."

She nodded. "My name is Inge."

"Inge. Well, I'm glad to meet you." He shook her by the hand. He was warming to his role as a Canadian businessman, and the challenge dissipated his fatigue.

They talked further—about his business, about hers, about their private lives. She was unmarried. He was divorced with two difficult adolescent children. Eventually Inge looked at her watch and said, "I suppose I should be going."

"OK. Me too." He called the barman and asked for the bill. Again the barman glanced at Inge—a fleeting, familiar look, hard to interpret. Without presenting an account, he asked Gerasimov for DM 100. Gerasimov swallowed but paid up; if he wanted the woman, he could not seem to be cheap.

"Can I drop you off at your hotel?" Inge asked.

"That would be kind."

She led him to a shiny blue Audi 80. Gerasimov got in beside her. "The Trebizond. Do you know where that is?"

"It's only a block away."

"Is it? I'm sorry. I'm kind of lost. I guess I could have walked."

Inge said nothing but turned to see if she could drive out into the stream of traffic. "The Trebizond is not very elegant," she said.

"It's pretty basic," said Gerasimov. "It was booked by the German company, and I guess they were feeling stingy."

"The Germans are stingy," said Inge, swinging her car out into the street.

When they reached the hotel, she drew up by the curb fifty yards from the door.

"Would you like a nightcap?" asked Gerasimov.

She gave him another cool look. "Why not?"

Gerasimov could hardly believe his good fortune. They went into the lobby and she waited by the elevator while he fetched his key from the desk.

They were alone going up to the tenth floor. In the harsh fluorescent light Gerasimov noticed a faint line of speckled gray at the roots of her hair and adjusted his estimate of her age.

In his room he went to the minibar. "What would you like?"

"Later, perhaps."

He turned back. Inge came toward him, raised her arm, and loosened his tie. "Five hundred marks. OK?"

Gerasimov swallowed and opened his mouth but did not speak.

Inge pulled his tie away from his neck and started to undo the top buttons of his shirt. "It's usually more," she said.

He nodded.

"If you would give it to me now, it would make me more relaxed."

Gerasimov reached into the inside pocket of his jacket, took out the grubby envelope containing a month's expenses, and counted out the banknotes.

She took the money and handed Gerasimov a condom in exchange. "You won't be disappointed."

She was as good as her word. She did not have blue eyes, blond hair, or long legs, and her breasts and skin had the slackness of a woman well over forty, but her underclothes were clean and lacy and she smelled superb. Deftly she slipped off her own clothes and helped Gerasimov out of his, and when they started to make love her movements and murmurings persuaded him that she was transported against her will. Her eyes became bleary, her murmuring became groans, her groans gasps, until finally involuntary cries came from her mouth: yes, yes, yes! *ja, ja, ja!* or was it—he could not believe it—not *ja, ja, ja!* but *da, da, da?* With a grunt, he collapsed. She eased out from under his body and went to the bathroom.

"You're Russian?" he shouted in Russian.

"*Koneshno.* Sure."

Gerasimov groaned and hid his face in the pillow.

Chastened by the fiasco of the night before, Gerasimov spent the next morning reading through Inspector Kessler's file. As he proceeded through its many pages, he felt a certain patriotic pride at the way Orlov and his team had frustrated the pedantic investigators of the German police. There were no footprints or fingerprints, only the bullet that had killed Grigori Maslyukov and the fragments of tobacco from the cigarettes that may have been used to burn his wife.

The bullet had come from a Beretta, and they must know that Berettas were sometimes used by the KGB. But they were a common enough weapon; if this was all that had led them to invite Gerasimov to Berlin, Inspector Kessler and his friends were clutching at straws.

The cigarette burns surprised him. Orlov was trained for any eventuality, but torture seemed uncharacteristic. The woman must have known something he was determined to find out. Orlov smoked—it was in his file—probably BTs when he could get them, but so did several million others from the former Soviet Union, not to mention Bulgaria itself and other neighboring countries. Gerasimov did not know about Partovski or Kastiev, the Chechen. Partovski seemed even less likely than Orlov to have stubbed cigarettes out on the wretched woman. It was probably the Chechen; those savages from the Caucasus thought nothing about that kind of thing.

The papers from the file were spread out over Gerasimov's unmade bed. The whore's scent lingered on the sheets to remind him of his humiliation. He wished now that he had made her give the money back, but she might have made a fuss, brought in some pimp, and caused a rumpus in the hotel that would get back to Kessler, who might complain to Interpol, so that eventually it would come to Savchenko's ears, which would mean demotion, possibly dismissal, and certainly an end to assignments abroad.

The bitch. With some relish, Gerasimov began to visualize stubbing cigarettes out on her flaccid skin; more than the pretense that she was German, he resented the cool way she had led him to believe that she was going to give him a free ride. All the same, even if she was not worth DM 500, she had learned some tricks of the trade in Berlin; she was in a different class from the sluts in the Cosmos Hotel in Moscow.

Gerasimov went back to the files. The junior detective, Dorn, had checked the comings and goings from Schönefeld airport, but they must know that no trained agent from the First Chief Directorate would fly in from Moscow on a Russian passport, murder the Maslyukovs, and then fly out again the next day. Orlov had almost certainly traveled as the German Hans Lauch, and would now be in Switzerland as Franz Grauber, in France as Marcel Jeanneret, or even in the United States as Edward Burton. The best way to trace him would be through hotel registers, apartment leases, or car-rental companies. There might also be bank accounts in any of these names. The bulk of the Maslyukovs' money, if he had retrieved it, would be in a secret numbered account, but he would have had to establish some facility for his everyday requirements.

The names would have to wait. If he gave them to the Berlin police now, they might find Orlov within a week. They would also find him before Gerasimov did, and Savchenko's orders were most emphatic. On no account was Orlov to be allowed to talk to the German police. Gerasimov must find him and if necessary kill him, and the best way to do so was through the Volkswagen dealer in Leipzig. But that, too, could wait.

That night, Gerasimov went to the movies: *Terminator 2*. He turned in early and was ready in the lobby of his hotel at eight the next morning when Inspector Kessler came to take him out to Zehlendorf to visit the scene of the crime.

"Were you able to read the file?" asked Kessler.

"Of course."

"What do you think?"

"Your investigations have been most thorough."

"Could it be the work of this man you call Ivan the Terrible?"

Gerasimov shrugged. "As you know, there are no real clues to point in any particular direction."

"There is the tobacco."

"Yes. Bulgarian tobacco. A favorite smoke in the former Soviet Union. But also in Bulgaria, Romania, Hungary—"

"Of course."

"It seems extraordinary," said Gerasimov, "that if large numbers of icons were stolen they have not reappeared in the Berlin art market."

"Agreed," said Kessler. "That's why we think it's not a simple burglary."

"I see that the Maslyukovs had foreign bank accounts?"

"We assume so. Numbered bank accounts in Liechtenstein and Switzerland."

"Is there no way to discover whether anyone has used them since the murder?"

"We don't even know the numbers or where they are."

"Could anyone, knowing the numbers, make withdrawals?"

"With a certain type of numbered account, yes."

"To obtain the numbers was perhaps the reason for torturing the Maslyukov woman?"

"Yes." Kessler paused, then said bluntly, "The job was so expert that some have suggested an intelligence angle."

"Ah."

"Perhaps Maslyukov was a conduit for funding secret operations?"

"For the CIA?" asked Gerasimov innocently.

"Or perhaps some Soviet organization?"

"The KGB?"

"Is it possible?"

"I gather some of their people have been involved in icon smuggling. . . ."

"And they use Berettas."

"Yes. But then so does James Bond."

Kessler grunted. "You heard nothing in Moscow?"

"The KGB never did confide in the militia, and now, as you may know, there is no KGB. However, the influence of the Lubyanka is still there, and I would not have been sent here if the KGB had anything to hide."

"I see."

"It seems more likely, in my opinion—if this really has the hallmark of an intelligence operation—that it is the work of some former officers in the Stasi who have been obliged by their reduced circumstances to turn to crime."

Kessler scratched his cheek. "We thought of that. The hypothesis was rejected."

"Why?"

"The ex-Stasi agents are under surveillance."

"All hundred thousand of them?"

"The important ones. Anyway, there's no evidence to suggest it."

"There's no evidence to suggest anything."

They arrived at the house in Dubrowstrasse where the Maslyukovs had been killed. The house was still empty. Kessler opened the front door. "It was only rented by the Maslyukovs," he said. "The owners have not succeeded in finding new tenants." He sniffed the musty air. "It still smells of murder."

They made a tour of the house. Kessler pointed out to Gerasimov where Grigori Maslyukov's body had been found and where Vera Maslyukov had been tied to the chair. The chair had been removed long ago to the police laboratories; so had the tape deck and cassettes. The two men went to the kitchen, then to the bedroom. "Their correspondence?" asked Gerasimov.

"At the lab, what there was of it."

"Some of it in Russian?"

"Yes."

"You have people who read Russian?"

"Of course."

"It might be useful if I looked through the letters." Another time waster.

"Very well."

They came down the stairs. "It's a pity," said Gerasimov, "that we weren't informed earlier."

"Applications through Interpol take time."

"Of course. And I don't wish to suggest that our technical expertise is equal to yours. However, trails are more difficult to follow when they are cold."

"I agree."

"Our friend Ivan the Terrible—"

Kessler frowned. "You think it might have been him?"

"It's certainly a theory worth pursuing."

"We shall see what we can do when we get your file on Ivan the Terrible from Moscow."

"Of course. In the meantime, I might pursue some inquiries among the Russians living here in Berlin. You never know. They may be willing to say things to a compatriot that they would not tell the German police."

Kessler left Gerasimov at the police laboratories to look through the Maslyukovs' correspondence and drove back to his office in Schöneberg, where he summoned Dorn.

"The Russian tart. What did she say?"

"That he claimed to be a Canadian called Turner and thought she was German. She said she charged him DM 200, but she had DM 500 in a roll in her purse. I tell you, chief, if that man's KGB, it's no wonder the Soviet Union went down the drain."

"Are you sure she isn't a contact?"

"For the clap?"

"For the KGB?"

Dorn shrugged. "Ask your friend in the BfV. As far as I know, she's a shop assistant who moonlights as a part-time whore."

"Odd that he should choose a Russian."

"Berlin's crawling with them." Dorn looked down at his notes. "He spent yesterday in his bedroom. The maid said there were papers spread out all over the bed. In the evening he went to a movie."

"Did he meet anyone?"

"Not unless he slipped a note to the person sitting next to him. Our man was three rows behind."

"So he may be just what he seems?"

"What do the BfV say?"

"Leave him on a long leash. Go on with surveillance, but keep it discreet."

Dorn left, and Kessler called Grohmann. "So far he's behaving as if he's just what he says he is, a plodder from the Moscow militia."

Grohmann did not reply.

"Are you there?"

"Yes. I'm thinking."

"We keep an eye on him, right?"

"Yes. But he mustn't know. If the Maslyukov murders were one of their operations, he'll do what he can to throw dust in our eyes. Or simply obstruct by inaction."

"That seems to be his tactic so far."

"What about this Ivan the Terrible?"

"Nothing in our files, but there are new groups from Russia arriving all the time."

"We've nothing to lose by leaving him to his own devices, if that's what he wants. Check on everyone he goes to visit. If there is an Ivan the Terrible, he may find him. If it was a KGB operation, he may expose it by trying to cover up the trail."

"I don't have the men for twenty-four-hour surveillance," said Kessler.

Grohmann hesitated. "I'll see if I can arrange some help."

14

It quickly became known in the Excursus office that Dr. McDermott and Professor Serotkin were now more than colleagues and friends. Francesca tried to act normally in Andrei's presence but inevitably gave herself away—not to Günter Westarp or Julius Breitenbach, or even that dedicated academic Frau Doktor Koch, but to Dora and Gertie, the two secretaries, who were quick to note her changed manner and passed on their discovery to the incredulous Julius, with whom they were on gossiping terms.

The first person to get confirmation of the suspicions that she had harbored for some time was Sophie Diederich. She realized at once that there could be no other explanation for Francesca's metamorphosis in so short a space of time from a brisk, ambitious academic to a gentle, dreamy, cozy girlfriend who, instead of going on about Kandinsky and Malevich, brought every conversation back to Serotkin.

"So you are more than just good friends?" Sophie said to Francesca one day when they met for lunch.

"Can you be more than good friends?" asked Francesca with a sly smile.

"Yes, of course you can. Stefi and I were friends, and then we were more than friends. We were lovers."

"Isn't it better to be friends first and then lovers?"

"I suppose so. Unless he is also a friend of your husband's."

"I haven't got a husband."

"So?" Sophie waited.

Francesca nodded. "Yes."

"You're lovers?"

"Mmm."

"You're crazy."

"I know."

"He only wants an American passport," Sophie blurted out.

Francesca looked offended. "That hasn't come up."

"So what does he want?"

"Me, I guess."

"Don't believe it."

"Thanks!"

"I don't mean that you aren't attractive, but . . ."

"What?"

"Stefi mistrusts him."

"He's certainly mysterious."

"If . . . if he fancied you," said Sophie, "then why did he wait for so long?"

"I was the one who waited."

"What made you change your mind?"

Francesca sighed as she considered. "I don't know. *Le coeur a ses raisons que la raison ne connaît point,* I guess."

"I don't understand French."

"That's Pascal. The heart has its reasons that reason cannot comprehend."

"I admit he's handsome," said Sophie reluctantly.

"Dashing," said Francesca.

"And he did save you from those Turks."

"That must be it," said Francesca, laughing. "I just melted before his machismo, except—"

"What?"

"He was the one who took the melting. I had to hit him when he was down."

"*You* seduced *him*?"

"It's always the woman who decides."

"So what happened?"

"He was sick, in bed. I . . . ministered to his needs."

"When he was *sick*?"

Francesca smiled as she remembered. "He was getting better."

"Even so."

"Kill or cure."

Sophie shook her head. "But what do you know about him?"

"Next to nothing. But I like that. In America, men give you their life story on the first date and generally never talk about anything except themselves. Unless they feel they have to give you a turn to get you into bed."

"So what does the professor talk about when you are alone together, Kandinsky?"

"Yes. Kandinsky. And his own ideas about life and history, Russia, women. He recites poetry. He has a phenomenal memory. He can quote whole chunks of writers like Dostoyevsky. In America, art historians only talk about art."

"So you love him for his mind?"

"His body's not so bad."

"Francesca!"

Francesca's expression became serious. "*You* should understand, Sophie, because there's something mysterious about Stefi too."

"Of course. And the trouble with Paul was that he was so honest and transparent that you always knew what he would think and what he would say."

"So you got bored."

Sophie shrugged. "Yes. I did."

"Love only lasts if there is mystery."

"And will yours last?"

"I hope so."

"Will you marry him?"

"He hasn't proposed."

"He will."

Francesca frowned. "I'm not so sure. He seems decisive, but inside there are areas where he's really confused. I mean, here he is, an expert on modern art, yet I get the impression from some of the things he says that he actually hates it. He loves me but hates America; he seems to agree with Dostoyevsky that there's not much to choose between emigrating to America and committing suicide. He loves Russia. He hates the suffering of the Russian people. But he's ambiguous about the re-forms."

"He doesn't like Gorby?"

"No."

"He'd like to rebuild the Berlin Wall?"

Francesca laughed. "No, I'm sure he wouldn't go as far as that. He just loves Russia and its traditions and its values, and I guess he's afraid they'll get swamped now as it opens up to the Western world."

"Shall I tell you something interesting?" said Sophie. "That's just what Paul used to say about the DDR."

"Would he say that now?"

"I don't know. We only talk about arrangements for the children. But a friend said she had heard him preach at Bechtling, and he was warning his congregation of Ossies against the fleshpots of the West."

Andrei Serotkin now slept in Francesca's apartment. He kept a pair of pajamas in the cupboard in her bedroom and a toothbrush in her bathroom. The Odol and the Polyman Color remained on the ninth floor.

After sleeping alone for so long, Francesca found it difficult to get used to sharing her bed with a man. Andrei did not snore, and he had the decency not to smoke in bed, but he slept fitfully; often she would wake up at three or four in the morning and see in the dim light that came through the blinds from the streetlamps that he was lying on his back, his arms clasped behind his neck, staring at the ceiling.

Sometimes, if she snuggled up to him, a strong arm would come down around her shoulders, but there were occasions when he would rebuff her, turning away to face the wall. She could not fathom his moods. At times he was boyish and cheerful, at others somber, almost grim. Frequently he would tease her with evident affection, but on occasions he would become moody and silent, behaving as if he loathed her. He had dreams from which he awoke grinding his teeth; even in the midst of making love, a look of hatred might come onto his face and a physical ferocity replace the gentleness that had inspired his ear-lier caresses.

After one or two solicitous inquiries about his insomnia and bad dreams had been rebuffed, Francesca came to appreciate the truth of what Stefi had said about Russians: they had learned to keep themselves to themselves. Unlike most of her American friends, Andrei disliked analyzing his feelings or discussing the past. He made a number of deprecating remarks about the debilitating effect of psychoanalysis; introspection, he seemed to think, was unworthy of a man.

Whenever Francesca touched on his marriage, she found Andrei reluctant to discuss it. He would not even tell her the name of his wife. "You are now the only woman in my life."

"But before you met me—"

"Love is eternal, and eternity has no before or after."

He was equally reticent about his family. She sensed that he was fond of his parents, of his sister, and of his son, but she gained no impression of the kind of life he led in Moscow, a subject that particularly interested her since it was a life she might come to share. She made some oblique references to the future but found that here too he was unwilling to be drawn, even into conjecture. She saw only too clearly that their time in Berlin would soon come to an end, and, while she had no wish to test a bond so freshly formed, she could not bear to imagine that they would simply go their separate ways.

Although they were able to spend their nights together, the days were hectic and were often spent apart. Then there came a lull before the storm—when the catalog had gone to press, the works had all arrived at the warehouse in Tegel, but there was still a week to go before the hanging could start. That Sunday was one of the first in the past eight months when Francesca had not gone into the office or worked at home. Both she and Andrei therefore had the luxury of lying in bed until ten, making an American breakfast with English muffins and bacon and eggs, and reading *Die Zeit, Welt am Sonntag,* and *Time* while listening to a compact disc of *Tosca.*

It was one of the first hot days of June, when the sunshine seemed to insist upon an excursion of some kind—to Charlottenburg, Potsdam, Köpenick, or the Grosser Müggelsee. However, they had lingered so long over breakfast that it was twelve before they were dressed, so they decided simply to take the S-Bahn to the Friedrichstrasse station and from there walk to Museum Island. In the Pergamon Museum they studied the superb displays of classical antiquities: the gate of Ishtar from Babylon, the Sumerian temples, and the great Pergamon altar itself, all brought to Berlin by German archaeologists in the nineteenth century. Later, as they walked back down Unter den Linden toward the Brandenburg Gate, Andrei spoke to Francesca about the rise and fall of empires and the fickleness of destiny. She only half listened; she was happy simply to be leaning on his arm. They passed the Brandenburg Gate, crossing the great swath of no-man's-land where the Wall had once stood.

"I guess that in terms of world history," said Francesca, "the Berlin Wall will hardly rate a mention."

"Not, certainly, if you compare it to the Great Wall of China."

"Unless to compare and contrast: a wall in China to keep the barbarians out, a wall in Germany to keep them in."

"You are confident that history will see the Communists as barbarians?"

"Isn't shooting people who want to emigrate barbaric?"

"Two hundred people were shot trying to escape from East Berlin over a quarter of a century. In Detroit the same number are shot in a week. Add to that the number who die as a result of drugs, and one is entitled to wonder what is meant by civilization."

"People cannot be civilized if they are not free."

Serotkin looked at her with amused condescension. "The Roman empire was a military dictatorship. The barbarians were democratic."

Francesca was getting out of her depth. "Let's not argue," she said, clinging tighter to his arm.

They were now walking down the long boulevard leading from the Brandenburg Gate to the column surmounted by the Goddess of Victory. The whole area was redolent with history. To their right, through the trees of the Tiergarten, they could see the Reichstag, burned down at the time of the Nazis, now rebuilt. A little later they came to the Soviet War Memorial, a stone monument flanked by two tanks and two cannons from World War II and surmounted by a huge bronze statue of a Soviet soldier, a rifle with fixed bayonet slung over his back.

Here Serotkin stopped amid the cluster of tourists and looked impassively at the two live Soviet soldiers who remained guarding this monument to their country's dead.

"I didn't realize," said Francesca, "that there are still Soviet soldiers in Germany."

"Some have left, but others must wait until homes have been built for them in Russia."

"And what will the Germans do with this memorial when they go?"

"Demolish it," said Serotkin grimly.

"Or move it to the Pergamon Museum," said Francesca. "After all, it's the nearest thing to a Soviet altar."

"No, they will demolish it," said Serotkin again. "They will not want a constant reminder in the middle of their capital city of who it was who freed them from fascism."

"Wasn't it kind of a joint effort?"

"Yes. American money and Russian blood."

"There were the British."

"Marooned in Britain."

"And the French."

"Defeated."

"The Americans, then."

"Neutral, until Hitler declared war on *them*."

"It was Stalin who made a pact with Hitler."

"He had no choice."

Francesca did not want to get into an argument about the past, nor, it seemed to her, did Andrei. She could tell from the movement of his jaw under the skin, as he clenched and unclenched his teeth, that he was biting back words—not words directed at her but some dispute that was going on in his own mind.

She took his arm, a gesture that was meant to signify that she loved him whatever their differences of opinion. He did not shake her off but turned and looked at her with an expression bordering on contempt. "Tell me, Francesca, since you know so much about history, when have Russian soldiers marched through the Brandenburg Gate?"

"At the end of the war, I guess."

"And before that?"

She shook her head. "I don't know."

"Chasing Napoleon on his retreat from Moscow."

"I thought he was defeated by the British at the Battle of Waterloo."

"Finally, yes. Wellington dealt with an ad hoc army, assembled in a hundred days. But it was the Russians who defeated his *Grand* Army in 1812. Just as with Hitler, we are employed by the West Europeans to dispose of their tyrants."

"While unable to get rid of your own."

Serotkin frowned. "We disposed of the czars."

"But Stalin died of natural causes."

"Under Stalin," said Serotkin, "we were admired by many and feared by all. Now that we are democrats, Russia is universally despised."

"At times," said Francesca, "you sound as if you wished that Stalin was still around."

Serotkin hesitated. "Stalin was ruthless, but any government is ruthless when it comes to its nation's vital interests."

"He was more than ruthless," said Francesca. "He was cruel."

"For cruel necessities you sometimes need cruel men," said Serotkin. "It used to be thought that the Russians could only be governed by terror."

"But not now."

"We shall see."

"*You're* not governed by terror, are you?"

He paused, then said, "It is always preferable to be governed by love, but sometimes one has to choose between two different loves."

"Maybe you think you have to choose when in fact you can have both."

He turned and once again looked at her, but this time the expression in his eyes was sad. "I think you know, Francesca, how much I love my country. When . . . all this is over, I shall have to go back."

"Would you like company?"

He hesitated.

Francesca blushed. "I'm sorry. I didn't mean to put you on the spot."

"What about your job? Your tenure?"

As a reply, she simply squeezed his arm.

"Francesca." He hesitated again, as if searching for the right words. "Francesca, there are things about me . . . things that I have done and things that I must do. You don't know me. I am not what I seem."

Thinking of the hair dye, Francesca smiled. "Didn't you say that a woman's conscience is her intuition? Well, when I'm with you I feel it's right, and when I'm not I feel it's wrong."

"There are other things than love." As he said this, he sounded uncertain.

"A month ago I would have agreed."

"The exhibition, the paintings . . ."

"Who wants art when you can have life?"

Serotkin turned and looked at her as if to see whether or not she was sincere in what she said. "If you had to choose," he asked, "between me and all those paintings in the exhibition, one or the other—not to *have*, but to *exist*—which would it be?"

She did not hesitate. "You."

He looked away as if this was not the answer he wanted. For some time he stood silently staring up at the bronze soldier towering above the memorial. "Valentin Rasputin once wrote, 'Truth is remembering. He who has no memory has no life.'" He turned back to face Francesca. "There are things in our past, you see, that no Russian can forget, and the memory leads him to a certain course of action. But in time that action also becomes a memory, just as our being here will become a memory."

He turned to walk on, took a few paces, then stopped and once again looked directly into her eyes. "In a month's time," he said, "on July fourteenth, Bastille Day, I shall come back to this Soviet altar, and if you are here I shall ask the same question, and if your answer is the same then I promise you we shall remain together for the rest of our lives."

15

After two weeks in Berlin, Nikolai Gerasimov could no longer postpone his trip to Leipzig. It was clear that Inspector Kessler was beginning to wonder whether or not to cut his losses and send him back to Moscow, and General Savchenko, to whom Gerasimov spoke from time to time on a secure line from the former Soviet embassy on Unter den Linden, now the Russian consulate, was also impatient. His excuse—that the Germans were keeping him busy—was beginning to wear thin.

Kessler appeared happy to let him conduct investigations on his own; indeed, he encouraged him to do so. When Gerasimov told him he was going to Leipzig, Kessler informed the city's police and provided him with a letter To Whom It May Concern, asking for full cooperation. A room was reserved in a hotel, a first-class ticket provided by Kessler's office, and Gerasimov was met at Leipzig's palatial railway station by a plainclothes detective from the city's police.

Leipzig depressed Gerasimov. From his study of German literature at the Institute of International Relations in Moscow, he remembered that the city had been described by Goethe in his *Faust* as "a little Paris." Now, after nearly fifty years of socialism, it was more like a large Nizhni Novgorod or Dnepropetrovsk. Many of the older edifices still showed traces of the war; some bombed-out buildings had not been rebuilt, and others had the pockmarks left by Soviet shells. The post-war buildings were mostly tawdry and shabby, as yet untouched by the transfusion of hard currency from the West.

The young Leipzig detective who met Gerasimov at the station had clearly been molded by the old regime. Inadvertently he addressed Gerasimov as "comrade" and drove him with some pride to a modern high-rise hotel. Gerasimov recognized it at once as a Soviet-style Hilton. They waited for more than a quarter of an hour in the crowd around the reception desk as a sullen girl slowly searched for their reservation among scraps of paper scattered over the broken-down computer. Gerasimov felt at home.

After handing the visitor his card and promising any assistance should it be required, the Leipzig detective clicked his heels and departed. By now it was midafternoon. Not wanting to stay in Leipzig any longer than he had to, Gerasimov left his suitcase in his room, returned to the lobby, and bought a map of the city from the hotel shop. If he was watched, it would look as if he meant to do some sight-seeing before settling down to work.

Gerasimov did not even look around to see if he was followed as he walked to the center of the old city; he took it for granted that he was under surveillance. He looked at the old town hall, the old stock exchange, went into the Church of St. Thomas, and, on coming out again, paused to look at the statue of the church's former organist, Johann Sebastian Bach.

Opposite the church was a café. He went in, sat down, and ordered a cup of coffee and a slice of strudel. One of the tourists by the statue of Bach looked around every now and then to make sure he was still there. Gerasimov paid for the coffee and strudel and, when the tourist's attention was distracted, went into the kitchen of the café and out through the back.

He went to a tram stop and climbed onto the first one that came along. It took him along the Martin-Luther-Ring and Harkortstrasse. He got off at the Fine Arts Museum and waited on the traffic island in the middle of the road. No car had stopped when he got off the tram, nor did one alter direction when Gerasimov got on the next tram traveling in the opposite direction. As it approached the center, he got off again by the new town hall, hailed a taxi, and asked the driver to take him to the corner of Goldschmidt and Nürnbergerstrasse, a block away from the showroom of the Volkswagen dealer G. Bedauer.

Again no car was hovering as Gerasimov paid for the taxi. To be doubly sure, he walked around the block and stopped at a shopwindow. He was not being followed. He reached the forecourt of the Autohaus Bedauer just as a rubicund fifty-year-old man was closing up.

"Good evening. Herr Bedauer?"

The man turned. "Yes? How can I help you?"

He was not a local; Gerasimov could tell from the accent. He was probably a Wessie come to give his country cousins a lesson in free enterprise.

"I am sorry to have come so late in the day," said Gerasimov in a slangy western German. "And I'm not even here to buy a car."

"Never mind, never mind. We are here to serve. That is what the people here will not understand." He opened the door to the showroom, invited Gerasimov to enter, and then led him between two shiny new Golfs to his office at the back.

As the two men sat down, Herr Bedauer behind his desk, Gerasimov handed him the letter from Berlin's chief of police. "I'm working on a special investigation," he said. "All in confidence, of course."

The dealer read the letter and handed it back to Gerasimov. "Always happy to help the forces of law and order."

"We are interested in a white Volkswagen van, sold by you a little under two years ago, probably in July, possibly June."

"It can't have been before July 'ninety-one."

"Why not?"

"Because that's when I started in business. My first sales were in July." Herr Bedauer stood and went to the filing cabinet behind his desk. "Have you the registration?"

"Unfortunately not."

"Chassis number? Engine number?"

"No."

"There will be more than one," said Bedauer. "When the Ossies got their deutsche marks, they went crazy. I sold everything Wolfsburg sent me." He thumbed through the files. "If my secretary were still here, she would know where to look. Commercial vehicles . . . here we are. July before last, you say?"

"Yes."

Bedauer took out a file and sat down at his desk. He went through the papers. "We sold twenty-two vans that July."

"How many were white?"

"Wait a moment." Bedauer went through the file once again, removing some of the papers. "Here we are. Eight of them white."

"Do you happen to know if any of them are still in Leipzig?"

"Most, I should imagine."

"The van that interests us is not in Leipzig."

"Stolen, eh?"

"Used for an illegal purpose. So if you could remove, for example, those vans that have been serviced here."

Bedauer looked through the invoices. "Grützner . . . that's still in Leipzig. So is Dunklebeck. He's opened up a building-supply business. Doing well. And Kuhn, the flower shop. I see that one almost every day. But these five, I don't know. I'd have to check the service department, but the garage is closed."

"Could you do it in the morning?"

"Of course."

"And if, in the meantime, you could give me the names and addresses of the five?"

"Now?"

"I would be grateful."

Bedauer took out a pen and started to write, slowly and methodically, on a pad. "Telephone numbers?"

"If possible."

"They will be on Dieter's Rolodex."

"Dieter?"

"Our sales manager." Bedauer stood and went out to a desk in the showroom. He returned a few minutes later and handed the list to Gerasimov. "If you leave a number," he said, "I'll call you tomorrow when I've had a look at the service records."

"I'll be out and about," said Gerasimov. "I'll call you, if I may."

"Give me a little time."

"Around eleven?"

"Fine."

Gerasimov took a tram back to the center of Leipzig, watched the news on television in his hotel room, and then went out again to have supper in the restaurant beneath the old town hall, Auerbach's Cellar. This too brought back memories of his study of Goethe's *Faust;* however, he had not chosen it for its literary connotations. It was, he thought, the kind of place a tourist would choose, and so might persuade his shadow that, after they had lost him that afternoon, he had disappeared into an art gallery or a museum.

Gerasimov also wanted to find a place where he could talk to someone unobserved. The trouble with Leipzig, or any of the other cities in East Germany—or Eastern Europe, for that matter—was the homogeneity of the population. Under the Communists, it was almost as difficult to enter East Germany as to leave it. As a result, there was no national or racial diversity in the population of Leipzig. All the people you saw in the shops or the streets had the same white faces. In a local *Gaststätte,* Gerasimov would have stood out in the crowd, just as Faust and Mephistopheles had in Auerbach's cellar in Goethe's poem:

> Those two travelers coming from afar,
> Their foreign fashion tells you what they are.

He could still remember the lines. Now, as he ate roast pig's knuckle, he observed, as he had suspected, that the very celebrity of Auerbach's Cellar had drawn foreign tourists and visiting businessmen, so that no one stranger was more noticeable than any other.

While Gerasimov was eating and drinking, he concentrated on his food and his beer. It was important to savor the taste so he could take back memories to Moscow. Between courses, he opened a copy of *Der Spiegel,* sometimes reading the magazine, sometimes studying the list of names, addresses, and telephone numbers he had been given by Bedauer.

Two of them were commercial enterprises, three private individuals. Rather than wait for Bedauer to look at the service records, he could try telephoning the private buyers that evening on the pretext that he was looking for a secondhand van. The chances were good that this would reveal whether or not it was still in Leipzig. The danger here was that the buyer who was Orlov's associate might not only lie, he would also be alerted by the inquiry and might warn Orlov that someone was on his trail. There seemed no alternative but to see each person face-to-face.

Gerasimov rose early the next morning and took a tram out to the St. Alexis Church on Philipp-Rosenthal-Strasse, built to commemorate the 22,000 Russian soldiers who died fighting Napoleon in the battle of Leipzig. But he was more interested in German launderers than in Russian glory. He walked past the premises of the St. Alexis Wäscherei, one of the two commercial premises on the list. He did not care whether or not he was being followed by the Leipzig police; one could not know what he was doing from the cursory way he glanced into the yard behind the laundry and saw bags of dirty linen being unloaded from a white Volkswagen van.

Mentally, Gerasimov crossed that name off his list. He walked on for half a mile or so, then caught a tram to a stop a short distance from 52 Giesenstrasse, the second address on his list. This was the painter and decorator, and Gerasimov expected to find a small shop. Instead it was a large apartment house; clearly the man worked from home. He went into the building. The elevator was new; an illuminated number showed it was now on the seventh floor. If Gerasimov waited, anyone following would know to which floor he had gone. Wearily, he started up the stairs.

On the thirteenth floor, he came to the flat. He rang the bell. As he waited, he heard the screaming of a child. A bedraggled woman came to the door, a sniffling one-year-old saddled on her hip.

"Is Herr Thiele here, by any chance?"

"He's out on a job."

"Ah, I was wondering . . ."

"He'll be in this evening."

"I have his address but not his number."

"OK. Hold on."

The woman went back into the flat, leaving the door ajar. Gerasimov waited. She returned with a card.

"I can't remember who gave me his name," Gerasimov began.

The child wiped its nose with the back of its hand. The mother looked restless. "He put an ad in the paper."

"Or could I have seen his name on the side of his van?"

"Perhaps."

"A white one? A Volkswagen?"

"That's right."

"That must have been it." He put the card in his pocket. "Many thanks. I'll give him a call."

By now it was eleven. Gerasimov called Bedauer from a public box.

"Yes," said Bedauer, "I've been through the records. St. Alexis Wäscherei has their van serviced here regularly. Rolf Rosegger—you can cross him off. Apparently he traded his van for a Suzuki jeep three months ago. He's a friend of one of my lads. The painter hasn't had his van serviced here; they think he may do it himself. No one knows about Dieter Bleicher or Manfred Kraus. Neither one has been back."

After thanking Herr Bedauer, Gerasimov put down the telephone, irritated that he had been told largely what he knew already. The laundry and the painter had already been crossed off his list. Rosegger was a possibility—the trade-in could be a ruse—but if he was a friend of one of Bedauer's young mechanics he was unlikely to have worked for Orlov. That left only two, Bleicher and Kraus.

Bleicher's address was out on the road to Torgau and Dresden, farther from the center of Leipzig. Gerasimov decided to tackle him first; he could call on Kraus on his way back to his hotel. He took another tram, changing several times on the way. It was almost one before he reached Bleicher's address. It turned out to be a bookshop that was closed for lunch. There was no sign of a Volkswagen van.

Gerasimov settled down in a *Gaststätte* with a glass of beer and a plate of sausage, sauerkraut, and roast potatoes. At two, he walked back to the small square in the center of the suburb, looking into one or two shopwindows before returning to Bleicher's bookshop. He sauntered past the entrance, then stopped as if something in the window had caught his eye. In point of fact, there was little on display to tempt anyone; it appeared to have been, and perhaps remained, a state-owned shop selling dusty titles from the days of the DDR.

A young woman sat on a tall stool behind the counter, tying up bundles of books with old-fashioned paper and string. She had dark untidy hair and steel-rimmed glasses.

"Is Herr Bleicher here?" asked Gerasimov.

The woman looked up. "One moment." She continued with her work, and only when the knot was tied and the loose ends of string trimmed with scissors did her attention return to Gerasimov.

"You want to see Herr Bleicher?"

"Yes."

"What about?"

"A private matter."

The woman frowned, got off her stool, and went through to a room at the back of the shop. A moment later she returned, followed by a small, balding man.

"Yes?" he asked.

"I represent Allied Insurance," said Gerasimov.

"And?"

"A white Volkswagen van was involved in an accident—"

"That has nothing to do with us," said Herr Bleicher. "It was stolen several months ago."

"Ah. When was that?"

"When was it, Lisl?" The older man turned to the young woman, who was sitting once again on her stool.

"October or November."

"Did you report it to the police?"

"Of course."

"And your insurance company?"

"Yes."

"And did you replace it with another Volkswagen van?"

"No, with a Ford. But what has that got to do with the accident?"

Gerasimov's mind was working quickly. The theft could well have been a way to cover up the fact that the van had been given to Orlov, but they would hardly have waited so long to report it. "Nothing as such," he said. "It has nothing to do with the accident, but in insurance we are always interested in whether or not claims are settled—"

"Interested! I should say so. They knocked twenty percent off the price for wear and tear when the van was almost brand new."

"Your policy was not new for old?"

"Who knows what it was? All that damn small print. If you ask me, we were better off before when we didn't have to worry about that sort of thing."

"Indeed," said Gerasimov. "My superior, Khrulev, would agree." He studied the man's face for any recognition of the name. There was none.

"Insurance, taxes," muttered Bleicher. "A fat lot of good that's done us, eh, Lisl? No one wants to read books anymore. They're all watching TV shows and videos."

"So you can't help me with the van?" asked Gerasimov.

"Help you? I thought you were meant to help us!"

"Try our company next time."

"Allied, you said? Give me your card."

"Alas, I've run out. Business is so good."

"For you, perhaps."

"You don't know where the van is at present?"

"Oh, of course. The thief sent me his name and address!"

"I'm sorry. A silly question."

"Ask the police. I filed a complaint, but they'll never find out who stole it. They never do now. They're too busy fighting the skinheads. What a mess, what a mess!"

More or less satisfied by now that the bookseller was not the man he wanted, Gerasimov began to move toward the door. "I'm sorry to have taken up your time."

"You don't want to buy a book? Something by Lenin, perhaps? We are selling his collected works at half price. Or Engels or Marx or Ulbricht? They'll be collectors' items in a year or two."

"Thank you, no. Perhaps some other time." Gerasimov fled into the street.

Gerasimov's hopes now rested on Manfred Kraus—hopes not just of finding Orlov but of getting back to the fleshpots of West Berlin. The day, starting cloudy, had now cleared. The late-afternoon sun shone on the dilapidated buildings and colorless shops passed by the tram that took him back toward the center of Leipzig. In Russia he found such shabbiness tolerable because it was familiar, and the familiar was even lovable, like an old pair of slippers; here in Germany it somehow seemed like a mirror held up to the face of the eternally slothful Slav. Gerasimov imagined a reproachful voice saying, The Romans left roads, the British left railways, but what will remain from the Russian empire?

This line of thought brought on one of Gerasimov's occasional fits of depression. East Germany had always seemed the showpiece of the eastern bloc, ahead of the Soviet Union in every way, so the shabbiness of socialist Leipzig appeared the best he could hope for from the future. If he played his cards well, he could hang on to his job and perhaps put some icing on the cake of his basic pay and conditions by doing favors here and there, or by using trips abroad to import some Western electronic goods, but he knew he would never have the vision or determination to cut loose and stay in the West as Orlov had. It was not that he had much to go back to in Moscow: the slut Ylena, a son he rarely saw, and possibly some kind of revenge from Georgi's gangster friends. But to succeed in the West, he knew, you had to be the type to get yourself out of bed in the morning; actually to work in your office rather than simply pass the time of day; to have ideas and follow them through, instead of waiting for orders and then carrying them out with only a semblance of zeal. Gerasimov could comprehend the concept of professionalism—being good at one's job as an end in itself—but initiative was another matter. It was not the sort of quality a Russian had in his bones.

As he pursued Orlov, Gerasimov grew increasingly convinced that his quarry must have foreign blood. It was not like a Russian to sustain a covert scam over so long a period of time. The émigrés after the Revolution had mostly settled passively in the big cities of Western Europe and America, working as waiters and taxi drivers or, if they were lucky and had an aristocratic name, marrying an indigenous heiress. The only Russians to have made their fortunes were the Russian Jews. Perhaps Orlov had some Jewish or German blood, like Lenin.

Gerasimov changed trams at the railway station on the Platz der Republik. Avoiding surveillance was almost second nature to him, which in itself, had he thought about it, might have told any surveillant that he was not what he seemed. But the chances were that Kessler suspected it already. It did not matter; what was important was to find Orlov before they did. He got off the second tram on the Petersteinweg, a block from his destination, which he then approached on foot by a circuitous route. Turning a street corner, he waited once again in front of a shopwindow to make sure he was not followed. Reassured, he walked down the street of tall nineteenth-century apartments, their walls still black from the soot blown from factories since the time of the Kaiser.

Even before he reached it, something caught his eye: a glint of gold that was the only color in the otherwise gloomy street. When he reached it, he found it was a small brass plaque that had caught the reflection of the setting sun. On the plaque, in black lettering, was MANFRED KRAUS, PRIVATE INVESTIGATOR.

The entrance to the office was not through the courtyard but through a door that led directly off the street. There was a bell. Gerasimov pushed it.

"Yes?" A woman's voice.

"To see Herr Kraus."

There was a short silence, then, "Have you an appointment?"

"Unfortunately, no."

Another silence. "What is it about?"

"A personal matter."

"Your name?"

"Kessler."

"One moment."

Gerasimov waited. Then came a buzzing and the door clicked open. He walked up some steps and came to a second door just as it was opened by a small, frumpish, middle-aged woman. She nodded, stood back to let him enter, pointed to a faded blue sofa, and asked him to wait.

Gerasimov did as he was told. The woman returned to her seat behind a desk and continued to type on a heavy manual typewriter. When she had finished, she put the letter into a folder and then stood to put the carbon copy in one of the brown filing cabinets behind her desk. Gerasimov noticed that the drawer ran easily and with a rumble, as if it was empty. It seemed likely that if Kraus was a private detective he had not been in business for long.

The furniture in the office was familiar. The desk and the cupboards had the same beech veneer found in the offices of every state enterprise from the river Elbe to the Sea of Japan. The green plastic telephone had an old-fashioned dial, and the heavy plastic intercom with black cloth over the speaker might have been a radio from before World War II.

There was a click, and from the speaker came a man's voice. "Please ask Herr Kessler to come in."

The frumpish secretary got to her feet, beckoned to Gerasimov, and opened the door to the inner office. Gerasimov smiled to thank her; she did not smile back.

A tall man, over fifty and wearing a suit, rose reluctantly from behind his desk. He did not offer to shake hands but, as the secretary closed the door behind him, pointed to a chair, saying, "Please sit down." The impression he gave was of a busy doctor seeing a tiresome patient at the end of a difficult day. The pedantic, mildly irascible expression on his otherwise unexceptional features, together with his neatly trimmed gray-flecked hair and rimless spectacles, led Gerasimov to promote him

209

from general practitioner to hospital consultant; had one passed him in the street, one might also have taken him for a company director or senior civil servant. The only anomaly Gerasimov noticed was an underlying nervousness that contradicted his authoritative manner, which in turn seemed inappropriate in this two-room office on a back street in Leipzig.

"How can I help you, Herr Kessler?" Kraus asked.

"I was wondering whether you could undertake some investigative work on behalf of a client?"

Kraus had a ballpoint pen poised over a pad. "You are . . ."

"Acting for this client."

"A company?"

"Yes."

"Named?"

"Khrulev."

Kraus hesitated for a second too long before noting down and repeating the name Khrulev. "And what is the nature of the investigation?"

"We wish to find a vehicle."

Kraus frowned. "Perhaps the police—"

"A white Volkswagen van, purchased here in Leipzig in July 1991."

In the fading light of the afternoon, it was difficult to see the expression on Kraus's face.

"More important," said Gerasimov, "there is also a man—"

Kraus held up his hand. Gerasimov stopped.

"Ah, yes, I remember," said Kraus. "You wrote to me about it. Let me find your letter." He scrawled on the pad, then turned it to face Gerasimov: *Don't talk here.* "Here we are. Yes. Your client, if I am not mistaken, owns a Bulgarian import-export agency which formerly bought shoes from a factory in Weissenfels—"

"Correct," said Gerasimov, writing on the pad *Auerbach's Cellar, 7 P.M.* He turned it to face Kraus.

"After the change from reichsmark to deutsche mark, the shoes became too expensive for the Bulgarian market, but their quality was not sufficiently high for the Western market. As a result the factory closed down."

Kraus scrawled on the pad *This is madness—I am watched.* He turned it back to face Gerasimov and pointed to the outer office.

"As far as I remember," he went on, "your client offered a Volkswagen van to pay for the residual stock, and while the management took possession of the Volkswagen, they were unable to deliver the shoes because in the meantime the factory had been taken over by the Treuhand organization."

"Quite correct," said Gerasimov, pushing the pad back to Kraus, having merely underlined his original message: *Auerbach's Cellar, 7 P.M.*

Kraus shrugged. "Very well. We will see what we can do."

"I would be most grateful."

"I shall make some calls. We can talk later."

"Many thanks."

Both men stood up. "By the way," said Kraus. "I had heard that your managing director was . . . not well."

"That is true. Herr Khrulev is indisposed. But the new management is still most interested in the business in hand."

"Of course."

As Kraus escorted Gerasimov to the door of the outer office, the secretary remained at her desk.

"Thank you for calling."

"Thank you for receiving me without an appointment."

"I am the one who has been remiss."

"I look forward to hearing from you."

The young Leipzig detective greeted Gerasimov in the lobby of his hotel. "Good evening, Herr Inspector. I just called on the off chance that there was something you would like me to do."

"Thank you, no."

"Inspector Kessler telephoned to ask whether you had made any progress."

"Disappointing. It has been disappointing. One or two leads, but they have led nowhere. In fact, there is nothing more I can do in Leipzig. I shall return to Berlin in the morning."

"Would you like me to make a reservation?"

"That would be kind. A midmorning train."

"And this evening? Can I offer you our hospitality?"

"Thank you, no. I must read the material provided by Inspector Kessler. I'll grab something to eat in the hotel or in town."

"Very well." The young man bowed and clicked his heels. "I shall come in the morning with your reservation."

"Many thanks."

Back in his room, Gerasimov took off his jacket and shoes and lay down on his bed. What line should he take with Kraus? Clearly, he had been one of Khrulev's agents and had provided the van for Orlov. What else had he done for Orlov? What had been his cover at the time? The shiny new plaque and the empty drawers of the filing cabinet suggested that he had not been a private detective for long. Nor did he look like a man who had spent his life on petty investigations. His manner was too imperious; he was a man who was used to command.

An executive? Not under socialism. An army officer? Too cunning. The speed with which he had concocted the story about the shoes in Weissenfels had impressed Gerasimov. Here was a man accustomed to thinking on his feet. Why was he watched? And by whom? If his cover was blown as a Soviet agent, he would not have been afraid to mention Khrulev. It seemed more likely that he had worked for the Stasi under East Germany's Communist regime.

That was it! Kraus must have been an Eleventh Department agent within the Stasi, probably recruited by Khrulev and answerable to the general alone. To recover the icons, Khrulev could not trust ordinary KGB channels; too many agents had done business with Maslyukov. The team had been Orlov, Partovski, and the Chechen, with Kraus providing support in the field. By then the Stasi had been disbanded, and Kraus, starting up as a private investigator, would have been under some kind of surveillance. But even if Kraus had been an officer in the Stasi, there had been so many Stasi operatives it was unlikely that a close watch would be kept on him. Probably it was left to the secretary to make reports to the BfV. He could understand now why Kraus had been afraid to talk. It was one thing to have been in the Stasi, quite another to have spied for the KGB.

What approach should Gerasimov employ? Quite possibly Kraus had held a commission in the old KGB, with a higher rank than Gerasimov's. Was he still committed, or was he keen to end that chapter of his life? Had he helped Orlov in obedience to an order from Khrulev? If so, would he be prepared to take orders from the new Security Service of the Russian Federation? Or was he a hard-liner who still shared Khrulev's Communist zeal? Would Gerasimov have to blackmail him with the threat of exposure, or simply rely on the man's Prussian sense of duty to accept that, with Khrulev dead, Savchenko was now in command?

As Gerasimov had observed, most of his fellow guests in Auerbach's Cellar were tourists or businessmen from outside Saxony: some from western Germany, others from farther afield. There was a group of Italians and an American couple with two bored adolescent children.

Gerasimov chose a table between the Italians and the Americans. Promptly at seven, Kraus came down the steps in the restaurant, looked around as if looking for a spare table, came up to Gerasimov, and said, "Do you mind if I sit here?"

"Please."

Kraus sat down and studied the menu. "If we are watched," he said softly, "we will fool no one."

Gerasimov nodded and leaned forward, as if to introduce himself. "Whoever watches you may not know me, and whoever watches me may not know you."

Kraus nodded. "We can only hope so."

The waiter came. "Together or separate?" he asked.

"Separate," said Kraus.

They ordered and sat in silence until the waiter returned with two glasses of beer. Then, as if they were indeed two solitary businessmen, Gerasimov began talking, at one point opening his copy of *Time* to point to an article, as if it had something to say about the issue under discussion. "There are changes in Moscow," he said to Kraus as he did so.

"So I read."

"Khrulev is dead."

"Yes."

"His place has been taken by General Savchenko."

Kraus said nothing.

"You are to answer to him."

This last remark was a gamble but it seemed to pay off. "You must explain to the general," said Kraus, "that my position is precarious. Mielke is under arrest. Wolf is also insecure. Either of them could expose me to improve their own chances. They are prosecuting officers who gave orders to shoot fugitives trying to escape over the Wall. And my links with the Dzerzhinski brigade are already known."

"But they have not prosecuted you?"

"No. By and large, Stasi officers are being left to their own devices. No pension, of course, even though they honored the Nazis' pension commitments after the war—"

"Scandalous."

"But the files in the Runscestrasse still exist. There is no knowing what they may find there."

"It will take them years to sort through those."

"I know. And my links with Moscow will not appear in those files. Only Mielke knew, and perhaps Wolf. But General Savchenko should understand that there is little I can do now for Moscow, and really the risk I run in performing an auxiliary logistical role, as I did that July, is out of all proportion to the value of the service."

"I understand."

"Khrulev offered me a post in Moscow, but I have a wife and children here in Germany. Moving to Leipzig from Berlin was bad enough for them; they certainly do not want to move to Moscow. But if I remain here, it is imperative that contacts be kept to a minimum, if not terminated altogether. If the BfV ever discover the connection with the Lubyanka, they could put me under great pressure. A charge of treason is not unknown—as a means of persuasion, you understand, to tell all I know. That is why a meeting like this is so dangerous to everyone concerned."

Ah, thought Gerasimov; he is trying to put a little pressure on me to leave him alone. "I am here for two reasons," he said. "The first is to reassure you that your past services are not forgotten, and will not be forgotten, by the new Security Service of the Russian Federation."

"It would be better—"

Gerasimov raised his hand. "Let me finish. Your past services are not forgotten, but any future participation is a matter for you to decide."

A look of great relief came onto Kraus's face. "It would be infinitely preferable for me simply to be left alone."

"Of course. That is what we supposed. Which brings me to the second point. The help you gave to Comrade Orlov two years ago was much appreciated, but his more recent demands are quite unauthorized."

Kraus turned pale. "Unauthorized? He told me he was acting under orders."

"Whose orders?"

"Khrulev's."

"Khrulev is dead."

"I know that now. But not then."

"No one will hold you responsible," said Gerasimov slowly, "if you can help us to limit the damage."

"The damage?"

"Where is Orlov?"

"I don't know."

"What is he doing?"

"I don't know."

"What did he want from you?"

"Names."

"Whose names?"

"Names of men, former officers and men in the Dzerzhinski brigade whom he could recruit for an operation."

"What operation?"

"He didn't say."

"Did you give him these names?"

"Yes, two. An officer and a sergeant."

"How did you choose them?"

"For their commitment, their zeal, and their loyalty to the Soviet cause. It was my job at the Runscestrasse to know who was ideologically sound."

"Did you contact them?"

"No."

"Did he?"

"I believe so."

"Why?"

"I was called by one for confirmation."

"Of what?"

"His credentials."

"From where?"

"Bautzen."

"What did Orlov want them for?"

"I don't know."

Gerasimov frowned. "He must have given you some idea of what he had in mind."

Kraus looked perplexed. "It was not customary to ask questions. I simply obeyed orders."

"If they *were* orders."

"Two months earlier, he had been sent by Khrulev. I assumed the general had sent him again."

"Two men," Gerasimov repeated. "What on earth could he want with two men?"

"I believe two was only the start. He intended to call upon the two to recruit more."

"Up to how many?"

"Twenty or thirty. I am not sure."

"Did he propose to pay them?"

"I don't know. He appeared to have ample funds at his disposal, but the quality he looked for was not venality but commitment. He realized there were still some who remain dedicated to the Communist cause."

"What were the names of the two men?"

Kraus hesitated. "I have destroyed the file. It was too dangerous for me to keep it."

"Can you remember them?"

"The names, but not the addresses." He took out a note pad and started to write them down.

"He told you nothing about the operation or about who was involved?"

"I assumed it was the same team as before."

"Partovski? The Chechen?"

"I never knew their names."

"Anyone else?"

Again Kraus hesitated. "He was in touch with someone with the code name Chameleon."

"Who is Chameleon?"

"An unofficial collaborator of our state security who also worked for Khrulev, but not under my control."

"Do you know his real identity?"

"No. But I got the impression from Orlov that it was someone now in a position of some influence."

"But surely his cover is blown?"

"No."

"His file?"

"It has gone."

"Who saw to that?"

"According to Orlov, Chameleon saw to it himself."

"A clever fellow."

"Not clever enough. Orlov could prove he had been controlled by Khrulev, so Chameleon had no choice but to cooperate."

"Orlov blackmailed him?"

Kraus shrugged. "In effect."

The two men had finished with their food. Kraus's was mostly uneaten.

"Another beer?" asked Gerasimov. "Dessert? Coffee?"

"I had better go," said Kraus. "My wife will be expecting me. I told her only that I was working late."

Gerasimov called the waiter to pay the bill. "If any of the opposition should ask you about Orlov, say nothing."

"And if they ask me about you?"

"I was after the consignment of shoes from Weissenfels. They might even believe it."

The two men rose to go. "When you saw Orlov that second time, had his appearance changed?"

"No. I don't think so. A little unkempt, perhaps."

"What do you mean?"

"My daughter tells me it is now in fashion."

"What?"

"The unshaven look. Designer stubble, I believe it is called."

16

As the day approached for his great patriotic gesture, Colonel Nogin grew increasingly ill at ease. Keminski's nephew, Perfilyev, had come back to the base at Waldheim three or four times. Nogin had been delighted to see him, not least because he always arrived with a case of vodka, but five months after their first meeting he did not feel he knew him any better or could altogether trust him. Perfilyev was intelligent, amusing, and a good listener—qualities of value to a bored veteran of the Great Patriotic War—but, while the colonel had told Perfilyev everything there was to know about himself, his visitor had given away very little. He was also one of those men who make others feel that it is somehow improper to inquire, so Nogin did not feel he could ask Perfilyev, for example, how he obtained the deutsche marks to buy the vodka or the chocolates and other delicacies that he always brought for the officers' wives.

Nogin knew well enough that everyone involved in the dismantling of the Soviet military machine in East Germany was making what he could out of it, from the private soldier who sold his cap to the nuclear engineer who hawked plutonium from the trunk of a car, so it would not have surprised him if he had learned that Perfilyev, despite his denunciation of corrupt reformers, had some deutsche-mark-earning scams on the side. Such contradictions had always been part of the Soviet way of life, and if he had suggested to Nogin some modest scheme for selling surplus weapons systems to Third World countries, or tanks for scrap, as a way of bolstering the colonel's pension when he finally retired, Nogin would have been happier than he was with his promise to destroy highly secret equipment from Jena.

Of course Nogin recognized that there was a world of difference between selling weapons to Arabs or Africans to kill one another and selling sophisticated systems to the potential enemies of Russia. For this reason he did not intend to renege on his commitment to place the base at Perfilyev's disposal, even though he could reasonably argue that he had been drunk when the promise was made. But the whole plan made him feel uneasy. If schemes to raise currency were uncovered, the money could be used to escape the consequences; where the rewards were purely political, noble motives would not save one from the Lefortovo prison.

There were other reasons for Nogin's unease. The first was that the scale of the thing was greater than he had been led to expect. Perfilyev now talked of several van loads of equipment arriving on a single night. The second was the sense the colonel had gained, for no particular reason, that it would be less dangerous now to proceed than to change his mind. He had always known that the engineers working for the Ministry of Medium Machine Building might be more than they seemed, but the mystery surrounding Perfilyev had taken on an element of menace. He did not give the impression of being a man who would take kindly to being thwarted.

The third reason was the realization that there were others in Jena besides Perfilyev who were involved. On the last two occasions that he had come to Waldheim, Perfilyev had been accompanied by a Chechen. As a rule, Nogin disliked Chechens, along with Azerbaijanis, Armenians, Georgians, and Jews. He had to tolerate them—many of his troops now came from the Muslim republics of the Russian Federation—but he never trusted them. Behind the shifty expression in their narrow Asiatic eyes lay centuries of resentment of Russian rule.

Nogin realized that his visitor may have had to bring the Chechen into the conspiracy because it would be dangerous to leave him out. Perfilyev introduced him as a friend and fellow engineer, working on the same project in Jena, but he did not look like an engineer to the colonel; nor did the two men behave as if they were friends.

Nogin had left the detailed arrangements for the operation to Captain Sinyanski; it had occurred to him that if the whole affair blew up in their faces, Sinyanski would make a suitable scapegoat because of his earlier links with the KGB. Nogin could argue that he had cooperated at the request of Sinyanski, who had led him to believe that the operation had been authorized by the Security Service of the Russian Federation.

It became apparent, however, that Sinyanski was thinking along the same lines. After the last visit of Perfilyev and the Chechen, the captain had reported to Nogin that Perfilyev had changed his instructions; the machinery was not to be destroyed on arrival but was to be hidden in the empty hangars pending Perfilyev's further instructions. Sinyanski pointed out to Nogin that this increased the risk; ashes could be scattered, but what was hidden could later be found. He insisted that Nogin decide whether or not to go ahead with these new arrangements.

Nogin reached for his telephone but then remembered that he had neither an address nor a number for Perfilyev. Should he call Keminski in Moscow? It seemed too risky. He told Sinyanski they would have to wait until Perfilyev returned.

Sinyanski now raised another odd aspect of the whole matter, already noticed by Nogin—the apparent disharmony between Perfilyev and his Chechen friend. On their last visit they had stayed with Sinyanski; he was not married and had two spare rooms. After the two visitors had supposedly retired to their respective rooms for the night, Sinyanski had overheard some acrimonious exchanges in Perfilyev's bedroom. He had picked up only scraps of their conversation and from them had gained the impression that they were quarreling about some woman.

Nogin laughed and felt relieved. The best of friends could quarrel about a woman. But Sinyanski went on to add some other words that he had picked up through the wall of his bedroom: "CIA . . . jeopardy . . . if necessary . . . the whole enterprise," spoken by the Chechen, interspersed with Perfilyev's mollifying "Of course, of course."

"And there is something else," said Sinyanski. "When they were arguing, the Chechen addressed Perfilyev not as Piotr Petrovich but as Andrei Anatolyevich, which leads me to suspect that quite possibly he is not the man you suppose."

Nogin remonstrated. Sinyanski must have misheard. Perfilyev had been sent to him by Keminski, Nogin's old comrade-in-arms. But the more he heard, the less he liked it, and he started to chide Sinyanski for getting them involved.

Sinyanski reminded his commander politely that it was he who had introduced Perfilyev and who had agreed to destroy the equipment on the base, at which Nogin exploded, blaming all the misery and misfortune of his country on the machinations and skulduggery of chekists and Jews. But before Sinyanski left, he had calmed down. The two men were in this together, and neither saw any alternative but to see it through.

V

1993
June–July

17

Four days before the hanging of the Excursus exhibition was to start, Andrei Serotkin told Francesca that he had to fly back to Moscow because his father had suffered a stroke. This was not a catastrophe so far as the exhibition was concerned; he had never shown much interest in the hanging. It was sad for Francesca but she did not complain. She knew Serotkin was close to his father and could see that he was anxious. He promised to return to Berlin as soon as he could, almost certainly for the official opening in the Old Museum by President von Weizsäcker and definitely by July 14, Bastille Day.

For the rest of that week, Francesca was kept busy at the office. There were no other crises. The invitations had gone out: for the reception to be held by the City of Berlin following the opening and for the more exclusive lunch at the New National Gallery the next day. All the works of art were ready in the OZF warehouse for distribution to the two galleries on the following Monday morning. The first finished copies of the catalog came into the office on Friday. They looked superb.

Only when Francesca awoke on Saturday did she start to pine for Serotkin. If she had had a photograph of him, she would have been able to gaze at it; as it was, she had only his toothbrush and pajamas to remind her that he was not a figment of her imagination. She lay on her bed, musing about him, tantalized as always by the residual mystery in the man whom she by now should know so well.

She recalled her first impression, that he had been dashing, reminding her of the Bulgarian patriot Insarov in Turgenev's novel *On the Eve*. She went into her living room, took the book from the shelf, and started to reread it. She laughed when she came to the passage where one of the characters, Bersenyev, comes to see the heroine, Elena, saying, "Fancy, our Insarov has disappeared."

"Disappeared?" said Elena.
"He has disappeared. The day before yesterday he went off somewhere and nothing has been seen of him since."
"He did not tell you where he was going?"
"No."

This could well have been an exchange between Günter Westarp and Francesca. She also smiled when she reached the scene where on a picnic a drunken German who pesters the ladies is thrown into the river by Insarov. A prophetic passage, thought Francesca, if you set the scene in Berlin's Englischer Garten and replace the German with three Turks.

She read on and was struck by other similarities that made her feel her love for Serotkin had in some strange fashion followed the same pattern as Elena's love for Insarov. Andrei was as mysterious as Insarov and had the same sense of dedication to a greater purpose, even if it was not clear what that purpose was. When Insarov tells Elena that he must go and fight for his country's independence, she volunteers to go with him. When he falls ill, she goes to visit him. And when he is still weak, they make love just as she and Serotkin had done.

It was extraordinary, now that she reread the novel, how many similarities there were between the fictional and the real situations. Then she frowned. How did it end? Stopping, briefly, to make herself some lunch, she raced through the pages. On the broad lagoon separating Venice from the narrow strip of accumulated sea sand called the Lido, Elena and Insarov lie in a gondola. In Insarov there is a cruel change:

He had grown thin, old, pale and bent: he was constantly coughing a short dry cough, and his sunken eyes shone with a strange brilliance.

Consumption, thought Francesca, munching an apple: the AIDS of the day. They go to the opera in Venice. Insarov grows weaker.

It's all over . . . I'm dying. Good-bye, my poor girl, good-bye, my country.

Elena sends for the doctor. The doctor comes. "Signora, the foreign gentleman is dead."

Francesca shuddered. That was not how *their* story would end. Soon they would return to the Soviet War Memorial and make a commitment to each other for life. Then either she would go to Russia with Andrei or he would change his mind about leaving his country in the lurch and return to America with her. The first solution was the more romantic, the second the more practical. Francesca was not sure what she would do in Moscow, or how they would live on a salary paid in rubles. Nor did she like the sound of Russian obstetrics; she took it for granted that they would want a child.

Knowing that Serotkin was away, Sophie Diederich invited Francesca to supper that Saturday evening, a small private celebration for the creators of Excursus now that the donkeywork was done. "Everyone said it was impossible," said Sophie, "but we did it, and it would be nice to have one last quiet evening together—just you, Günter, Stefi, and me—before all the public celebrations begin."

Francesca felt a little sad that Serotkin's name was not included in this inner circle, but she had to concede that it had no right to be there. She also acknowledged that if it had not been for Stefi and Sophie, she would not have been chosen to organize Excursus, and if she had not been so chosen, she would not have met Andrei Serotkin. For this, she owed the Diederichs at least one last tedious evening at their flat in the Wedekindstrasse.

Francesca felt mildly ashamed that she now found the Diederichs a bore, and as she drove across Berlin that evening she tried to analyze why it was so. Undoubtedly Andrei was part of the reason; the bright light that shines from one's lover always makes others seem dim. Stefi could be witty and undoubtedly had a lively mind, but Francesca still found him insubstantial and unconvincing. She realized that politicians were inevitably insincere, but Stefi gave the impression that he was untrustworthy through and through. It was partly this that had led to her growing exasperation with dear, sweet, slightly stupid Sophie: how could she love so uncritically a patent shyster, particularly when she had been married to a man like Paul?

Perhaps in a way Paul had been to blame. His very nobility had encouraged in Sophie the kind of hero worship that came naturally to the traditional German wife. When Paul had had his nervous breakdown, showing he had weaknesses too, Sophie had simply transferred her loyalties to the understudy waiting in the wings.

The memory of Paul gave Francesca a twinge of guilt. She thought of him, she realized, as if he were either dead or locked up in a lunatic asylum, when in fact he was alive and an evangelical pastor at Bechtling, a village only an hour or two's drive from Berlin. Why had she not been to see him? She had been too busy. Then, when the work eased up, there had been Andrei. At the back of her mind, a niggling prick of conscience told her that if Paul had been in a position to further her career, she would certainly have found time to pay him a visit. Now, with the hanging starting on Monday, followed two weeks later by the opening of the exhibition and God knew what thereafter, she wondered whether she would ever get to see him unless she drove out to Bechtling the next day.

Stefi was drunk. This surprised Francesca, because she had never seen him drunk before. Sophie tried to cover it up as soon as Francesca arrived by whispering that her husband was "in a filthy mood," but what was wrong was quite apparent from Stefi's bloodshot eyes and slightly slurred speech, as well as the glass of vodka in his hand.

"So, the American," he said as soon as he saw Francesca, bowing with an ironic flourish. "So elegant, as always, as befits a princess from the triumphant superpower."

Francesca frowned. She had, in fact, dressed down (black trousers, a blue shirt); if her wardrobe lacked the versatility to plumb the depths reached by Günter Westarp, who sat despondently on the sofa, it was hardly the costume of a princess.

She decided to rise above the irony and try to make her mood match his. "Forget the super*power*, Stefi. Let's drink to the super*man*, Stefan Diederich, who has done what everyone said could not be done: planning and staging a major exhibition in under a year."

"Thank you." He bowed again, then lurched to the bar on the sideboard. "You will drink vodka, yes? We are all drinking vodka here."

"I'd rather have a glass of white wine."

"So you have a taste for Russians, but not for Russian drink."

"Stefi!" said Sophie.

Francesca laughed. "Oddly enough, Andrei doesn't drink that much."

"Most dangerous," said Stefi. "A Russian who doesn't drink." He handed Francesca a glass of white wine.

"Why?"

"A symptom of megalomania."

"I don't get it."

Stefi refilled his glass with vodka. "A man who conquers his own weaknesses thinks he can conquer the world. Look at Lenin, Stalin, Gandhi—"

"Gandhi was hardly a conqueror."

"On the contrary. He thought he could conquer the forces of evil, like that megalomaniac of all megalomaniacs, Christ."

"Phooey," said Sophie. "You're just trying to justify getting drunk."

"What was it Caesar said? 'Let me have men about me that are fat; sleek-headed men, and such as sleep o' nights.' Does he sleep o' nights, Francesca?"

"Stefan," Sophie scolded again. "You go too far!"

"He sleeps very well, thank you," said Francesca.

"But he is not fat?"

"No. As a matter of fact, he is exceptionally fit."

"*Exceptionally* fit! Have you never paused to wonder why?"

"I guess he feels better that way."

"And can dispose of Turkish rapists just like that." Stefi gave an impression of a kung fu fighter, spilling the vodka he held in his hand.

"It certainly came in useful."

" 'Would he were fatter,' " said Stefi.

"Why?"

" 'Such men as he are never at heart's ease while they behold a greater than themselves, and therefore are they very dangerous.' "

Francesca frowned. She knew Stefi disliked Russians in general and Serotkin in particular, but that was no reason to bad-mouth him in her presence. "I don't think Andrei is dangerous," she said.

"Why should he be dangerous?" asked Sophie.

Stefi turned to Westarp. "Why should he be dangerous, Günter? Tell us."

Günter looked at him mournfully. "You tell me, Stefi. You always know best."

This jibe seemed to annoy their host. "Know best? How can one know best? We either know or we don't know, and what we know often turns out to be lies. First it is socialism and the dictatorship of the proletariat; then it is capitalism and democracy. What can we do, Günter, but be picked up and blown hither and thither by the strongest gust of wind?"

Günter did not answer.

"Gloomy riddles," said Sophie. "We are meant to be celebrating, and all we get are these gloomy riddles. Well, let's eat and see if some food won't improve our morale."

Sophie's veal fricassee and potato dumplings had a sobering effect on her husband and improved the mood of Günter Westarp. Over strudel and coffee, Günter even made a short speech saying that, "whatever the outcome," he felt privileged to have been associated with Excursus and in particular to have worked alongside Francesca McDermott. Her example had taught him how professionalism and hard work could be combined with courtesy and charm. He raised his glass, the Diederichs following, and drank to her.

Feeling ashamed of the contempt she had felt for Günter, Francesca replied to the toast, saying how working on Excursus had changed the course of her life, not just professionally but also from a human point of view (giggles from Sophie). Stefan had taught her how an artistic phenomenon could be turned into a political message that would enlighten and inspire the nations of Eastern Europe, dispossessed by communism of their culture and tradition; Günter had shown how the indomitable spirit of a single man could survive decades of intellectual oppression in one of the most efficient totalitarian states known to history. The lights had seemed to go out behind the Iron Curtain, but small, flickering flames had remained alight in men and women like Stefi, Sophie, and Günter Westarp, and only a small spark was needed to ignite the spiritual conflagration represented by the works of art now in the Excursus exhibition, the greatest collection of modern Russian painting that the world had ever seen.

It was overdone, and Francesca's images got a little out of hand, but her speech led Sophie to clap her hands and Günter to mumble, "Thank you, thank you," as a big tear ran down his cheeks into the brush of his Günter Grass mustache.

For a moment Stefi remained silent, his head bowed, his eyes staring down at the table. Then he looked up. "Excellent," he said. "You must make such a speech at the opening of Excursus. When I am in Bonn I shall make sure you are included in the program. *Spiritual conflagration*. I like that. Von Weizsäcker will like it too."

At nine the next morning, Francesca set out in her car to visit Paul Meissner. She had not told Sophie or forewarned Paul; since it was a Sunday, she felt reasonably certain that she would find the pastor at Bechtling. The traffic was light. She quickly reached Neuruppin and then drove north to Dierberg, where she turned off onto a side road that led through beautiful forests and past numerous small lakes. A second turn took her out of the forests into vast pastures with large herds of cows.

The brick church at Bechtling was visible a mile or two away, its pointed black spire like a witch's hat. When Francesca reached the village, she felt saddened that a man who had held such promise should now live in such an obscure parish, ministering to the needs of peasants from the local collective farm. She stopped her car in the village square, embarrassed that it should seem so conspicuous beside two shabby Trabants and a rusty Skoda. There was no one in sight to ask for directions to the house of the pastor. The single shop was closed, and there was no café or *Gaststätte*. She looked at her watch; it was twenty to eleven. The pastor was probably in church.

When Francesca opened its huge creaking door, a dozen people in the congregation all turned to look at the intruder. She almost fled, but in the pulpit above the row of gnarled faces she saw one that she knew; Paul was preaching. Seeing her, he stopped in mid-sentence and said, "Please come in." He smiled; he had recognized her. She sat down in the back pew and Paul continued his sermon.

Francesca could not concentrate on what he was saying because she was too shaken by the change in his appearance. He had aged twice the number of years that had passed since she had last seen him. Yet despite his lined face and gray hair, she saw how much the boy she had seen at the Diederichs' looked like him and realized how hard it must be to have been separated from his children.

Paul was preaching about love and forgiveness—a predictable homily, perhaps, but a controversial message in a once-Communist country where the victims were now the victors. It was up to God to punish the wicked for their sins, he said; it was Christ, not man, who should judge the living and the dead. Vengeance is mine, says the Lord. I will repay.

When the sermon ended, Paul came down from the pulpit and went to the altar. Francesca, who generally only entered a church for the odd funeral or wedding, did not know when to kneel or sit or stand, but neither, it seemed, did most of the congregation, and since she sat at the back, her confusion was hardly noticed.

At the end of the service, they sang a hymn. Again, few of those present appeared to know either the music or the words. There was no organ, and the only voice that guided them was that of the pastor himself, far stronger than his enfeebled appearance would lead one to suppose.

The hymn over, the villagers shuffled out of the church, glancing slyly at Francesca as they passed her. Paul Meissner had left the altar, and Francesca thought perhaps she should go around to the back of the church to intercept him as he left, but as she rose from her seat he came out of the sacristy wearing gray trousers, a shirt, and a sweater. When he reached her, he smiled again. "Come," he said, putting his arm around her to lead her out of the church.

He closed the door with a large key and set off toward the village, Francesca walking beside him. "I had hoped to see you," he said. "I heard that you were in Berlin."

"I have been arranging an exhibition."

"Yes. Excursus. I look forward to it."

"It was thanks to Sophie—"

"And Stefi. I know."

"I wanted to see you, but we became so busy. . . ."

"Of course. That doesn't matter. For God, a day is the same as a year and a year the same as a day. So long as you remembered me."

"How could I forget?"

"*You* could forget, I am sure. There must have been many other things going on in your life."

"Nothing like that year in Berlin."

"You saw us at our best. After you left . . ." He laughed. "Not *because* you left but *after* you left we were not quite so heroic."

"You fell ill."

"Is that what you heard?"

"Yes, that you had a nervous breakdown."

Paul nodded. "I suppose you could call it that."

They came to a low one-story house indistinguishable from any of the others in the village. Paul led Francesca into the narrow hallway. There was the smell of cooking.

"I don't want to impose myself," said Francesca.

"My mother will be expecting you," he said. "She saw you in church."

They walked down the short hallway to the kitchen. A frail old woman stood at the stove, a look of suffering and distinction on her thin, pale face.

"Mother," said Paul, "this is my American friend from ten years ago, Francesca McDermott."

Frau Meissner wiped her hands on her apron and reached forward to greet Francesca. "Paul has often spoken about you," she said.

"I am so sorry to surprise you like this."

"We are delighted. Our life is usually rather quiet."

"I didn't mean to turn up for lunch."

"It is an old tradition," said Paul, "to cook enough for the unexpected guest."

He turned and led Francesca back into the small living room of the little house. At once Francesca recognized some of the furniture and pictures from the flat in the Wedekindstrasse ten years before.

"Do the children visit you?" asked Francesca.

"Yes, from time to time. They find Bechtling a little dull."

"It must have been hard to lose them."

"Of course. But in the DDR, given who I was, I could not hope to win custody."

"And you were not well."

Paul hesitated. "I was not perhaps quite as ill as some people thought at the time."

"Sophie said you were in a clinic."

"Yes, that is certainly true. But we have now discovered that some clinics in the DDR were not there to help their patients get well."

Francesca looked puzzled. "I read something about harassment—"

"The Stasi had a way of dealing with dissidents which they called *Zersetzung*. It was a program for the annihilation of anyone who opposed the regime. They preferred not to arrest us or imprison us; that earned them bad publicity and produced martyrs. They preferred to wear us down with petty privations and above all to demoralize us so that we would lose faith in ourselves. We know this now because we have had access to their files."

"Have you seen your file?" asked Francesca.

"I will come to that in a minute." Paul had always had a slightly pedagogic manner. "At the time, we had no idea of how thoroughly we were being manipulated by the Stasi. Every now and then, I would be called in for questioning and threatened with prosecution for speaking out against the state. They were particularly enraged because of my success with students, but it was difficult for them to pin anything on me because, as you will remember, I was always careful *not* to speak out against the state. I always insisted that we must render unto Caesar the things that are Caesar's, reserving for God only the things that belong to God."

"I remember."

"But they were clever at twisting what I said to make it sound seditious. What was demoralizing was not the number of times that I was called in for questioning but the discovery under interrogation that they were so well informed about what I had said. I began to feel paranoid, imagining that there were radio transmitters in our living room, our bathroom, even under our bed. The alternative—that it was not secret microphones but my closest friends who were relaying everything I said to the Stasi—seemed too dreadful to contemplate.

"I was also on my guard against disinformation. I knew the Stasi would do what they could to sow distrust in our group. It was therefore essential, in order to preserve our sanity, to be open with one another within our inner circle of friends. We sustained one another by holding prayer meetings and readings, reciting poems and stories that could not be published, and by finding work for those who lost their jobs because of their political opinions. But all the same, the pressure was sometimes intolerable. I was not given much support by my bishop. His secretary was of the opinion that we should avoid all open criticism of the regime. It now emerges from the files that the secretary was a Stasi IM—*Inoffizieller Mitarbeiter,* or unofficial collaborator—reporting back after each meeting everything I and the bishop had said.

"Inevitably the strain took its toll on our marriage. You will remember how Sophie was in those days: cheerful, brave, very loyal, but not at heart"—Paul groped to find the right word—"not much interested in intellectual or spiritual ideas. She sometimes felt, I know, that I put my conscience before my wife and family and that life would be much easier if I would only compromise with the regime.

"As you can imagine, the fear that there were radio transmitters under our bed, and perhaps cameras hidden in the walls, poisoned the physical expression of our conjugal love. I must also recognize, in view of what happened, that Sophie was always more appreciative than I was of the carnal side of our married life—something for which I, not she, was to blame. My anxiety led to long periods of abstinence which, Saint Paul warns us, permits the devil to do his work. Frustration made Sophie irritable, and her irritability made me anxious. I felt she did not support me in my work. Persuading young people to put God before the state, to prefer confirmation in the evangelical church to the Communists' pagan ceremony, the *Jugendweihe,* was setting them off on a path that would entail great suffering. It was an awesome responsibility. My nerves suffered. I slept badly and started to have persistent headaches. Sophie urged me to go to a doctor, a particular doctor, recommended by one of our closest friends.

"I believed, of course, that one should try and bear suffering as Christ bore his cross on the path to Calvary, but in the end I was persuaded. I went to see the doctor—a Dr. Friedemann—who recommended a course of pills. These made me feel worse; on top of the headaches came long periods of black depression. My inner doubts grew about my work. To my friends, you will remember, I was something of a hero, and in West Germany stories were written about me as a dissident leader and champion of democracy. This gave ammunition to the Stasi. Time and again I was brought in for questioning and threatened with prosecution and imprisonment in Hohenschönhausen or Bautzen. Time and again my bishop warned me to take care. The irony, of course—and you may remember this too—was that in my homilies to the students, I preached as vigorously against Western materialism as against Marxist materialism. I was emphatic in my criticism of the greed and injustice that sustain the market economies of the West. That further enraged the Stasi, for whom only communism could be permitted to hold the moral high ground; it also irritated visiting West Germans, and Sophie too. I would never accept gifts from Western visitors such as cigarettes or toilet water. Sophie accepted my decision—she accepted everything I said—but her morale was low because of my depressions, and she started to suggest that perhaps they had a psychological cause. So did Dr. Friedemann. He had read Freud and Jung, which was unusual in the DDR, and thought that perhaps I lived in the shadow of my father, that I drove myself too hard to win his approval, or perhaps to do better than he had done to win my mother's love. To me this was nonsense, but Sophie thought there might be something in it, and so did our friend, that closest friend, the one who had recommended Dr. Friedemann. They urged me to trust Friedemann, so when he suggested that I go for treatment to a clinic, I agreed.

"There, dear Francesca, there—" Paul stopped. His face, which until then had held the benign expression of a patient teacher, became twisted for a moment as if the memory rekindled some kind of terror.

"There I was given a course of injections, supposedly part of a therapy which—" He shook his head. "I cannot describe the effect those drugs had on my mind. When I slept, I had grotesque nightmares; when I awoke, they continued and if anything became worse. I was pursued, tormented; my anxieties grew out of all proportion. I began to fear there were microphones hidden in my pillows and mattress, so I took a knife and tried to cut them to shreds. They put me in a strait-jacket and tied me to the bed. I raved. I was deranged. But all the while I kept a kernel of sanity, not by thinking of liberty or democracy or the church or even of God, but by remembering Sophie and the children. It was for them that I was determined to pull through.

"When the course of injections came to an end, the nightmares ceased and I became calm. Whatever fears remained, I kept to myself. All I wanted was to go home. In time, they agreed. A date was fixed. They said that Sophie had been informed and had arranged for a friend from Leipzig to come and fetch me in his car. He drove me back to Berlin and carried my small overnight bag up the stairs to our flat. He had a key—many of our friends had a key—and we went in. It seemed to be empty. The door to our bedroom was ajar. I pushed it open. On our bed was a naked couple making love, Sophie and our closest friend."

"Stefi?"

"Yes. Stefan Diederich."

"And the man who brought you to the house?"

"The friend from Leipzig? Günter Westarp."

Francesca was silent. She could think of nothing to say. The story Paul had told, and told with such conviction and apparent pain, was not only horrifying in itself but quite as terrible in its implications. "But does that mean that Sophie was working for the Stasi?"

"Sophie? No. She was weak but innocent."

"But Stefan? And Günter?"

"I don't know."

"In your file—"

"My file has not been found. Nor has a file been found as yet for Stefan or Günter, even though the three of us were prominent dissidents."

"Why not?"

"It seems that someone removed them in good time."

"But who? And why?"

"When the regime collapsed, gangs of skinheads broke into the Stasi headquarters on the Runscestrasse. A committee was formed by the dissidents to take charge. One of their first resolutions was to destroy the files because they thought the Soviets would intervene and the Stasi would return. Later, of course, they realized they were destroying evidence against the Stasi."

"Stefan was on that committee?"

"A leading member."

"So he could have destroyed the files?"

"Mine, Sophie's, Günter's, his own."

"Is there no reference to him in any of the files that have been found?"

"Investigators are going through them now. Dr. Friedemann's file has been found; he was working for the Stasi. So was the director of the clinic. In several files there are references to an unofficial collaborator among the dissidents code-named Chameleon. It is possible that this is Stefan."

"But has no one exposed him?"

"There is no proof."

"Surely the West Germans suspect?"

"I am sure they do, but they are in a difficult position. Stefi is an elected member of the regional assembly. He is also a leader of the New Grouping, upon which the Christian Democratic government depends. Further, there is a growing resentment among the East Germans against the high-handed behavior of the officials from Bonn, and a feeling—which I share—that it is best for us all to forgive and forget."

"To forgive? After what you went through? Can you bring yourself to do that?"

"Me? No. But for God nothing is impossible. I love my children and I must think of their future, not my past."

"But a future with a Stasi spy for a stepfather—and a minister in the regional government?"

"As a stepfather he has not done badly, and as Prussian Minister of Culture he can do no harm."

18

Francesca drove back to Berlin with her mind in confusion. Could what Paul had said be true? Or was he creating a myth in his own mind to explain Sophie's leaving him for Stefan? Paul himself had said he had no proof, yet the more she thought about Stefan Diederich, the more plausible Paul's story became. There had always been something shifty about Stefi, and Sophie was as gullible as a goose.

Before she left Bechtling, Paul had asked Francesca not to tell Sophie what he had said. It would only make her unhappy and destroy the stability of his children's home.

"But you," Francesca had said. "How can you bear to see them flourishing in that way?"

"God rewards us for our suffering," replied Paul, "in a way it is sometimes difficult for others to understand."

Francesca was not a Christian, but she could see that from a Christian perspective it might jeopardize Paul's terminal bonus in the next world if he were now to seek revenge. However, she had to consider the implications of what she had learned for the here and now. If both Stefan Diederich and Günter Westarp had been unofficial collaborators for the Stasi, what bearing did this have on their decision to put on a major exhibition of Russian experimental art? She remembered her first meeting with Stefi nine months before, when he had talked with such enthusiasm about the cultural rehabilitation of Eastern Europe after almost half a century of Communist rule. Had it been bogus or sincere?

When Francesca had put the question to Paul Meissner, he had come up with no satisfactory answer. Perhaps Stefi had had a genuine change of heart and wished to atone for his past wrongdoing. Or perhaps he had thought an exhibition like Excursus would help cover his tracks. As she drove through Neuruppin, it seemed to Francesca that there must be more to it than that. Paul's judgment was distorted by compassion. She needed the advice of someone she could trust. But who was there? Only Andrei, and he was in Moscow. She cursed herself for not getting a telephone number from him before he left.

There remained Sophie. Whatever doubts she may have had about Stefi, Francesca was convinced that Sophie was straight. She was naive, and perhaps had cultivated this quality to avoid resolving painful contradictions or facing up to disagreeable truths, but if she knew more than she let on, it would also be more than she let on to herself. She had to talk to Sophie. Remembering that Stefi had flown to Bonn, she decided to look in at the apartment on the Wedekindstrasse on her way home.

When she saw Francesca at her door, Sophie kissed her without embracing her because her hands were covered with flour. "I'm making pastry," she said, leading her visitor into the kitchen, where her two children were eating their supper. "I always cook when Stefi's away so I can spend more time with him when he returns."

Once the children left the table, Francesca helped clear up. Then Sophie opened a bottle of wine and, while filling two glasses, asked Francesca how she had spent her day. For a moment Francesca hesitated; then she told Sophie she had been to see Paul.

Sophie turned to Francesca. "Paul," she repeated in an almost reproachful tone of voice. "How was poor Paul?"

"He was . . . fine. I mean, as well as can be expected."

"You should have told me you were going to see him."

"I went on impulse; anyway, I thought you wouldn't want me to go."

Sophie said nothing.

"But I had to, Sophie. He was also my friend, after all, and once we start hanging there just won't be time."

"What did he say?"

"Nothing special."

"About me?" Sophie's brow wrinkled as if she was preparing herself to rebut some terrible slur.

"He was very nice about you. He seemed to me to be extraordinarily . . . understanding."

"Yes." Sophie said this as if it was not necessarily a good thing to be.

"He is a good man," said Francesca.

"Yes, but he is not the only good man."

"Of course not."

"Stefi is a good man too."

"I daresay."

Sophie's face went a shade pinker. "He thinks of others, does kindnesses that no one knows. He got Günter his job—"

"I know."

"And he insisted that you should be the one to organize the exhibition when everyone said it should be a German."

"I appreciate that, Sophie."

"And only today, before he left, he said that if anyone asked, I was to say the Excursus exhibition had been your idea."

"My idea?"

"Yes. Because he is now sure it will be a success and he wants all the credit to go to you."

Francesca was dumbfounded. She sat, silent and frowning, trying to work out what might be going on in Stefan Diederich's mind. "Sophie," she said eventually, "are you sure . . . are you absolutely sure. . . ." Her voice petered out.

"Yes, I am sure. He is a good man. He was always our friend, and when he saw how terrible things were for me, he . . . he . . ."

"He made love to you."

"Yes."

"And you let him?"

"Yes."

"Even though Paul was still your husband?"

Sophie's face was now flushed, either from emotion or from the wine. "He was not my husband, not really. How could he be my husband when he was so ill, so depressed?"

"Didn't you ever suspect, Sophie, that it was the Stasi who made him ill?"

241

Sophie looked confused. "Now, yes, because we know that the doctor was an unofficial collaborator, it is possible that they made him worse, but he was always so gloomy and spiritual, worrying about God and Hell, and never any fun." She started to sniffle.

"He was serious," said Francesca, "but he wasn't gloomy."

"Stefi was fun."

"Yes, but"—it was too late to turn back—"Paul told me that what finally broke him, what pushed him over the edge, was coming back from the clinic to find you in bed with Stefi."

Sophie looked dumbfounded. "That is a lie," she said, her sniffles turning to sobs.

"Paul said he was brought back by Günter just at the moment—"

"Oh, God, oh, God," moaned Sophie. "That can't be true, it can't. Why do you tell me this? It can't be true!"

"Sophie"—Francesca tried to remain composed—"I am only telling you what Paul told me."

"He is lying. He must be lying. He is so jealous. He has never forgiven me. He makes up such stories just to punish us. And now you too, you say these terrible things about Stefi, who has been so good to you."

Francesca was a little taken aback to find that *she* was the one in the dock. "I'm sorry, Sophie. Perhaps I should have kept quiet. But, well—"

"You don't like Stefi. You never did. So now you spread these lies about him."

"It's not that I don't like him, Sophie. It's just that I don't . . . well, if what Paul said was true, there would be serious implications."

"Implications? What do you mean, implications?"

"Well, possibilities."

"I know what you mean. You think Stefi worked for the Stasi. Of course. It's easy to say that, isn't it, because his file is missing so he can never disprove it. Other people say it behind his back because they are envious that he is Minister of Culture and they are nothing. But if Stefi was an IM, why did he marry me? Was he ordered to do it? Is that what you mean? Are you suggesting that for ten years I have been making love to a man who does not love me? Do you think a woman cannot tell? I tell you, Francesca, that Stefi has loved me in a way Paul never did, for all his talk about holy matrimony. Paul did not love my body as Stefi loves my body, and certainly, *certainly,* he never loved my soul."

Francesca left the flat on the Wedekindstrasse as soon as she reasonably could, but if she and Sophie did not part enemies, they hardly parted friends. Francesca's disclosures had served no purpose. All that had been established was that Sophie still loved Stefi and that she was still a fool.

All at once, in the drab dusk of East Berlin, Francesca felt frightened and far from home, surrounded by Germans, none of whom she could trust. She wished Andrei were there, if only to tell her that her anxiety was absurd. It was quite possible, after all, that Stefan had had nothing to do with the Stasi and that Paul's suspicions were, as Sophie suggested, a way of demeaning his rival in his own mind.

But if Stefi *had* worked for the Stasi, why would he want to put on an exhibition of Russian art? And why did he want Sophie to say it had been Francesca's idea? Sophie assumed it was to give her all the credit, but if anything went wrong she would also be there to take the blame.

The realization that she had been instrumental in bringing such a unique collection to Berlin at Stefi's instigation filled Francesca with unease. Many of the world's finest modern paintings were now sitting in the warehouse in Tegel. Who had recommended the warehouse to the committee? She had—at Günter's suggestion. She had checked the security, which seemed superb, but she knew nothing about the company that owned it or the staff that was employed to guard its contents. Who had reassured them about Omni Zartfracht? She could not remember. Either one of Stefi's officials or Günter Westarp, who, Paul suspected, had also collaborated with the Stasi.

The brighter streetlights and shopwindows told Francesca that she was now in West Berlin. She was still making for her flat in the Hansa quarter, but she now realized that she could not possibly simply go home. She must pass on her anxieties, but to whom? The police? The American consul? What could she tell them, that she did not trust the provincial Minister of Culture? They would think she was crazy.

Andrei was the only person who would listen without laughing and then either reassure her or know exactly what should be done. But without him, she had to do something herself, and the only thing she could think of was to drive out to Tegel and make sure the paintings were safe. She was well enough known by the Omni Zartfracht people; she could say she had come to make some last-minute checks before the hanging started the next day.

She drove down the Hardenbergstrasse, joined the Stadtring at Charlottenburg, and a short time later reached Tegel. By now it was dark, and outside the center of the city there were few lampposts and no shopwindows to light up the streets. Francesca was distressed and exhausted. She took a wrong turn and lost her way. She had to stop the car, take out her map, and read the street sign to take a bearing. She found where she was and memorized the route to the warehouse. A light blinked on her fuel gauge; she was almost out of gas. She had never been to the warehouse in the dark and could not see any familiar landmarks. Then suddenly she saw the line of lights illuminating the fenced perimeter and came at last to the gate.

Francesca stopped her car and got out to ring the buzzer to announce her presence to the guard, but before she pressed it she saw that one of the gates was open. The gap was not wide, perhaps five or six inches, but it was nevertheless odd. She looked down toward the warehouse. Its doors were closed. There were no vehicles outside the office, but a light came from its window. She knew that normally at least three security guards were on duty through the night. She feared they were all drinking coffee or playing cards.

She pressed the buzzer and waited, but there was no answer. She tried again: still no answer. She went back to her car, switched off the engine, and walked through the open gate and down the fifty-yard drive to the office door. She knocked, waited, and heard nothing. She turned the handle, the door opened, and she went in.

The lights were on in the anteroom but no one was there. Francesca shouted "Hello!" There was no answer. She went through to the office. Here too the lights were on but the room was empty. Assuming that the guards were doing their rounds in the warehouse itself, she went through to the enormous space where the paintings were kept. This was in darkness but she knew where to find the switches and turned on the lights.

It was empty. The works of art were gone. Francesca stepped back, trembling, saving herself from falling only by grabbing the edge of the table on which the paintings had been examined after being unpacked.

Her first thought was that they had been stolen, her second that this was impossible and they must have been taken in advance to the museums or perhaps moved to a different area of the warehouse. She recovered enough to stand without the support of the table and walked forward toward the racks at the back of the warehouse. It was dark, and she did not know where to find the switches for the lights back there. She peered into the gloom, and her eyes slowly adjusted to the poor light. She could see the bare wall. There was nothing. The warehouse was empty. All the pictures and sculptures had gone.

She was about to turn away and run to the office when her eyes made out the face of a man standing in the shadow of one of the racks. He was so still that for a moment she thought he was a statue or a tailor's dummy. But the eyes moved; they were watching her like those of a lizard waiting for the best moment to seize and swallow its prey. As she stepped back, he came forward, and she recognized the dark features of the man who had been with Andrei when he was sick.

Her first impulse was to turn and run; her second was to behave as if nothing unusual had happened. "Hi," she said. "Aren't you Andrei's friend?"

He said nothing, and Francesca remembered Andrei saying that he spoke little of anything but Chechen and Russian.

"The paintings," she said, gesturing toward the empty spaces. "They seem to be gone."

Again he did not answer, but pointed toward the entrance to the office.

Francesca turned and walked as he had instructed. He followed close behind. They went into the empty office. "Is Andrei around?" she asked.

He pointed to a chair. "Sit," he said in English.

Francesca glanced toward the telephone but thought it prudent, while his eyes were on her, to sit down. The Chechen moved behind her. She thought it would suggest alarm and therefore suspicion if she looked to see what he was doing. She heard a crack, and the light dimmed. She turned to see him approaching with the electric cord from a lamp. She leaped to her feet and ran toward the door, but he was there before she was. She backed away. He came forward, no words coming from his mouth and no expression on his face. She came up against a desk and looked toward the window, but before she could move farther he was upon her. He grabbed her and turned her savagely to face away from him, her arm behind her back.

When she felt the cord encircle her wrist, she struck out with her free hand but could not reach him. A moment later, he took hold of that hand too, pulled it behind her body, tied her two wrists together, shoved her back to the chair, and pushed her down. She was forced to lean forward as he lifted her arms over the back of the chair and secured them. Then, with a second strand of cord, he bound her ankles to the legs of the chair.

She shrieked for help. He stood and slapped her face. She closed her eyes and was silent; when she opened them again, he had gone. She turned her head as best she could to see if he was standing behind her; then, sensing that she was alone in the office, shouted again. He came back through the door from the warehouse, sauntered across to where she was sitting, and slapped her again. In his hand was a roll of packing tape, which he now stuck over her mouth and wound around her head.

Francesca sat, half suffocating as she inhaled air through her narrow nostrils. The Chechen sauntered back to lean his body against a desk and light a cigarette, watching her as he did so. She became calmer and breathed more easily. Slowly, rational thoughts supplanted instinctive terror. If this was Andrei's friend, perhaps Andrei would appear. But time passed, Andrei did not appear, and all the while the Chechen watched her, his body propped against a desk, smoking unfiltered cigarettes. His eyes still had no expression, but their glance had a direction, studying her neck and breasts and legs. She felt fear and then, oddly, a certain shame, as if she had somehow invited his lingering looks.

She heard a car. The Chechen looked toward the door and at the same time took out a gun. They heard the catch of the entrance to the anteroom. He held the gun ready. When the inner door opened, Francesca turned her head and saw Andrei. She started to cry. Tears ran down her cheeks as she waited for him to cut her loose and take her in his arms.

Andrei Serotkin glanced at the Chechen, then at Francesca. Neither man spoke. The Chechen's arm went down but he did not put away his gun. The two men started talking in Russian, words Francesca could only half understand. The Chechen seemed angry, Andrei uneasy. At one point, with an unpleasant leer, the Chechen took the lit cigarette from his mouth with his left hand and offered it to Andrei. Andrei frowned, looked at his watch, and shook his head. His right hand went to the inner pocket of his jacket. For a moment Francesca thought he was going to take out a gun. Instead, he removed a small black case. He turned his back to Francesca and put the case on the desk. When she could see his hands again, one was holding a syringe.

He crossed to where she sat and looked down into her imploring eyes. "This will send you to sleep," he said in English, his tone indifferent.

She shook her head and tried to speak.

He held the syringe up to the light to make sure no air was left in the needle. "I am sorry it had to come to this," he said quietly, "but as I tried to explain a number of times, no individual can be allowed to frustrate the destiny of a nation." He moved behind her. "Don't you remember, that afternoon in front of the memorial?"

She felt a sharp pain in the muscle of her neck and at once began to feel drowsy.

"If you remember, you will understand why things have to end in this way." He came around to face her once again and looked down into her eyes. *"Truth is remembering,"* he whispered. *"He who has no memory has no life."* Her muscles grew weak; her head slumped forward; her eyelids closed. *"Truth is remembering. . . ."*

She felt his hand raise her chin. With a great effort she opened her eyes and looked into his. It seemed, in Francesca's last moment of consciousness, that Andrei Serotkin smiled.

19

Because he ate too much on Sundays, Inspector Kessler always felt dyspeptic and therefore irritable on Monday mornings. His mood was made worse on the morning of Monday, June 21, by the report he found on his desk from the Leipzig police describing their failure to trace the movements of the Russian, Gerasimov, whenever he left his hotel. It read as if they were proud that one of their former masters could outwit them with such ease. It was particularly humiliating for Kessler because a second report from the BfV passed on by Grohmann described succinctly every move Gerasimov had made, from the visit to Bedauer, the Volkswagen dealer, to his dinner in Auerbach's Cellar with the private detective Manfred Kraus, formerly Generaloberst Franz Riesler of the Stasi.

Clearly Gerasimov was not a policeman: they had realized this from the start. It was natural enough that he would use old contacts in the Stasi. But what was the relevance of Riesler? Why had he bought a Volkswagen van two weeks before the murder of the Maslyukovs? If the KGB had been responsible, why would Gerasimov need to find this out? Even the BfV had been unable to eavesdrop on the two men's conversation in Auerbach's Cellar, but the secretary had overheard what had been said at the office. From this, it appeared that Gerasimov was less interested in the murderer of the Maslyukovs than in the barter of a Volkswagen van for a consignment of shoes! Certainly Grohmann had drawn this conclusion, appending an acid note on the report to the effect that in his view Gerasimov was not an undercover agent but an undercover black marketeer.

Kessler looked at his watch. A meeting was scheduled with Grohmann and Gerasimov at 10 A.M. It was in the BfV report that on his return to Leipzig Gerasimov had gone straight to the Soviet consulate on Unter den Linden. If he did not come up with anything interesting today, Kessler would suggest that the time had come for him to return to Moscow.

The inspector left his office to get a cup of coffee from the machine. He usually waited until midmorning, but it was Monday and he would need his wits about him to deal with both Grohmann and Gerasimov.

Dorn passed him in the corridor. "Know anything about those paintings, chief?"

"What paintings?"

"You know. The big exhibition of Russian rubbish they got planned."

"I saw something about it."

"Apparently they're lost."

Kessler went back to his office and looked through the BfV report once again. Could it be that Gerasimov himself was part of a group within the KGB involved in the import and export of icons *and* shoes? In that case, he had probably been sent to do what he could to obstruct them. And they were paying his expenses!

A junior officer, a girl, looked through the door of Kessler's office. "Did you get the message?"

"What message?"

"They called while you were getting coffee. You're wanted urgently upstairs."

He glanced at his watch. "If Herr Grohmann and the Russian turn up, ask them to wait."

"Understood."

Kessler swallowed what remained of his coffee and went down the corridor and up a single flight of stairs to the office of Berlin's chief of the criminal police, Commissar Edgar Rohrbeck. From the look on his superior's ashen face, Kessler assumed that he too suffered from dyspepsia on Mondays. Then he saw that three of his senior colleagues had been called in and realized something serious must be going on.

"Gentlemen," said the commissar, "we have had a call from the New German Foundation to say that the paintings and sculptures for the Excursus exhibition have disappeared."

There was a baffled silence from the assembled officers. "Disappeared from where?" asked Kessler.

"The exhibition was due to open in two weeks' time. The hanging of the paintings was to start today. In the meantime the works of art had been stored in a new warehouse at Tegel belonging to Omni Zartfracht. Omni Zartfracht was due to start delivering the paintings to the galleries at eight A.M. today. When they failed to arrive, the organizers called OZF. There was no reply. Two of the organizers drove to Tegel to see what had gone wrong. They found the warehouse deserted and the works of art gone."

"It must be a joke," said one of Kessler's colleagues, Inspector Allerding.

"Or they've been taken to the wrong location," said another, Inspector Hasenclever.

"Or they're stuck in traffic," said Kessler.

"Unfortunately," said the commissar, "none of these hypotheses can be true. There was never any intention to move all the works of art in a single day. Moreover, several vans were seen on Sunday at the OZF warehouse. None of those vans are there today."

"Isn't there an office for OZF?"

"No one answers the phone. Officers have been sent to investigate."

"But they can hardly have been stolen," said Allerding.

"I fear we must work on that assumption," said Rohrbeck.

"But you can't fence world-famous paintings like that."

"No. But you can threaten to destroy them."

"Are they insured?"

"They are covered by an indemnity by the Federal government."

"For how much?"

"I don't know precisely, but their total value may be as much as a billion marks."

The four officers looked stunned.

"But no government would pay a ransom," said Hasenclever.

"That remains to be seen," said Commissar Rohrbeck. "Our job is to make sure it does not have to make that choice. I want you all to drop whatever you're doing until we find the paintings. I shall take overall command." He turned to Kessler. "What are you working on?"

"The Maslyukov case."

"Drop it. You've wasted too much time on that one already. Get out to Tegel. There were over three hundred works of art. They cannot have disappeared without a trace."

Kessler ran down to his office, two steps at a time. Grohmann was waiting. "Listen," said Kessler, "there's been some gigantic heist, so the Maslyukov case will have to wait—"

"But Gerasimov is coming."

"Do me a favor. Deal with him."

Grohmann frowned. "I can't do that. This is a police matter, not a question of national security."

"He went to see a *Generaloberst* from the Stasi. That puts it on your plate."

Grohmann hesitated. "I shall have to get advice." He turned to go, but just as he did so, Dorn ushered Gerasimov into Kessler's office.

Gerasimov had a look of great self-importance, like a magician about to produce a white rabbit from under his hat. "Good morning, gentlemen," he said.

Kessler looked past Gerasimov to Dorn. "Are you ready to move?"

Dorn looked surprised. "When you are."

Kessler turned back to Gerasimov. "I'm afraid something has come up. My boss has taken me off the case—temporarily, I hope. Herr Grohmann will explain."

Grohmann gave an exasperated splutter. "This is impossible!"

"But I have the names," said Gerasimov. "The names and passport numbers of Ivan the Terrible."

"Good, good," said Kessler. "Give them to Herr Grohmann." Shaking the Russian by the hand, he pushed past him and out the door.

Dorn switched on the siren as he weaved through the traffic around the Innsbruckerplatz, up the Stadtring, and then on the Schumacherdamm to Tegel. They were at the Omni Zartfracht warehouse only fifteen minutes after leaving police headquarters. Four patrol cars were already there, their lights still flashing. The large doors to the warehouse were closed, and two uniformed policemen stood guard. Inside, in an anteroom, three others waited, their bulky leather jackets cramming the small space.

"Outside," said Kessler.

He went through to the inner office to find a uniformed sergeant and three men. Kessler knew the sergeant. "Who are these men?" he asked.

"The art people," said the sergeant.

"Günter Westarp," said the first, an older, bedraggled figure, from his appearance clearly an Ossie.

"Julius Breitenbach," said a younger man. He looked not only pale but likely to vomit at any moment.

"Dr. Kemmelkampf, from the Ministry of Culture," said a third, a tall thin-faced figure who looked like a schoolteacher, the eldest of the three.

"Who was first on the scene?" asked Kessler.

The young man raised his hand. "I came here with Herr Westarp from the New National Gallery. We were expecting the works of art. We telephoned—"

"How did you get in?"

"The gate was closed but not locked."

"The office?"

"The same."

"There was no one here?"

"No."

"How did you discover the paintings were gone?"

"We looked," said Günter Westarp. "We had been here many times before. You see, they had to be sorted and arranged so that they could be moved out quickly when the moment came—"

"Quickly, yes," said Kessler with some sarcasm. He turned to Dr. Kemmelkampf. "Have you been in touch with the company?"

"Yes—that is to say, they have only a small office here in Berlin."

"And?"

"Apparently it is closed. We are trying now to make contact with the head office in Zurich."

"Looks like a dummy company," said Dorn.

"Impossible," said Dr. Kemmelkampf.

"You chose the company?"

"Yes. That is, the Ministry—"

"You *knew* the company?"

"This warehouse was newly constructed. We were most fortunate in that. . . . The large number of works of art . . . there was nowhere else suitable."

"Was the company known to you?"

"Known? Well, not personally, because that was not the responsibility of my department."

"Who chose it?"

"Who? I am not sure. I would have to look at my papers. But certainly the Ministry endorsed it. We all thought . . . it seemed so convenient. Everything was so rushed, you understand."

Kessler looked around the office. It was unusually tidy; nothing seemed out of place. He turned to the sergeant. "Has anything been touched?"

"Nothing. Except the letter."

"What letter?"

Günter Westarp stepped forward. "There was a letter on the desk addressed to me."

"You opened it?"

"Yes. I thought—"

"What did it say?"

"It was a business letter, saying that we would be told how we could recover the paintings."

"Signed?"

"Raskolnikov."

"Code name," said Dorn. "So when we get the ransom demand, we'll know it's for real."

"Do you know anyone called Raskolnikov?" Kessler asked Günter Westarp.

Westarp shook his head.

"It's the name of the hero in a novel by Dostoyevsky," said Julius Breitenbach.

"Which novel?" asked Kessler.

"Crime and Punishment."

"So our thief has a sense of humor," said Kessler, reading the letter, which was typed on a plain sheet of white paper:

Dear Dr. Westarp: In respect to the paintings we have removed from the warehouse, kindly await instructions as to how they may be returned.

The name R. R. Raskolnikov had also been typed, not written. He turned to Dorn. "Check it for prints."

"Some hope."

Kessler looked around the office again. Dorn was right. He could tell at a glance that it had been wiped clean. He opened a filing cabinet. The waybills were neatly placed in their files. They were unlikely to give any clues about where the works of art had gone. Their best hope was of some tipoff from the underworld, but the complexity and the audacity of this heist—the planning and money that must have been required to set it up—made it unlikely that this was the work of ordinary thieves.

"Chief." Dorn called Kessler from across the room. Kessler joined him. "Something odd here. Two lamps with no cords." He pointed to where they lay on the floor.

"Why odd?"

"Well, everything else is so orderly."

Kessler turned back to the civil servant. "Dr. Kemmelkampf, I would be grateful if you would return to your ministry and assemble all those who had anything to do with this exhibition."

"Certainly, except—"

"What?"

"The Minister is in Bonn. I daresay he will return when he hears the news. It was a project in which he took a personal interest."

"Then we shall have to wait until he comes back, but in the meantime I should like to talk to anyone else involved." He turned to Günter Westarp and Julius Breitenbach. "I would like you to do the same. Return to your office in the New National Gallery."

"It is at the New German Foundation on the Schöneberger Ufer."

"Go to the Schöneberger Ufer, then. Assemble your staff, the entire staff, everyone who has had anything to do with the Excursus exhibition. I shall be along later in the morning to question them."

"There is one problem," said Günter Westarp.

"Yes?"

"The Russian member of our staff, Dr. Serotkin, is absent; he is in Moscow. And we have been unable to locate another, Dr. McDermott."

"Who is he?"

"A woman. An American. She was expected at the New National Gallery but did not turn up. We telephoned her at home but there was no reply."

Kessler turned to Dorn. "Call headquarters. Ask them to try and locate this Dr. McDermott, and tell them that the fingerprint boys can move in. Not that I expect they'll find much. Whoever is behind this certainly knew what they were doing."

On his own territory in the Prussian Ministry of Culture, Dr. Kemmelkampf regained his incisive, bureaucratic manner. He showed Kessler and Dorn into his office before going into the conference room where four other officials were waiting. "We have informed the Minister," he said. "He has canceled his appointments in Bonn and is returning at once to Berlin. He suggests that the matter be kept out of the news for as long as possible. The Federal Ministry feels the same. If the lenders become aware that their works have disappeared, it will do incalculable damage to our cultural relations with other nations. Excursus had the personal endorsement of the Federal Chancellor; it was to have been opened by President von Weizsäcker himself. Everything has to be done to ensure that the paintings are recovered before it becomes known that they have been stolen."

"I don't control the press," said Kessler, "and we were not asked to ensure the security of the paintings."

"Of course."

"The thieves have a twelve-hour start. The works could be anywhere in Germany. They may even have left Germany. Checks are being made on the frontiers, but as you know, controls over EC borders are now loose."

"I understand."

"The most likely way of recovering the paintings is by finding out who stole them, either from a tipoff or by investigation. Our job is the investigation. Technical experts are examining the warehouse, but to be honest I don't expect them to find many clues. In my experience, cases that involve fraudulent companies have one thing in common: someone on the inside has put the business their way. So our best bet is to follow the trail back from the owners of OZF."

Kemmelkampf looked uncomfortable. "My colleague, Dr. Giesenfels, has tried to contact their head office in Zurich, but apparently . . ." His voice tailed off. "He had better speak to you himself. Come."

The three men entered a conference room where three other civil servants sat at a table, as if waiting for the start of a departmental meeting.

Prompted by his chief, Dr. Giesenfels, a small, bald, bespectacled man, delivered his report in a high-pitched voice. "We have had considerable correspondence with Omni Zartfracht," he began, peering into a folder open on the table in front of him. "The invoices were always sent by the Berlin office and were paid into an account at the Berliner Bank. We also had correspondence with their head office in Zurich and many calls. But this morning there was no reply from the Zurich number. I talked to the management of the building and was told that no one had come to the office there this morning."

Kessler shook his head, as a sign of incredulity. "If I may say so, gentlemen, it seems incredible to me that you would entrust paintings of such value to an unknown company."

"Unknown?" said Kemmelkampf. "It was new, but it was not unknown."

"Whose idea was it," asked Kessler, "that OZF should be employed to store the works of art?"

"Yes, well"—Dr. Giesenfels looked down at his file—"You must understand, Herr Inspector, that because of political considerations, the exhibition had to be organized in a very short period of time. Normally an exhibition of this size would take three, four, even five years from start to finish. Excursus had to be arranged in less than one. The two galleries involved had already made arrangements for the summer. We had to cancel two exhibitions and curtail four others. This left a minimum amount of time for the hanging of Excursus, and of course the storing of so many paintings was also a problem, so it was suggested that they be assembled at an outside location."

"Suggested by whom?"

"I am not sure. By Dr. Westarp, I believe."

"And who chose OZF?"

"Again, I cannot be sure. But a preliminary examination of the minutes of the Excursus committee indicated that the recommendation of OZF came from Dr. McDermott."

As they drove from the offices of the Prussian Ministry of Culture to the Schöneberger Ufer, Kessler and Dorn heard from headquarters that the Swiss police had been to OZF headquarters in Zurich. It was a single room with a telephone and was now empty. They were looking at the register of companies and the OZF bank accounts and would report back as soon as they had any useful information.

"They'll find nothing," said Dorn. "False names, false documents, numbered bank accounts."

At the Excursus office, the exhibition organizers were waiting in the conference room for the arrival of the police. It was clear to Kessler that some of them were in a state of shock. The two secretaries had been weeping, and at the sight of the detectives they burst into tears once again. The young man, Breitenbach, still looked nauseated; Westarp was like a dog that has been whipped and fears it is about to be whipped again. An older woman, introduced as Frau Doktor Koch, had her face set rigidly in an expression of self-righteous indignation, as if the world had finally reached the sad state she had so often predicted.

At Kessler's suggestion—their sobs were distracting—the two secretaries were sent back to their desks. The four who remained sat down with the two detectives, Kessler taking the chair at the head of the table.

"Is this the entire staff of the Excursus exhibition?" Kessler asked Westarp.

"Yes, apart from the Minister, Dr. Serotkin, and Dr. McDermott."

"Still no word from Dr. McDermott?"

"No."

"The Minister is on his way back from Bonn?"

"Yes."

"And Serotkin is in Moscow?"

"Yes."

"When did he leave?"

"Four days ago."

"Why did he leave?"

"For personal reasons," said Westarp.

"Do you know what these were?" asked Kessler.

"His father suffered a stroke."

"And when is he due to return?"

"At the latest, for the opening on July sixth."

"I would like you to tell us, from the beginning, of your contacts with the freight and storage company, Omni Zartfracht," said Kessler.

"Of course," said Westarp. "You see, we were faced with a difficult situation because of preexisting schedules in the two museums—"

"That I know. But why OZF?"

"They offered us just the facilities we wanted: an air-conditioned, climate-controlled warehouse near Tegel, custom-made to handle works of art."

"Who suggested OZF?"

"I can't remember. I imagine it was the Ministry."

"Dr. Kemmelkampf has told us it was first mentioned here."

Westarp looked confused. "Here?"

"At a meeting of the organizing committee, by Dr. McDermott."

"That is possible," said Günter Westarp. "I cannot remember who first made the suggestion."

"You will appreciate," said Kessler dryly, "that it is a matter of some importance."

"Yes, of course. But it was some months ago."

"For your information, it now seems that Omni Zartfracht was a bogus company set up simply for the theft of the paintings."

The four around the table were silent. Then Frau Doktor Koch suddenly blurted out, "It's too valuable."

"I beg your pardon?" said Kessler.

"Art. It is now too valuable. Too expensive. People no longer think of it in terms of the spirit, only in terms of cash."

"But they cannot sell the paintings," said Julius Breitenbach. "They are too well known."

"It is more likely that they will demand a ransom," said Kessler.

"And if the ransom is not paid?"

"Destroy the paintings."

"I cannot believe that," said Julius Breitenbach. "In that warehouse were all the best Kandinskys, the best Chagalls, the best Maleviches, El Lissitzkys, Gabos, Pevsners—all that exists in the world of modern

Russian art in the twentieth century. It would not be a criminal but a madman who could bring himself to destroy that."

One of the secretaries came into the room to say that there was a call for Inspector Kessler from police headquarters. Kessler nodded to Dorn to take it.

"Which of you here," asked Kessler, "had contacts with the staff of OZF?"

"The Ministry dealt with the contractual side," said Günter Westarp. "I talked occasionally with the director of the Berlin office. We all went down to the warehouse from time to time to examine the works of art before we signed for them."

"Whom did you deal with?"

"The warehouse director, Herr Taub."

"And the younger one, Mishi," said Julius Breitenbach.

"They were very tight on security," said Westarp. "Do you remember the first time? They wouldn't let us in."

"Were they Germans?" asked Kessler.

"Yes."

"East or West?"

"Ossies."

"Accents?"

"Saxon, I would say."

"Leipzig?"

Breitenbach shrugged. "Somewhere down there."

Kessler turned to Westarp. "What would you say?"

"About what?"

"The accents?"

Westarp looked confused. "They were . . . yes, Saxon, perhaps. From Halle, maybe, or Leipzig. But they were not all the same."

"How many of them were there?"

"It varied. Half a dozen or so."

"Would you recognize them again?"

"Taub, certainly."

"And Mishi," said Julius Breitenbach. "I had quite a few chats with him."

"Can you think of anything unusual about them?"

Günter Westarp shook his head. "No."

"They were very good at their job," said Frau Doktor Koch. "Very efficient."

"Disciplined," said Julius Breitenbach. "When Taub gave an order, it was carried out immediately."

"They really did not seem like criminals," said Frau Doktor Koch. "Those I saw were so young and so earnest."

"I agree," said Westarp.

Dorn came back into the conference room and handed a note to Kessler. Kessler glanced at it, then looked up. "I am afraid appearances can be deceptive. A call to the Chancellery in Bonn from Raskolnikov has said that all the paintings will be destroyed at midnight tonight unless a ransom is paid of one hundred million dollars."

Back at police headquarters on the Gothaerstrasse, Kessler was called into conference by Commissar Rohrbeck together with the two other inspectors, Allerding and Hasenclever. Kessler reported what he had found at Tegel and described his preliminary interrogation of the Ministry and Excursus staffs.

"Any leads?" asked Rohrbeck.

"Not to speak of. From the description of the OZF people, it's possible that some may have come from the Leipzig area, but that's little more than a hunch."

"We've alerted the police of the different *Länder*," said Allerding, "as well as Interpol and the French, Swiss, Italian, and Austrian police. There are several reports of vans leaving Berlin on Sunday night, but they come from all the different exits. None reports a convoy. We have strict instructions not to say what's been stolen. If Bonn decides to pay, they don't want it known in advance."

"It will leak out," said Kessler.

"It won't matter after the event, but no one wants to argue about it beforehand. If it's got to be done, it's got to be done."

"What about the American?" asked Kessler.

"We've searched her apartment and checked airline departures, and her picture's been circulated to our men on the street. No sign of her as yet."

"The FBI?"

"Bonn doesn't want them to know what's going on."

"What about the Ministry of Culture?"

"We've run the names of the civil servants and the Excursus staff through the database," said Hasenclever, "and we're keeping them all under surveillance. We're now working on the staff of the New German Foundation. The database hasn't told us much. The Minister, several of the civil servants, and Westarp are Ossies, so we don't have their records. The young man, Breitenbach, was a student activist and got pulled in after a number of demonstrations, but there's no suspicion of any links with the Red Brigades, and he seems to have been quiet for the last five years. The Russian, Serotkin, was the witness in an attempted rape in the Englischer Garten three months ago. He dealt with three Turks who had attacked his American colleague, Dr. McDermott. And that's about it."

"I've had the Chancellor's office on the telephone," said Rohrbeck. "It has been decided that it is preeminently in the national interest to get those paintings back."

"Then they'd better pay," said Kessler.

"A hundred million dollars?" said Allerding.

"The indemnity will cost them more."

"But the precedent!" said Hasenclever.

"Of course," said Rohrbeck. "The Chancellor's office is mindful of that. But against the precedent you have to balance not just the cost of the indemnity but the dreadful damage to Germany's reputation that would result from the destruction of a unique collection of this kind. Our relations with both Russia and the United States would be seriously affected, not to mention the nations of the other lenders. Thus, the decision has been made to pay the ransom if this is thought to be the only way to get the paintings back. The deadline is midnight tonight."

Back in his office, Kessler received a call from Inspector Noske, the officer in charge of the fingerprint team. As Kessler had suspected, everything was clean. "Incredible discipline," said Noske. "Incredible. They seem to have worn gloves the whole time or wiped everything down before they left. And methodical. The way the waybills were filed, cross-referenced. . . . Why take so much trouble with things you're going to steal?"

Method. Efficiency. Discipline. None of this sounded to Kessler like the work of even the most experienced thieves.

"What about those lamps without their cords?" he asked Noske.

"Someone just ripped the cords off, but we haven't found them and there are no prints."

"Is there *nothing* else unusual?"

"The only odd thing we've found," said Noske, "since they were otherwise so tidy, were some cigarette butts on the floor by one of the desks. Dark tobacco. Unfiltered cigarettes."

As he replaced the telephone on its cradle, Kessler's eye fell on his open diary and the entry *10:00 Gerasimov*. A pang of remorse made him call Grohmann.

"Grohmann?"

Silence.

"It's Kessler. I'm sorry."

A further sulky silence; then, "I understand. I heard about the paintings. But don't expect me to take on this case for you. We are not the criminal police."

"I know. It can wait."

"Never again do I want to see Gerasimov."

"Did you talk to him?"

"Briefly."

"And?"

"He was pretty angry about being stood up."

"Understandably."

"He said he had made a major breakthrough. He had the names being used by this Ivan the Terrible, names and passport numbers. Apparently the man speaks five languages and is a master of disguise."

Kessler laughed. "He learned all this while bartering for shoes in Leipzig?"

"Or he was given the names over the phone from Moscow. I've left the list on your desk."

"What do we do with him now?"

"That's your affair."

"Send him back to Moscow."

"Or give him more money to spend on whores. But not BfV money. It has nothing to do with intelligence. I lent a hand and was left holding the baby. Now I'm off the case. It's over. *Schluss. Fertig.* Goodbye."

Grohmann slammed down the telephone; Kessler replaced his more gently on its receiver.

"Grohmann?" asked Dorn.

"Yes."

"Pissed off?"

"Yes. He's had enough of our Russian friend."

"I don't blame him."

"Apparently Gerasimov came up with some names and passport numbers for Ivan the Terrible. They're in the in-tray." He nodded at the shallow wire basket on the right-hand corner of his desk.

The telephone rang and Kessler picked it up while Dorn leaned forward for the list.

Kessler slammed down the telephone. "Diederich's back. Come on."

"The list?"

"It'll wait."

Kessler and Dorn were met by Dr. Kemmelkampf at the door of the office in East Berlin where they had been earlier that day and were shown straight into the minister's office. Before Kessler could open his mouth, Stefan Diederich went on the offensive.

"So, gentlemen, this is a fine kettle of fish. I have had calls from the Chancellor's office in Bonn every half an hour asking for a progress report, and so far I have not been able to tell them anything. What, please, am I to say the next time they call?"

Kessler was flabbergasted by this audacious greeting. "I . . . we . . . there have been investigations, naturally, but there are no real leads."

Stefan Diederich gave a snort of exasperation. "You must forgive me, sergeant—"

"Inspector," said Dorn.

"Inspector. I'm so sorry. You will forgive me if I express a certain disillusion. As you know, I was until recently a citizen of the German Democratic Republic. There were many unpleasant aspects to life in that totalitarian state, but it would have been inconceivable for a collection of some of the greatest art the world has ever produced to simply disappear overnight."

"Herr Minister—" Kessler began.

"I am sorry. I realize you are not the one to whom I should address my complaint. You are merely a humble inspector. And you?" He turned to Dorn.

"Detective sergeant."

"Detective sergeant. Excellent. Well, neither a detective sergeant nor even an inspector can be held responsible for the abysmal failure of the Berlin police to protect a unique collection of this kind. However, you are here, as I understand it, to clear up the mess."

"To investigate—"

"Yes. To investigate and, I hope, to find—because if the paintings are not found, we are all in the soup, gentlemen, *all* of us, from the Chancellor of Germany down to the humblest police inspector and detective sergeant."

"As far as I know," said Kessler, "the Berlin police were never asked to ensure the security of the paintings."

"Ah," said Diederich. "So we have to *ask* for our property to be protected? It is not an automatic right?"

"Of course it is a right," said Kessler, "but in particular cases—"

"Yes, yes, I understand. Undoubtedly an inquiry will discover that since the reunification of Germany, the theoretic unity but actual diversity of administrative powers in the eastern part of Germany can partly be blamed for this fiasco. The very fact that the exhibition was being organized by the government of a former province of East Germany, yet had its offices in West Berlin, meant that certain areas of competence fell, as it were, between two stools. Actions to be taken by one or another of the different authorities were in fact taken by none. This is an accident of history, and from a historical perspective, the hundred million dollars—if indeed it is paid—will be added to the total cost of the reunification of our country and, as a percentage of the whole, will be seen to be very small indeed. Naturally, we have already instituted such an inquiry, and if any of *my* officials are held to be responsible, then of course disciplinary procedures will be taken against them. But this will only be done in some months' time and it is unlikely to placate, say, the Museum of Modern Art in New York or the Musée d'Art Moderne in Paris, not to mention the Tretyakov in Moscow and the Russian Museum in St. Petersburg. I tell you, gentlemen, my thinking and that of the Chancellor are at one on this question: The destruction of these works of art is *unthinkable*. Everything must be done to recover them."

"Certain features have started to emerge," said Kessler.

"Features? Do you mean clues?"

"Not clues, no, but clearly the robbery was planned over a long period of time."

"Clearly."

"The company, Omni Zartfracht, was bogus, set up simply to assemble the paintings."

"So Kemmelkampf told me. Unbelievable."

"It is therefore important to know who chose OZF."

"Not important. Essential."

"Essential, then."

"Kemmelkampf has already been through the correspondence and minutes and says that the idea came from the Excursus committee."

"Yes. Apparently it was suggested by Dr. McDermott."

"Who, I understand, has disappeared."

"Presumably the Ministry checked the company's credentials?"

"Here we may have been remiss," said Diederich. "Kemmelkampf left it to a subordinate, Dr. Giesenfels, who now tells us he thought Dr. Westarp had taken that in hand. I have to say, Inspector, that this is my responsibility as minister, and I do not want to duck it, but for various reasons that I am sure *you* appreciate—the Chancellor's office and the Ministry in Bonn are less conscious of local conditions here in Berlin— but for various reasons it was important to give certain posts in the Ministry to people from the former DDR who were not only inexperienced when it came to mounting an international exhibition of this magnitude but who, in particular, knew little or nothing about vetting companies with headquarters in Switzerland. As I understand it, the OZF people here in Berlin were efficient and cooperative, so they saw no reason to look into the Swiss parent company. I have to say, and this is not meant to be in any way a criticism of Dr. McDermott, but my officials were somewhat dazzled by this handsome art historian from the United States and hence worked on the assumption that she knew what she was doing when she recommended this company, Omni Zartfracht."

Kessler nodded. "What about Professor Serotkin?"

"What about him?"

"He has apparently returned to Moscow."

"Yes. His father is ill. He hoped to be here for the opening."

"How did he become involved in the exhibition?"

"It was thought necessary to have a Russian to ensure Soviet cooperation. Many of the works, you understand, were in Russian galleries."

"Did you choose him?"

"No. We were advised that if you ask for one man, they are certain to send another. And to be blunt, we did not really care who came, as long as he could arrange for the loan of the paintings. We made a request through the usual channels and they sent Serotkin."

"Did you know him?"

"No, but I know the type only too well. An apparatchik. He knows very little about modern art."

"But since the coup—"

"At that level of bureaucracy, nothing has changed."

"Could we get hold of him if required?"

"Of course. Kemmelkampf has the number of the Ministry in Moscow."

"And he became involved *after* you decided to hold the exhibition?"

"Yes."

"So he had nothing to do with the choice of OZF?"

"No."

Again, Kessler paused. His notebook was open on the table in front of him, but the page was blank. "Can you tell me precisely when it was that you decided to put on the exhibition?"

The Minister looked embarrassed. "It was last summer, but—this is awkward but, you will understand, politics is politics—although I have been credited with the idea, and have not sought to disown that credit, the very germ of the idea was not in fact mine."

"Whose was it, then?"

"Dr. Westarp will confirm this, and my wife, that the first mention of a comprehensive all-embracing exhibition of modern Russian art was made at a dinner in our home last summer by Dr. McDermott, who was a friend from ten years before and who in the meantime had made this field her specialty."

"*She* suggested Excursus?"

"It was a brilliant idea. We jumped at it, Dr. Westarp and I. It was just what was needed: politically, culturally, in every way. But things are serious now, so we must keep scrupulously to the truth, and the truth is that Dr. McDermott suggested the exhibition, with herself as the chief organizer. It was only for this reason, in fact, that we insisted she be given the job. There were many Germans better qualified, but since it was her idea it seemed only just."

It was now 4 P.M. and the two detectives, who'd had no lunch, stopped off on their way back to police headquarters at a stall for a quick currywurst and a glass of beer.

"It all points to the American," said Dorn.

Kessler chewed his sausage without answering.

"Although . . ." Dorn hesitated.

"What?"

"A woman? I mean, I know that these American women are a new breed, but all the same . . ."

"She wouldn't have been on her own; she'd be working for someone else. You need big money to set up a dummy company like OZF."

"Who's behind her, then? The Mafia?"

Kessler finished his sausage and wiped the ketchup off his fingers with a paper napkin. "I don't know. She might have a boyfriend, or she may have been blackmailed. But I'm not entirely convinced it's her. I feel we're being nudged in that direction."

"Don't you believe the Minister?"

Kessler hesitated. "Do you?"

"I don't trust any politicians. They always sound false." Dorn finished his sausage.

"What's curious about Diederich," said Kessler, turning to go, "is that he's only been a politician since the fall of the Wall."

Dorn hesitated. "I'm still famished, chief. Mind if I buy another?"

"Better bring it back to the office."

Dorn ordered another currywurst and, while it was being prepared and put in a bag, drained his glass of beer.

At 5 P.M., the three inspectors were called upstairs to report to Commissar Rohrbeck. "Time's running out," said Rohrbeck.

"Still nothing from the frontier police, the state forces, or Interpol," said Allerding.

"The Swiss have come back on the OZF company," said Kessler. "Bogus names for the directors. Current account fed from a secret numbered account."

"Can we freeze it?" asked Allerding.

"It would be a waste of time," said Rohrbeck. "Raskolnikov has faxed the numbers of different accounts for the ransom to the Chancellor's office in Bonn, and the OZF account isn't on it."

"Are those accounts in Zurich?" asked Kessler.

"Zurich, Luxembourg, Jersey, the Cayman Islands—all over."

Rohrbeck turned to Hasenclever. "What about the American, Dr. McDermott?"

"We've checked on her as far as we can without telling the FBI what's going on," said Hasenclever. "She's cleaner than clean. No known criminal connections. They have her flagged only for the year she spent here in Berlin."

"Her background?" asked Kessler.

"Father's a professor of some sort."

"No Italian family connections?"

Hasenclever shook his head. "Not that we know of."

"Why do you ask?" asked Rohrbeck.

"Diederich says it was Dr. McDermott who first came up with the idea of the Excursus exhibition."

"I thought it was him."

"He took the credit—"

"But doesn't want the blame."

"He says Westarp and his wife will confirm it. McDermott is also on record as first suggesting the OZF warehouse."

"We found nothing incriminating in her apartment," said Allerding.

"What about the Russian?" asked Kessler.

"We're trying to locate him," said Hasenclever. "No luck so far."

The commissar waved them away. "I won't keep you. Press on."

Kessler returned to his office. Dorn was waiting by his desk. "Did you know that our Dr. McDermott was screwing the Russian, Serotkin?" he asked Kessler.

"Where did you hear that?"

"That bloke Breitenbach just called to tell me. Said he thought it might be relevant. They lived in the same building near the Englischer Garten. Apparently he's been spending most nights in her place."

Kessler frowned. "Did they know each other before?"

"Apparently not. It was an office romance, or perhaps a reward for saving her from the Turks."

"They never met before they came to Berlin? We're sure of that?"

"According to Breitenbach, no one knew Serotkin. He was just sent here by the Russians. Initially the American took a dislike to him. They avoided each other for the first six months."

"Slow fuse."

"Or calculation." Dorn took his second currywurst out of its bag. "Do you mind?"

"Go ahead."

"We've got to find the Yank," said Dorn, with his mouth full. "She's our only lead."

"But even if we find her," said Kessler, "what evidence have we got against her? The exhibition was her idea. So what? It was a good idea, even the Federal government thought so. She suggested OZF, but she was in no position to insist on it and certainly wasn't responsible for checking it out. The thieves planned this thing in such detail that it's unlikely that they would build a warehouse on the assumption that the Ministry would take up her idea."

"Sure." Dorn took another mouthful of sausage and roll.

"We've got to get the FBI to go deeper into her background."

"Then the Yanks will get suspicious."

"There must be someone who can do it off the record."

"Not before midnight tonight."

Dorn put the last piece of currywurst in his mouth and licked the ketchup off his fingers. "Got a tissue, chief?"

Kessler looked in the second drawer of his desk. The box of tissues was empty. "No. Use scrap paper."

Dorn picked up a piece of paper lying next to the in-tray on Kessler's desk. "This OK?"

"What is it?"

Dorn squinted down at a row of names and numbers. "A list."

"What list?"

"Burton, Lauch, Grauber . . . it's the names used by Ivan the Terrible."

"Put it back in the basket. Use this." Kessler tore the top sheet out of his spiral notebook and handed it to Dorn. But Dorn did not take it; he was staring at the list. Then he put it on the desk in front of Kessler. "Look at this, chief. The last name. It's the same as the Russian on the Excursus committee, Andrei Serotkin."

Kessler snatched the list. "Shit!" he said. Then: "Where's Gerasimov?"

"I don't know."

"Call Grohmann—no, call Gerasimov's hotel. And get a picture of Serotkin from the Excursus people or the visa office."

Inspector Hasenclever stood in the doorway. "The boss says you're to get back to Tegel. They've found the American."

"Where?"

"Trussed up in the trunk of her car parked in a side street near the warehouse."

"Dead or alive?"

"Alive but unconscious. They're bringing her around now."

20

On their way from Gothaerstrasse to Tegel, Kessler and Dorn picked up Nikolai Gerasimov from the Trebizond Hotel. Seated in the back of the car next to Dorn, he was told about the theft of the paintings.

"Ah," said Gerasimov. "That was what all the fuss was about this morning."

"Do you think Ivan the Terrible is the art historian Serotkin?"

"Have you a photograph?"

Kessler showed Gerasimov the picture of a bearded man that had been faxed from the personnel department of the New German Foundation.

"Possibly. Yes, I should say so. Orlov with a beard."

"Orlov? Who is Orlov?"

Gerasimov looked confused. "Because of the seriousness of the situation, I feel you should know that the real name of Ivan the Terrible is Andrei Orlov. He was responsible for the theft of the icons and the murder of the Maslyukovs, and although now a major criminal he was at one time a member of a certain security agency of the former Soviet Union."

"The KGB?"

"In a word, yes. The KGB. Of course he was dismissed."

"When?"

"Some time ago."

"Because he was a thief?"

"More or less."

"But he still has the training and the contacts," said Dorn.

"Certainly," said Gerasimov. "He was one of our best men."

"If we had known this sooner," said Kessler, "the robbery might not have taken place."

"It is only now," said Gerasimov, "that we have learned what names he was using on his false documents. If you had listened to me this morning—"

"Does he know that you know?" Kessler interrupted.

"Possibly not."

"But possibly yes?"

"You have to understand, inspector, that things in my country are somewhat confused at the present time."

"I understand. But does that mean this man Orlov may be getting some backup from the present Security Service of the Russian Federation?"

"Officially, no. Quite the contrary."

"But unofficially?"

"Unofficially, of course. There are a number of people in my country—a large number of people—who are unhappy with the reforms. Unhappy, also, to have no power, no privileges, and no currency."

"Would he have links with agents here in Germany?"

"Yes."

"With former Stasi officers?"

"Undoubtedly."

The method, the discipline. . . . Suddenly an understanding of what had happened began to take shape in Kessler's mind. "Is it possible," he asked Gerasimov, "that someone in the Ministry of Culture in Moscow intercepted the request of the Excursus committee and sent Orlov posing as Serotkin to Berlin?"

"Quite possible, yes. It is also possible that no request was ever received in Moscow."

"Can you look into that tomorrow?"

"Of course."

"If there was no request to Moscow," said Dorn, "that would point a finger at the provincial ministry here in Berlin."

"Yes," said Kessler.

"What about Dr. McDermott?" asked Dorn.

Kessler turned to Gerasimov. "Would this man Orlov be capable of seducing a woman to involve her in his scheme?"

"Of course. That would have been part of his training."

"He would be that cold-blooded?"

"Come on, chief," said Dorn. "Stubbing out cigarettes on a woman—that's cold-blooded. Fucking a good-looking Yank—that's a piece of cake."

Julian Becker, a detective constable, had brought a Styrofoam cup filled with coffee for Francesca McDermott; sitting in an armchair in the office, she held it between her hands. Her blond hair was disheveled, her white shirt grubby, her green skirt creased. Encircling her wrists and ankles were stripes of blue bruises and broken flesh.

Kessler went up to her. "Dr. McDermott?"

She looked up. "Yes?"

"I am Inspector Kessler of the Berlin Criminal Police."

She showed no interest.

Kessler drew up a chair and sat facing her. "I am sorry for what has happened. We have sent for a doctor."

"I don't need a doctor."

"Do you feel able to answer some questions?"

She looked up. "What has happened?"

"The works of art have been stolen."

She shook her head. "I hoped it was a dream, but . . ." She looked down at her wrists.

"There has been a demand for a ransom of one hundred million dollars. If it is not paid, they may be destroyed."

A look of alarm came into her eyes. "Will it be paid?"

"I don't know. It is not for me to decide. My job is to find the paintings."

She nodded.

"Do you know where they are?"

She shook her head. "No."

"Do you know who has taken them?"

She stared ahead into the middle distance. "No."

"Can you tell me what happened last night?"

Francesca opened her mouth to speak, but no words came out.

"Why did you come to the warehouse?"

"I was afraid."

"Of what?"

"I don't know . . . that something would happen to the paintings."

"Why?"

"Because Paul had said . . ." Her voice petered out.

"What?"

"He told me he thought Stefi had worked for the Stasi."

"Stefan Diederich? The Minister?"

"Yes."

"Who is Paul?"

"Paul Meissner. He was married to Sophie Diederich . . . before. He said that Stefi and Günter . . ." She waved her hand as if she did not have the energy to go on.

"So you came here to the warehouse?"

"Yes."

"What did you find?"

"No one. Nothing. The gate was open. The paintings were gone."

"Why didn't you call the police?"

"I was going to."

"What stopped you?"

"A man."

"Serotkin?"

She looked away to avoid his eyes. "Another man. He took me and tied me to that chair." She pointed but did not look.

"Who was this man?"

"I don't know."

"Was he a German?"

She shook her head. "No. An Arab or a Turk."

"And then?"

"He stood there watching me, smoking, and then—" Her face fell into her hands and she started sobbing.

Kessler rose to comfort her. As he put his hand on her shoulder, he noticed a red spot on her neck. "Did you feel a pain in your neck?"

"Yes. He had a syringe. I thought I was going to die."

Dark tobacco, unfiltered cigarettes, and, as on Vera Maslyukov, the mark of a needle. "Yes," said Kessler. "What is odd is that you are alive."

"Was I poisoned?"

"I don't think so. A strong sedative, that's all." He beckoned to Dorn. "Where is the doctor?"

"I don't need a doctor," said Francesca again.

"Are you sure?"

"Yes. I'm fine."

Kessler started toward the telephone, then turned back. "Are you sure you had never seen the man before?"

This time she looked straight into his eyes. "Quite sure."

Kessler called Commissar Rohrbeck from the warehouse director's office. "It's Serotkin and possibly Diederich too."

"The Minister?"

"Some sort of scam by a former Stasi and a rogue KGB man."

"Can we prove it?"

"Not yet, but it's falling into place."

"We've put a call out for Serotkin."

"We'll never find him. Our only hope is Diederich."

"Very well. Put it to him. See what he says. But if you have it wrong, we may both lose our jobs."

Kessler called the Prussian Ministry of Culture and was told that the Minister had gone home. He turned to Francesca McDermott.

"How are you feeling?"

"OK."

"If you feel up to it, I'd like you to accompany us to the Diederichs'."

She hesitated. "Very well."

Dorn sat in front next to the driver, Kessler in back between Gerasimov and Francesca McDermott. The car darted through traffic, its lights flashing, its siren loud.

Kessler turned to Francesca. "What can you tell me about Andrei Serotkin?"

"He was my colleague on the Excursus committee."

"Did you know him before?"

"No."

"You met him only when you came to Berlin?"

"Yes."

"Who introduced you?"

"I was told by Herr Diederich that he would be working on the exhibition. I met him when he came to the office."

"I believe you lived in the same building?"

"Yes. We were both provided with apartments there by the Ministry of Culture."

"Would you describe Professor Serotkin as a friend?"

"Yes."

"Anything more?"

"Yes. We were lovers."

"Would it surprise you, Dr. McDermott," asked Kessler, "to learn that Andrei Serotkin is not the professor's real name?"

She thought for a moment, then answered, "No, it would not surprise me."

"Why not?"

"There was always something mysterious about him."

"Part of his attraction, perhaps?"

"Perhaps." In a tone of casual curiosity she asked, "If he is not Andrei Serotkin, what is his real name?"

"Orlov," said Gerasimov. "Andrei Anatolyevich Orlov."

"So he was always Andrei."

"Yes, but that may be the only thing that Orlov and Serotkin have in common. He was not an art historian—"

"I guessed as much," said Francesca.

"He was a criminal."

She turned away.

"Known by the Russian police as Ivan the Terrible."

"Why that name?"

Kessler reached into an inside pocket of his jacket, took out a photograph of the corpse of Vera Maslyukov, and handed it to her. "Almost two years ago, a Russian couple, dealers in icons, was murdered here in Berlin. The husband, Grigori Maslyukov, was shot dead. The wife, Vera, was tortured by being burned with cigarettes before she was killed by an injection of potassium cyanide in her neck. We have good reason to believe that this was done by Orlov, alias Andrei Serotkin."

Francesca's face, already pale, turned white. "That's impossible," she whispered.

"I am afraid there is little doubt."

Francesca was silent.

"Dr. McDermott," said Kessler. "Before we go any further, there is one important question I must ask you, a question perhaps only you can answer. You knew Andrei Orlov. You knew him better than anyone else in Berlin. From what you know of him, do you think it possible that if the ransom is not paid he will actually destroy the works of art of the Excursus exhibition?"

Francesca did not hesitate. "Yes. Yes, he will."

"And if the ransom *is* paid, will he return them?"

For a moment she did not reply. She was thinking, concentrating, remembering. Then she said, "Yes. Yes, I think he will."

"You are less certain?"

"No. I am certain."

Kessler leaned forward to speak to Dorn. "Radio the commissar and give him Dr. McDermott's answer." He turned back to Francesca. "You are so sure, I presume, because he informed you of his intention?"

"Yes. That is to say, no, but he said things which, looking back, now make it clear."

"That he meant to steal the paintings?"

"Or destroy them."

"And you were to help him do this?"

"Help him? No."

"It was your expert knowledge that enabled Serotkin to assemble such valuable works of art, your reputation that reassured lenders in the United States, and where they led, others followed. You recommended the fine art warehouse at Tegel owned by the fraudulent company, OZF, and you were present in the warehouse at the time the paintings were stolen."

Francesca nodded. "I can see how it looks, but I never thought . . . I never realized . . ."

"That they were being assembled simply to be stolen?"

"How could I know that?"

"But we have been told, Dr. McDermott, that you are the one who first suggested a major exhibition of modern Russian art."

"Me? No. I was asked to help organize it, that was all."

"Then who first suggested it?"

"As far as I know, it was Stefan Diederich. The Excursus exhibition was his idea."

The two detectives who had been tailing Stefan Diederich were waiting in their car on the Wedekindstrasse opposite the entrance to the

Diederichs' apartment. They reported that the children had left with an older woman earlier that afternoon and that the Minister had only just returned.

Kessler, Dorn, Gerasimov, and Francesca McDermott walked up the two flights of stairs and rang the bell at the Diederichs' door. It was opened by Stefan Diederich. He looked mildly surprised, almost annoyed, to find visitors at that hour in his home. "Ah, inspector! You have found Dr. McDermott. Did she tell you that you would find the stolen paintings on the walls of my home?" He beckoned them in and led them down the corridor to the living room. "I am afraid that at this rate you are hardly going to save the state one hundred million dollars."

Sophie Diederich got up from the sofa as they entered, her face wet and red from tears. Seeing Francesca, she crossed to room and, sobbing, fell into her arms. "Stefi has just told me. The paintings are gone!"

"We have made more progress than you might suppose," said Kessler to Stefan Diederich.

"You have found the paintings?"

"No, but we have found the thief."

"Who is he?"

"Serotkin."

"Serotkin? The Russian?" He laughed. "Surely not."

"His real name is Orlov. We believe he was also responsible for the Maslyukov murders."

Diederich frowned. "I remember. Murder, I believe, and torture."

"We have been after him for some time," said Gerasimov.

Diederich turned. "And who are you?"

"Gerasimov. Moscow militia."

"Another Russian! I might have known. Well, you must forgive me, Herr Gerasimov, if what I say appears implicitly to denigrate your nation, but from my own long experience of Russians, it seems unlikely that a Russian could single-handedly accomplish a crime which"—Diederich looked at his watch—"in a few hours' time will earn a place in the *Guinness Book of Records*."

"We know he had accomplices," said Kessler.

"Good. Who were they?"

"That is what we were hoping to elicit from Dr. McDermott."

"Do you think *she* was an accomplice?"

"Don't you?"

"Have I ever suggested any such thing?"

"Clearly, if the same person suggested the exhibition *and* the OZF warehouse, that person becomes the prime suspect, or at least an accomplice."

"Clearly."

"You told us earlier today that the idea of the exhibition was first put to you by Dr. McDermott."

"As I recall—"

"It was not my idea, Stefi," said Francesca. "It was either Günter's or yours."

Diederich looked puzzled. "No, Francesca. You came to us, don't you remember? You came to supper here and suggested an exhibition of modern Russian art—"

"That's not true, Stefi."

"That's certainly how I remember it, and Günter confirms it. Don't you remember? He was here too. And of course Sophie was here. You remember, don't you, Sophie? It was Francesca's idea."

Stefan Diederich turned to look at his wife, but Sophie did not meet his eyes. She was sitting like a sack on the sofa, her head slumped over her bosom. There were damp patches where tears had fallen on the front of her dungarees.

"Sophie," Diederich repeated slowly, like a teacher talking to a child, "tell them what you remember. Francesca came to us, after ten years' absence, to say she was now a specialist in Russian experimental art and it would be wonderful if I could use my influence as the regional Minister of Culture to put on an exhibition she could organize—"

Sophie looked up. "What . . . did . . . you do to . . . Paul?" she asked between her sobs.

Diederich faltered, for the first time uncertain. "To Paul? What has Paul to do with this?"

"To destroy him. That was why you said you loved me. You were under orders . . . and Günter brought him . . . and he saw us . . . and he fled . . . and I did not even know."

"Sophie! What are you saying? Have you seen Paul? What has he told you?"

"I saw Paul," said Francesca. "He told me. You worked for the Stasi. You seduced Sophie as part of their campaign against him."

"But this is absurd!" said Stefan, turning to the three other visitors as if to appeal to them. Again he faltered. The actor had forgotten his lines.

"The important point at the moment," said Kessler to Sophie, "is to establish precisely who first had the idea for the Excursus exhibition."

Sophie sniffed. "It was him. It was Stefi, not Francesca. He invited her over from America. It was all his idea."

A look of shock, and then of pain, came onto the face of Stefan Diederich. "Sophie! How can you talk like that? I am your husband!"

"Paul was my husband!" shouted Sophie. "And I helped you to destroy him, and you cannot say that anyone lies because you do not know truth from falsehood, Stefi. You don't, you don't!"

"Sophie!" Diederich spoke hoarsely and looked at her with an expression of genuine anguish.

She turned away, and suddenly Stefan Diederich appeared to pull himself together. "Her mind has clearly been poisoned against me by Dr. McDermott," he said to Kessler. "You have only to talk to Günter Westarp. I shall tell him to come over. He will confirm everything I have said." Diederich moved toward the door.

"I should like to ask you some further questions," said Kessler.

"Of course. Let me just call Westarp. I won't be a moment." Diederich went into his study.

Kessler turned to Francesca. "Dr. McDermott, you will appreciate the urgency of the situation we are in. You knew Orlov better than anyone else in Berlin. Can you remember anything—anything at all—that he might have said at any time to suggest where he would take the paintings?"

Francesca pondered, then shook her head. "No."

"Did he give you an address or a telephone number where he could be contacted in Moscow?"

"No."

"Before he left," said Kessler, watching Francesca closely, "did you make any arrangement to meet with or speak to Orlov again?"

Francesca hesitated. Then she looked at the photograph of Vera Maslyukov, which she still held in her hand. She opened her mouth to answer, but before she could speak the sound of a shot came from the study.

Dorn ran to the door and looked in. "Shit." He looked back at Kessler. "Better call an ambulance, chief. The Minister's blown a hole through his head."

At 11:30 P.M., a conference call from the office of the Federal Chancellor in Bonn was put through to Commissar Rohrbeck in Berlin. Present were inspectors Hasenclever, Allerding, and Kessler and two men from the BfV, one of them Grohmann. First Rohrbeck spoke. He reported that the stolen works of art had not been found. It was now clear that the robbery had been planned and executed by a Russian named Andrei Orlov, posing as art historian Andrei Serotkin. He had suborned former members of the Stasi to assist him, among them the Prussian Minister of Culture, Stefan Diederich, who was now dead.

"Diederich is dead?" The speaker had not introduced himself, but the voice was unmistakably that of the Chancellor himself.

"Yes. He committed suicide."

"It seems unbelievable that I was not warned that Diederich might be a traitor."

Grohmann leaned forward. "It was known he might have collaborated with the Stasi, but nothing could be proved. His file had disappeared from the Runscestrasse."

"And no one suspected he had been working for the KGB?"

"No."

"What about the other two, Westarp and Riesler?"

"They are in custody," said Rohrbeck, "and have been questioned. It is difficult to make out how much either knew of what Orlov planned to do. It is our judgment that neither knows the whereabouts of the stolen works of art."

"And what do we know about Orlov?"

"Formerly an officer in the KGB," said Grohmann, "apparently dismissed after the coup. His father-in-law, Ivan Keminski, was at one time a top official in the Secretariat of the Central Committee. It is possible that the robbery is to raise funds for the Party now that it is no longer paid for by the state."

A jumble of voices now came from the console as the Chancellor and his advisers conferred. Then: "Commissar Rohrbeck?"

"Herr Bundeskanzler?"

"Our decision rests on your answers to three questions. The first: Can you recover the paintings before midnight tonight without paying the ransom?"

Rohrbeck did not hesitate. "No."

"The second: Is it your view that if the ransom is not paid, the works of art will be destroyed?"

Rohrbeck looked at Kessler. Kessler nodded. Rohrbeck said, "Yes."

"The third question: Is it your view that, if the ransom *is* paid, the works of art will be returned?"

This time Kessler looked less certain, but again he nodded.

"We think so, yes," said Rohrbeck.

Once again, the sound of a subdued discussion came from the console. Then: "Herr Kommissar Rohrbeck?"

"Yes."

"The view taken here is that we have no choice. We shall instruct the Bundesbank to pay the ransom. But no word of this must ever reach the outside world."

"Understood," said Rohrbeck. Then he added, "I am sorry."

"You did your best. But please remain on hand. We will inform you as soon as there is any word from Raskolnikov."

The five men waited in the commissar's office; not all of them were needed, but none wanted to go home. Hasenclever went off to telephone Frankfurt from his office, dragging a police specialist on banking fraud out of his bed to question him about whether money paid into numbered bank accounts could be traced and subsequently recovered. The answers he received brought him back to Rohrbeck's office in a pessimistic frame of mind.

At dawn, Kessler made one more trip down to the coffee machine on the floor below, returning with five cups on a tray. At seven the new shift arrived, at eight-thirty the clerical workers, and at nine the first cart with fresh coffee and buns. By then Grohmann and Allerding were both asleep, slumped on their chairs.

Every now and then Rohrbeck's telephone would ring or other officers would look through the door to bring different matters to the commissar's attention. Rohrbeck curtly dismissed them and gave orders that only a call from the Chancellery was to be put through.

At 9:40 A.M. the telephone rang. Rohrbeck snatched it up and switched on the speaker. It was Bonn. Raskolnikov had made contact. A fax stated that five vans containing the Excursus works of art were parked in a railway siding at Tucheim, fifty miles north of Berlin.

21

The postponement by one week of the opening of the Excursus exhibition meant that neither President von Weizsäcker nor the American ambassador could attend. The reason given for the delay was the technical difficulties of hanging so many works of art. There were some rumors of more serious complications, and even a story in the Berlin *Morgenpost* linking the delay to the bankruptcy of the Omni Zartfracht Company, ending with a speculation that some of the paintings had been mislaid for a short period of time.

This was immediately denied by the Excursus organizing committee and the Prussian Ministry of Culture, but all the same it gave rise to inquiries from other papers, and Francesca McDermott had to take some difficult calls from museum directors around the world. At one point MOMA in New York requested the immediate return of their works, a demand that was only withdrawn after reassurances from the American embassy in Bonn.

Despite the absence of the president of Germany and the ambassador of the United States, the opening of the Excursus exhibition was a glittering occasion. For political reasons the official ceremony was in East Berlin, under the cupola in Schinkel's Old Museum. The Christian Democrat Minister President of the provincial government made a moving speech about the tragic death of his Minister of Culture, Stefan Diederich, killed when confronting an intruder in his apartment.

This enabled him to make several political points at the expense of the Social Democrats and to call for a change in Germany's liberal asylum laws that had led to an unprecedented influx of criminals posing as refugees.

Sophie Diederich was not present; she was in a clinic recovering from the shock of her husband's violent death. Dr. Kemmelkampf had been summoned to Bonn. Professor Serotkin had been unable to get back from Moscow, and Günter Westarp was also absent, thought to be suffering from some kind of nervous exhaustion caused by the stress of mounting such a major exhibition. As a result, Francesca McDermott became the sole representative of the organizing committee and, as such, joint hostess with the Minister President's wife at the reception given after the official opening at the Old Museum on July 13 and at the more exclusive lunch the next day at the New National Gallery in West Berlin for lenders, curators, and diplomats. Only the French cultural attaché was unable to attend because it was his country's national holiday, the anniversary of the storming of the Bastille.

Despite all the horrors to which she had been subjected two weeks earlier, Francesca rose to the occasion. The show was stupendous; to see the work of so many great artists assembled from all over the world, to "bathe in the form and color of their inspired vision" (words from her introduction to the catalog), to receive at the same time the effusive praise of the world's most distinguished curators and critics who a year earlier had never heard of her, and—though this was only a minor consideration—to be able to wear for the first time some of the more elegant clothes she had brought from Boston: all this was a good antidote to the discovery that her lover, Andrei Serotkin, was a murderer.

Kessler, Dorn, and the Russian detective, Gerasimov, were present at the opening of Excursus at the Old Museum and also at the lunch at the New National Gallery the next day. After the earlier debacle, which had cost the German exchequer one hundred million dollars, the governments at both the national and provincial levels had insisted upon unprecedented security. The three detectives were wearing suits and mingling with the guests. To Francesca, the two Germans were unmistakably policemen; no one could possibly suppose that they had anything to do with art. Both looked uncomfortable in these surroundings, and so Francesca went over to talk to them in an attempt to put them at their ease.

"Well, inspector," she said to Kessler, "what do you think of the exhibition?"

Kessler looked embarrassed. "I was never one for modern art."

"If I had a hundred million dollars—" began Dorn.

"You don't," said Kessler, "and you won't even have a job if you don't keep quiet."

Francesca, who had been questioned half a dozen times by Kessler while hanging the Excursus exhibition, had become fond of the middle-aged Berlin inspector and his sergeant. She supposed they knew, or at least suspected, that she could have told them more about Orlov, alias Serotkin, and was grateful that they showed no rancor. She had followed their investigation and knew what little progress they had made. No prints had been found on the vans found at Tucheim: no admissions had been gained from Westarp or Riesler or from suspects among former members of the Stasi's Dzerzhinski brigade, and there was no word from Interpol about any Burton, Lauch, Grauber, Jeanneret, or Serotkin.

"Any news from Russia?" she now asked Kessler.

"They deny the existence of Serotkin."

"And Orlov?"

"They say the evidence is insufficient to extradite him. A number of witnesses attest that he never left Moscow."

"Do you still think the paintings were hidden in a Russian base?"

"Yes. Almost certainly at Waldheim, a kilometer from Tucheim. But the Russians have refused us access, and its senior officers have been sent home."

"But not the detective," said Francesca, nodding toward Gerasimov on the other side of the room.

"No, he's still here. He'll hang on until his allowance runs out."

To Francesca, Nikolai Gerasimov seemed even more out of place than the two German policemen. She had disliked him from the first moment she had seen him in Kessler's car. He had thick, fleshy lips and a pockmarked face but clearly thought he was irresistible to women. On the pretext that he was protecting the security of the works of art loaned by Russian collections, he had loitered around the galleries during the hanging, his eyes always on Francesca, never on the paintings. He followed her wherever she went and one evening had the audacity to ask her out to dinner. Francesca had said she was much too busy. "Perhaps after the opening?" he had asked, to which she had replied, with all the disdain she could muster, "Perhaps."

She should have said no. The possibility of a date sometime in the future had encouraged him to pester her. He had followed her from gallery to gallery, watching her every movement with lecherous eyes, popping up at odd moments to offer to lift a painting, move a ladder, or drive her home in his rented car. Francesca recognized that the revulsion she felt toward Gerasimov might have something to do with her confused feelings about that other Russian, Andrei Serotkin. Gerasimov's vulgarity made her wonder whether she perhaps had been mistaken about Serotkin's nobility. Was it possible that he had only seduced her to involve her in his plot? This seemed unlikely, because she had always thought it was she who had seduced him. But it was possible, as Sophie had suggested, that Andrei had hired the Turks to pretend to rape her simply so he could present himself in a heroic role. "How convenient, when you think of it," she had said to Francesca, "that he happened to be running past at the time! I tell you, Francesca, if he was once in the KGB, he would be capable of anything. They are trained to seduce American women!"

Sophie had said this the morning after Stefi's suicide, when she was still in a state of shock and may have been unconsciously looking for a scapegoat on which to vent her grief and rage. Francesca was in her kitchen in the apartment on the Wedekindstrasse, and it was she who had been the bearer of the tidings that had set off the chain of events ending in Stefi's death.

When her husband had asked her to confirm his lie about who had first suggested the exhibition, Sophie had impetuously told the truth. Why? Because she had realized instantly that if he could lie so easily about something as big as that he could have lied about everything else, and suddenly the mystery of why Paul had never come home from the clinic was solved. The monstrous thought that all Stefi's loving words and gestures over the past decade had been simply to comply with a Stasi controller's command made her want to kill him, and at that moment, in front of Kessler, telling the truth was an easy and obvious way to take revenge. But the look in Stefi's eyes—the look of real anguish that had appeared as though through two holes in his mask—had confounded her. Had he loved her after all? She had been about to follow him into his study when she heard the shot. Now she would never know.

It was for this reason, a perfectly understandable one, that over breakfast the next morning Sophie had not only told this story but had done her best to persuade Francesca that Andrei Serotkin also had been insincere. "It was the system. There were so many lies, and lies within lies, that it was quite impossible for any of them to be truthful."

Francesca had agreed, for it seemed prudent to seem to accept that she had been used. But from the moment she had regained consciousness in the OZF warehouse, her swollen wrists and ankles in great pain, her body aching in every joint, the memory foremost in her mind was not the dead look in the eyes of the Chechen but Andrei Orlov's smile.

She had realized at once that she was still living because Andrei had spared her life, and intuitively she understood all that this implied. He had spared her because he loved her, and because he loved her he would spare the paintings too. This was why she had been able to assure Kessler that Orlov would keep his side of the bargain.

Truth is remembering. He who has no memory has no life. Why had he said this? What was she to remember? Their words at the Soviet Memorial. But what had they said? He had asked her to choose between him and the paintings. She had chosen him. He had said they would return there on Bastille Day, and if her answer was still the same they would never be parted again.

Today was Bastille Day. Would he be there? Reason told her he would not. He was now one of the world's most wanted men. With one hundred million dollars and a safe haven in Russia, it was unlikely that he would linger in Western Europe, let alone return to Berlin. But her intuition argued otherwise.

It was only a short walk from the New National Gallery to the Soviet Memorial. Smiling, Francesca excused herself from the group of admiring dignitaries, critics, and curators that surrounded her and made for the cloakroom. She went down the flight of stairs, past the bookshop and restaurant, through the administrative offices, and out past the parking lot by the back door.

She did not hurry. She walked between the Philharmonia Hall and the new National Library, garish modern yellow buildings that lay between the gallery and the Tiergarten, the second built close to what re-

mained of the Wall. She crossed into the Tiergarten and took the path
that led to the Soviet Memorial. Her mind was calm and reflective, as
if she were indeed going to the memorial to honor the Russian dead.
It was warm; young people lay on the grass in the shade of the silver-
barked birch trees. Would he be there, she wondered, or was he now
in Russia sitting beneath the branches of just such birch trees as these?

She came to the wide boulevard leading from the Brandenburg Gate
to the Goddess of Victory. On the other side was the Soviet Memorial,
beyond it, shrouded by trees, the Reichstag. Francesca waited for a
break in the traffic and then crossed the road. A cluster of Scandinavian
tourists was looking up at the tanks and the cannon and the great
bronze statue of a Soviet soldier on top of the memorial.

Francesca stood quite still, remembering what he had asked her a
month before and the answer she had given, with no inkling of what
the question involved. Now, as she put the question again in the full
knowledge of what he had done and what he had been planning—the
theft and destruction of all the works of art—she realized the answer
she would give now would be the same. Life, her life, did mean more
to her than all that dead art, and even if Andrei was a murderer, a tor-
turer, and a thief, she was committed to him for better or worse. He
was a man who loved his country and was tormented by its fall from
power. He had done terrible things—the image of the tortured woman
remained imprinted in Francesca's mind—but for her sake he had
spared the works of art. If she was given the chance, she had no doubt
the savage Muscovite could be tamed and ennobled by her love.

From the group of tourists behind her, someone stepped forward
and in a quiet voice said her name: "Francesca."

She turned but at first did not recognize the bespectacled man.

"I did not know if you would remember," he said.

Now she saw who it was.

"Or that you would come if you did."

She smiled. Tears came into her eyes. She longed to embrace him
but dared not.

"Are you all right?" he asked.

"I'm fine."

"It was a terrible thing to do, I realize, but it was the only way. The
other man—"

Smiling, she interrupted him. "So it is gray after all."

"What is gray?"

"Your hair."

"No, it's brown." He took off the rimless glasses as if to show her what he really looked like. "But it could be black again if you like, and I could grow another beard."

"I like you . . ." She raised her hand and touched his cheek. "I like you any old how."

"I have little to offer you, Francesca. Here in the West, I shall always be a fugitive. Even in Russia, my future will depend upon how history unfolds. I shall be poor; all the money has gone to the cause. It's a wretched prospect when compared to the life that awaits you back in Boston."

"No life awaits me back in Boston. You are now my life."

"Francesca." The sound of her name was a cry of joy.

"Can we live by Lake Baikal," she asked, "like a couple in one of Rasputin's stories?"

"Of course."

"In a wooden house surrounded by birch trees?"

"Protected from the outside world by the vastness of the forests and the infinity of the skies."

She heard a sound from somewhere behind him like that of a ball hitting a bat. As she looked over his shoulder to see what had caused it, he moved forward, and for an instant Francesca thought he was taking her into his arms, but his arms remained limp and his eyes turned to look up at the sky. His mouth opened, but only a gurgle came from his throat. He began to fall. She held him up. Over his shoulder she saw the other Russian, Gerasimov. In his hand was a revolver. On his face was a grin. He came closer, poked his gun into the nape of Andrei Orlov's neck, fired a second shot, stepped back, and ran off toward the Russian consulate on the other side of the Brandenburg Gate.

ACKNOWLEDGMENTS

For the material in this novel relating to Russian art in the twentieth century, I am indebted to *The Great Experiment: Russian Art, 1863–1922* by Camilla Gray (London: Thames and Hudson, 1962). Much of my knowledge of the internal organization of the KGB comes from *KGB Today: The Hidden Hand* by John Barron (London: Hodder & Stoughton, 1984).

ABOUT THE AUTHOR

PIERS PAUL READ is the author of twelve novels and three works of nonfiction including *Alive: The Story of the Andes Survivors*. Research for his most recent book, *Ablaze: The Story of the Heroes and Victims of Chernobyl,* took him to Russia, Belorussia, and the Ukraine. He has also traveled extensively in Eastern Europe and lived for a time in West Berlin. He now lives in London.

ABOUT THE TYPE

This book was set in Galliard, a typeface designed by Matthew Carter for the Mergenthaler Linotype Company in 1978. Galliard is based on the sixteenth-century typefaces of Robert Granjon.

12-10
7-15

Date Due

JUL 1 2 2010		
AUG 0 6 2010		
SEP 1 3 2010		

BRODART, CO.   Cat. No. 23-233   Printed in U.S.A.